PENGUI

73 Dov

'Touching, entertaining, hopeful. A vivid sense of time, place, people's attitudes and fragilities' *Sunday Times*

'Psychologically astute and emotionally absorbing, this is a heartfelt read' *Daily Mail*

'*73 Dove Street* is a pacy and evocative account of the struggles facing women of that era' *Herald*

'Gripping . . . Julie Owen Moylan vividly recreates drab, grey, post-war London and her characters are convincing to the end' *The Times*

'From the Rivoli Ballroom to the seedy nightlife of Soho, the characters leap off the page in this compelling mystery' *Woman & Home*

'An incredibly vivid rendering of post-war London and the complicated lives of three woman whose fates intersect at a boarding house. This was an engrossing read; emotional, immersive and utterly absorbing' Jennifer Saint

'A corker. It's the story of three working class women in 1950s London. I loved how the strands came together, very satisfying' Kate Sawyer

'A wonderfully evocative, immersive novel that brings 50s London to life, from the smog and the nightlife to attitudes towards women. It's a vivid, absorbing and ultimately uplifting read' *Sunday Express*

'A vivid and propulsive story of three women and three dangerous secrets, *73 Dove Street* so brilliantly and evocatively captures Soho in the 50s that I really feel I was there' Sophie Irwin

'Powerful, poignant and so beautifully drawn – every single scene comes alive' Frances Quinn

'Once again, Julie Owen Moylan has created a mid-century world that feels completely real and vivid. A hugely enjoyable book' Jodie Chapman

'Set in my end of 1950s London, the sense of time and place is beautifully evocative, the ghost of the war, and the sense of societal change about to come' Laura Shepherd-Robinson

'Stark choices and dangerous secrets disrupt the lives of three damaged but resilient working-class women in this compelling emotional drama' *Mail on Sunday*

'A beautiful story of friendship and new beginnings' *Best*

'Gripping and atmospheric, this novel will worm its way into your heart' *Red*

'Brimming with 1950s detail and atmosphere, pacy and evocative, authentic and well-drawn. An enjoyable read' *Independent*

'Superb' *Sun*

ABOUT THE AUTHOR

Julie Owen Moylan is the author of *That Green Eyed Girl* and *73 Dove Street.* Her debut novel *That Green Eyed Girl* was a Waterstones Welsh Book of the Month and the official runner up for the prestigious Paul Torday Memorial Prize. It was also shortlisted for Best Debut at the Fingerprint Awards and featured at the Hay Festival as one of its 'Ten at Ten'. *73 Dove Street* was named as one of Waterstones' Books of 2023 and a *Daily Mail* Historical Fiction Book of the Year. As a filmmaker Julie won the Celtic Media Award for her graduation film *BabyCakes* before going on to win Best Short Film at the Swansea Film Festival. Her writing and short stories have appeared in a variety of publications including *Sunday Express*, *Independent*, *New Welsh Review* and *Good Housekeeping.* She has a Masters in Filmmaking and an additional qualification in Creative Writing & English Literature. Julie is an alumna of the Faber Academy.

By the same author

That Green Eyed Girl

73 Dove Street

JULIE OWEN MOYLAN

PENGUIN BOOKS

PEGNUIN BOOKS

UK | USA | Canada | Ireland | Australia
India | New Zealand | South Africa

Penguin Books is part of the Penguin Random House group of companies
whose addresses can be found at global.penguinrandomhouse.com

First published by Penguin Michael Joseph 2023
Published in Penguin Books 2024
001

Typeset by Jouve (UK), Milton Keynes
Printed and bound in Great Britain by Clays Ltd, Elcograf S.p.A.

The authorized representative in the EEA is Penguin Random House Ireland,
Morrison Chambers, 32 Nassau Street, Dublin D02 YH68

A CIP catalogue record for this book is available from the British Library

ISBN: 978–1–405–94944–6

www.greenpenguin.co.uk

Penguin Random House is committed to a sustainable future for our business, our readers and our planet. This book is made from Forest Stewardship Council® certified paper.

For my grandmother Lilian, 'Lil'

She is clothed with strength and dignity, and
she laughs without fear of the future.

Proverbs 31:25

I

London, October 1958

Something was burning. A tall plume of black smoke curling high up into the air, accompanied by the crackling of bright orange flames.

Edie blinked twice, slowing her pace before finally coming to a halt next to a rusty garden gate. The fizz of sparks climbed upwards, and just to be sure she blinked again – but there it was . . .

Someone had set a bonfire right in the middle of the pavement.

It was one of those London streets that had become a canvas of tatty boarding houses: windows filled with crooked pieces of cardboard saying 'Room to Let'. The houses all looked the same: bay-fronted with scruffy front gardens filled with dustbins, and children loitering on doorsteps with their runny noses and scraped knees. In one front garden sat an abandoned pram still bearing the thick, dark traces of the coal it had recently carried, while a surly cat leapt from an open dustbin where it had been ferreting for scraps.

Up ahead, the flames crawled high into the air and the heavy black smoke turned to grey as it drifted over the upper part of the street, which was quite empty now, apart from a barefoot child playing hopscotch, the chalky-white squares of the game scratched over the grey stones of the pavement.

Edie watched as the girl tried to turn without putting her foot down. The sole was caked in grimy black dirt, and Edie couldn't help but stare. The child stuck out her defiant arms, wobbling violently but forcing herself to hop back to safety. Suddenly aware she had an audience, her head jerked upwards. Pushing her wild tangled hair out of her eyes, she glared at Edie, sticking her little pink tongue out.

'What *you* looking at?' the girl cried and Edie hurried on, embarrassed by her own curiosity.

She began to walk towards the strange bonfire up ahead of her, a furious blister forming on the back of her left heel. It was unseasonably warm for October and she felt hot and tired. A trickle of sweat ran down the channel between her breasts. In her arms, she clutched a small cardboard suitcase to her chest as the handle had broken. The suitcase was bound up with string because the lock didn't work either – a neat little knot holding it all together. An old leather handbag nestled softly in the crook of her elbow.

Edie was gripping a crumpled scrap of paper between her fingers; the skin around her fingernails was raw and broken where she'd been gnawing at them. From time to time she checked it anxiously, although she knew the words off by heart now: '73 Dove Street'.

Pressing on, she glanced nervously behind, but there was nobody following her. The smoke began to claw at her eyes and Edie didn't really want to go any further, but she couldn't go back either. It was too late.

'You've made your bed, Edie Budd . . .' she muttered to herself while mentally checking off the numbers of the houses one by one. There was number 65, with its sooty bushes either side of a bright green front door. The fire was getting closer now, and the smoke surrounded her. A few more steps, and Edie was standing outside number 69: the front garden a graveyard of wheels, most of them buckled, surrounded by the remains of broken prams and bicycles. A child's red scooter had been abandoned on the ground. She checked the piece of paper one last time, counting out loud – it must be . . . *that one*. Her mouth fell open as she gazed at the fierce blaze right there on the pavement outside her destination. Number 73, Dove Street.

The house was a dirty red brick with a mud-brown front door, a black iron gate creaking back and forth on its squeaky hinges every time the wind blew. The front garden contained only weeds and a path leading to a grey metal dustbin, its lid fastened by means of a house brick carefully placed on top of it. The surly cat strutted past, with its questioning tail, and jumped over the low wall that separated number 73 from the neighbouring house. Next to the dustbin was a dirty white step leading up to that mud-brown front door with a brass knocker in the shape of a lion's head. The brass lion was roaring and seemed to indicate that casual visitors should not bother knocking.

Edie hesitated, trying desperately to find some welcoming feature about the house, then turned back to the fierce blaze on the pavement in front of her. Underneath the dense smoke and leaping orange flames was a small mattress – which had seen better days even before someone had seen fit to set it on fire. On top of the single mattress lay the smouldering remains of a man's suit in navy blue, along with a funeral pyre of assorted belongings.

Vinyl records melted into the mattress, black and tarry. To the side of the flaming bonfire was a blackened pan; clearly, blazing lard had been thrown over both these belongings and the bodily fluids of whoever had last laid down on that mattress.

Edie was about to turn around and walk away from number 73 when suddenly a stout middle-aged woman wearing a furious expression on her face appeared at the front door and shouted, 'If you've come about the room, best get inside . . .'

The two women eyed each other cautiously. After a long few seconds, Edie gulped down an anxious breath and slowly picked her way past the crackling whip of sparks in the air and a lone sock, whose mate was lost in the fire.

Five Years Earlier

The first time Edie laid eyes on Frank Budd, she was on the other side of the city: dancing on a table with a sailor in the Rivoli Ballroom. She hadn't intended to dance in front of everybody, but the music had carried her all the way up there, every drumbeat and trumpet blast giving her feet an energy they didn't normally possess. Her arms couldn't stop moving, and when a passing sailor grabbed hold of her, twisting her under his arm and back again, Edie could only laugh and throw her body into it. At some point the crowd parted a little as people watched them jive, then the sailor jumped up on a table to carry on dancing. For a moment, Edie stood there all alone in the middle of the dance floor being cheered on by strangers, not knowing quite what to do until two pairs of strong arms hoisted her up, and suddenly there she was: swinging her arms in time with the music and tapping her feet, while the sailor spun her around and around until she was dizzy.

Eventually the music stopped and everyone went wild, clapping and cheering. Another sailor put his arms around her waist and picked her up, showing her off to the crowd for their applause before placing her delicately back on to the dance floor. Edie laughed and turned her head to look for her friends but she couldn't see them. The thirsty sailors wandered off to the bar to fetch more drinks and she was left alone, her heart still racing and a sheen of sweat cooling on her forehead and arms.

There he was, standing in front of her, watching everything with those pale blue eyes. They were smiling, mischievous eyes and he nodded, staging a funny little bow to her.

'Quite the little dancer, aren't ya?' he said with a soft voice. It didn't sound entirely like a compliment.

'I like that song, that's all.'

He made her feel she had failed some kind of a test that she hadn't known she was sitting. Strangely, she found that she wanted to pass it. This handsome stranger with the pale blue eyes was watching her, and, unlike the other boys, he hadn't asked if he could get a dance, or if she'd like a gin and lime. He was older than the rest and there wasn't that feeling of desperation which sometimes poured off them, or that sense of it all being a game to see if they could get her to go outside for some 'fresh air', where they would demand kisses as the price to light her cigarette, or even to let her go back inside the dance hall again.

Frank just leaned back against the wall and watched her. Edie giggled nervously and then when he didn't join in the laughter, she stopped.

'I can't work you out,' she said.

'Ahh, you're not alone there. I've been trying to get to the bottom of me for years. If you get there before me, I'll be quite upset.' His eyes glinted and he grinned at her.

Edie laughed with him this time, moving closer to where he was standing. It was hot inside the dance hall and she could smell soap and sweat, cigarettes and the sour tang of Brylcreem on his hair. From the corner of her eye, she could see other girls eyeing him up but he carried on smiling softly at her.

'You're a funny one . . .' She inched closer, feeling as if he was pulling her to him.

'What's your name?' he asked.

'Edie.'

'Pretty name.'

'What's yours?'

'Frank.'

Edie stared up at him, her lips curling into a smile. Somewhere deep inside, part of her was already attaching her name to his: *Edie and Frank* . . . as if they belonged together.

'I'll walk you home, if you like?' He took her arm gently and she let him lead her towards the entrance. Edie hadn't even wanted to go home before that moment but once she felt his fingers pressing against the warm skin of her forearm, she didn't want to stay without him either.

As they reached the door Frank paused next to a

lanky dark-haired man who had trapped a small red-haired woman against the wall and seemed to be trying his best to persuade her to go outside with him. Frank tapped him on the shoulder.

'Pete, I'm off. Catch you tomorrow.'

Reluctantly, the man turned his attention away from the redhead, turning to look Edie up and down, before grinning at his friend. 'Don't do anything I wouldn't do . . .' Pete laughed at his own joke but Frank was already walking away, with Edie following behind him.

The streets were scattered with people coming and going from the dance hall. As they walked along, car headlights lit up couples tucked in doorways or alleyways, their mouths open and their hands inside each other's clothing. Frank made no attempt to pull Edie into one of the dark openings and do likewise with her. They just walked in silence; the only sound was the click-clack of her heels hitting the paving stones. She wasn't usually stuck for words, but for some reason this man made her want to choose what she said carefully.

'I haven't seen you there before,' she said eventually.

'I haven't seen *you* there before,' he said and took hold of her hand.

His fingers wrapped around hers, feeling warm and solid, as if he was something that she could hold on to. Edie liked the feeling of him touching her and to her surprise thought she wouldn't mind if he did pull her into one of those dark doorways to kiss her.

The pub on the corner was kicking out, and Edie could see her neighbours and her Uncle Bert wandering slowly back to their houses, shouting goodnights and sharing the last moment of the joke that had no doubt kept them chuckling for much of the evening. As their laughter faded away into the night air, Frank's pace slowed, as if he had no wish to get caught up in their chatter. On either side of the street, the little houses leaned one against the other, as if they'd all fall over if someone moved the pub on the corner. As they approached Edie's front door, the street was quiet again, with only the sounds of muffled arguments going on inside the little houses as drunken husbands were greeted by their wives.

Edie could hear the sound of her own breathing as she waited for Frank to kiss her goodnight. Instead, he just kissed the hand he had been holding, pressing the back of it to his lips. Soft, warm lips they were too. She gazed up at him, wanting to fall into those smiling blue eyes, but finding something steely and unrelenting about them. He wasn't smiling now. She snatched her hand away from his lips and stood there pouting with her chin jutting forward.

'Goodnight then. Thanks for walking me home.' She put her hand to the letter box, pulling out the piece of red wool they kept the front-door key on. The key rattled up against the wood of the door until it was in her hand and she slotted it into the lock.

'I'll pick you up next Friday at seven o'clock,' he said. Edie turned to face him, puzzled now and a little annoyed. She didn't like the game he was playing, keeping her off balance and wanting her never to be sure of him.

'Oh, is that right? I think I'm washing my hair that night.' Edie regained her composure and stood there, staring him down. She wouldn't be taken for a fool.

'If you like . . . I'll be here though – seven o'clock.' And with that he started to walk away, whistling softly under his breath.

'Hang on a minute there. I haven't said I'll go out with you.'

'Then you won't answer the door when I call, will ya?' he shouted over his shoulder and raised his hand to wave as he walked away. Edie watched him go; the memory of his mouth still tracing the skin on her hand.

2

London, October 1958

The hallway of 73 Dove Street had an olive-green carpet, which was curling at the edges and looked as if it hadn't been cleaned for a very long time. There was no lightshade, and the bare bulb swayed slightly with the smoky breeze blowing through the front door.

'Close the door if you don't mind. Come into the parlour. That's where I like to discuss my business,' the woman said and opened a door that was painted in army green.

The parlour was a dusty room with heavy red furniture and thick, moth-eaten curtains. There was a strong smell of camphor but, judging by the state of the curtains, it was too late for such measures. Edie wrinkled her nose.

The red velvet sofa had lost one of its little feet and was lopsided. Next to the sofa was a small table with a black Chinese vase that had clearly been glued back together: the top of the vase was chipped and a large crack ran down the centre of it, as if somebody had dropped it at some point. On the wall facing Edie as she entered the room was a picture of the Queen in her ermine robes, and on the opposite wall a watery landscape in blues and greys, all tumbling seas and cloudy skies. There were photographs in wooden frames along the top of the mantelpiece, but their faces were all turned downwards. Edie wondered if somebody had died.

Edie had never rented a room on her own and her courage, with which she had started the day so well, had long since run out, leaving her in a nervous state. Everything had happened so quickly that she hadn't had time to think. Standing to attention, she tried to steady herself. She just needed a few days to work out what to do next.

Her plan had been quite clear in her mind when she'd nervously scribbled down the address of a house with 'Rooms to Let' from a newsagent's window earlier that morning. She would lie low for a while, maybe a week, and then she would buy a train ticket and leave London for good. The buying of the train ticket seemed like such a simple thing, but the problem was that the destination kept changing in Edie's mind as possibilities came and went. She'd never been further than Margate – in fact, she'd barely set foot outside Deptford in her entire life. Her world had been small and she had liked it that way. Familiar houses; people she'd known her whole life. It had been all she needed until things had gone so terribly wrong. Apart from the odd shopping trip or day out, Edie had never strayed very far and she had no idea how you might go about choosing a place to live far away from everything you'd ever known. Even 73 Dove Street, lodged firmly as it was in the shabby hinterland between Notting Hill and Ladbroke Grove, seemed quite far to travel in Edie's mind.

There were just too many choices. Presenting themselves as sunny seaside resorts, or dark industrial cities filled with strangers, playing like images on a movie screen, and all she had to do was choose. But the choosing confused her. One choice presented all the worries of refusing the other choices, and every time Edie reached the same conclusion: she'd think about it tomorrow.

'I'm Mrs Collier but my tenants usually call me Phyllis. I'll answer to either . . .'

The sound of the woman's voice cut through Edie's worrying and she snapped to attention.

In front of her, Phyllis stood with her arms folded, droning on and on about rules. Apparently, it was very important that Edie understood the kind of respectable house she was running, as the woman carried on explaining without drawing breath. Meanwhile, Edie's hands continued their trembling no matter what she did. Her little cardboard suitcase felt heavy in her arms, and there was a faint whiff of burning in the air from the mattress that was still ablaze in the street. The wallpaper in the parlour was peeling due to the damp and Edie couldn't help wondering: if this was the parlour then what on earth would her room be like?

'Come along then . . . I'll show you up.'

Edie scurried along behind the older woman as they walked out of the damp-smelling parlour and started to climb the stairs. They were covered in the same awful olive-green carpet, which looked as though it had been nailed on to the bare boards. The wallpaper was light brown with large yellow chrysanthemums flecked with damp spots and peeling at the seams. It had one of those annoying light switches that plunged you into darkness if you were too slow reaching the next floor.

One flight up, they passed by a small shared kitchenette for the tenants, with the bathroom next door. The kitchenette had an old sink stained with dirty brown streaks, a Formica cabinet in lemon yellow for storing groceries and dishes, and a Baby Belling cooker stuffed away in the corner. The bathroom smelled of carbolic soap but was clean enough. On the back of the door was some kind of cleaning rota, but several of the names had been crossed out, so it made little sense. Just across the landing was a small room containing the lavatory with its thick wooden seat and long metal chain. On the wall beside it, a pile of old newspapers was cut up and stuck on a nail for toilet paper. Edie exhaled softly, a quiet disappointment. It would have to do for now.

By the time they climbed to the top of the house

Edie was beginning to worry about what she might find behind the closed door, but in fact it was so small there wasn't space for anything too offensive. A single bed pushed up against the wall with a tiny attic window. A wooden chair acted as a bedside table. In the cheap hotel where she'd stayed last night there had been bed bugs, and she'd spent hours hunting them down with a bar of soap, watching black dots scatter across the mattress as soon as she put on a light and pulled back the covers. At least this room wasn't that bad.

Against the other wall was a small closet and a single gas ring with a tin kettle sitting on top of it, although the tap to fill it was downstairs in the kitchenette. Two dull blue cups hung precariously from metal hooks over a shelf.

The window had a small painting of a Victorian child playing with an old-fashioned hoop leaning against it, but no curtains. Edie doubted that anyone could see in, anyway, as they were so high up and the window was so small. The room seemed quite gloomy even in the daytime. On the floor by the gas heater a meter was whirring around, even though Edie couldn't see that anything was being used at that moment.

Phyllis sniffed loudly, 'I had two tenants leave in a bit of a hurry so there's another room downstairs I can show you if you like, but it's an extra ten bob a week.'

'No, this will do . . .' She gazed around the tiny attic room that was to be her new home, at least until she could get herself sorted out . . . whatever that might mean. Today was a fresh day, although the same dark cloud of worry nagged at her constantly. Tomorrow, tomorrow she would decide what to do. The tiny sliver of hope soothed her nerves a little.

She nodded to Mrs Collier and finally set the small cardboard suitcase on the floor. She shook out her aching arms and decided that this would do for the time being, so reached inside her handbag and handed over two crisp pound notes.

'Gas meter takes penny pieces, so you'll need those. I don't keep spares otherwise I'd be up at all hours feeding the meters for my paying guests, and I can't do it, you see. The electricity meter is in the passageway just outside your door. Same thing. You'll soon get the hang of it. I'll fetch your change up later . . .'

The woman rubbed the pound notes between her finger and thumb, and finally took a moment to inspect Edie, who was standing nervously in front of her.

She stared for so long that Edie began to worry what she might see. *Too much make-up and horribly bitten fingernails, the outline of a faint purple bruise on her cheekbone.*

This in turn made her even more nervous, but her money was real enough and so, eventually, Phyllis handed over two small brass keys.

Edie curled her fist around the keys, suddenly overwhelmed with the idea that she could lock her own door and do whatever she pleased.

Her sense of freedom was short-lived as, suddenly, the door flew open and a young woman burst into the room, gabbling away nineteen to the dozen and reaching for a small cardboard box that was sitting on top of the bed.

'Won't be two ticks, Phyllis. Just getting the last of my things . . . Oh! Is this the new girl?'

'Yes, this is my new tenant . . . Miss Budd, wasn't it?' said Phyllis before Edie could so much as open her mouth.

'Yes. Edie.'

'How d'you do? You can call me Tommie.'

The other girl was all sharp wits and weary eyes. Around the same age as Edie and slightly taller, she was wearing a loose blue dress with her hair tied back in a bright red scarf; a cigarette dangled from her bottom lip. Tommie, she'd called herself – and she embarked on a stream of chatter, all delivered without so much as a glance at Edie. Snatching up her cardboard box, she rushed back out of the room, only hesitating in the doorway long enough to give Phyllis a knowing look.

'What about . . . *my mattress*?' Tommie raised her eyebrows as she emphasized the words. Phyllis folded her arms and pursed her lips.

'My brother will sort it out later. Well, I think that's all for now . . .' Phyllis scowled at Tommie, and then turned on her heel and walked out of the room, leaving her two tenants to get on with things.

'*Matrimonial* . . . Should have heard 'em – went on for *days*. Welcome to Dove Street,' Tommie whispered, rolling her eyes and grinning at Edie, before pulling the door closed behind her.

Edie listened as the footsteps clattered away down the stairs, before taking out the two brass keys that Mrs Collier had given her, turning one in the keyhole and sinking back against the locked door.

She stared around the room, taking it all in. It had happened so quickly – the awful look on Frank's face, those men hammering on the door, last night in that awful hotel, the long walk to Dove Street. She'd only left her home in Deptford yesterday morning but it seemed so far away now. Another life entirely.

Edie moved towards the bed to finally sit down, when suddenly a thought flitted across her mind and she hesitated. There was one thing she had to do first. Opening her old leather handbag, she carefully took out a small brown envelope, crammed full of cash, all tied together with a thick elastic band. She held it by her fingertips as if holding it more tightly would make everything real. It was more money than she'd ever seen in her life, and Edie didn't want to touch it or carry it with her for one minute longer than she had to.

She searched around the room for hiding places and then gently lifted up the mattress from the metal springs underneath it. Getting to her knees, she shoved the envelope as far as it would go, so that it was wedged firmly between the mattress and the wall. It would be safe there for a little while. Edie knew that she would have to face the fact of the small brown envelope at some point . . . but not today. She smoothed down the eiderdown, making sure that it covered the edges of the mattress, carefully checking that the money was safely tucked away out of sight. Fussing with the salmon-pink quilt, she picked at the edges of it nervously until she was completely satisfied. Only then did she let out a long sigh and sit back on her heels. When she looked down, Edie saw that a tiny cloud of glittering spangles had settled on her lap in silver, gold and blue.

Five Years Earlier

Edie tried on her two dresses, twirling around madly in front of the mirror to see which one she preferred. There was the pale green dress she'd worn out dancing with its frilly petticoats and sweetheart neckline, or a black wool dress that was tight fitting but covered everything up nicely. The black, she thought . . . after all, he'd already seen the green one and she wanted to look like a serious person. A girl you could get serious with, that was. She poured a nip of gin into her pink Bakelite toothmug and downed it in one go. He probably wouldn't even turn up. Men like that were all charm until they got what they wanted, then you'd be left knitting booties out of lemon-yellow wool and not see sight or sound of them again. It had happened to her friend Margaret. Just the once it was too, she'd said. Her back pressed against the alley and her knickers around her ankles. 'I wouldn't have minded,' she'd said, 'but they were my best ones and I got dirty black oil on them.' As it turned out, Margaret had got a lot more than oil on her best silk drawers. Nine months later she had a baby boy weighing in at nearly ten pounds. 'Like a prize turkey,' she'd exclaimed when Edie visited her at home. The baby was wrinkled, rash-ridden and smelled of something nasty but Edie nodded and said he was handsome as could be and Margaret seemed satisfied. She couldn't remember the last time she'd seen Margaret out and about now.

'And let that be a lesson to you, Edie,' she said to herself in the mirror.

Her hair was not behaving itself as it should: one curl was sticking out at an awkward angle and refused to be pinned or flattened back down. Apart from that, she looked quite nice in her black wool dress. She admired herself for a bit, the curve of her waist and her large hazel eyes. She wasn't bad when she made an effort . . . not that she was making an effort for him.

Edie told herself that she honestly didn't care about Frank as she checked the clock again. It was nearly seven but there was no sign of him. She looked nice and she might pop into the King's Head and treat herself to a gin and lime if he didn't come. She knew everyone who drank in there and was sure to find one or two of the girls from the biscuit factory. She'd been moved from plain to fancy biscuits but all her old mates were 'cracker packers' and she missed the fun they would have telling stories about their dates, or husbands in the case of the older women. Yes, that's what she would do, and then it wouldn't matter whether he turned up or not. She checked the clock once more, then sat down on her bed to wait.

At exactly seven o'clock there was a loud rat-tat-tat on the door and Edie counted to ten before slowly – as slowly as she could possibly manage – walking downstairs to open it. She was glad her Uncle Bert had gone out to the pub already, as he took great pride in inspecting any male callers and teasing her about them for days afterwards.

'I'm only doing what your father would do if he was here,' Uncle Bert would say as Edie protested her embarrassment. She wanted to keep Frank all to herself though . . . for a while at least. He wasn't like the others. She reached for the front door and took a deep breath.

There he stood, as handsome as she remembered, carrying flowers no less. Pink carnations, wrapped in brown paper. Edie couldn't remember anyone ever bringing her flowers before. There was Martin, the boy who worked at the butcher's in the High Street, who took her to the pictures once, picking a dandelion off a crack in the street before handing it over to her to blow the head off it. He said it was good luck, and Edie didn't ever argue about things to do with luck so she had done it, but it hadn't been lucky for Martin who had the most awful breath and never got to take her out again.

But these flowers were something else – and so was

Frank, standing there holding them in his navy suit and a clean white shirt. Those blue eyes twinkling just for her.

'So, not washing your hair then?' he said and Edie felt a flare of annoyance. Not *You look nice* or *Where would you like to go?* but like he'd trapped her in a game that she'd lost. She regretted the black woollen dress, and wished she'd answered the door with a towel draped around her head in a turban, wearing her old flowery dressing gown with its mismatched belt.

'Oh, it's you . . . I was just going out as it happens.' Her smile was secret and spiteful, and a small frown appeared between his eyes for a brief second. Edie knew she'd struck a small blow: knocked him off balance for a moment and revealed that he wasn't quite so sure of himself as he made out.

'Are they for me?' she said, reaching a hand towards the pink carnations.

'No, they're for my grandma. That's why I called, actually . . . to tell you I'm going to visit my poor sick grandma so I can't take you out after all.'

Edie's face must have registered the same shock and surprise as Frank's face had just a few moments ago. It was a game of chess and now she was the one checkmated. She pulled a face and withdrew her hand, feeling rather foolish. This man was constantly knocking her off balance and she both liked the challenge of it and disliked how stupid it made her feel.

'I'm kidding . . . that's all. Are you coming or not?'

He laughed and his face relaxed. The frown was gone now and his pale blue eyes sparkled with the fun of teasing her. The pink carnations came towards her and this time she took them, burying her face to smell them for a moment to hide her embarrassment.

'OK then, but I can't be out too late. I've got an early shift tomorrow.'

'Don't worry, Cinders, I'll have you home before midnight.'

'Where are you taking me anyway?' Edie pouted slightly, but in a way that she knew men generally found attractive.

'I thought I'd take you to the pictures. Might even spring for the Circle and a box of chocolates if you're a good girl. You look beautiful, by the way . . .'

His face turned serious, all the teasing faded away and Edie saw that he liked her. She gazed up at him for a moment, feeling a faint blush spreading across her cheeks, and then they both smiled shyly at each other.

'So, pictures it is then,' he said firmly and she nodded.

Edie liked going to the cinema, and going upstairs to the Circle, where she could look down on everyone she knew, might be nice. She silently gave thanks that she'd chosen the black woollen dress over the pale green, which would have been quite wrong for this.

She abandoned the pink carnations on the side table by the front door where they kept the mail. She wanted to take a moment to put them in water but Frank was hurrying her along.

'Let's get going then – don't want to miss the start, do we?' he said, moving away from the doorstep towards a large black motorbike that was parked in the street.

'I'm not getting on that thing,' she said, faintly horrified that he would expect her to.

'But it's my pride and joy!' Frank laughed as he sat astride it.

Edie edged gingerly towards the motorbike. 'Suppose I fall off it . . . ?'

'Then I'll have to find myself another date, won't I?'

Her mouth opened and closed again as she searched for a witty retort. His face softened and he reached out his hand, pulling her towards him. 'You won't fall off. I'll look after you.'

She hesitated but Frank gently squeezed her hand. 'Climb on then!'

To her surprise Edie found herself lifting up her black woollen dress so she could straddle the bike. Raising her feet away from the ground, she clamped both arms around his waist as the engine burst into life with an awful roar.

3

London, October 1958

The room on the first floor of 73 Dove Street was much bigger than the one Edie was busy making herself at home in. Tommie used to have the top room herself, but she hadn't hesitated to grab a better room as soon as the old tenant, Trudy, had left. It was worth paying out an extra ten bob a week as far as she was concerned. As she put her cardboard box down on the table, she looked around approvingly while flicking cigarette ash into the palm of her hand.

The room had a large bay window and the same light brown wallpaper with yellow chrysanthemums as the hallway, but at least here it appeared to be firmly attached to the walls. It was less gloomy than the tiny room upstairs, and that pleased her. There were two wooden chairs and a small table, plus a gas ring to make tea. There was a gas fire on the opposite wall and next to that a single bed that was missing its mattress. Tipping the cigarette ash from her hand into an empty cup, Tommie eyed the bare metal springs of the bed, shrugged her shoulders, and turned her attention to the small cardboard box.

On top of various old photographs and assorted souvenirs lay an old postcard. Picking it up carefully, she hunted around in the box for a drawing pin. The postcard was of an old tearoom somewhere in the English countryside. It was surrounded by beautiful purple wisteria and had leaded windows outlined in black. Tommie stared at it for a few moments and then pinned the postcard up next to her bed, so she could look at it before she put her light out at night.

Walking over to the bay window, she pushed back the greying net curtains with one finger so she could see what was happening. Outside in the street, the flames were dying out, leaving only the charred remains of the mattress that had once belonged to the single bed in the corner of her new room . . . and all of Mr Collier's worldly possessions. A small boy rattled the front gates of all the houses with a long wooden stick, the clanging noise filling the air as he dragged his stick against the metal bars. If one gate made a particularly pleasing noise the boy returned and hit it again. His very own metal orchestra.

The fruit and veg man had parked up on the other side of the road, the back doors of his van flung open and a small queue of neighbours gossiping as they picked out their carrots and potatoes, or a nice bit of cabbage.

Tommie plonked herself down in one wooden chair and rested her feet on the other. Sucking in a lungful of tobacco, she blew a chain of delicate smoke rings into the air.

As she stretched out her limbs, Tommie began to consider the possibilities for the rest of her day. A familiar ache grew as she contemplated her plans for the evening. It was as if a string were attached to the centre of her chest, so that whenever she took a breath, it pulled her closer to where she wanted to be . . . closer to *him*.

Leaning back in her chair, Tommie closed her eyes, imagining the narrow Soho streets, neon lights flickering on and off, the thump of loud music, the smell of greasy food and strong coffee in the air. The aching hunger grew, blooming inside her until she bit down on her bottom lip. Her eyelids fluttered open as her lips parted. Another smoke ring crawled slowly towards the yellowing ceiling and then disappeared. She began to hum a happy tune – her favourite song. Her lips curled into a hopeful smile.

Somewhere deep inside her, the ache won. There was only one place she wanted to be tonight.

Upstairs, there was the sound of a stern click and then the room plunged into darkness. Edie was curled up on her single bed having barely moved. She felt rigid, as if her muscles wouldn't work properly. All she wanted to do was lie still and be very quiet. Everything felt strange: the mattress under her weight, the furniture, the unfamiliar smell of the musty pink bedspread. Edie couldn't quite take it all in yet, and so she lay there staring at everything in the room, trying to understand that she lived here now.

The moment the penny in the electricity meter was all used up, Edie realized that she didn't have another one. She could either carry on lying on her bed until morning or go in search of change. Wearily, she got to her feet, rubbing at the blister on her heel and standing at the little window looking out at Dove Street. If she stood on tiptoe, Edie could just about peer out at the red-brick houses slashed by rain. She searched the street for signs of anyone she recognized and, finding only people scurrying out of the rain, decided to risk going outside again.

The unseasonably warm October day had turned into a cool drizzly evening and Edie reached for her coat and handbag, buttoning her coat all the way to the throat before tying her navy-blue headscarf firmly in a knot under her chin.

She opened her bedroom door a few inches, carefully checking if anyone was around, before creeping out on to the landing and locking the door behind her, then tucking the little brass keys deep into the bowels of her handbag to keep them safe.

Her mother had always kept the front-door key threaded on a loop of red wool that you could pull through the letter box to let yourself in. When Edie married, she had done the same thing, only with a piece of blue wool – but number 73 wasn't the type of house to have anyone put their hand through the letter box to let themselves in, and for that she was grateful. Remembering the piece of blue wool made her think about Frank, and Edie shook her head, as if she could make the thoughts go away. The last time she'd seen him . . . She couldn't think about that now.

She had to look to the future, make plans . . .

As she crept down the first flight of stairs, Edie heard the sound of somebody opening the bathroom door and stood quite still as Tommie wandered back to her room, humming a little tune as she went. She waited until the bedroom door clicked shut before running quietly down the rest of the stairs, hoping not to bump into anyone else in the house.

Edie had no idea where she might go to get change for her meter but she was certain that she had no wish to knock on any of the other doors. It was best not to mix with people. She didn't mind if the other tenant wanted to keep herself to herself. That suited her quite nicely as she wasn't one for gossip at the moment, and she certainly didn't need anyone to be interested in her.

As she reached the front door, Edie could hear the strains of Mantovani seeping through the kitchen door. It was open a crack and she could see Phyllis mopping her kitchen floor. She hesitated for a moment, wondering if she might ask her for change just this once to save her going outside. Then Edie remembered her stern warning about the stock of penny pieces and hurried away, silently clicking the front door shut behind her.

Outside, someone had removed the burnt mattress from the street, and all that was left was a black stain on the pavement where the flaming pan had landed. Mrs Collier wouldn't be frying for a while. There was a café a few doors down from the Electric Cinema on the Portobello Road that Edie remembered passing on her way to see the room – she could pop in quickly and ask for some change for the meter, if it was still open. She hadn't given much thought as to how she would manage for meals, but she supposed that tomorrow she would need to buy some things: tea and powdered milk, maybe a few ginger biscuits to settle her stomach. The worry was making her ill.

The café was small and greasy. There was no name over the door, just 'CAFÉ' written in large brown letters. A fug of condensation misted up the grimy windows and the door stuck when you pushed it open, so that Edie imagined nobody ever felt truly welcome as they forced their way inside.

'What can I get you?' The woman behind the counter had coal-black hair and arms filled with gold bangles that rattled and jangled as she worked. She spoke in a thick Middle Eastern accent. Edie stumbled over her words, undecided as to whether to stay or to go. The café was warm and the idea of lingering there for a cup of tea was tempting. There was only one other customer, an old man who was busy reading his newspaper and had paid her no attention when she came in.

Edie eyed a corner seat away from the window where she could see without being seen, and ordered a cup of tea and a currant bun.

'I'll bring it over . . . Sit down.'

She asked for the change in pennies and then settled herself at a table, untying her headscarf and brushing the raindrops from her coat. A cigarette lay burning away in a large glass ashtray to one side of the woman who barely glanced at Edie as she poured tea from a large grey metal pot and slopped in the milk, tiny drops of it landing on the counter. The woman sighed and wiped them up with the tea-towel she carried slung over her shoulder, before slipping a currant bun on to a small white plate.

Edie nervously moved the sugar bowl from side to side, and watched the tops of umbrellas and bowed heads walking briskly past the large misty windows. The old man kept clearing his throat loudly, and slurping his tea from the saucer where he'd poured it to cool down. On the table in front of him was the evening paper and Edie strained her neck to try and see the headlines, but he kept the pages folded over, studying something she couldn't read. Her heart raced as for the first time she considered the very real possibility that by now there might be something in the newspapers, and other people could have read it. The old man felt her staring and glared at her. She shifted her gaze to the nicotine-yellowed ceiling until he went back to reading his newspaper and slurping his tea.

Her miserably pale cup of tea arrived, and the currant bun tasted stale, but Edie took mouse-like nibbles at it and tried to think of what she might do next. She stirred a large teaspoon of sugar into her cup and took another tiny mouthful of the bun. Her stomach churned and she pushed the plate to one side.

The freedom she'd craved to do as she pleased felt overwhelming – endless possibilities stretching out before her, lonely and slightly bleak. Gnawing nervously at the skin around her fingernails, Edie tugged at it until it bled and then hid her hands away under the table, as if she were ashamed of them.

The old man's chair scraped back across the linoleum floor and he staggered to his feet. Edie held her breath, waiting to see if he might leave the evening paper behind him. She was desperate to check if there was anything in there. Gathering up his donkey jacket and grey cap, the old man waved to the woman behind the counter, who was now sitting on a high stool, smoking cigarettes and watching the rain fall. Behind her head was an old, rusted advert for Gold Flake.

'See you in the morning then,' he said cheerily on his way out of the door, all thoughts of his newspaper seemingly forgotten. The woman waved a careless hand in his direction and crushed out her cigarette in the ashtray. The café door opened and a wet breeze drifted inside, causing Edie to shiver.

As she watched the old man leaving, Edie noticed Tommie from the room downstairs passing by the café on her way out somewhere. She was all dressed up now and wearing a lot of red lipstick. The loose blue dress she'd been wearing earlier had been abandoned in favour of a low-cut yellow frock and a pair of stiletto heels, and she held a red umbrella over her head. She had to hold up one side of it with her hand to stop its little broken spoke flapping about and to keep the rain out, as it was the only thing saving her from being soaked to the skin. As Edie watched, Tommie started to run after a bus that was crawling to a halt across the street. The girl hopped on just as it started to move away from the bus stop, and Edie stared after it, watching as the broken red umbrella gradually collapsed and disappeared inside.

The woman behind the counter had turned her back now and was clearing away plates and wiping down the back of the counter, moving her cloth around the large metal teapot and the urn of boiling water.

Edie pushed back her chair as quietly as she could manage, not wanting to attract attention to herself. Reaching out, she grabbed the edges of the old man's newspaper between her fingers and pulled it over to her own table.

Carefully unfolding it, she flattened the pages under the palms of her hands. The crossword was half completed and the greasy dribble from a bacon sandwich trailed across the page. The front-page headline was about Princess Margaret's new love affair, but Edie anxiously flicked past it and on through the pages, searching and searching. There was nothing. She got to the part of the newspaper that was all racing form and things she cared little about, before starting again from the front page, checking to see if she'd missed anything. She even checked the lists of obituaries thoroughly but there was nobody she recognized there. Edie sat back in her chair and sighed with relief. She was all right for now, but it could only be a matter of time.

Draining the dregs of her tea, she abandoned the rest of the stale bun and fixed her clothes to go back outside into the rain. Edie felt like walking now even if she got wet. She could put on her little gas fire when she got home, stocking the meter full of pennies so she was lovely and toasty warm. Tucking her hands in her pockets, she slipped quietly out of the café door without the woman behind the counter noticing that she'd gone.

On the corner of the street the Admiral pub was bustling with drinkers but Edie couldn't bring herself to go inside to order a gin and lime or a bottle of stout. It was too much of a risk. In the distance she could see a fish and chip shop just by the railway bridge, and she decided to buy herself a bag of chips, which she smothered in salt and vinegar, feeling the hot grease of them in her mouth. Sheltering from the rain under the railway bridge, she ate them greedily, licking her fingers when she was finished.

Edie stood there listening to the rumble of trains

and the shouts of passing drunks echoing around her. Eventually, the drunks disappeared and the street fell silent, except for the fat drips of rain falling from the edges of the railway bridge. She felt perfectly peaceful for the first time that day. The darkness under the bridge hid her from view, and there was nobody around to disturb her, nothing except the splish-splash of raindrops. Edie licked the salt from her lips and watched the rain falling.

Suddenly, the shrill peal of a police siren ripped through the silent street. Edie dropped the damp vinegary newspaper as she searched the gloom for oncoming lights. There was nothing but darkness. Her heart thumped in her chest as her breathing became sharp and jagged. Then, out of the shadows, a pair of blazing headlamps streaming light and the loud burst of a tinny siren came racing down the road towards her.

A wave of fear flooded through her and Edie pressed back into the shadows, letting the darkness hide her from view. Water dripped down the brick columns of the railway bridge, and the cold wetness of it soaked through her winter coat as she leaned against them. She took a breath and waited. Feeling the whoosh of air as the car sped past her, the siren fading away as it disappeared from view. With the road silent again, Edie let go of the breath she'd been holding on to and then moved forward slightly, checking to make sure there wasn't another police car coming fast on the heels of the first one. Only when she was convinced the coast was clear did Edie move, running as hard as she could down the street, her heels echoing as they hit the pavement.

As she reached the corner of Dove Street, Edie was gasping for breath – but she didn't stop, only slowed to a walk and carried on walking briskly to the front door. The rain was easing into a dull drizzle and a pale crescent moon poked through the clouds and followed her until she arrived panting on the doorstep of number 73, fumbling in her handbag for the little brass keys, wanting to be hidden away behind locked doors where she felt safe.

As Edie turned her key in the lock she could hear the sound of mournful ballads coming from Mrs Collier's back kitchen, but the door was closed. There was no sign of Tommie; Edie presumed she was out for the night. The house felt too big and empty suddenly.

Edie hesitated at the bottom of the stairs for a moment, listening to the strains of sad orchestral music coming from Mrs Collier's kitchen. There was nobody left to care where she was now. She sighed and put her foot on the bottom step. Tomorrow she could start again. Tomorrow she would make a plan.

As she climbed the stairs to her own little room, the thoughts came rushing through her mind like autumn leaves kicked up by a fierce breeze, her initial wave of relief turning to worry.

There was nothing in the newspaper – why was there nothing in the newspaper?

Five Years Earlier

The lights were already down by the time they'd bought their Circle tickets, and Frank hadn't bought her a box of chocolates at all, but a bag of toffees – which she didn't like to eat because they got stuck in her teeth and made such a noise when they were unwrapped, especially during the sad bits of the film. When she'd tried, people had turned to stare or muttered '*shh*' under their breath until she'd given up, and now Edie sat awkwardly with the crinkled white paper bag on her lap not wanting to touch them, but unable to find anything else to do with them. She wished they hadn't come to the pictures now. It wasn't even any fun being in the Circle, as they'd arrived so late that nobody could see her with him anyway.

Edie wished they'd gone straight to the pub where she knew people. She could have nursed a gin and lime and not had to worry about making a noise. She wanted a cigarette too but she hadn't brought any, and she didn't want to ask him for one. The cinema was crowded and the black woollen dress felt too hot. Edie kept pulling the collar away from her neck with her finger but it made no difference. She felt a slight itch caused by the heat but she really didn't want to start scratching like a flea-ridden cat next to him.

On the screen, Deborah Kerr was rolling about on the sand with Burt Lancaster and Edie's mind started to wander, wondering if all that sand was uncomfortable. It was probably quite damp, but if you had the right person did damp sand not matter that much and the passion just take you over? Edie had not really encountered such passion, and given that all she really wanted at that moment was a gin and lime with a cigarette it was unlikely she'd feel it that evening . . . or possibly ever with Frank.

The whole date felt wrong, awkward, and she didn't like how he always seemed to win at the little games he played, as if he were a big old cat and she was a tiny mouse. She sighed out loud, and he turned to look at her. Frank must have mistaken it for something other than frustration with her situation, because he placed his hand on her knee.

His fingers nibbled at the edges of her skirt, his thumb rubbing back and forth against her leg, drawing circles that got gradually bigger until she felt herself loosen. She could see him grinning at her in the darkness, his eyes glinting with mischief and a kind of intensity that Edie didn't know what to do with. She caught a wave of longing but then quickly pushed his hand away, crossing her legs so that her body turned away from him and her feet protruded out into the aisle. She couldn't see his face now but she knew he was still grinning.

Edie found herself remembering the curve of his mouth when he'd smiled at her and then she started to wonder about when they reached her front door later . . . thoughts of what might happen, or how much she might allow. He hadn't tried to kiss her the last time he'd walked her home and if he tried tonight, she decided she wouldn't let him. Not this time. Make him wait.

'Gin and lime for the lady . . .' Frank placed the glass on the table and squeezed into the seat beside her.

Edie took a sip gratefully and exhaled smoke from a cigarette she'd managed to cadge from one of the factory girls while he was at the bar.

'He's a looker that one . . .' Violet Crim had said as they'd watched him walking back to where Edie was waiting, raising her eyebrows in a knowing way as she'd cupped her hand around a flame to light her cigarette. Violet was all peroxide blonde hair and low-cut frilly blouses. She always had eyes for the other girls' fellas and so Edie said nothing, just expelled a small cloud of cigarette smoke through her nose and plucked a strand of tobacco from her bottom lip, but a blaze of pride flared inside her that she was the subject of envy. The girls were all watching Frank as he sat there but he only had eyes for Edie.

Away from the cinema and surrounded by familiar

faces, she felt back on solid ground, in control once again. Frank drank a half-pint of dark bitter out of a thick glass with a handle, slurping at it a little and then wiping the creamy foam from his top lip.

'So . . . what do you do when you're not dancing on tables or letting strange men rub your knee in the dark?' His voice was soft as he took another gulp of his beer. He studied her from under his brows and she saw he was teasing her again.

'I work at Marshall's biscuit factory. I was a "cracker packer" but now I'm on "fancies". It's more delicate work so the pay's better . . . although I miss my mates. I was on crackers for a long time.' Edie worried he might be bored by this. What did he expect her to say? She wasn't going to turn out to be a fashion model or a rich girl hanging around for fun. Nearly every girl in this pub worked for Marshall's Biscuits. It was good money and the work wasn't bad.

'What do *you* do?' Her tone implied that she had no intention of being impressed no matter what he said.

'This and that . . .' He sniffed and took a long gulp of his beer.

'What does that mean? You could be a burglar for all I know, or a Peeping Tom creeping into girls' bedrooms.'

Frank laughed, loud and hearty, so that people turned to look at them. Edie was trying to sound smart but she knew it had come off as daft.

'Maybe I am – or maybe I don't need to creep anywhere. Maybe I get invited . . . What do *you* think?' He grinned, as if he knew the conversation had taken a turn that would leave her wondering what to say next. When she said nothing, he winked at her.

Edie sipped at her gin and lime, her cheeks flushing under the weight of his teasing, suddenly aware of the solid warmth of his body next to her.

'Come on, let's get you home. You've got that early shift in the morning and we can't have you missing out on your beauty sleep, can we?' And with that he took the cigarette out of her hand, crushing it into the ashtray on the table between them.

'Oi, I was smoking that.'

'Dirty habit . . .'

'You smoke!'

'I do a lot of things I shouldn't.'

He leaned towards her as if he was going to whisper something in her ear. She felt his thumb drawing circles on her knee under the table, only on top of her skirt this time. It was a reminder that he had felt her loosening under his touch and he wasn't going to let her pretend that she didn't like him. He looked at her as if he knew every thought she'd ever had. As if he could peel her back layer by layer, and there was nothing she could do about it.

Edie didn't know what to say to him. Nothing sounded smart or clever, like it did when she was flirting with the lads in the factory. Sometimes the drivers liked to have a bit of a joke with her and she never minded, but this was different.

She gulped down her gin, feeling grateful for the Dutch courage, and gathered her things, following him out of the pub. Now he would see she wasn't a pushover. She'd work him out just as she worked out all the lads with their sweaty hands and Old Spice ways. No matter what happened, she would not kiss him goodnight. She wouldn't even make another date with him.

As they walked back to her house, Edie was planning exactly the right type of clever remark to leave him with – a proper zinger to send him home with a flea in his ear. She could see her front door in the distance now and she pursed her lips ready to tell him his fortune. The cheek of him, with his game-playing and knee-rubbing. Who did he think he was?

Frank had not attempted to hold her hand and they walked along side by side, not speaking for several steps. The silence was neither comfortable nor uncomfortable. Edie watched his shadow on the ground next to hers, broad and solid, and felt the same loosening as before. They were nearly at her door now and her rehearsing of smart remarks was suddenly overtaken by the very real fear that he wouldn't ask to see her again.

Her feet slowed a little and for a moment it was perfectly quiet, just the sound of their breathing and the gentle click-clack of her heels hitting the concrete.

One of her shoes was a bit worn down on one side and made a little scraping noise like sparks on metal.

'You know you're quite rude. Marching me out of the pub like that. I don't know who you think you are . . .' Edie felt the need to assert herself, despite the risk he might not ask to see her again.

Without warning, he grabbed her elbow, spun her around to face him and pushed her back against the wall of her neighbour's house. She could feel his warm beery breath on her face, and then he reached to the side of her, kissing her gently and too slowly on her neck. Before she knew it, her arms were wrapped tightly around his shoulders, clinging to his back, while he moved up her neck and on to her cheek. He held her face between the palms of his hands and they stared at each other for the longest time before he finally kissed her. The heat of his mouth seeking hers. He wasn't smiling now. The games were over. The kiss lingered raw and truthful on her lips.

'You're a beautiful girl, Edie. I could really like you. What time do you finish your shift tomorrow?' he said, his voice gruff and urgent now.

'Two o'clock.' Edie's heart pitter-pattered as she gazed up at him, her mouth forming a shy smile.

'Pick you up at two then. Factory gates. Don't keep me waiting.'

'I haven't said I want to see you again . . .' The words were lost as Frank's lips touched hers before pulling away, leaving her panting slightly against her neighbour's wall.

'Oh, I think you did . . .' he whispered, his breath hot against her ear. Edie opened her mouth to speak but nothing came out. 'Two o'clock then.'

He winked at her, and then walked away without looking back.

4

London, October 1958

The narrow streets of Soho were already packed with a night-time crowd when Tommie checked her lipstick in her compact mirror under the lamplight. She fluffed her hair out and then patted it back down again, unable to decide exactly what she was trying for. In front of her the bright neon signs flashed on and off, announcing coffee, music or girls. That familiar ache inside her turned into a fizzing excitement at the possibilities now she was here.

Tommie knew exactly where she was heading. She walked quickly down Meard Street, passing Le Macabre coffee bar where a crowd had spilled out on to the pavement, before finally arriving at her destination: a small, easily missed shopfront with an ever-open door. Once you stepped inside, the sweet steam of the espresso machine enveloped you, and the blast of the jukebox quickly sorted those who belonged there from those who didn't. Tommie straightened her shoulders, ran her tongue over her lips and made her entrance.

There was a padded wooden bench running along one wall with three small white tables in front of it.

Most evenings, dating couples or singles looking for fun had to squeeze past each other to get in and out of their seats. Occasionally a young woman would be toppled into the lap of a Brylcreemed stranger, and sometimes she stayed there for the rest of the evening. As Tommie glanced around the room, the sound of someone playing guitar riffs on the jukebox filled the air and young men drummed along using the palms of their hands on the Formica tabletops.

At first, as she stood in the doorway, Tommie couldn't see the person she was looking for. A man she didn't know offered her his seat, but she shrugged her shoulders and ignored him. Then the crowd surrounding the jukebox parted and she could see Cassie standing there in her grey work skirt and white blouse, a tray of coffee in her right hand. Cassie waved her over but Tommie wasn't in the mood for a gossip tonight. She was looking for someone and he wasn't there. Cassie knew instantly by Tommie's hesitation and she shook her head.

So, he hadn't been in yet? Tommie wondered if it was worth hanging around to see if he would arrive later. A crowd of girls pushed past as she stood there hesitating, making her mind up for her. Tommie raised her hand to wave at Cassie, but she'd already turned back to the jukebox to feed it someone else's coins.

Out on the street the rain dripped down the broken spoke of her red umbrella and Tommie cursed the fact that her hair would be ruined now, after she'd spent the night sleeping in her curlers to get it just right. She dashed into the red telephone box on the corner of the street and had barely picked up the receiver before a hand banged on the glass, and a man gestured to her that he needed the telephone.

'I was here first!' Tommie mouthed through the glass. 'Bloody cheek.'

The man pulled a face but started to walk away towards the telephone box in the next street. Feeling in her pocket for some change, she dialled the number that she knew off by heart. The pips sounded urgently in her ear and she pushed coins into the slot.

'Hello,' the voice said.

'Are you alone?' Tommie whispered into the mouthpiece.

'Oh . . . it's you.'

'Yes, it's me.' The waiting was excruciating. This was always the worst moment. The pause for approval or rejection. Tommie already felt the sting of humiliation but part of her liked the challenge of taming him. All those other sharp-shoed boys were so eager – too eager. Pulling out chairs for her and buying her chocolates.

'I was going to meet a friend later.' Past tense. Tommie's heart leapt and she exhaled softly. Then her stomach tightened as she realized 'a friend' might be a woman. There were many such 'friends', usually peroxide blonde with shabby second-hand fur coats and worn-down heels. She was different though . . . not like the others. He was coming around to that way of thinking – she was sure of it.

'Up to you . . .' She knew how to play this game, was practised at it now. Withhold just enough to make it interesting and then reluctantly give herself up. She knew he liked it that way.

She could hear him breathing down the line. Weighing it up – the offer. That annoyed her: the fact that she had offered and he was weighing up if it was worth it to him. Was *she* worth it to him? It never occurred to her to ask if he was worth it to her. It was *all* worth it – or at least it would be . . . one day. She was winning this game; she just needed a little patience.

Then, somehow, the decision was made and it didn't involve her at all. Something came down on her side over the others. A small voice buried deep inside Tommie wondered if it was just the convenience of home delivery.

'Come round . . . I'll leave the door open.' And the phone went dead.

Ten minutes later, Tommie stepped into a dimly lit passageway and closed the front door behind her. She was expected but she still didn't know if she was welcome. The hallway was whitewashed and empty as if nobody lived there. It was the kind of place where people picked up their post rather than let it linger for others to nose at. She climbed up the familiar stairs, past the door with the elderly Jewish man who screamed in his sleep so loudly they could hear him on the next floor. Reaching the second floor, Tommie found that his apartment door was also ajar.

He was sitting on a sofa wearing a wine-coloured bathrobe. As Tommie slipped off her coat, he offered her a sip from his glass of brandy. Not even her own glass of brandy, but his leftovers. She wished she hadn't called now but she couldn't stay away. His moods drove her crazy. He could be sweet though . . . when he felt like it.

Tommie lit a cigarette and he frowned.

'You know I hate it when you smoke in here,' he said.

'It's the price you pay, I'm afraid,' she replied, and then wondered why she made it sound as if she didn't mind when he wasn't nice to her. Tommie took a gulp of his drink and felt the warmth spreading out through her veins. She smiled at him and he stared back at her. The cigarette was crushed into an ashtray, which she regretted instantly, her mouth feeling empty and awkward as her hands fussed by her sides.

'I could go if it's not convenient,' she said without meaning it.

'No . . . stay for a while.'

Ah, 'a while' then, that was the offer, not 'stay the night' or 'be mine forever'.

Tommie felt a pang of disappointment. She would change his mind though. He put his hand up to pat her leg as if she were his pet and then he stood up to face her.

'You go on in – I need to piss.' He gestured to his bedroom and Tommie looked at him coyly.

'Well, aren't you the charmer?'

He sighed. 'You caught me at a bad moment.'

'Then maybe I should leave you to it?' Tommie placed her hand on her hip and waited.

'No . . . I'm sorry, I've had a long day. Don't go.'

Tommie smiled. The radio was playing softly in the background, a song she liked. She began to sway her hips from side to side. 'I'll cheer you up . . . Come dance with me. I like this song.'

He shook his head but Tommie was already moving towards him holding out her arms to gather him in. He threw his head back and laughed but he didn't resist as she swayed right into him.

'See? Isn't that better?'

'You smell nice . . .' He pulled her closer.

The bedroom door was open and she could see the familiar red covers of his double bed. There was a moment where she caught a glimpse of her jacket thrown carelessly over the back of the chair where she'd abandoned it, and Tommie thought about picking it up and leaving him wanting her. She thought something like this every single time yet she couldn't walk away. It was a drug pulling her towards him, intoxicating in the moments before the reality and then afterwards . . .

He grinned at her, knowing she wouldn't leave now. She pouted a little and then shrugged her shoulders.

Tommie slipped out of her shoes and walked slowly across the living room towards the open door of his bedroom. The bed had been made neatly, all hospital corners and smoothed-out pillow cases, and Tommie knew he hadn't done that. Nothing meant anything to him – except her. He'd told her that once. She'd amused him and he'd said that if he wanted to get himself tied down then he liked a girl who made him laugh. Tommie had placed herself at the top of his list at that moment. It had been a long time ago. Now she waited . . . and relied on one fact. In all the time they had been seeing each other, he had never once turned her away. That's how she knew that, deep down, he really did care something for her.

By the time he closed the bedroom door she was naked under his covers. He flicked off the light and climbed in with her. Tommie stared up at him in the darkness. Outside the window, a neon light advertised the bar on the corner. The bright outline of a champagne glass made shadows on his bedroom wall. Flashing on and off and then on again.

His skin felt smooth under her fingers and she could smell the brandy on his kisses as he began his usual routine. His kisses were always in the same order so Tommie was never surprised by anything he did. Even when sometimes he hurt her a little it didn't come as a surprise. She thought of it as the way in which he alleviated his own boredom and was able to tell one woman from another. The ones he could hurt a little and the ones that he couldn't. Tommie didn't want to be a woman that it was all right to hurt a little along the way but it was better than being alone.

His mouth moved down, tracing her collar bone, and she ran her fingers through his hair, imagining what it would be like to have the right to touch him casually whenever she felt like it, instead of tracking him down after dark in Soho and making an appointment to do this.

Tommie thought too much for a while and the anger started to pool in her belly. White-hot rage, but she damped it down until all she could feel were his kisses on her bare skin and then he was inside her and she ceased to exist. Tommie knew that. He couldn't have told you who was under his weight. It was afterwards she lived for . . . the softness.

Eventually, he rolled off her and on to his back. Tommie crawled towards him, leaning over his damp chest and burying herself under his arm. She posed them as if he really were her boyfriend. An arm around her shoulders and then nothing but peaceful breathing and the warmth of him, his heart quietly beating against her ear, and she wanted to cling to him and beg him not to move. Not ever to move. The ticking thrum of her anxiety stopped and Tommie relaxed, nuzzling closer. His breathing started to slow and she felt certain that he'd fallen asleep. She stroked his chest with her fingers and breathed in his scent. This was all she'd wanted.

5

London, October 1958

At number 73, Phyllis put the empty milk bottles out on the doorstep for the morning, with a note for the milkman rolled up carefully and tucked inside the bottle. She supposed she'd need one less pint now. Phyllis was a patient woman under normal circumstances, but these were certainly not normal circumstances. She had been made a show of and that was for sure. People were gossiping about her and the goings on. Her husband. And *Trudy* of all people. Nasty little tart, she was. All big eyes and too much cheap perfume. Stank the place out with it. Like living in a bloody rose garden.

Phyllis stood there, eyeing the blackened stain on the pavement gleaming under the street lamp and wishing the rain would make it go away. Water trickled down the drain and pooled over the front garden. The pavement turned grey and slick with water but the defiant black stain stared back at her.

At least she'd found a new tenant quickly. She seemed like a strange, nervous girl, but as long as she paid on time Phyllis didn't care what her tenants got up to. At least now they wouldn't be getting up to it with her old man.

'Phyllis, you're imagining things.' He'd said that to her before she found them. Stood there, as large as life, and told her it was all in her mind. Then she'd come back early from her sister's house one day. Not feeling well at all. Terrible cramping in her belly and a headache. Proper sick she'd felt . . . until she turned the key in the door.

Their rooms on the ground floor were all empty, but his coat was on the back of the door so she knew he hadn't gone far. She'd only been fit for bed all the way home, yet for some reason she took off her shoes and crept up the stairs to the first floor in her stockinged feet. It was the giggle that did it. A certain type of low giggle, and just like that she knew.

He had stood there in nothing but his vest and pants looking ridiculous, and as for her . . . lying there on the bed that Phyllis had bought and paid for, naked as the day she was born. Their faces shocked as could be. Like a painting, she thought, as she started to throw things.

She grabbed that Trudy by her arm and dragged her off the bed. The girl held the sheet up to hide her nakedness and the commotion got so loud next door that her friend Iris appeared in the doorway smoking a cigarette.

'What's all the racket about?' When Iris saw Phyllis standing there with the naked Trudy and Mr Collier in his vest and pants, she started to laugh. The peal of her amusement ringing out, on and on.

Phyllis was not going to be a laughing stock, not in her own house. Out they all went, bags and all. Served them right.

But now, with this being her third night on her own, loneliness began to tug. Not that she wanted him back. No, she was done with Terry Collier once and for all – but still, there was nobody to warm the bed now, or occasionally (and it had been very occasionally) make her a cup of cocoa at night. 'Here you go, love,' he would say, holding out a steaming mug, and she would act surprised, as if it was a bouquet of roses, even though he'd been clanging pots in the kitchen for the last ten minutes.

Truth was, Phyllis missed the essence of Terry without actually missing the person. She didn't miss the constant clean shirts, neatly pressed just as he liked them, and the way he used to slurp his morning tea or perch his reading glasses on the end of his nose to see the paper. On those days his breathing annoyed her and she would have given anything to be alone. 'If I win the pools,' she would mutter to herself and make plans immediately to depart for somewhere with sunshine. She didn't know *where*. Phyllis was never very good at geography. Wherever they have sunshine was good enough for her. She'd never won the pools, though, and now he was gone and she had no need to escape to the sunshine on her own.

She could hear the old clock ticking on the kitchen wall and she stood there in her slippers on the freshly mopped linoleum and watched the seconds ticking away.

'Well, this won't win the war . . .' she muttered to herself, although the war was long gone. She turned the radio up and sat down at the kitchen table. She didn't know what to do with herself. The night before, she'd taken herself off to the pictures and watched Audrey Hepburn all dressed up as a nun until she fell in love. *There you go*, thought Phyllis. You could be happy as a nun and then some man takes your fancy and the next thing you are out in the street with your little suitcase. Although she could see why being a nun might not suit everyone. They had to get up very early, for a start.

A mournful ballad started playing on the radio, followed by another one, and Phyllis thought she might like a bottle of stout, but she wasn't sure that she had any in the house. What's more, they usually only drank it on special occasions, and she wasn't sure that this counted. She opened the cupboard doors and started searching at the back for the small dark brown bottles, but there were none. As she came up empty-handed, Phyllis leaned back against the kitchen door and for a brief moment caught sight of herself in the small mirror pinned on the wall. It had a gold frame. It was a cheap thing, but she'd won it at a funfair years ago when she was a young girl, and she was fond of it. There'd been a boy named Billy and he'd taken her around all the stalls. She'd thrown hoopla and taken pot shots at floating tin ducks. Billy had been a nice lad.

Phyllis pulled at the bags under her eyes and sighed. She should have married Billy, although he'd never asked her. Come to think of it, he'd never asked her for another date after the night at the fair. She wondered about that for a few seconds and then went back to pressing the skin around her neck, holding it back and imagining herself young again. What would she do with it though? *All that youth wasted on the young*. Someone had said that – Phyllis couldn't remember who.

The evening was gone and it was dark outside the kitchen window, but Phyllis went on standing there in the gloom, listening to the cats fighting in the back garden and thinking about what would happen to her now. She was too old to start again. She was too tired for it. *What was he doing tonight?* she wondered. Probably at his mother's house, being waited on like a king.

'There you are, Terry, eat up . . .' the old woman would say. Plonking slabs of meat on his plate as though he owned the place. Phyllis wouldn't treat anyone as if they were a king inside her own house, and why should she? Nobody thought of her as being a queen.

The darkness bothered her now. How long had she been standing here? Long enough that she couldn't see herself in the pretty gold mirror any more. Phyllis reached for the box of Swan matches that she kept by the cooker. She could just turn the light on but she didn't want to see herself under the glare of the bulb. She struck a match and watched the little yellow flame burn down, blowing it out before it burned her fingers.

She could go to bed. She could stretch out on that double mattress and say, *Sod you all.* The house felt cold and empty, though, and Phyllis carried on standing there, striking matches one by one, watching them flare and burn until they were just black and charred.

She felt tired most days now. A sadness rolling over her the moment her eyes opened. It pulled at her all day long. She wasn't sad about losing Terry but she definitely felt the sadness at losing something that belonged to her. Maybe it was her hope. That was it: all her hope had gone out of the door, packed up in his little suitcase along with his freshly ironed white shirts and his clean socks. There was nobody left to care for. Phyllis was quite alone.

Somewhere deep inside a dark grief rose up from her belly and suddenly she couldn't bear the pain of the loss. The emptiness . . . She'd lost everything now. *Why?* She'd lived a good life, always tried to do the right things, but now the future stretched out before her, bleak and lonely.

The thought came to her out of nowhere. She had never considered it before that moment but when the idea occurred to her, Phyllis knew it was the right answer.

'That's it,' she said – and did the strangest thing. She took off her pinny and hung it up on the back of the kitchen door. Her handbag was in its usual spot by the kitchen table and she took out her comb, running it through her hair even though she couldn't see what it looked like. Then she put the comb back inside her handbag and snapped it shut.

There was a pile of washing waiting to be done in the laundry basket underneath the kitchen table. Phyllis tipped it out on to the floor and then got down on her knees, pushing bits of clothing around the doors, sealing the gap underneath them as tightly as she could manage. Satisfied that she'd done the best she possibly could, Phyllis sat back on her heels and started to murmur a little prayer that she'd learned in Sunday School.

'As I lay me down to sleep . . .' She couldn't for the life of her remember the rest of it. She thought of Terry and what he might say but all she could see was him looking ridiculous, half-naked in his underpants, and that girl laughing at her. Humiliating her like that was unforgivable.

The oven door squeaked a little. It had done so for ages. All it needed was a little bit of oil, but nobody had bothered to do it and it was too late now. Her hand shook as she turned the knob as far as it would go to the right. Pulling out the metal trays, she stacked them neatly on the floor to the side of her. The gas hissed like steam escaping.

Phyllis bent down and put her head inside the oven but she could smell the grease that had gathered on the bottom and didn't want her cheek to touch it. The stench of gas was all around her but she sat back up and wiped a greasy hand across her cheek while she thought. Then she took off her yellow knitted cardigan, folding it into quarters so that it formed a soft pillow for her head. Placing it carefully on the bottom of the oven, Phyllis shuffled forward on her knees and pressed her cheek against her cardigan, hissing sounds filling her ears as she started to take little breaths.

Tommie watched him wake up, his face a mask of confusion, rubbing at his eyes until he felt fully awake. He wriggled away from her embrace, uncomfortable now as he reached out a hand for his watch on the bedside table. The neon light had stopped flashing outside his window, which meant that it must be nearly midnight.

'Shit . . . I need to go. I'll give you the money for a cab,' he said.

'I could wait here for you to come back?'

'No, it's just business, love. You go on home and get your beauty sleep like a good girl.' He kissed the top of her head, dismissing her. Tommie recognized her cue and rolled away from him. When he got out of bed, she stole a book of matches from his bedside table. She liked souvenirs.

She was dressed and out of the door before the clock struck ten past the hour, the taxi fare shoved hastily in her coat pocket along with her stolen matches. It had been all too brief but she knew she would do it again. Not the next night, that would be too soon, but maybe in a few days. She needed to give him a chance to miss her. Wouldn't do to make herself too available. Naming a day made her feel better as she could count down the hours to their next meeting.

The cab driver was in a grumpy mood and they rode in silence through the dark, wet streets. Tommie felt a tear slide down her cheek and she didn't try to stop it. She wasn't going to make herself feel worse by naming her loneliness or how pathetic she felt suddenly. She wiped away the tears and blew her nose into her handkerchief. The cab driver looked at her in his mirror and shook his head. He was always driving home crying women.

Already Tommie was thinking about the next time and what she might do differently, as if he were a puzzle and all she had to do was find the key to him. She'd said that to him once and he hadn't let her visit for two weeks. Most of the time, he didn't want her to solve him. At other times he seemed reluctant to let her go and she lived for those nights.

Tommie wondered where he was now. He'd put a fresh white shirt out on the bed, next to the money he'd left for her cab fare. While he was in the shower, she'd pulled a button off his shirt cuff. Whoever he was going to see wouldn't have him with all his cuffs buttoned up . . . as if that mattered. Tommie leaned her head against the glass window of the taxi cab and watched the rain falling.

Four Years Earlier

This was the third weekend that Edie had spent with Frank in Margate. They were staying in one of those 'no questions asked' bed and breakfasts, in a little street right by the railway station. The rooms overlooked the sea: sparkling blue in summer but freezing grey-green through winter.

After a year of courting, Frank had become the centre of Edie's life. Every day, he met her at the gates of the biscuit factory to the cheers and teasing of the girls who told her 'What a catch!' and 'That fella is so handsome he could be a film star.' Something happened to Edie when she walked down the street with Frank. She felt taller, somehow beautiful in a way she'd never felt before, proud that she had been chosen and was – as far as she knew – the only girl that Frank Budd was seeing. That made her special, she was sure of it, and it was the only reason she agreed to their weekends.

She found herself twisting the cheap brass ring that Frank insisted she wear for appearances' sake, so the staff would not be alerted to the fact that she wasn't in fact Mrs 'Smith'. The receptionist was a young woman with smudged eyeliner and a sour-puss expression on her face. She looked bored, playing the radio too loud until the owner of the establishment told her to 'pack it in' and the silence was filled with a long cold sulk. Their room key was pushed across the desk without a glance – in reality, Edie knew that she cared about their fake married names no more than their need for directions to any nearby pub. The girl sighed and pointed them to the stairs and a glass-fronted door marked 'Breakfast Room' for the morning.

Frank carried their suitcase up three flights of stairs. There was nothing much in it. Toothbrushes, a change of underwear, a warm sweater for Edie, and night-clothes that felt strange and unnecessary under the circumstances but she'd insisted on bringing in case there was a fire alarm in the night.

Edie walked up the stairs and stood waiting as Frank unlocked the room with its wide bay windows and grey-green sea views. There was a boat in the distance bobbing about and she thought how cold they must be out there crashing about on the icy waves.

As soon as they were safely inside, Frank locked the door and put the little gas fire on to heat the room up. Someone had left the top window open to air the room out, causing a damp misty chill to wrap itself around everything. Edie shivered slightly as she stood there in her winter coat, not wanting to move.

'Soon warm up,' he said although the windows

rattled with the wind outside and the bedding looked thin and inadequate. She waited patiently for Frank to finish making the room warmer for her; for the moment when he would turn and look at her, his smile, the words he whispered – all the things that made the shabby, cold hotel room worthwhile. A tingle of anticipation rushed through her.

As soon as the top window was closed and the gas fire roaring away, Frank didn't hesitate. He peeled off her winter coat and hung it carefully on the back of the door. Slipping off his own jacket, he unzipped her best blue dress, letting it fall clumsily to the floor so that Edie had to step out of it. She wanted to hang it up so it wouldn't crease, but Frank had already pulled her down on to the pink candlewick bedspread and had his hand clamped across the left cup of her black brassiere.

'Look at you . . .' he whispered softly in her ear.

His other hand slid underneath the suspender belt that was holding up her only pair of stockings and Edie prayed he wouldn't snag them. As it was, she would have to rinse them out in the basin, and let them dry overnight.

She was still shivering although Frank felt warm on top of her and she pulled at the weight of him to cover her half-naked frame. When that didn't work, she managed to ease herself away from him long enough to slide under the covers, while he struggled out of his shoes and trousers, throwing his clothes carelessly behind him. They landed on the small red velvet armchair that had pride of place in the bay window.

Edie eyed her best blue dress in its rumpled heap and bit her lip. The candlewick bedspread was thin and there was only a sheet and an equally thin blanket underneath it. The blueish flames of the gas fire seemed a long way from the bed and she wondered if she would ever get warm. Frank was now naked apart from his underwear and Edie slipped closer to him, grabbing at his warmth and pressing him to her. The palms of his hands swept her hair back off her face so he could look at her. Searching her face as if he couldn't believe his luck. They gazed at each other for a few moments before their lips touched and Edie felt a familiar heat spreading over her. This was all that mattered.

A dull bluish light blinked through the windows and Frank switched the bedside lamp off. In the late-afternoon gloom, she could see his pale outline looming over her. The milky whiteness of his skin. The touch of his hands unfastening her, sliding clothing away from her as if he were an archaeologist removing layers to get at some long-buried treasure. Edie felt like treasure under Frank's touch.

He was her first lover, truth be told, and although she had endured the amateur fumbling of several young men in recent years, this was entirely different.

She'd never felt anything like what she felt when Frank slid his hands over her. That first loosening had turned into a complete giving over of herself. It was all his to take as he pleased and Edie couldn't stop herself from wanting him as much as he wanted her.

The room that just moments ago seemed cold and miserable now glowed with colours she'd never seen before. Shades of warmth came and went as Frank moved over her, pressing himself into her. His eyes were closed as he whispered endearments in her ear. The things he wanted to say – what she meant to him. Edie lay there, blinking up at him and felt wonder that, out of all the girls in the world, he had chosen her.

6

London, October 1958

It was fair to say that Phyllis Collier felt like a fool. A week after her close encounter with the gas oven she was still reeling from the shame of her tenant coming home and catching her on her knees in front of it. Tommie hadn't been taken in for a moment; she could see that all right. Standing there in the kitchen, listening to her spout a pack of lies about how the pilot light must have gone out, and she'd let her ramble on and on about it too.

Having to make up such a silly lie made her flush crimson. Then when her tenant made her way upstairs to her room, she'd noticed the yellow sleeve of her cardigan hanging out of the oven. Tommie must have seen it, and why would a wool cardigan be in a gas oven . . . well, not many reasons that she could think of.

She grew more and more upset over the embarrassment of it and the cheek – that Terry Collier had very nearly driven her to the brink. Why, she could be . . . *elsewhere* . . . Quite where was food for thought, as Phyllis had not been anywhere near a church for a long time now. She wasn't really a believer as such, although she thought of herself as a 'good Christian woman' in all things except the part where you needed to have faith in it.

She could hear footsteps coming down the stairs so she peeked around her kitchen door. It was Tommie on her way out and Phyllis, still smarting with humiliation, hid behind the kitchen door until she heard the front door slam shut.

'Well now . . .' she said to nobody in particular and at that precise moment she had a pang of regret and longing, remembering Terry Collier sitting at her kitchen table in his grey-white vest, slurping his tea and studying the crossword puzzle in his newspaper, a cigarette burning to nothing in his nicotine-yellow fingers. He'd listened to her 'well now's a thousand times and never once responded, except one time with 'Any more tea in that pot, Phyllis?'

She stared bleakly out at the back garden but found no answers there. She should get a wash going before it started to rain again. The yellow cardigan lay there on top of her laundry basket, a dark grease stain on one side of it. Phyllis picked it up and hugged it to her chest for a moment.

'Silly woman,' she muttered to herself, 'what were you thinking?' It was all too much to bear. She imagined Terry Collier standing over her grave with the rain falling, him all dressed in black, clutching a wreath of white lilies. She hated lilies. The stink of them in the house – the smell of death on them.

Phyllis took a deep breath, exhaled it with purpose, and then rushed out of her kitchen and into the hallway, the yellow cardigan still clutched tightly in her right hand. Looking around for signs of life, she opened the front door and headed to the dustbin, where she carefully removed the old house brick that was supposed to keep out the sly neighbourhood cat who was the bane of her life.

Pulling the metal lid off, Phyllis pushed the yellow cardigan deep into the dustbin, burying it under potato peelings and grey ash from the coal fire. She didn't want to look at it. The shame of those grease stains . . . the evidence for everyone to see. How silly she'd been. A moment of weakness, that's all it was. Phyllis slammed the metal lid back on top of the dustbin and secured it with the brick. She felt lighter as she walked back to the kitchen, as if a weight had been lifted and her shame temporarily removed.

Phyllis turned the radio up and thought she might listen to the play if it was any good. Voices were company, even if you couldn't get them to talk back to you.

Earlier that morning, on the top floor, Edie woke to the strangest sight in her single bed under the eaves. A magpie was spying on her, his beady little eyes watching her from the windowsill as she lay there in her white flannelette nightgown. Her head ached from worrying. Tossing and turning every night in the gloom. Several times since arriving at Dove Street she'd got out of bed in the small hours and looked down into the street, convinced that someone was watching the house – but there was nobody there. Now she dug her fingers into her temples and tried to ease the tension as she stared around the little attic room.

The wallpaper was peeling off a patch of damp in one corner, fat browning chrysanthemums coming away from the wall. The house was so quiet – too quiet. It made her nervous. She sat up, swinging her legs over the edge of her bed until her bare feet touched the cold linoleum. The thought occurred that she'd better buy a little rag rug for her feet in winter. It shocked her, the idea that she might still be here in this room when there was snow on the ground outside, or ice forming on the one small window, where the bird was still watching over her.

She didn't feel well. The lack of sleep was making her ill. She couldn't stay here – and yet she hadn't done anything except lie on her bed and fret about her future. She was no closer to choosing a place to go. All she did was hide away in her little room and occasionally, when she felt particularly brave, visit the café, stealing glances at other people's newspapers.

In the quiet moments before she opened her eyes each morning and realized where she was and what had happened, Edie felt as if she'd dreamed her entire life. Then thoughts came rushing in, regrets lined up like little carriages on a steam train, one after the other in a neat line.

Since the day she moved into 73 Dove Street she hadn't spoken one word to anybody in the house. At first Edie had been quite happy to be ignored by everyone, but now it crossed her mind that the only people she'd spoken to were the shopkeepers who sold her tea and ginger biscuits, and occasionally the woman in the local café. Edie had overheard other customers refer to the woman as Mrs Salim. She had not as yet tried using the name herself, mainly because she had no wish to share her name in return. Her life was reduced to a series of whispered thank yous to strangers.

Tying the mismatching belt around her flowery dressing gown, Edie wandered down the stairs. It was really more of a summer robe and the autumn chill made her shiver. Her feet were like blocks of ice and she regretted leaving her bedroom slippers behind. They were still neatly stacked under her old bed where she'd left them before she'd moved out.

The kitchenette was empty as usual, but she could smell Tommie's perfume. Edie rarely saw her fellow tenant, but a heavy jasmine scent lingered in the rooms long after she'd gone.

She set about filling her kettle with water to make her morning tea. The water dribbled out of the tap, giving Edie time to stare out of the window at the grey wet rooftops and overgrown back gardens, with their damp leaves strewn across garden paths. A black cat sat licking its white paws on the fence and then disappeared behind a thorny bush, leaving Edie to turn the stiff brass tap off and carry the kettle back up to her room. When she was halfway up the stairs, the light timed out and plunged the landing into darkness, leaving Edie feeling her way along the damp wallpaper until she reached her door.

As the kettle started to splutter on her small gas ring, Edie warmed herself up by wrapping the eiderdown around her shoulders. She stood on the end of her bed to look out of the attic window. Unlike the quiet of the back gardens, people were scurrying past, their faces hidden under umbrellas. The milkman was doing his rounds, crates being unloaded. The empty bottles clinked and the garden gates clanged up and down Dove Street as people were allocated their Gold Top or pint of sterilized milk.

At the sight of the paper boy racing from door to door, a half-whistle on his lips, Edie's mind began its frantic daily churn about the news. Leaving the boiling kettle, she darted down the stairs as quietly as she could manage. This had become her new morning routine: catching the newspaper before the letter box clanged its arrival.

Racing back upstairs, Edie locked her door carefully and exhaled softly. The kettle was steaming up the room now and Edie turned it off, abandoning her dull blue teacup, the little tin of loose black tea, her jar of powdered milk and her small bag of sugar.

She laid the newspaper on top of the bed, turning

the pages and running her fingers over each line to check. Once she reached the very back page of the paper, Edie folded it up again, running her fingers over the sharp creases, trying to make it look fresh and unused. She'd deliver it safely back to the door-mat for Phyllis to find.

There had been nothing in any of the newspapers so far and the silence was starting to bother her. It had been days since she'd left home . . . surely it would be a big enough story for a reporter to write up? Then again, she wasn't really sure what made stories big or small. Maybe things didn't matter to newspapers if you weren't important.

Edie gnawed anxiously at her fingernails. She was taking too many chances by staying so long. She had a tin of mushroom soup and some ginger biscuits, and that would have to do until she came up with a plan. Edie leaned back on the bed and shoved her left hand down between the mattress and the springs, feeling around for the small brown envelope held together with a thick elastic band.

The single magpie sat on the windowsill watching her as she felt the envelope with her fingers. Judging her, she thought, as the bird's head turned from left to right and back again.

She would deal with it today. She would deal with everything today. *She would.*

Edie had been telling herself this every day for a week.

Four Years Earlier

Edie studied the wiry muscles of his back and the sharp jutting outline of his shoulder blades as he leaned past her to grab his pack of smokes from the bedside table. In the dull orange glow of the bedside lamp, the grey sea just visible through the bay window, she watched him flick his lighter open and catch his cigarette with the flame. He lay back on the pillow, smoking his cigarette, and she folded herself under his arm, her hand reaching across his bare chest. Everything felt soft and warm. It was all perfect. This handsome man, the things they did, the way they slotted together effortlessly as if they were meant to be. He wasn't a particularly tender lover but Edie felt the power of him and took it as a sign of his passion for her. That happiness made her feel powerful in return. She was Frank's girl and everything was all right. He kissed her tenderly on top of her head as she nestled into him.

'I'm starving . . .' he announced before leaping up and wandering around the room searching for his pants, his cigarette dangling out of the side of his mouth. Edie smiled up at him.

'You're always hungry. Come back to bed for a minute.'

He leaned over her and began to tickle her until she begged him to stop.

'Stop it . . . Frank . . . behave . . .' She giggled and pulled the sheet up to cover her breasts.

He began to pull his pants on, impatient now. 'Come on, lazybones. Let's go out for a bit.'

'Oh, I've just got nice and warm . . .'

'And I'll warm you up again later if you're a good girl.' He leaned over, kissing her tenderly on her mouth.

Edie stirred and was about to get out of bed when the sight of him standing there half- naked alerted her to something that had not crossed her mind until that very moment.

'Where's the johnny?'

'What do you mean?' He was zipping himself into his trousers now with the cigarette still hanging out of his mouth, a fingertip of grey ash threatening to fall at any moment.

'The johnny . . . We always use the things you get . . . from the barbers. Where is it?'

'Oh, that . . . I didn't have time to get anything.'

'You didn't *use* anything?'

'We'll be fine. I was careful. Don't worry.'

Edie felt a ripple of panic rush over her. She loved Frank but she didn't want to end up like her friend Margaret, knitting lemon-yellow booties.

'Don't worry, *he says.*' She sat up in bed, glaring at him, trying to think about what she should do. Frank tucked his shirt into his trousers, moved across to the bed and leaned down to kiss her mouth. His cigarette was in his right hand now and the ash fell, scattering over the bedspread.

'Hey . . . hey, c'mon now. Everything will be fine . . . Now, if you're a good girl I'll buy you a gin and lime and a fish supper.' He slapped her playfully on her thigh and began to button his shirt.

As Edie started to say something, he silenced her protests with another kiss but this time she turned her face away from him. He stank of cigarettes and a blaze of anger seared right through her. She was furious at him for not telling her, for just going ahead and fucking her without a thought. It was OK for him to say everything would be all right but she was the one who might be knocked up. And then what? Suppose he didn't want to marry her . . . a mother and baby home with some nuns somewhere, or worse? Frank sat down next to her and tried to kiss her again. She remained stiff and defiant, refusing to look at him. Her arms folded against him. He nuzzled against her and she pushed him away.

'No, Frank, it's not fine.'

He sighed and got to his feet. 'Edie, don't be like this. It was just a one-off. I'll get some in the morning. Come on . . . I've been looking forward to this weekend. Don't spoil it, eh?'

He tried to pull her to her feet to hug her but Edie's anger was just beginning and she pulled away from him.

'Get off me. I don't want to go out. You've spoiled everything now.'

'Edie, come on, don't be like that. I said I was sorry. It was just one time. I was careful . . .'

'You should have *told* me.'

'Come on, sweetheart . . .' Frank planted kisses all down her shoulder and arm but she shrugged him off.

He was standing over her, trying to pull her to her feet. It was a battle of wills with Edie still rigid with white-hot anger, her face turned away from him. Suddenly Frank leaned down, his face dark with fury, spitting his words at her and tightening his grip on her wrist so that it began to hurt.

'I brought you away for a nice weekend and *you're* spoiling it now. This is the thanks I get. I've worked hard all week for this. You're making a big fuss over nothing.'

'You're *hurting* me . . .' Edie cried out but she was halfway off the bed and her feet had reached the floor.

'Say you're sorry! SAY IT!' he screamed.

She crouched in front of him, naked, her wrist throbbing with pain.

'*I'm sorry* . . .' Edie cried as he yanked her to her feet but he didn't let go.

Her wrist twisted under his grip. Breathing hard, Frank gave a deep sigh of exasperation and suddenly released her, shoving her roughly down on to the bed. She lay there naked and shivering, rubbing at her wrist, not daring to say another word to him as he walked over to her best blue dress, picked it up from the floor and threw it at her.

'Get dressed,' he said.

7

London, October 1958

In a quiet Bayswater square, Tommie spent all morning watching people's legs passing by the iron railings outside the basement window without giving Edie so much as a passing thought.

The kitchen was always slightly gloomy, as it lay below street level, but it had the advantage of being spacious and removed enough from the main residence to allow Tommie a degree of privacy. The bolt on the kitchen door was old and rusty and Tommie often used this as an excuse for locking Mrs Vee out. She'd quickly hide her bottle of cooking brandy or throw her cigarette out of the back door and wave at the smoky air while Mrs Vee stood on the other side of the door, shouting, 'Tommie, the door's stuck again,' or, 'Tommie, can you grease the bolt?'

By the time the bolt was greased the air would be clear and the brandy removed from plain sight. These were Tommie's only little moments of rebellion and she clung to them as proof she was still young and not just another plain cook, found in the advertisements of *The Lady* along with 'Companion Wanted' or 'Dog Walker Required'.

Tommie had been working for Mrs Vee for five years now. Her employer was left over from a bygone age. She lay in bed on peach satin sheets with matching eiderdown, a cream telephone pressed to her ear, until midday, when she took her bath and dressed. She would then take a walk around the small gardens in the square where she lived and afterwards lie down on her bed once again for a nap before dinner. She spent her mornings inviting reluctant guests to join her for dinner and her evenings feeding the reluctant guests. Whether the reluctance was due to Tommie's poor cooking or Mrs Vee's poor hosting, nobody was brave enough to say.

From time to time, Mrs Vee would wander down to the kitchen and sit drinking tea while telling stories about her life with Mr Vee, who was by all accounts quite the catch.

Mrs Vee had been a renowned society hostess once upon a time and she would tell Tommie stories about the other cooks and their elaborate dinner parties. Her claim to fame was having once entertained the King and Mrs Simpson and she loved to tell of the time he'd congratulated her on a fine egg custard. The compliment had become engraved on her memory over the years, enlarging and expanding to fill the empty space in her life. 'A fine egg custard,' Mrs Vee would murmur, flushing with pleasure as if she had laid the egg herself.

Tommie, on the other hand, had no interest in an old king and his passion for egg custards. The past was deathly dull. She was only interested in the future. Although her days passed quietly in the basement of Mrs Vee's large Bayswater house, there was one part of London that seemed fresh and exciting to her. She lived for her nights out there. The rest of the time she tolerated Mrs Vee and failed to meet her exacting standards. Tommie was actually quite fond of the 'old bat' as she called her, and occasionally went so far as to try and please her, although she didn't often succeed. But it was a comfortable job and the most settled Tommie had been for a long time – for now, she had no wish to leave Mrs Vee and look for more exciting work. They suited each other quite nicely and Tommie had come to think of her as some aged relative she had the care of, rather than the woman who paid her wages. Meanwhile, Mrs Vee didn't enquire about Tommie's ridiculously long grocery lists, and nor did she seem to mind the burnt edges of puddings or the curdled nature of Tommie's custard. They lived in mutual appreciation of each other's flaws.

That morning, Tommie had her feet up on the old Belfast sink and her back studded against the kitchen chair as it was poised, somewhat precariously, on two legs. It was a habit she was always getting told off about. 'Watch out, you'll fall over,' people often said to her, but she paid no heed. She stretched out her stockinged feet, wanting to rub them but not wanting to risk moving until all four chair legs were back on the safety of the green tiled floor.

In her hand she twirled a pencil as she tried to remember what she needed for the weekend dinner party that Mrs Vee was planning. The boy from Kendricks' Grocers ('Purveyors of fine goods since 1856') was constantly forgetting things, leaving Tommie, who often didn't make time to check his deliveries, to change the menu at the last minute.

Tommie's back was aching from several days sleeping on the awful lumpy mattress that Phyllis's brother had sourced. As she sat with her feet up and a cigarette dangling from her lip, Tommie paused for a moment to watch people passing by outside. She liked to make up lives for them and guess what their evenings might look like. Heavy brogues – a swift half in the local and then home to meat and two veg. Fancy court shoes – a gin and orange and the pictures to swoon over someone. She watched young couples walking by arm in arm and imagined herself strolling down the street with *him*. Him opening a car door for her or walking on the outside of the pavement so she didn't get splashed by the rainwater in the gutter. Ordinary things, and Tommie firmly believed that one day they would all be hers. All she had to do was play her cards right . . .

That evening, Mrs Vee would not be entertaining, so Tommie was only required to put together a supper tray consisting of a piece of haddock and one slice of lightly buttered bread. She'd be finished early tonight . . . and the aching inside her had returned after her last visit. For days Tommie had replayed every moment with him. What he'd said to her . . . the way his fingers felt on her skin. She didn't dwell on the lovemaking itself but rather the aftermath: his arm tightly wrapped around her; the way the aching just left her at that moment and everything was peaceful. She knew she could have the most wonderful sleep there, but he never let her stay the night. And now the ache was back. She could feel it, pressing behind her ribs, filling her chest. Maybe she could go to Soho again tonight? It had been a week . . . Was that too soon? An urgent need tugged at her.

The front legs of the chair hit the tiled floor hard, causing a jolt that hurt her back a little. She felt a small flip of excitement in the pit of her stomach. The smell of coffee and greasy food in the air, music playing and the girls in doorways giving her dirty looks as if she was taking their trade . . . Tommie would give them dirty looks back. She had as much right to be in the West End as anyone else. She'd seen some of those girls gathering around, smelling the money on him. Yes, she would go back tonight, and early this time.

The bell tinkled on the kitchen wall and Tommie sighed. Mrs Vee probably wanted her morning tea.

The old girl had an appointment that morning and she'd been fussing over her clothes and hair more than usual, driving Tommie mad with her requests. She wet her cigarette under the tap and threw it in the bin.

She was in a grumpy mood already with not sleeping properly in the awful new bed and now Mrs Vee was behaving quite strangely. Twice she'd dragged her up the stairs to order breakfast tea and eggs, and then dragged her all the way up again to tell Tommie not to bother.

She ran up the stairs to Mrs Vee's bedroom, shoving her hair sloppily back into hairpins as she did so. Mrs Vee was sitting at her dressing table, putting on too much make-up. Her eyes were ringed in smoky black, while her lips were a dark purple. She was dressed in a silk kimono with her hair hidden under a green turban and had the look of an old silent movie star uncovered too quickly by daylight.

'Oh, Tommie, there you are. I've been ringing and ringing. Anyone would think we lived in Buckingham Palace the time it takes . . . Bring some tea, would you?'

Tommie rolled her eyes but ran all the way back down to the basement kitchen, cursing the very many steps along the way. By the time she'd carried the tea tray all the way back up the stairs, Mrs Vee was wearing her best sable fur coat and waltzed straight past her, out of the bedroom door, without a word.

Tommie stood there with her mouth open and the tea tray in her hands until she heard the sound of the front door slamming shut.

'Well, I'll be damned . . .' she muttered wearily. Flopping down on the peach satin eiderdown, Tommie poured a cup of tea, before helping herself to a large spritz of Mrs Vee's expensive French perfume and a violet cream from a fancy ribboned box on the bedside table.

As it turned out, Gladys Vee's appointment that morning was an important one with a Harley Street doctor who was not her regular man. She'd barely registered Tommie coming and going with a tray of tea in her hands. Mrs Vee's mind was firmly focused on other matters. The doctor was a specialist in areas of medicine that had led her to a small waiting room, where she now sat with her feet together and her back stiff. She kept her large black handbag on her lap, gently undoing the clasp and snapping it shut again while she waited. A thin woman with wispy grey hair sat behind a solid oak desk answering the telephone more quietly than Mrs Vee thought possible. Names were delicately written into a large leather appointment book. Mrs Vee could see that there was another empty column next to their names but couldn't think what it might be for.

Eventually, the doctor appeared in the doorway. He was wearing a dark suit, and it surprised Mrs Vee that doctors in this most expensive of streets went out of their way to look like ordinary people, as if she were visiting her lawyer or accountant. She was ushered into an office and offered a comfortable chair on the other side of the desk, which she accepted, before placing the large black handbag close to her feet so she wouldn't keep playing with the clasp. Her hands, however, had taken on a life of their own, clasping and unclasping.

The doctor smiled as he said, 'Mrs Vee . . .' but then his eyes couldn't meet hers and she knew what he was about to say. As he continued, he scrutinized the papers on his desk, even though surely he knew there was no mistake at all. Mrs Vee stared at him and tried to imagine what it must be like to do this kind of thing day after day. She found reservoirs of pity for the poor man until it suddenly occurred to her that he was talking about *her*.

'Maybe Christmas . . . probably not spring.'

Mrs Vee thought that was a strange way to put it and thought of last spring and how she had squandered it, eating chocolates and making telephone calls from her bed. She realized that she should have done more things, but what?

The doctor was silent now, and eventually he looked up at her, as if trying to gauge her reaction. Mrs Vee nodded. Her hands clasped and unclasped once again. She had a tiny stain on the finger of one of her kid-leather gloves that she hadn't noticed until now. She reached for the large black handbag and stood up to go. The doctor shook her hand, and said he was very sorry.

Afterwards, Gladys Vee went to the Savoy and ordered a lunch of lamb chops and boiled potatoes with butter but, when the food arrived, she found that her mouth was unable to chew properly and she pushed the plate to one side. *What did one do under these circumstances?* she wondered, and then the answer came to her: a last supper. She would tell Tommie to prepare a spectacular menu – pheasant or venison – and she would invite . . . ? Gladys Vee didn't know. She had very little family left, one or two distant cousins; most of her old friends were gone. The lovers were so long ago she couldn't bear for them to see her again. If only her darling Bertie were still with her. That was the problem with living to a great age: the losses. So many she had lost count. No, Mrs Vee couldn't work out the finer details just yet, but that's what she would do. A grand dinner party the likes of which she had not thrown since the old King was on the throne.

'Are you quite all right, madam?' the waiter said as he scooped up her untouched lunch plate from the table.

It was only then that Gladys Vee realized she was crying.

Four Years Earlier

In a Margate pub, a few doors away from the Dreamland funfair, Edie was sullen and miserable. Normally she loved to go on the rides and Frank would buy her a stick of candyfloss but not tonight. Her gin and lime lay untouched on the table next to a small brass ashtray. Her wrist was swollen, turning pale mauve under the skin. Frank swilled his pint glass empty in two great chugs and was now smacking his lips together and looking around to see how busy the bar was. He couldn't quite bring himself to catch her eye. The words that fell between them were stumbling and broken, as if they were strangers meeting for the first time.

They were squashed on a tiny table in the far corner of the pub surrounded by locals. It was one of those places with no carpet on the floor and horse brasses over the spot where a fireplace had once existed but was now boarded up and covered in yellowing woodchip paper. From time to time, she could hear loud cheers go up as somebody hit a double top on the dart board in the public bar. They were sitting in the lounge bar where men brought their wives. Most of them didn't look all that happy about it. The couple on the next table stared blankly into space and drank as though they had nothing left to say.

Edie was watching Frank and then pretending to glance around the room as if there was nothing wrong. Their eyes met across the table and he attempted a smile.

'Drink up. I'll get you another one. Might as well, eh?' he said as if they were having a good time and had nothing to worry about. Edie put her head down and stared at her bruised wrist, laying it across her lap like a trophy. She shook her head, biting down on her bottom lip, wanting to say something, but then not wanting to cause a scene in the bar that was already packed. She felt the tears welling up in her eyes as their romantic weekend turned sour. She wanted to go home. Frank eyed her anxiously for a moment and then got up, making a fuss of carrying his empty pint glass back to the bar.

Edie watched him go. Studied him as he smiled and laughed with the barman. Turning on the charm. He'd tipped him, Edie could tell. 'Have one yourself,' he'd have said as they shared a joke together. Then Frank returned with a full pint of bitter and a fresh gin, which he placed gently in front of her, before reaching across to put his hand over hers.

He caught her wrist and Edie flinched in a quite obvious way, which in turn made Frank withdraw his hand but move his chair closer. 'Did I hurt you?'

Edie nodded but she didn't look up at him.

'I don't know my own strength sometimes,' he joked while she carried on sullenly gazing at her bruises.

His fingers, gentle now, reached for her. 'I am sorry, Edie. I never *meant* to hurt you . . .' He raised his eyebrows a little and his expression had a pleading look about it. She moved her hand away so he couldn't touch her, but he looked so unbearably sad, as if her unhappiness caused him such enormous pain, that Edie felt herself softening almost against her will. She didn't speak or acknowledge his words until Frank leaned across the table, whispering to her, 'I've made a right mess of things. I don't know why I lost my temper like that. I would *never* do anything to hurt you . . . I don't know what came over me.'

Edie didn't speak but her eyes never left his face.

'I wouldn't blame you if you packed me in now. All I can say is I'm sorry and if you give me another chance then I'll never hurt you again. We were playing . . . and then I didn't realize how hard I was holding you . . . I just lost my temper . . .' His voice trailed off and his face crumpled into misery.

As their fingers touched, Frank let out a long sigh and she was startled to see that his eyes were filled with tears. Her anger dissolved as she tentatively reached her hand across the table to comfort him.

She couldn't stay angry with him. It was just a stupid mistake – the kind that anyone could make in the heat of the moment. Her eyes met his and there was a glimmer of a smile; Frank picked up her wounded wrist and pressed it to his lips over and over again.

'Kiss it better . . .' he murmured as he placed delicate tiny kisses all over it. His mouth was hot against her skin.

Edie almost smiled but managed to keep her stern face, which in turn made Frank carry on planting kisses all over her wrist and then up her arm until she squealed for him to stop.

'People are looking.'

'Let them look. I don't care.'

'I care . . .'

'Are you still angry with me?'

'A bit . . . You're daft, you are.'

'Not so daft I don't know a good thing when I see one.'

'Oh, so I'm a good thing now, am I?' Edie scowled in mock exasperation but Frank could see the smile hiding behind it.

'You are . . .' His voice was soft now . . . beguiling.

Frank let go of her wrist and took a gulp of his beer but his eyes never left hers.

'I am really sorry, Edie. It will *never* happen again. You know that?'

Edie exhaled softly; then she reached across the table to take his hand. She lowered her voice so the bored couple next to them couldn't listen to their conversation and whispered, 'I was just worried . . . you know . . . about not using anything. I don't want to get caught out.'

'I should've told you. I got a bit carried away. You looked so beautiful in that little blue dress and, well . . . I've never felt like this about someone . . .' His voice trailed away.

A rush of love swelled inside Edie and even though her wrist was starting to throb now, she realized that it was just a misunderstanding. Frank would *never* mean to hurt her. She'd just been stubborn and things had gone too far. She could see that now. He was staring across the table so intently that she wanted to reach over and kiss him right there in the pub and let the other couples have a good old stare. She edged closer to him, threading her fingers through his. Their hands entwined across the tabletop and Edie took a sip of her gin and smiled.

His pale blue eyes were fastened on her now and she couldn't look away. In that moment, he was everything she'd ever wanted.

'And how *do* you feel, Frank?' Edie's voice sounded small, like a child wanting something, wheedling, and she didn't understand why it did. She found she was holding her breath waiting for him to speak and then he did.

'I *love* you . . . that's what. I love you more than anything.' The words seemed to take Frank by surprise but once they were out of his mouth there was no way to take them back again. The words lay between them, inviting and slightly dangerous.

Frank waited for Edie to speak but she didn't say anything and his expression changed . . . forlorn now, as if he'd been left stranded on a high wire and had only just realized that everyone had abandoned him. His head dropped and he stared dismally into his pint of beer. The silence, unbearable . . . and Edie couldn't stand it for one more minute.

Leaning across to him, she reached out to stroke his face. 'Me too, Frank . . . me too.' All wrongs were righted and the past forgiven. His face lit up as all traces of his former misery disappeared.

His chair scraped back on the floor and the next thing she knew, this man that she loved so deeply was on his knees in front of her, his face intent and serious as the grave. He cleared his throat and the people around them started to cheer and egg him on. Shouts of 'Go on, fella . . .' or, in one case, 'Don't do it, mate . . .' swiftly followed by jeers, laughter and the mutterings of an unhappy wife who clocked her husband with her handbag for his cheek.

Frank's pale blue eyes never left Edie's face. Pleading with her without saying a word, desperate to make everything right between them. 'Will you marry me, Edie? Say you will . . .'

The words tumbled out before Edie could stop and think about them. 'Yes, of course I will.'

Her arms wrapped around his neck; her good wrist covering the bruises on the other one. His mouth felt tender and warm on hers and for that moment she couldn't hear the daft comments or applause from the pub. It was just her and Frank, and they were going to be so very happy.

8

London, October 1958

Tommie was in the middle of putting her make-up on, sitting at the table in her room with only her pink hand mirror to see what she was doing. The radio was playing her favourite song of the moment and she pulled faces into her mirror as she mouthed the words:

'I'm in love and it's a crying shame (stupid Cupid)
And I know that you're the one to blame (stupid Cupid) . . .'

She laughed at herself in the mirror, tapping her feet along with the melody.

Tommie was chewing over a problem – whether to take the chance on *him* being available as he was last week, or to try and find someone to come out with her so that any encounter could look as casual as possible. It was a delicate game and she felt that the other night had shifted the balance away from her. Trouble was, most of her gang didn't want to go out on a weeknight any more. Most of them had settled down long ago. Tommie sighed but she had to go now no matter what the cost to her pride. She'd left him alone for long enough to miss her and now she needed to see what he was up to.

As she twisted up the tube of red lipstick, pulling her mouth into a perfect 'O' as she began to apply it, the room was quite suddenly plunged into darkness and the radio fell silent.

She cried out, although there wasn't anybody to hear her. Her pack of Woodbines lay on the table and she struck a match while feeling around for her purse. She knew as she picked it up that she didn't have the right money for the meter, since all she had in change was half a crown and an old thrupenny bit.

'Oh, Mother Mary and Joseph . . . what a carry on . . .' Tommie, exasperated now, sucked her teeth and shook her head.

The match burned down towards her fingers, almost singeing the tip of her thumb before she hastily blew it out and got unevenly to her feet. Tommie had been nervously jiggling one of her stiletto heels around with the toe of her foot, a habit she'd got into while sitting with her legs crossed; now the shoe had fallen off and disappeared somewhere under the table and she couldn't see it.

Tommie scrambled to her hands and knees and felt around the shabby bit of carpet until her fingers caught hold of a stiletto heel and she was able to slide her foot back inside her shoe. It didn't solve the problem of the lights, though, and she was wondering what to do for the best when she heard the floorboards creaking above her head – and thought of the girl upstairs for the first time since she had moved in a week ago.

Edie had been telling herself all week that she had to make some decisions quickly: to find somewhere permanent to live far away from London, where she could get on with her life. But first there was one thing she needed to do. She had been putting it off for long enough now.

As usual, her resolve weakened the moment that she was faced with actually doing it and Edie found a way to pass the hours washing out her smalls, or heating up a tin of mushroom soup for her supper. Eventually she couldn't put it off any longer. The money in that envelope couldn't be ignored. It was all she had now.

After several laps of her tiny floor, she got down on her knees, crouched by her bed and slid her hands under the mattress, feeling around for the bulky envelope. Having retrieved it, Edie sat back on her heels before carefully opening it up and pulling out a large bundle of what appeared to be ten-pound notes wrapped in a thick elastic band.

Edie hadn't touched the bundle of cash since it had been in her possession. She hadn't dared – and so in fact she had no idea how much was there, or how long it might last. She meant to count it all out on her bedspread, licking her fingertips to separate the notes, but somehow, she still couldn't bring herself to touch them.

It had only been a week but it might as well have been a thousand years. It was another lifetime. A cloud of dark thoughts settled around her and then a sudden burst of terrible fear caused her to start gnawing at her poor fingernails once again.

'First count the money . . . then we'll see . . .' Quite what Edie might see she wasn't sure but she was suddenly filled with a determination to get on with it.

She pulled at the elastic until it released the notes and let them fall into her lap. It was a great deal more money than she had originally thought; there were at least two fifty-pound notes, an amount Edie had never even seen before in her entire life, and the idea of that being tucked under her mattress made her chew on her fingernails even more frantically, biting the skin around them until it was red and sore.

She was just about to lick the tips of her fingers and start to count when there was a knock at her bedroom door and the sound of someone rattling the door handle.

'Hello . . . Hello . . . Is anybody there?' called out a woman's voice that at first Edie didn't recognize. She hastily crammed handfuls of the notes under the mattress and straightened the salmon-pink eiderdown over the top of it.

Edie unlocked her bedroom door and opened it a crack. In the hallway outside, she was surprised to see

Tommie looking all dressed up, but with only her top lip covered in red lipstick. It gave her face a strange clown-like expression and Edie started to giggle.

'What you laughing at?' Tommie asked quite innocently.

'Your lipstick . . .' Edie replied and with that Tommie spied a small mirror hanging off a hook on the wall and pushed past her to get a glimpse of the problem.

'Oh, would you look at the state of me?'

'Was there something you wanted?' Edie asked timidly, wondering why Tommie had inserted herself into her room and interrupted something she had been putting off for days.

'Oh yes. Sorry to barge in like this, only the meter's run out. You couldn't be a love, could you . . . only I'm due to go out tonight.' Tommie had such a comical pleading look on her face that Edie found it hard to say no.

'I can spare you sixpence worth. That should keep you going for a bit,' Edie offered and moved towards the small jar that used to hold mint imperials but now contained her diminishing stock of coins for the various meters. 'I'll need them back though . . .'

'Sure thing. I'll let you have them back tomorrow, I promise, soon as I've finished work.'

Edie counted out the pennies into the palm of her hand as Tommie's eyes glanced around the room, coming to rest on what she was quite sure was a fifty-pound note under the bed. Edie didn't seem like the type of person who would happen to have fifty quid hanging around but you couldn't always judge by appearances, and anyway it was none of her business.

'You might want to pick that up. Don't want old Phyllis getting her hands on it when you're at work,' Tommie said, pointing to the note.

Edie was busy fastening the lid back on the jar so it took her a moment to realize what Tommie was referring to. The minute Edie saw it she moved swiftly to collect it and shoved it deep inside her pocket.

'Does she come into the rooms when we're not here?' This had never occurred to Edie and, now it had, she wondered how she could ever go out again.

'I was just teasing. I don't think Phyllis cares about much these days. She's not herself at all . . .' Tommie's voice trailed off and she stopped talking.

'Oh, right.' Edie didn't feel quite as reassured as she'd hoped.

'I'll be off then. I'm going down to Soho for a night out,' Tommie said and started to move towards the door. There was something about Edie that made her feel a bit sorry for her and she couldn't quite put her finger on what that was. Tommie wasn't given to natural bursts of sympathy towards people but this girl seemed strangely nervous and a little bit lonely. An idea formed at the back of her mind.

'Come along if you fancy it?' Tommie hesitated,

halfway out the door into the passageway and Edie couldn't help but smile as her lipstick was still slightly askew. Tommie seemed to take that as a friendly sign and carried on talking. 'There's a bar there where I like to hang out sometimes. I got a fella I see in there . . . So, you could just come along, if you wanted?'

'But if you've got a fella . . .' Edie shrugged.

'No, no. Girls' night out. No . . . I was just saying I might see someone I know, if he's about. Just to say hello.'

Tommie thought that Edie might make the perfect alibi. What could be more casual than two girls popping in for a drink or a chat? Do a bit of flirting. Let *him* get jealous for a change. If things worked out the way Tommie was hoping, she could always stick Edie in a cab home. It wasn't as if the girl couldn't afford it if she had fifties lying around the floor.

'We'll just stop for a few drinks and maybe go dancing later. There's a club I know with a good band. Keep you dancing half the night if you let them.' Tommie, having decided in favour of this odd girl, now felt the need to persuade her.

Edie chewed the inside of her cheek and thought about it. She didn't want to leave her room but it wasn't until Tommie had barged in that she'd realized how desperately she missed company.

She used to love a night out . . . She hadn't been out dancing for years – since before Frank. Edie thought about how she used to be, a girl who couldn't wait to finish her shift on a Friday so she could get to the Rivoli Ballroom with the girls from the biscuit factory. The music playing and her feet moving.

'All right then, but I'll need to get changed.' Edie surprised herself with her decision but Tommie just nodded.

'Sure – pop down to mine when you're ready . . . and thanks for these.' Tommie raised her fist full of penny pieces and grinned at her.

One night couldn't hurt. She deserved that, surely?

Four Years Earlier

Edie had been sitting in the back seat of her Uncle Bert's borrowed car for a good twenty minutes, waiting. The rain streamed down the windscreen of the car in thick ribbons of water. From time to time, Uncle Bert used his wipers to clear it away, but it only started again, enormous fat raindrops hammering against the shiny black metal of the bonnet.

Inside, Edie shivered a little in the thin summer suit that was all she had suitable to wear, and picked a leaf off the bouquet of flowers wilting in her lap. Frank was late, maybe because of the rain but quite possibly because of her. She rubbed the small ball of her fist in circles against the back window and smeared the condensation until she could get a clearer view of the red-brick and white stone steps of the deserted registry office. Nobody got married on a Tuesday. Edie grimaced because it was quite possible that she wouldn't be getting married on a Tuesday either.

They'd had words only last night. Silly bickering over the number of wedding guests . . . and now here she was, fretting that he'd changed his mind about her.

He *loved* her though – she was sure of that. Deep down, Edie knew that although he might occasionally rage at her, or worse go into one of his cold, dark sulks, he would never *ever* hurt her again. He'd promised that – solemnly sworn on the Gideon bible in the Margate bed and breakfast that night.

She studied the back of her Uncle Bert's balding head and wished that she could just run away.

Bert cracked open the front window an inch and lit a Capstan cigarette. Then he coughed deep from his lungs before saying, 'Nasty bit of rain. The lad needs to hurry up. We should go inside in case the registrar thinks we aren't coming.'

Edie studied the frown between her Uncle Bert's eyes. She knew he wanted to say things to her. He'd already tried but she'd told him off about it. 'You're not my father. You've no right to say those things about Frank.' An uneasy silence lay between them as he puffed away on his cigarette and swallowed his words.

'He'll be here.' Her voice sounded so sure of it.

'You are sure about this whole thing? Because once it's done you can't undo it . . .' Uncle Bert grimaced and bit down on his bottom lip to stop himself saying any more.

'I'm sure. We should go inside. Come on.' Edie patted at her hair and then laid a hand across the thin material of her suit, feeling each button as if it were a lucky charm.

Uncle Bert forced his half-smoked cigarette through the open window and watched it drown in the pool of rainwater on the road. A bus swished by, throwing up dirty puddle water.

Edie sighed and opened the car door nearest to the registry office. 'We'll have to make a run for it.'

The skies were bruised purple and steel-grey and the rain showed no signs of stopping. Edie thought about other weddings she'd seen with sunshine and white dresses made out of parachute silk. Brides with roses in their hair and the smiles . . . so many smiling faces.

She didn't have roses in her hair, just a small bouquet of sad-looking flowers from a neighbour's garden all tied up in an old blue hair ribbon. The ribbon had once belonged to her mother. She couldn't bring herself to wear it in her hair but carried it about with her for luck. It didn't seem to be working.

The minute the car door swung open, a spatter of thick raindrops pelted her face and clothes. She ran as hard as she could up the stone steps, pulling open the thick wooden doors. Inside was a dingy passageway leading to the registrar's tiny office and a grand wooden staircase leading upstairs to the function room where marriages were held. Edie had been here once before, for the wedding of a neighbour. The whole ceremony only took about ten minutes before they were back in the local pub for beer and sandwiches. The mother of the bride had brought out a fruit cake covered in royal icing with a tiny bridal couple on top. They were leaning slightly to one side, and Edie remembered the bride's mother trying to straighten them up with her finger, hoping nobody would notice.

The thick wooden door swung open and Uncle Bert arrived behind her, panting and wiping his face with a stiffly pressed handkerchief. A pink carnation in his buttonhole glistening with raindrops. The door closed silently behind him and they both stood there not knowing what to do now.

Uncle Bert looked at his watch when he thought Edie wasn't looking but she saw him anyway. She didn't need to look at a watch to know that Frank was nearly twenty minutes late. She wondered whether to sit down on the chairs in the dingy passageway or to go on up to the function room. Edie needed the lavatory but there wasn't anyone to ask and she didn't want to go off wandering, trying to find it on her own, in case Frank turned up.

Suddenly the registrar appeared on the staircase and peered over the banisters at them both. 'Ahh, here you are! Better late than never, as I always say. Bit of a downpour, eh? Never mind, what's a bit of rain between chums, I always say. Come on up.'

The registrar seemed to *always say* a lot of things but even he couldn't tell Edie where the hell Frank Budd had got to. Edie put her hand on the banisters and started to climb up the wooden staircase. She had to see it through now, whatever happened. If he didn't come, then what? A surge of dread rose from deep inside her chest and for a moment Edie thought she might be sick. She paused on the steps and took a deep breath, closing her eyes to gather her courage. Suppose he'd changed his mind after all the beautiful words he'd whispered to her that night in Margate?

After the fight he'd been tender as could be. He'd kissed her over and over again, begging for forgiveness for hurting her wrist, even though Edie had already forgiven him for it. 'Hush now,' she'd said, pressing him to her.

Suddenly the door creaked open and there he was, shaking off the rain, his mother standing there in her best mauve dress with a little feathered hat perched on one side of her head. She didn't smile, but just sniffed loudly as if the air wasn't quite to her satisfaction. Edie didn't mind at all because she was just gazing at Frank, and those pale blue eyes were smiling back at her. Edie felt relief flood through her. He looked so handsome in his suit, and even though, truth be told, there was a musty damp smell coming off the navy wool, Edie didn't care a bit. Her face broke into a wide grin and she couldn't take her eyes off him. He turned to look at her and offered his arm.

'Ready then?' he said, smiling down at her. Edie nodded and threaded her arm through his. Her little worries about the rain and her thin summer suit melted away.

They were going to be married.

9

London, October 1958

'Come on quick or we'll miss all the fun,' Tommie said. Edie giggled, feeling something she hadn't been allowed to feel in a long time. Tommie had lent her a little white bolero jacket to go over the top of her old pale blue dress and Edie felt quite fancy. It was cold but neither of them wore their coats, preferring to shiver and look stylish.

As the bar loomed closer, Tommie suddenly pulled Edie into a doorway and took out the compact mirror from her handbag. She spent a few seconds patting her hair and rolling her lips together, and ran her fingers around the edges of her mouth to scrub away any stray lipstick marks. Puffing out a tiny breath, she then handed her compact to Edie. 'Here . . . can't be letting the side down.'

Edie ran an index finger under her eyes where flakes of mascara were sprinkled over her skin. Then she removed a stray curl off her face and clipped the compact shut, before handing it over. As Tommie was shoving it back into her handbag, a noise sounded behind them. Edie hadn't even noticed they were standing in front of a large black door until the man coming through it nearly knocked them out of the way. He was much older than Edie, in his sixties, she thought, but still muscular. He took stock of the two women cluttering up his doorway and then, recognizing Tommie, leered at them, holding a cigar between his fingers.

'Lovely evening, ladies. Would you like to come inside? I've got a cancellation.'

Tommie sighed and turned away. 'In your dreams, you dirty old man . . .'

He laughed and took a deep mouthful of his cigar, sucking and sucking before blowing a cloud of smoke towards them. 'It's good money. You never know when you might need a few quid, Miss Hoity-Toity there.'

'Yes, well, must be going . . . *so lovely to chat.*' Tommie pulled a face at him and slipped her hand through the crook of Edie's elbow, pulling her away.

They could hear the man's deep laugh followed by a spluttering cough as they walked away. Edie whispered, 'Who was that?'

'Oh, that's Monty Daniels. He takes mucky pictures . . . you stay away from him. He's got all kinds of rackets going on down here. He's not wrong, it's good money, but you don't want to go down that road.'

'Oh . . .' Edie was shocked by this new world but even so she could feel a pulse of excitement racing inside her. She'd never been to Soho at night like this.

She'd once spent a couple of hours browsing at Berwick Street Market on a Saturday morning when everything was bathed in sunshine, but there were people all around jostling to get their hands on a bargain. She'd known there was another side to it, and to get up close to the cigar-smoking man who did who-knew-what behind that hidden black door made her nervous, but also gave her a thrilling sensation. She felt safe with Tommie, as if she was a protected tourist being shown around by a local guide. The girl seemed to know everybody, and everybody knew her.

As they entered the bar, Edie clung to Tommie, terrified of losing her in the crush. As they shoved their way through the crowd, she could hear her chattering away.

'Yeah, you too, love . . .'

'Good to see you . . . How's your mum? Tell her I said hello.'

'Cheeky bugger, less of that if you don't mind.'

'Can I what? I don't think so . . . You should be so lucky.'

On it went until they reached the bar, by which point Edie felt overwhelmed with the noise and the smell of sweat and smoke.

Tommie braced herself as they reached the bar. *He* might be here with someone else. That was always the risk of turning up unexpectedly. She squeezed Edie's arm for support and looked around. People were squashed together, clinging on to their glasses and shouting loudly over the top of the crowd to whoever had been sent to buy drinks.

Two barmaids were busy pulling pints and mixing shorts while a dense cloud of cigarette smoke hung over everything. Tommie inserted herself between two men who towered over her and waved at one of the barmaids. The woman smiled cheerily and then signalled for her to move away from the bar and wait. Tommie and Edie slipped into the far corner where they were unlikely to be spotted easily, until the barmaid put on a great show of collecting some dirty glasses right in front of them, whispering, 'Evening, Tommie. Usual?'

'Yeah . . . and what about you, Edie? What you drinking?'

'Gin and lime, please. I'll get the next round in.'

'Oh, don't worry about that. On the house . . . the girls are friends of mine.' Tommie gave Edie a sly wink before turning back to the barmaid. 'So, brandy for me and a gin and lime for my friend here.'

The barmaid nodded and gave a signal to her companion behind the bar, who got busy pouring a brandy into a glass for Tommie and a gin for Edie, and then quick as a flash the two drinks appeared in front of them. 'Here you go. Don't let him upstairs see you at the bar. You know he don't like girls getting served on their own.'

Him upstairs was Reggie Vella, the owner, a man

with very specific rules of behaviour in his bar and a hot temper. Tommie was always careful not to get on the wrong side of him in case she had to move on to another bar and actually pay for her drinks.

'We'll be careful. Thanks, Mandy,' Tommie said and then, turning to Edie, she raised her brandy glass into the air. 'Cheers, duck.' She clinked her glass against Edie's and they both smiled at each other. The tall men soon disappeared back to their friends and the two women had enough space to stand elbow to elbow eyeing the scene.

Edie's glass had the faint imprint of somebody else's lipstick on the rim but she didn't want to cause a fuss, what with Tommie not actually paying for it. She tried to smudge it away by wetting her finger with the gin but it merely smeared it further along the glass and so Edie drank from the side that looked passably clean.

'So, what do you think about him over there? Your type?' Tommie pointed out a tall fair man in a suede jacket.

'Oh no, I'm not looking for a fella.'

'Yeah, but if you were . . .?' Tommie took a drag on her freshly lit Woodbine and laughed.

'He's nice . . .' Edie giggled, feeling the effects of the gin and her new freedom. 'Maybe more him at the back there?'

'Oh . . . tall, dark and handsome, eh? I got it.' Tommie laughed again and Edie felt as if they were having fun.

'What about him just coming in?' Edie nudged Tommie, but as her neighbour looked up, her smile faded away.

Tommie saw him before he saw her. He was coming through the door with a tall blonde who looked like Diana Dors in a bad light. All blonde hair and a tatty old fur coat long past its best. He was guiding the blonde with one hand on her waist and they were half-way to the bar when he spotted Tommie, his eyes flickering left and right. She knew he was checking to see who she was with, and Tommie didn't smile at him. She turned her back, swigging down her brandy quickly before giving Mandy a meaningful wave.

Despite her show, Tommie felt a hot pang of jealousy crawling over her. She stared across to the opposite end of the bar where *he* was now standing with the blonde. The blonde looked bored and possibly drunk, but she nuzzled her head towards him and cupped her hand around his to light her cigarette. Their drinks were refreshed, and Tommie spun around, thrusting Edie's drink into her hand despite her not having finished her first one, then leaning back against the bar and folding her arms with the brandy glass still tucked in her hand. Edie's chatter was beginning to irritate her as she glared across the bar, unable to take her eyes off him. A plan began to form at the back of her mind.

*

Edie wanted to ask Tommie things, about herself, about Soho, about life as she seemed to be so much more worldly, but Tommie didn't appear to be bothered with her. Her face looked sad and she was staring across the bar at someone.

'You must come here a lot then?' Edie shouted over the noise of the crowd but Tommie didn't reply. She crushed out her cigarette and said quite abruptly:

'I tell you what, why don't you mingle a bit? There's someone I need to talk to. OK?'

Edie had no wish to 'mingle' on her own. She didn't know anybody and this was supposed to be a girls' night out.

'But we're going dancing, aren't we?' It was only the thought of dancing that had tempted her from her attic room. But the other girl seemed distracted and sullen now.

'Sure, but I just need to say hello to someone first. You have a look around. I won't be long . . .' Edie started to protest again, but Tommie was already walking away.

Edie sipped at her gin and sidled around the edge of the crowd, avoiding the eyes of anyone who looked as if they might be staring at her a little too long. Her shoes were pinching her feet a bit and she wished that she could find a chair to sit down, but they were all taken. She'd felt safe with Tommie but now she was alone the stupidity of coming into town suddenly occurred to her.

The crowd moved like a wave, carrying her back towards the door, and Edie let herself be taken by the flow of it. She could see Tommie in the distance, moving towards a couple by the bar. The man was watching Tommie but the blonde woman next to him seemed oblivious to whatever was going on.

Edie took another gulp of her gin and, finding it suddenly empty, looked around for somewhere to stick the empty glass, but the nearest table was on the other side of a small crowd of young men. They looked full of themselves, all slicked-back hair, putting on silly Elvis faces. None of them came close to looking like Elvis so it was wasted effort as far as she was concerned.

Not wanting to get too close to them, Edie began to move back the other way. The crowd was crushing her into one small space now and she couldn't move left or right. Trapped by people laughing too loudly, she began to seriously wish that she'd stayed home. It was stupid to take the risk on a night out. She couldn't even see Tommie any longer. Another flush of anxiety enveloped her.

The crowd parted; in the distance, she could see the entrance to the bar and thought of heading outside for some fresh air. Squeezing herself between a group of girls drinking port and lemons, Edie took a step towards the door, desperate to get away from the crush. As she pushed her way past the crowd, a familiar voice called out her name and she turned around smiling . . . forgetting for a moment, before her stomach lurched and a wild terror clutched at her insides.

On the other side of the bar, Tommie was circling her prey. The blonde woman with him was older than she'd looked from the other side of the room, and, with some pleasure, Tommie noted the slight sagging of her chin and where her make-up had caked, drawing attention to the lines under her eyes. She had ugly hands covered in rings that appeared expensive at first glance but probably weren't, and her coat looked as if it carried passengers. The old familiar ache started to rise from deep inside her. Tommie took a long sip of her brandy and moved in for the kill.

'Well, fancy seeing you here . . .' She flashed a flirtatious smile; the furious need building inside her as he stared at her. His eyes were slightly mocking . . . but not, she noted, displeased to see her.

'Hello, Tommie. What's happening?'

'Not much. Just popped in for a quick drink with a friend.' Tommie gestured over her shoulder to where Edie was making her way gingerly around the edges of the crowd. 'What are you up to this fine evening?'

'I just bumped into Cheryl. She's an old friend of mine, aren't you, Cheryl?'

Cheryl didn't respond, but her eyes came to rest on Tommie and then skittered away to watch people coming and going.

'And later? Any plans?' Tommie could have kicked

herself, because her question didn't come out as casually as she'd intended, and she became flustered for a few seconds. A faint smirk passed over his face, his lips apparently considering a teasing smile but thinking better of it.

'No plans at all . . . yet.'

'Well, isn't that a coincidence . . . me neither.' Tommie switched on her most dazzling smile and took a cigarette from the packet that she carried around with her in a fancy embroidered purse with a snap-shut top. She'd once seen a very elegant lady do the same thing at one of Mrs Vee's dinner parties and immediately copied her. He flipped the top of his silver lighter and sparked the flame, allowing Tommie to lean right past Cheryl and whisper to him, 'See you later then . . .'

Their eyes met across the tip of the flame as he snapped his lighter shut. Vague promises made in a glance and then, turning away from Tommie, he said, 'Come on, Cheryl, I'll take you home.'

'We've only just got here – I haven't finished my drink.' Cheryl glowered at him like a petulant child.

'Well, now we're leaving, so drink up.'

Tommie felt a flush of delight pulse through her and not even Cheryl's flinty stare could make her feel anything but happy about the outcome of her night out. She was winning these little games and every victory brought her closer to the day she wouldn't need to play any longer. He was hers – he just didn't know it yet.

As he ushered the reluctant Cheryl back through the crowds, Tommie looked around to find Edie to tell her she'd need to find her own way home. It took a moment to locate her in the crowd but eventually Tommie caught sight of her deep in conversation with someone on the other side of the room.

Tommie began to push gently through the crowd but the bar was too full and she got stuck between a couple smooching as if nobody else was there and a very loud group of lads on a night out who tried to grab her waist as she passed them. The smell of hair cream and perfume lingered in the air and a cloud of tobacco smoke settled all around her. It was too hot now and she needed to get out of there. Tommie gave one last shove to get to the other side of the lads . . . but Edie was gone.

Four Years Earlier

The ceremony was over in a flash; no sooner had it begun than Frank was shoving the same Margate brass ring on to her wedding finger and the registrar was pronouncing them husband and wife. Frank pushed his lips roughly on to hers and held them there for what seemed like too long in front of their guests: the girls from the biscuit factory, Mrs Budd and Frank's best man Pete alongside her Uncle Bert, all clapping with silly looks on their faces.

They had nobody to take photographs but her Uncle Bert had splashed out on a bit of a do at a hotel just down the street. Edie had never been there, but it always looked nice from the outside. The kind of place that cuts the crusts off things and takes pride in their china.

'No point getting in the car,' Frank said as he pulled Edie along with him through the rain. 'It's only five minutes and a bit of rain won't kill us, Mrs Budd. Uncle Bert can take my mother in the car. She won't want to mess up her new hat.'

Edie swelled with pride at the words 'Mrs Budd',

but she wouldn't have minded taking the car. She felt slightly out of breath running so fast to get to the hotel and her hair was quite ruined. She'd taken such care with it too. Setting it into tiny pin curls and sleeping on her back so as not to disturb them. First thing that morning she'd combed them all out and then carefully clipped her hair back, so the waves framed the lower part of her face beautifully. Now she could feel damp tendrils slapping against her cheeks as she ran, and her thin suit was getting soaked. Finally, Frank pushed the hotel doors open and in they went, arriving at the reception desk bedraggled and dripping rain all over the polished wood floors.

They were greeted by a stern-faced man in a dark suit and tie who gave them the once-over with a steely eye, clearly deemed them to be unsuitable, but reluctantly showed them to the 'small bar'.

Frank immediately took umbrage at the man's attitude and refused to tip him even though the man stood in the doorway, clearly waiting and hoping. The 'small bar' was exactly that: a small room with a dining table shoved up against one wall, covered in plates with paper napkins draped over the top of them. Just across from the table was a corner bar where yet another stern-faced man was standing ready to serve them. As soon as Edie and Frank entered the room, a girl scuttled past, collecting up the paper serviettes to reveal the wedding buffet.

Rounds of sandwiches arranged delicately on white

china; two sherry trifles with some small glass bowls, and a great silver spoon laid out to one side for serving. A large iced fruit cake sat in pride of place, but there was no bride and groom on top of the cake, nor freshly starched linen tablecloth underneath it. The dining table was bare, slightly scuffed and stained, and not nearly enough of it was covered by the delicate plates of food for the number of guests. The sandwiches had been sitting out some time, as the crusts (which had indeed been left on) were starting to curl a little at the edges. Edie gnawed at her thumbnail, disappointed with how this day was turning out, but it was too late now.

The barman poured a pint of beer for Frank and she asked for a lemonade shandy as she hadn't eaten anything at all that morning. Before she could smooth down her damp skirt and settle herself in a chair by the only heater, the door burst open and in piled her wedding guests, chattering away nineteen to the dozen and heading straight for the sandwiches.

'Where's the blushing bride then?' Violet Crim shouted from the doorway but it was Frank she headed for, placing little kisses on his cheek and holding his hand just a touch too long. Frank didn't seem that impressed by Violet, a fact that Edie was grateful for.

'If you ever get tired of this one, you can send him my way. Lucky girl having him to go home to every night,' Violet said loudly, with a wide smile at Edie and an admiring lingering look at Frank. He mumbled something and turned away embarrassed, but it didn't put Violet off. She carried on her silly chatter until some of Frank's mates arrived and Edie made an excuse to get away. She didn't even remember inviting Violet, but here she was, shovelling down her fish-paste sandwiches and flirting with the groom.

Edie took her seat right by the heater and regretted it as her suit started to dry out and she began to feel too hot. The room was too small for the number of guests but had probably cost her Uncle Bert all of his savings. He wasn't going to let her go without, he'd said, and now here they were, packed like sardines in a stuffy room, with not enough sandwiches, and no piano for a bit of entertainment. Edie plastered a smile on to her face and sipped at her shandy.

Studying the factory girls and some of Frank's mates for a moment, Edie eavesdropped on their chatter.

'Is it anchovy? The fish paste – is it anchovy? I don't like anchovy . . .'

'Salmon, I think. I'll bring them over and you can try them.'

'Port and lemon? And you, Carol? *What?*'

'I'll have a large pink gin . . . easy on the bitters.'

'So, you seeing anyone then?'

'Might be. Depends why you're asking . . .'

'He'll have his hands full there . . .'

'She'll bleed him dry, I'm telling you. I took her up West for a night out. Left with my pay packet in my wallet and came home with only coppers.

Champagne tastes, mate, and nothing in return if you know what I mean. He'll be sorry.'

'I might like to take you out one of these nights . . .'

'Oh, might you now? Well, what did you have in mind?'

'Here she goes . . .'

'I thought maybe the pictures?'

'Oh, that's a bit dull. Everyone goes to the pictures. I like a proper night out me. Up the West End . . . Don't fancy that then, do ya?'

'I told you, didn't I?'

'I could take you up West if you like. How about next Friday. I get paid on a Friday.'

'Next Friday? Yeah, I think I can do next Friday. I'll meet you in the Red Lion for a quick one and then we can go from there.'

'They never learn.'

Her mate Pat from the biscuit factory had cornered Pete the best man and the sound of the girls squealing with laughter as he tried to chat her up drowned out everything else. He was busy telling her about his new job working the bars in the West End and she was busy working out how she might turn that into free drinks.

People had to shout now to make themselves heard. Somebody started a sing-song and there was a tuneless rendition of 'Roll Out The Barrel'. It was all very jolly but Edie felt quite alone suddenly. Her friends seemed to be having a good time and everyone was laughing and joking except her. Even Frank was smiling away on the far side of the room. Her fingers plucked at the knotted blue ribbon on her bouquet until it came loose from the green stalks.

'Penny for them, love . . .' Edie looked up startled at the sound of a friendly voice. Her Uncle Bert shoved a gin and lime into her hand, saying, 'Wishing you every happiness, Edie. You deserve it.'

Did she, though? Edie wondered about that. How do people deserve or not deserve their happiness? What had she done to deserve Frank? At the thought of him Edie looked around to see where he was and found him attending to his mother in the far corner of the bar. Mrs Budd did not look as if she was finding anything to her satisfaction, although Frank was pressing a small bowl of trifle on her, without great enthusiasm from the recipient. As Edie sipped at her gin and lime, smoothing down the damp creases of her skirt, she saw Frank striding across the room towards her and fastened a happy smile on her face to greet him. She was about to make a silly joke about being married but he didn't give her chance to open her mouth.

'We need to cut the cake now, love . . . my mother won't touch fish paste and the trifle seems a bit curdled to her so she fancies a nice bit of fruit cake.'

'But it's our wedding cake, Frank . . . we cut that later on after the speeches and things. It's too early to do it now.' Edie saw from his face that she'd said the wrong thing. His smile faded and he frowned at her.

'What does it matter when we do it? It's only a bit of cake. She's hungry.' His voice rose slightly and a few wedding guests turned to look at the happy couple.

The gin was making her feel worse and she slid her glass on to the carpet and tucked it out of sight under her chair. Daft to fight about a bit of fruit cake but it was *her* wedding. Surely, he should take *her* side now?

'Because we have to do things in the right order at a wedding. It's tradition . . .' Edie paused, her face pleading a little. He frowned at her.

'Nobody cares what order we do things in. She's my mother – and she's hungry.'

Edie couldn't give in and she didn't quite understand why. 'Maybe we could ask the hotel to get another sandwich – bit of cheese maybe. I'll ask them, shall I?' she offered, but Frank's face darkened, a surge of anger rising just under the surface. His lips tightened as he snapped at her.

'Please yourself, but if my mother wants a bit of cake, she's going to have it.'

In an instant he had turned away from her, taking great angry strides towards the buffet table where he snatched up a long-handled knife that was sitting at the side of their wedding cake.

Without saying a word to the assembled guests, or even a glance over to where Edie was watching him with a horrified look on her face, Frank hacked the knife right through the centre of the royal icing, his face red with fury. When he lifted the knife back out of the cake, he glowered across at Edie before declaring loudly, 'My mother would like a piece of cake now . . . if that's all right with everyone.'

Edie gasped. A hush fell over the room as everyone stopped their chatter and pushing food into their mouths long enough to watch Frank carve a ragged slice of his own wedding cake, which he then presented to Mrs Budd on a clean white plate. Tears prickled behind Edie's eyes.

Uncle Bert's mouth flapped open and then closed again. Then he sniffed and nodded, rising to his feet to take control of the situation. 'Good idea, Frank. We'll all have a nice bit of wedding cake and then do the speeches.'

The chatter restarted slowly, unsure at first but then rising to a background thrum of gossip and fruit cake. Edie bit down on her lip to stop herself crying and found that Violet Crim was studying her from across the room. Edie wouldn't give her the satisfaction of knowing she was upset so she leaned down to retrieve her glass of gin from under her chair and hoisted it into a cheery toast in Violet's direction.

'Uncle Bert, you start the speeches . . .' Edie got to her feet and swigged down the last of her gin. Her lucky blue ribbon floated from her lap as she got to her feet, becoming caught on a splinter of wood at the edge of the bar where nobody could see it. Violet turned away and Edie was able to take her Uncle Bert's arm and listen to him make his toast. His sweet, loving words pouring calm over the stuffy little room. Edie's glass remained empty as they drank to her fortune, health and happiness.

Frank's mother had long since gone to bed and Edie perched nervously on the very edge of a double bed that had once belonged to his mother and father but was now for them to use as a married couple. His father had died at a young age of a heart attack and Frank, being the only son, had taken over the care of his mother as the little man of the house.

Edie felt nervous about this new life. He was still angry with her and that had continued for most of the day. She had drunk that gin and lime and regretted it immediately. Her stomach churned with nerves and she'd tried to indicate as much to Frank but he was busy tending to his mother and barely said one word to her.

He appeared in the bedroom doorway, quietly closing the door behind him, undoing his cufflinks and placing them carefully on top of the dresser. He took off his shoes and then his trousers, hanging them with his suit jacket on the back of the bedroom door. Edie was still wearing her thin blue suit. She felt too shy to take it off, and she wasn't sure what had happened to her suitcase with her clean nightdress inside. Frank had brought it into the house but as for where it was now, Edie didn't want to ask him about it and risk another row.

When she'd sat down on the bed, the metal springs had creaked and made such a noise that Edie felt as if she'd rather sleep on the floor. The thought of his mother being on the other side of the wall bothered her, and Frank was still so angry, but for what reason she couldn't say exactly. She couldn't understand why his mood had shifted so quickly or where her charming Frank had gone.

'That's the old girl settled down for the night. You need to show a bit more respect for my mother next time, Edie. It was good of her to offer us a home for as long as we need it. She don't need us upsetting her.'

Edie began to protest but knew it was pointless and she really didn't want to fight any more. The whole wedding day had been ruined. First the rain and Frank being late, then the awful hotel and the episode with the cake. She took a deep breath and started to peel off her suit, undoing the pearl buttons on her blouse.

Her clothes stank of cigarette smoke and half a pint of beer that somebody had managed to spill over her as they were leaving. As she'd gone to the toilet to try and rinse out the worst of it, Frank's mother had appeared in the doorway, offering assistance. As the two women dabbed at the beer stains, the old woman had patted her arm and said quietly:

'Frank's a good boy . . . better than most . . .' Then, as she'd turned to walk away, Mrs Budd hesitated in the doorway for a few seconds. 'Marriage can be difficult, Edie . . . but I know you'll be a good wife to him.'

Then she was gone, leaving Edie in her damp beer-stained skirt wondering about her future.

She thought now about Frank's mother's words, what being *a good wife* meant as she stepped out of her skirt, leaving her clothes in a pile in the middle of the bedroom carpet to deal with in the morning, and slipping a strap of her white petticoat off one shoulder.

'Let's not fight, Frank. It's supposed to be a happy day. We're married now after all. I'm your wife . . .'

Frank took a step towards her and with one finger tugged the other strap of her petticoat down off her shoulder, filling the space with the warmth of his mouth. 'My wife . . . well . . . come here then . . .'

Edie wrapped both arms around his neck, pulling him down on to their bed and covering his face with kisses. The springs of the mattress made such a terrible noise, creaking and groaning with such an awful high-pitched squeak that they both burst out laughing.

'We might need to buy a new bed, Mrs Budd. Start as we mean to go on. This won't do at all, will it?' Frank's voice was soft now, beguiling her, and then he slid to the floor on his knees, kissing the insides of her ankles and up her thighs before pulling her down on to the pile of her discarded clothes to join him there.

10

London, October 1958

The noise of the bar seemed more overwhelming than ever as Edie found herself staring at the spiteful smile of Violet Crim, a cold trickle of fear pouring over her.

'Hello, stranger, fancy seeing you here! It's been ages. Where's that handsome husband of yours? Haven't seen him around lately . . .' Violet had a habit of looking away from you when she was talking, which gave the impression of always searching over your shoulder for a better option. Edie opened her mouth to speak but no words came out. The fact that it was just that easy to run into someone from before chilled her to the bone. Standing there with her mouth gaping open while Violet droned on and on until she couldn't stand to listen to her for one minute longer.

'Oh, Vi . . . I can't stop . . .' Edie didn't bother to check where Tommie was or what she was doing. She turned around and walked straight out of the doors, colliding with the blonde woman in the tatty old fur coat who had been standing by the bar earlier.

‘Sorry,’ Edie muttered and walked briskly in the opposite direction from the blonde and the man she was with. Edie didn’t know her way around these streets very well even in daylight and at night it all seemed so different. All the landmarks she recognized were closed and the places she’d never had cause to notice seemed to glare out at her under cover of darkness, as if they’d come alive.

She stopped for a moment on the corner of Brewer Street and tried to get her bearings. The neon lights of the Raymond Revuebar flashed brightly from a side street advertising ‘STRIPTEASE’ in enormous green letters. Surly men with greasy hair stood around in doorways, dressed in black, gold teeth glinting when they smiled, while scars left by the delicate slice of a switchblade decorated their cheeks. Punishment for some misdemeanour from the men who mattered.

Two young women in threadbare winter coats were outside a club sharing a cigarette. Underneath their coats they wore gold-spangled costumes that barely covered their breasts and they stood with their coats flapping open, not caring particularly. A drunken man with straggly grey hair and peculiar bowed legs started yelling something at the girls, making them draw their coats tighter around the glittery costumes, but he wouldn’t stop until a stocky black-haired man stepped out of the shadows of the bar and ushered the women back inside to finish their shift.

‘Get out of here and stop annoying my girls,’ he

yelled but the drunk pulled down his zip, reached a hand inside his pants and started to aim a stream of warm piss all over the posters of strippers in the entrance to the club.

'Dirty little fucker. I'll cut that off for you if I see you here again.' The drunk cackled and finished doing his business, in no hurry to move along. Edie stood frozen in the middle of the pavement, not wanting to walk past either of them. The stocky man put his hand in his pocket and the next minute the drunk was pinned to the wall with the tip of a sharp blade poking up his left nostril. 'Fun's over. Fuck off.'

The drunk quickly zipped himself up and shuffled away down the street grumbling, but not loud enough to persuade the other man to follow him. Edie began to walk quickly on the other side of the pavement, to get away from the men. When he was far enough away, the drunk turned around and began yelling at the other man. The switchblade disappeared with a click and slipped back into the man's suit pocket. The yelling stopped, replaced by angry mutterings as the drunk walked away.

Suddenly a sleek black car pulled up further down the street and two men got out. Edie could only make out the size of them and not their features but a sharp blade of fear ran through her. It must be *them* . . . Her mind flashed back to the last time she'd seen these two men, standing at her front door, demanding answers she couldn't give them. And Frank . . . that awful look on his face. Edie flinched at the memory of that day and bit down on her thumbnail.

Frozen to the spot, she watched the men laughing and joking with each other for a few seconds. Suddenly one of the men looked up and stared in her direction; Edie sucked in a lungful of air and began to run as hard as she could, back in the direction she'd just come from. Her heels slapping hard against the paving stones. Taking random turns into darker streets in her rush to get away from the passengers of that sleek black car.

Edie didn't recognize any of these bars or clubs. She was surrounded by signs offering things she didn't want. In the daylight they were just anonymous doors with nobody at home. She couldn't remember which way she'd come with Tommie.

As she turned another corner, she saw ghost-like figures of women tucked away in the doorways. Only the glowing tips of their cigarettes were visible until they heard footsteps approaching and shifted briefly into the light, their coats falling open and then snapping shut with disappointment when they saw Edie running past. There were open doors all along the street with handwritten signs boasting of 'MODEL UPSTAIRS' or 'MASSAGE AVAILABLE' and behind two steel grey doors the thumping beat of bongo drums.

Edie kept running until the streets became crowded again. Clubs and bars littered the pavement. Every time one of the doors swung open she could hear the faint strains of the musical revue going on; girls were singing a song about the British Empire and there was raucous laughter. But then the door swished shut and it was silent again.

Where am I? Edie took a left turn and stood in the middle of the street, turning around and around, trying to get her bearings. There was a huge 'CINZANO' sign hanging above a doorway, and an omelette bar that was packed in the daytime and strangely out of place at night. Edie slowed to a walking pace and then finally found herself standing outside Le Macabre coffee bar once again.

From the shadowy street she could see two middle-aged women with bottle-red hair were talking to Monty Daniels outside his place and Edie expelled a breath of grateful air. She knew where she was now, and all she needed to do was retrace her steps to the bus stop, unless she'd missed the last one, or maybe she'd treat herself to a cab. Yes, that's what she'd do. She had to get out of here before anyone else saw her.

If running into Violet had proven anything, it was that it wasn't safe to stay anywhere in London much longer, but where could she go? Edie gave herself a telling off for the time she'd already wasted. A whole week messing about like that – not wanting to count the money when she should have been making plans to get out. *Fool . . . fool . . .* she kept telling herself. She should never have come out for the night. *What had she been thinking of?*

'Changed your mind, darling? Always got room for a little one,' Monty Daniels called across the street to her and the two women laughed as if it was the funniest thing that they'd heard all night. The deep-throated laughter was followed by a coughing fit, a real smoker's cough, and then more laughter.

Edie scuttled away without a backward glance, pulling her little white jacket tight around her. On the corner was a black cab with his sign up and she slipped gratefully into the back seat, chewing on her fingernails all the way home and wondering how much longer she had before people came looking for her.

Tommie was walking quite purposefully towards a familiar apartment. She would wait outside until he'd tucked Cheryl in a cab and sent her on her way. She was pleased with her good fortune but, deep down, she knew that Cheryl wasn't much in the way of opposition, with her saggy face and tatty old fur coat. It didn't matter. All that mattered was that he'd taken the bait and now she might even get to stay the night. That scratchy hunger she carried around inside made her mean at times. Tommie knew it but she couldn't stop herself. Sometimes she imagined this was how drunks felt when they looked at the green bottles all lined up on a shelf. The hunger . . . the ache . . . the fizz of excitement and then . . . nothing.

As she turned the corner, Tommie could see the upstairs windows were dark and empty. She sighed and hoped he wouldn't be much longer. Her shoes were starting to pinch her toes and so she smoothed her skirt down under her and perched delicately on the steps to his building, trying to avoid the dog shit, and a Cadbury's wrapper that was tumbling past caught on a gust of wind.

After ten minutes or so Tommie was stiff with cold and getting irritated. It didn't take this long to find a taxi for someone. It crossed her mind that maybe he'd hopped in the cab with Cheryl and she could sit here alone until morning, but she pulled out her fancy embroidered purse and took out a cigarette, scraping flimsy matches across the soggy strip of her stolen matchbook. Each one dying on the wind until one sparked and burst into an orange flame just long enough for Tommie to light her cigarette. She flicked the match away from her, using her thumb and finger, before tucking the matchbook back into her coat pocket; then she stood up to try and get some blood back into her legs.

Tommie was just about to give up when she spied a dark, shadowy figure walking briskly towards her and her lips curled into a smile. The ache subsided – changed into anticipation as she blew a tiny smoke ring into the air.

'Sorry, love, got caught up. Get you inside, eh?'

'I've only just got here. Got chatting to someone.

You know how it is,' Tommie lied, smooth as butter. She knew he didn't care but her pride felt the need of it.

He was already slotting his key in the door and then they were both running up the stairs, Tommie's breath blowing white mist in the chill of the landings.

It was the same as it ever was. Brandy, but at least he poured one for her this time. Five minutes of chat where he scolded her about her antics in front of Cheryl.

'You've got no manners. Anyone ever told you that?'

'I've got manners when I need them. Anyway, you don't have very good manners towards me. Treat me any old how . . . and I don't tell you off about it.'

'You're not my missus, Tommie. You turn up here all hours. I don't hear you complaining. If you don't like it, you can go on home.'

He seemed exasperated with her, as if she was too much trouble tonight. His words stung but she couldn't leave. Deep inside she ached so much that it hurt and until that ache was satisfied then it didn't matter what he said or did, she couldn't stop coming around.

'No need to be like that . . . I'm here, aren't I?' Tommie's voice was soft now, barely a whisper. She gazed up at him, catching her breath at the thought he might ask her to leave. Her face soft and pleading. Waiting . . .

He walked towards the bedroom, calling her over his shoulder and she followed him obediently and silent.

Afterwards, when he'd taken his fill of her, Tommie rolled on to her side and placed his arm around her shoulders. She laid her head next to his heart and listened to its gentle beating. His breathing slowed to a sleepy crawl and Tommie felt tears start to trickle down her cheeks, splashing on to his skin.

She pulled on his arm, trying to tuck it around her waist, but it was limp and loose and that made it worse. Tommie held her breath but she knew it was too late to stop it. The familiar panic started deep in her belly and then a wave of it rose inside her, tightening everything as it flowed upwards. Her chest and her throat. She couldn't catch her breath properly and the room began to spin. There was a strange tingling sensation in her hands as Tommie started to puff out desperate jagged breaths. She felt like screaming, but then he'd wake up, and she didn't want him to find her like this.

She could hear the familiar roar in her ears.

When the bombs came, they would huddle together, just the two of them in the dark, holding on to each other so tightly, her mother whispering to her as she fell asleep, 'You're safe here. I've got you. You're safe here.' Her arms wrapped around Tommie, as if they would rather break than let her go. And gradually the planes would pass over; the roaring would stop, and

Tommie would wake the next morning safe and warm in her mother's arms.

'*You're safe here . . . You're safe here*,' Tommie whispered to herself and started to rock gently until the tightness of her chest eased. She felt him stir next to her and Tommie knew she couldn't stay now. It was all ruined. She slipped out of the sheets and picked up her scattered clothing, shutting herself in the bathroom where she fastened her blouse and wiped black mascara streaks from under her eyes.

Her limbs felt heavy and numb, her heart raced and the blood pulsed in her ears. Tommie clenched her teeth and tried to breathe normally. In . . . out . . . in . . . out . . .

Her arms wrapped around her chest as she sat on the edge of the bath, until slowly the fear began to subside. Only then did she collect her handbag from the living room and quietly click the front door shut behind her.

Tommie began to walk away from Soho and back towards Dove Street. She didn't mind how long it took as her mind churned with thoughts of the past. The same old memories haunting her. The thrill of Soho seemed far away, and her mood darkened.

She had a usual route that always led her back to the same place. All her memories of it were of grey people, dressed in the same shabby clothes, picking their way through rubble shortcuts, walking next to craters of their past. Huge unfilled holes where houses used to be, where families lived and children played, all dissolved in her mind as if not quite alive. A sort of twilight where people tried to make a life in colour again but mostly failed, over and over. Her feet traced her footsteps from that past. She had skipped along these streets as a young child. Eventually, they led her to a familiar spot where she stood in the darkness staring up at what remained of an old house.

Her face softened as she studied the building in front of her. At the top of the house was a window with a pair of pink curtains flapping in the breeze. The window itself was hanging from the wall of the house at a strange angle, and the rest of the wall that used to keep out strangers was completely missing, the bricks jagged like broken teeth. No matter how much Tommie tried to stay away, she always ended up back here at this same spot on the slick grey pavement. The other houses in the street were still intact. Net curtains carefully washed and put up at the windows, small front gardens tended or left to grow spiky weeds that forced their way through the concrete and into the light. Neighbours whose names she used to know. She glanced at her watch. It was late now, and she felt foolish.

The pink curtains floated through the air like a kite flying, and then caught on the broken window frame, billowing like sheets on laundry day. Tommie stared at the curtains one last time, and then slowly walked away.

Four Years Earlier

'Where are *you* going all dressed up?' His tone was calm on the surface but underneath was an irritation, an angry buzzing insect about to sting.

Edie had been married for two whole weeks and it was time to go back to the biscuit factory. She'd taken the two weeks off hoping she and Frank might get away to Margate again but he'd shown no interest in staying in a hotel now they had their own bedroom. Although he had bought a brand-new bed that didn't wake up the entire house as they rolled around in it, Edie couldn't shake off the thought of his mother being just the other side of the wall. She could hear the old woman coughing or getting up to use the chamber pot she kept under her bed, so God only knew what Frank's mother could hear at night, as apart from six inches of dividing wall they were practically lying head to head.

Edie couldn't wait to get back to work. She missed the gossip and the fun. As she brushed out the little sausage-like curls left by the tight pink rollers she pinned to her head, she felt excited to go back as a married woman.

She put on her usual blouse and plain skirt, which would soon be covered up with her white overall and net cap. After smoothing down the small pocket which lay over one breast with 'Marshall's' embroidered in pink letters, Edie slipped her purse into her handbag and ran down the stairs at a sprint, when she almost collided with Frank, who had just come in through the front door, carrying his racing newspaper and whistling the same old tune he always whistled.

'I'm off to work. There's a cold plate in the pantry under the cover for your lunch and I'll be back in plenty of time to cook dinner. I'll pick up a nice bit of liver, shall I?'

'You're not going back to Marshall's! What will people say?'

'What do you mean?' Edie reached for the front door, and Frank put his great paw over hers to make sure the door wouldn't open until he said so.

'I mean . . . *you're my wife.* You can't go back to working at the biscuit factory. People will think I can't earn enough to keep us. You don't want for anything, do you?' His voice had taken on the hard edge that always made Edie nervous. He was like storm clouds gathering and dispersing around her. Then they cleared and the sun came out, his face broke into a smile and he caught hold of her waist, pulling her to him.

'As you're all dressed up, how about we go for a spin on the motorbike? Haven't done that since we got wed, have we? It's a nice day for it.'

Edie couldn't find the words to refuse him. She felt confused, for surely it was up to her whether or not she carried on working at the factory. She'd banked on earning her own money just like the other women. They were always talking about 'hiding a little bit away for a rainy day'. Where would she get her *rainy day* money without Marshall's Biscuits?

'I *like* working there. It's good money too. We can go out on the bike at the weekend? Maybe go to Margate. I get paid on Friday and we could use the money for a nice time.'

Frank didn't even look as if he'd heard the words because his hand tightened on her waist and he started kissing her neck, working his way up from the bottom to her earlobes. 'My beautiful wife . . . come here, you . . .'

'I'm going to be late, Frank.' Edie wriggled out of his grasp but before she could turn to open the latch, he'd placed his body between her and the front door.

'We'll go out today like I said. We can take a spin down the coast. Then we can call in at Marshall's on the way back and tell them you're finishing up. Collect what's owed and that will be that.'

'I don't *want* to finish up there . . . I *want* to carry on working . . . at least for a bit.'

Frank stepped away from the front door, but the storm clouds had returned and his eyes glittered with anger. 'Go on then, make a fool of me . . .' he muttered.

'I'm not. I just . . . I . . .' Edie stuttered over her words, choosing and then rejecting them before she made the situation worse. She reached out her hand to stroke his arm but he shrugged her off.

'Get going then or you'll be late.'

'Frank, don't be like that . . . I won't go if you're going to be this way.' Edie stood there blinking up at him. She felt as if she were in trouble at school.

She hated it when he got like this. The coldness of his sulking could last for minutes or hours or even days. The rigid bones of his back turned away from her in bed at night. The punishment was never swift: the agony of waiting for *her Frank* to return with his charming smile and tender words. She reached out her hand and stroked his cheek, gently, trying to make amends. He wouldn't soften or even look at her. She moved closer to him, trying harder now.

'I'm sorry, Frank. I won't go, of course I won't go. Let's not fall out over it.' His face cleared and his gaze turned on her, loving and full of understanding now she had conceded.

'I don't *ever* want us to fall out, Edie. You're my girl, you are . . . and I love you more than my life. I *want* to take care of you. Let me do that. You're my world, Edie Budd.'

He reached into his pocket and pulled out a five-pound note which he offered to her. She didn't want to take it but his hand kept holding it right up close to her face until he was practically swiping the note across her cheek.

'Tell you what, we'll go up the High Street right now and buy you something nice.'

A smirk played upon his lips as he reached for her. Pulling her close, his hands sweeping the strands of her hair back and stroking her face. His mouth on her neck now, whispering how much he loved her. The sweetness of him pierced her heart and Edie was torn between giving in to whatever he wanted or allowing herself to deny him at least this . . . but there didn't seem to be any point, it would only make him angry.

She could hear the radio show his mother was listening to in the back kitchen blaring out – the familiar theme tune and strange jolly radio voices that didn't exist in real people. The audience was laughing hysterically. The strange jolly radio voices said things and they carried on laughing, the silly music playing over and over. It was a game or a quiz. There were no rules that Edie could understand.

Frank pushed her back against the front door, pulling at her skirt, his hands fumbling with her underwear, making room for himself inside her. His head buried in her neck now. Feverish kisses landed up and down her throat. The sour tang of his hair cream rubbed against her jaw. Edie, pinned to the front door, couldn't move for the weight of him. In the back kitchen the radio blared out the stupid quiz and his mother laughed along.

11

London, October 1958

Phyllis Collier was sweeping her front path, as if getting a layer of dead leaves off it would mean her fortune might change forever. She was boiling mad this morning and there was no particular reason for it. Even standing outside on a chilly day she was still too hot. Phyllis wondered if it might be 'the change of life', but she was only just fifty-three. Her skin felt as if she was being roasted alive but the worst part of all was the rage flowing through her like scalding water.

She attacked the path harder with her sweeping brush, watching soggy dark leaves sticking to it and dust being kicked up while she bundled it into the gutter. She began to sweep the wet leaves up into neat piles, but even then the strange white-hot fury was still flooding through her, as it had been since she'd opened her eyes that morning.

She'd spent days being sad. She'd played sad records. She'd pined. She'd looked right through the pictures in their old wedding albums. Her in a blue chiffon dress with a crown of flowers in her hair, and Terry in his best Sunday suit standing next to her looking so proud. When had he stopped looking proud to stand next to her? Phyllis felt the rage rising again and she swept faster and faster until there was nothing left to brush away on her front path. She hit the broom against the doorstep to get any loose fragments off it and pushed those to one side.

Another scalding wave of heat and fury flooded through her. All the anger she'd ever bitten down over the years had been released and she couldn't keep it inside.

She parked her broom in the cupboard under the stairs and caught a glimpse of her face in the hallway mirror. Phyllis surveyed the wreckage. Mousy greying hair hidden away in pink curlers, wrapped up with a mint-green headscarf and knotted on top. A face scrubbed clean with soap and water, a long nose red at the tip, and sallow cheeks riddled with spidery lines. A deep furrowed frown perched between her eyebrows.

'Miserable cow,' Phyllis muttered, and a little voice she didn't like popped up to condemn her: *No wonder he went after that Trudy . . .*

The little voice was a constant companion these days. It woke her up in the morning, pointing out every ache and creaking limb, and put her to bed every night reminding her about the cold sheet where Terry used to lie, filling her mind with where he might be and what he could be doing.

The sweat trickled under her armpits and down her back. There was a cold wind blowing in from the front door but still she couldn't get cool. She could be dead now; that was a fact. Why, if her tenant hadn't come home right at that minute . . . someone would have found her dead on her kitchen floor. Playing with gas like that – the whole house could have gone up and taken the tenants with it if they'd lit a match. The thought of it made Phyllis gasp and then the fury spilled over, making her hot again. Memories of Terry and that girl flooded through her mind as her anger flared into white-hot rage. She'd had quite enough humiliation.

Then she stopped, stared at herself in the mirror and said out loud to nobody in particular: 'You're a grown woman and you damn well deserve better than this.'

When she'd finished her sentence Phyllis nodded firmly at her reflection as if some kind of agreement had been reached. She was going to make some changes around here. There was going to be a brand-new Phyllis Collier – a woman not to be trifled with.

Edie sat up on her bed, leaning back against the wobbly iron bedstead that hurt her back. She'd begun to dream about choking – someone putting something around her neck and pulling it tight. She'd had the dream so many times now that she found herself waking up gasping for breath with both hands at her throat. Sometimes she saw Frank standing over her bed reaching out his hands towards her but when she opened her eyes there was nobody there.

Last night she'd woken up in a cold sweat, convinced that someone was watching the house. She'd stood at her tiny window, squinting down at the streets, searching every shadow for proof that she was right. The stress of it all was making her feel queasy and light-headed, living as she was on nothing but tins of thin vegetable soup and ginger biscuits.

Since her chance encounter with Violet Crim, Edie had stayed in her room, only venturing out to get something to eat, stockpiling tins of vegetable soup so she didn't even need to visit Mrs Salim's café. But staring at the yellow chrysanthemums on her ugly wallpaper every minute of the day didn't make her feel safe. It made her feel worse than ever.

For the thousandth time, Edie reasoned with herself. Violet had had a few drinks inside her when they met. She had probably latched on to some fella, and not given Edie a second thought. But as hard as she tried, not one part of Edie truly believed Violet would have such a lack of interest in her. After all, somebody would have missed her and Frank by now. They must have done. It somehow made things worse that, no matter how hard she searched, there was still nothing in the newspapers.

She had to get away . . . but the idea of travelling to a railway station filled with people, perhaps even being watched by people who might know she planned to leave, brought on an attack of fear. Every day, her indecision left her lying on her single bed at 73 Dove

Street, wishing she was somewhere else but unable to find a way to get there.

A creak on the landing outside her door alerted her to the fact that she was about to have a visitor and she swung her legs over on to the floor and stood up, bending over to straighten the bed so it didn't look as if she spent her days just lying on it and staring at the walls.

Sure enough, seconds later she heard a shy tapping on her door and opened it to find Tommie standing there.

'Hello, me again, like a bad penny . . .' She gave Edie a rueful look, almost apologetic and carried on, 'Speaking of which, I brought you these.' Tommie opened her fist to reveal six copper pennies in the palm of her hand. 'Sorry it's late.'

'Thanks. I'm sorry about the other night. I felt a bit sick, see . . . and thought it best to come home.' Edie was prepared for Tommie to not believe her lies, but to her surprise the other girl just seemed relieved by them. Edie gathered the six pennies into the palm of her hand, staring down at them rather than meet Tommie's gaze.

'Oh, don't you worry about that. I wondered where you'd gone but none of my business really.' The two women stood there shuffling awkwardly, then Tommie said brightly, 'You fancy a cuppa? I just made a pot if you want to share it . . . unless you're busy?'

Edie hesitated. Part of her wanted to send the girl away and get on with working out her escape plan, but the misery clawed at her, and to her surprise she heard herself say, 'No, I'm not busy . . .' She smiled. 'I've got some ginger biscuits left over. I'll bring them down. Be nice with a cup of tea.'

'Yeah, well . . . Come on down then.' Tommie grinned and scampered away down the stairs, leaving Edie to check her little brown envelope was still safely tucked away under the bed, before grabbing her ginger biscuits and carefully locking the door to her room.

Tommie felt bad about the girl upstairs, for although she hadn't abandoned her that night in Soho it was only because she hadn't had the chance to, what with Edie pulling a disappearing act like that. She seemed a nice enough sort, a bit nervy, and being stuck up at the top of the house in that gloomy little room couldn't be helping her. Back in her own room, Tommie turned her radio on so they'd have some background music to talk over rather than silence, and set out two cups next to a small brown teapot on her little table. She'd left her door ajar and after a few minutes Edie knocked and poked her head into the room, waiting for permission to enter, waving the packet of ginger biscuits at Tommie like some kind of a peace offering.

'Come on in then. I'll get a plate for them.'

The ginger biscuits were soon neatly spread out on a blue plate and placed in the centre of the table next to the teapot. The two women sat side by side at the small wooden table, Edie staring admiringly around the room, commenting on how much bigger and brighter it was than her little attic. Her eyes glanced over to the old postcard of a teashop pinned on the wall over Tommie's bed. Edie was about to ask where it was when the other girl interrupted her.

'Shall I be mother then?' Tommie said, picking up the teapot. 'Oh . . . did you want milk first? Only I know some people are particular about that.'

'Any way it comes really. I don't mind.' Edie always put the milk in first but as Tommie was hovering over the cup with the little brown pot, it felt like an inconvenience to stop her.

'So, what do you *do* with yourself all day, Edie?'

'What do I *do*?' Edie repeated puzzled.

'For work . . . you know . . . to pay the bills.'

Edie took a long, hesitant sip of her tea and tried to think of the right answer. 'I'm sort of in between things at the moment. I used to work at Marshall's Biscuits. We made these, actually.' She held up her half-dunked ginger nut for inspection and Tommie nodded.

'Oh yeah, I know it. That's down Deptford way, isn't it? I had a friend who worked there once – Shirley Banks? Do you know her?'

'I don't think so . . . Different section to me, I expect.'

'You couldn't miss her. The mouth on her – like a sailor. Shirley has a LOT to say for herself at the best of times.'

'No, like I say every section keeps to itself really.'

'So, what brings you to this part of the world?' Tommie had a way of asking questions in a friendly, casual manner, but Edie noticed that her eyes were always searching her face for more information than she wanted to give her.

Edie filled her mouth with a bite of her ginger biscuit and swiftly changed the subject. 'Oh, just felt like a change. What about you? What do *you* do?'

'I'm a cook and general dogsbody for an old lady. She lives in one of those fancy townhouses in Bayswater but she's all right, mostly. We rub along. I've been there for years now and just kind of fell into a bit of a rut. I used to think about opening my own little teashop . . .' Tommie looked wistful for a moment. 'Anyway, that's just wishing . . . but you know how it is. Wish in one hand, spit in the other and see which you get first.' She gave a weary chuckle, sounding older than her years although she was about the same age as Edie. 'Anyway, one job's very much the same as another. The money is steady and Mrs Vee's no bother most days. Don't get me wrong, she can be a handful at times, but I've just got used to her, I reckon.'

'It must be interesting work.' Edie had no idea whether it would be interesting or not, but the longer they talked about Tommie, the less likely they were to talk about her own life.

'Yeah, she used to invite all sorts around to her place to cook for. Once had the old King and Mrs Simpson – before my time, though. We used to do a lot of entertaining but not so much lately. Suits me . . . I do her lunch and a bit of supper on a tray and then leave her to it. Top you up a bit?' Tommie offered the teapot and Edie nodded, watching as she poured. She took another biscuit, dunking it until it was warm and soggy before letting it fall into her mouth.

Tommie sipped at her tea but left the biscuits untouched. She lit a Woodbine and blew the smoke out of the corner of her mouth. Edie warmed her hands on the teacup and stared into the murky brown liquid.

'Do you have family here?' Edie asked.

'Just my dad. My mother died in the Blitz . . . bomb hit our house.' Tommie took a deep gasp of her cigarette and blew a small cloud of smoke rings up towards the ceiling.

'I'm sorry. My mum died too – a few years back. Something on her lung. I don't know what. She wasn't very old.'

'And your dad?'

Edie shrugged. 'He never came home from the war. Missing . . .'

Tommie frowned and nodded. 'Mine came home. Married the local barmaid and started a new family. I don't get on with them. I look after myself – always have and always will.' Her chin jutted forward defiantly as she flicked a long chain of cigarette ash into the saucer. All the time she was watching Edie, studying her almost.

Edie felt herself squirming slightly under Tommie's gaze, wishing that they could chat about the weather or things that didn't matter. The noise of teacups being lifted from their saucers and put back down again filled the space between them. Edie took another bite of her ginger biscuit and tried to think of something to say.

'So, are you seeing that fella from the other night?' The moment Edie asked the question she regretted it.

'Yes, we've been courting for a while now but he likes to play hard to get. You know, one of those blokes who don't like to be tied down. He's coming around though . . .'

'That's nice.' Edie took another bite, searching for another topic of conversation but it was too late.

'What happened to your fella?' Tommie stared at Edie, who shovelled the damp biscuit mush from one side of her mouth to the other in panic.

'My fella . . . ?' Her voice trailed away as she swallowed the biscuit.

'You've been married?' Tommie pointed to Edie's ring finger where a pale circular welt marked the spot where her brass wedding ring had been worn until recently.

Edie folded the words around her mouth, hugging them to her before releasing them into the air. 'Oh . . . He . . . he died . . .'

It was the first time she'd spoken those words out loud. He died. *Frank was dead.* Even now, the words didn't feel quite real. The song on the radio faded away. She glanced around the room, not knowing what to say. Somewhere the sound of a clock ticked into the silence.

'Oh, I'm *so* sorry, love, and there's me being a nosy cow. You're on your own, then?' Tommie pulled an anxious face at having been so tactless and Edie tried to quiet her racing heart by taking small shallow breaths. Eventually she spoke.

'Yeah, it'll just be me now . . .'

Edie chewed her bottom lip and then took another gulp from her teacup. She would finish her tea, and then get up and leave. It was perfectly simple. She took a breath and gently placed her teacup back into its saucer.

Tommie leaned across the table and whispered to her, 'How long ago? If you don't mind me asking?'

'Not long . . . I'm just getting used to things – being alone again . . . you know how it is.'

'Of course, you poor thing. What happened to him?'

'Just collapsed one day – it was very sudden. His heart . . .' With this, Edie felt her own heart start to race again. She wanted more than anything to get out of the room and away from this girl who kept on asking questions when she needed her to stop. 'I don't really want to talk about it, if you don't mind . . . It's . . .' Her voice faded away.

'I'm so sorry . . . There's me babbling away and not thinking at all. Take no notice of me. I don't mean anything by it. Look . . . all I meant was anytime you fancy a chat or a night out just let me know, eh?'

Edie nodded gently at the other girl. 'That's kind. I don't go out much really. I mean . . . not since . . . The other night was a bit too much.'

'Oh, yes, I can see that. That's why you ran off like that. All makes sense now. You should've told me . . . I feel really bad about leaving you on your own. If you'd said . . . If I'd known it was your first time out – y'know, after? What was his name?'

'Frank . . . his name was Frank . . .' Edie's voice started to crack and she bit down on her bottom lip to stop herself crying.

'I didn't mean to pry . . . Like I said – any time you fancy a chat just pop down, eh? I'm usually about if I'm not working.'

'Sure . . . yeah. Of course, I will. Thank you . . . you've been very kind. Well, the day's getting on. I best get off. Got things to do. Thanks for the tea . . . and the chat.'

Edie hurried out of the room as Tommie called after her, 'Don't forget your biscuits . . .'

'You keep 'em . . . Bye now.' Edie ran up the stairs two at a time, cursing the key when it stuck in the lock and finally flinging herself on to her bed, burying her face in the pillows.

Three Years Earlier

'Pick up that prescription for my mother and don't forget to get some boot polish. We've run out,' Frank said without even looking up from the racing pages of his newspaper. Inwardly Edie seethed, but she bit back her reply. There was no point. He barked out lists of commands these days, expecting them to be done before he came home from the bookies or the pub, which is where Frank Budd spent his working life.

It had not taken Edie long to discover that when Frank had told her he did a bit of *this and that* it was mostly gambling. Occasionally there would be a day's proper work for a mate, but Frank largely spent his time selling on dodgy goods for equally dodgy mates, or making money by betting on dogs and horses.

His early mornings were spent poring over the names – Queen Christina, Blue Bird, Shirley Temple – trying to work out if there might be a sign to place a bet on or not. Frank was big on signs – mysterious forces that allowed him to make money or lose it. The gods decreed whether the rent could be paid, or if they all had to hide with the lights out when the milkman wanted his bill settling. Edie could have been bringing in a steady pay packet, but Frank believed in his magical ability to conjure money out of lame dogs and horses.

If he won there would be a fish supper, and gin and lime at the local, followed by kindness – and that look he got in his eyes which reminded Edie of when she'd first met him. The other nights, when he lost . . .

He raged at Edie for the smallest thing. It always started the same way, disappearing to the pub of an evening, where she'd picture him swilling beer until his mood darkened. Then the rattle of the key coming up on its string of blue wool through the letter box, and in he would come, demanding things Edie no longer wanted to give him.

In the mornings Frank would start again, sulking and poring over his racing pages at the kitchen table. Edie would fuss around him making sure he had what he needed. She would try to get it right. To not burn the lacy edges of the eggs in the lard, or cut the loaf too thin or too thick. She would use the plate he preferred, but he kept changing his mind. After a year of marriage, Edie had come to realize there was no right answer. Just as certainly as the sun would rise in the morning, Frank wanted to rage at her and keep raging at her . . . until when, Edie wasn't sure.

Their first Christmas as husband and wife had been a bleak affair of hot-tempered quarrels. Frank hadn't wanted her to go and see her Uncle Bert before they sat down for their dinner. Edie had only wanted to slip in with a bottle of stout and a pack of Capstan cigarettes. She'd written out a card from her and Frank, taking time to print out both their names carefully, curling the letters in an elaborate scrawl. And now they were heading towards yet another bleak Christmas. *What would they fight about this year?* Edie wondered. *The baby . . . ?*

The baby that had not arrived, no matter how hard they tried. It was a subject they rarely spoke of, but it was there between them all the same, like scar tissue covering a wound. The baby that Edie didn't want . . . or couldn't have . . . and that they couldn't afford anyway.

'Are you *listening* to me?' Frank's tone contained a bite of anger.

'Yes, get your mother's prescription and boot polish.' Edie washed down the kitchen counter and felt his stare but she wouldn't stop and meet his gaze. She kept on moving constantly, cleaning, shopping, using the Ewbank carpet cleaner or mopping up. She waited on his mother hand and foot, as the old woman was mostly bed-bound now. They'd got used to each other though. Mrs Budd was kind to Edie, after their frosty start at the wedding; the old woman always remembered to thank her and saved her a bit of chocolate now and again. She'd tell Frank off too when he spoke too harshly. Even so, the work of caring for her filled

Edie's days. Taking up trays of tea and poached eggs with lightly buttered toast. Stewing prunes to get the old woman's bowels moving, or putting senna pods in her morning tea. Edie was always busy doing something.

When there was nothing left to do, Edie made lists – endless lists of things to buy, or things to do, so she could start moving again. Edie couldn't stop moving because she wasn't sure what she might do if she sat down for long enough to start thinking about her life.

Edie loved the smell of the chemist's shop, medicinal but perfumed at the same time. All clean and safe. Nothing bad could happen to you in a chemist's, Edie supposed, as the woman behind the counter counted out tiny white pills while chatting away nineteen to the dozen. The woman had a starched white coat with a little name badge pinned to her lapel. 'Pamela', it said in large black letters. Edie studied the curl of the letters and the neatness of the starched white coat, not listening to a word that Pamela was saying. The tiny white pills were counted and dropped carefully into a brown glass bottle. Then the label was written out with 'Three times a day after meals', and the name of Frank's mother. Eventually Pamela had nothing left to say except, 'There you go, all filled up. Give my best to Mrs Budd. Shame she can't get out any more. Such a nice lady – always had time for a chat.'

Edie nodded and smiled. The bell over the door gave a sharp ring as she left the shop, the air changing in an instant from the sharp medicinal powdery smell to thick exhaust fumes from an old lorry trundling past. Edie held her breath until it had gone by. She rubbed her fingers over her temple to try and release a deep pulsing ache. Lately Edie had started to get such terrible migraines that she had to take to her bed. She could feel one building right behind her eyes. Sighing, she walked up to the cobbler's to pick up some boot polish and paused by the baker's shop to study the cakes in the window. Jam and cream doughnuts, apple turnovers and all manner of custard tarts. There wasn't enough money left over today for treats. They would have to hide from the people they owed money to again. Sitting there with all the lights out for hours on end, pretending to be out.

Edie stopped again by the dress shop. There was a pink taffeta frock in the window. The kind of evening dress that Edie might have bought with her wages once upon a time to go out dancing. There was an anger deep inside of her that dulled everything these days. She lived on the edges of Frank's moods now and all the time a white-hot fury made its home within her. There was nothing she wanted any more. She had no dreams about a future. It was a new thing that she'd only recently noticed. She wasn't going to get a pay rise or a promotion. There would never be a fancy holiday or a little terraced house that belonged to her.

She couldn't even walk into a dress shop and buy a pink taffeta frock, because she didn't have any money to call her own.

Edie's only indulgence was sometimes on Friday nights, when Frank had gone out, she would soak in a bath for an hour. Thoughts would rush in unbidden about what life would have been like if she had closed the front door on Frank Budd and his pink carnations. Then she would get out of her bath and tidy things away until the thoughts stopped.

It was nearly lunchtime now, and she began to walk briskly in the direction of home. Her head was pounding but Frank's mother would need her tray and probably her sheets washing out again. The old lady had started misjudging how long it took her to get out of her bed to the commode that lived in the corner of the bedroom. It was another of Edie's jobs to empty the commode pot and wash it out ready to be used again. She hadn't touched it that morning and it would probably be filled up by the time she got home. The old woman couldn't help it, but Edie didn't see why she had to handle a china pot of shit every morning.

The key bounced up the inside of the door on its blue wool chain as Edie tugged at it from the other side. She called out as she came through the door but there was no answer, just the sound of the radio playing upstairs in the old woman's bedroom. She was listening to her silly quiz again. Edie put the tablets from the chemist's on the kitchen table, along with the boot polish and a bloody packet of pork chops for Frank's dinner. She hung up her coat without bothering to look at herself in the hall mirror.

There was no sign of Frank but Edie knew where he was. The bookmaker's shop was three streets away, a small smoky room with a man behind a glass screen alongside a cash register. There were various stools placed around the room, so that men could sit and lean on the counter to fill out their betting slips while the sound of racing commentary blared out – always excited. The drama of the horses rising and falling as they took the fences. Galloping commentary ending in heartbreak as the sour-faced men would crumple up their pink betting slips and throw them in the bin. Occasionally somebody won and every face in the shop wore the same expression of hope and joy. It *was* possible to win – you just had to pick carefully. Queen Christina or Blue Bird or Shirley Temple. Try again and keep trying.

Edie sighed and moved the package of pork chops on to a plate covered by another plate in the pantry to keep cool. She set about boiling the kettle and poaching an egg while at the same time keeping an eye out for a slice of bread turning golden brown under the grill. She scraped butter over the toast and then gently placed a delicately poached egg on top. She put the teacup on a saucer and arranged everything neatly on the tray with a folded napkin. Edie went slowly up the stairs, balancing the tray so as not to spill the tea.

When she reached the top, she tapped gently on the bedroom door and breezed in as usual – moving, always moving.

'I've brought your lunch. Did you a nice poached egg with a bit of toast. I got some chops for later but if you don't fancy that there's a bit of vegetable soup left over. I'll do your commode pot now and then you're all shipshape again.'

Edie pulled back the curtains and opened a window to air the room. It smelled stale, like old clothes that were never washed. The old lady was asleep, her head lolling to one side of her pillow and the radio blaring out the stupid music for that quiz Edie hated. She switched it off, feeling the relief of the silence and tried to put down the tray, shaking the old lady to wake her up. Her hands were icy cold. Edie finally stopped moving and stood there staring at the blue-tinged lips of the now quite dead Mrs Budd.

She sat down on the edge of the bed and waited for a tear to slip from her eye or some feeling of sadness that the old lady was gone, but all she felt was a biting rage at being left alone with Frank.

12

London, October 1958

Val's Salon was barely big enough to be a front parlour, and yet she could fit one woman in the chair and three more under the dryers, all reading magazines and waiting for her to release them and comb them out. Val prided herself on her 'shampoo and set' and could have you washed and rolled up in ten minutes flat. You would then be seated under the dryer for a good forty minutes, scalp turning pink with the heat, until the blue curlers felt hot to the touch and the pins would burn your fingers as you removed them. Val would then tug at the curlers and dump them back into her black trolley to wait for the next customer. Thin wispy strands of fair or dark hair caught around their teeth but they were only cleaned when the Saturday Girl had nothing else to do, which wasn't often.

Phyllis was under the dryer, feeling distinctly uncomfortable. The blast of hot air was singeing her scalp and the little blue curlers were too tight. Val had dyed her hair using some purple paste that smelled of drain chemicals, then once that was rinsed out the too-tight blue curlers had been set, and now Phyllis was reaching the limits of her patience. The dryer hood was pulled down, and her only respite from the scalding heat was to sink down in her seat in an attempt to escape the blasts of hot air. Eventually a little pinging noise suggested to Phyllis that she was in fact cooked and the scalding heat subsided.

The girl whose job it was to listen out for the 'pings' then lifted up the hood and rubbed her sticky fingers over the purple net that held the blue curlers and their pins together, to decide whether Phyllis was 'done' or needed 'another five just to be sure'. After a pause, Phyllis thanked everything that was holy that the girl declared her done – and she was shifted along to Val to await her brushing out.

Half an hour later, Phyllis was standing in the hallway of number 73 Dove Street staring at herself in the blotchy mirror, trying to decide if the woman she was looking at was an improvement. This woman looked surprised to find her hair the colour of warm straw, rather than her usual mousy brown with grey strands. The warm straw made her eyes seem too big for her face. At first glance, she appeared to be all eyes and hair. The hair had been combed out, teased back on itself with a fine tail comb until it stood up on end, and then Val had shaped it into a large straw-coloured mound, spraying it with so much hair lacquer that the strongest gust of wind hadn't moved it at all. It was stiff and round like a small yellow helmet, decidedly odd, but Phyllis felt she looked . . . *better* than before.

She didn't look like the same woman who had knelt desperately in front of her gas oven. She was a new kind of woman. Ready for a fresh start.

Twisting up a tube of orange-red lipstick, Phyllis smacked her lips together and nodded her head in approval. She was about to do something quite different and possibly reckless. Phyllis Collier was going to have a night out.

After her strange conversation with the girl upstairs, Tommie had been running around after Mrs Vee for days. The woman was driving her crazy with her demands for the kind of fancy dinner party she hadn't held in years. Oysters and champagne were easy enough, although she'd need to order in slabs of ice and would cut her hands to shreds easing the shells open. It was the Beef Wellington which gave Tommie nightmares. She'd only made one once before and although it had looked beautifully golden on the outside, the moment the carving knife sliced through it, watery red blood had splashed all over the tablecloth. Tommie was dreading it. And if that wasn't bad enough Mrs Vee was demanding an egg custard to finish off. Tommie had tried to suggest other dishes – easier dishes – but the old woman was strangely defiant.

While Tommie fretted away in the basement with her Woodbines and cooking brandy, Mrs Vee spent her days sat in the middle of her peach satin bed, a box of violet creams on her lap, writing out scented invitation cards to people she used to know. It didn't seem to be going well, since every day when Tommie brought her breakfast tray up to her, there would be a pile of scribbled-out names and another list of people who had sent their apologies.

Now Tommie had taken Mrs Vee her lunch and tidied away, she was about to pop her list into the fancy butcher that Mrs Vee insisted on her using and was knocking off a bit early to do so. Tommie fastened her headscarf under her chin and did up all the buttons on her winter coat. There was a misty damp cold in the air – the kind that chilled your bones and meant you could never get warm, no matter how close you sat to a fire. Tommie walked quickly, hoping she wasn't too late to have a word with Mr Jackson the butcher. The cut of beef for the Wellington had to be just right and she was very much relying on him not to hack off some tough old bit of cow and send it to her.

The clouds were almost black and the light had been smothered out of the city by a swirling mist. Tommie could only see blurry orange lights in the distance where the shops were, one next to the other. Mr Jackson the butcher next to Mr Fry the fishmonger, and then Kendricks the grocer, all suppliers of fine produce to those who could afford their fancy products. Tommie's brown handbag jiggled back and forth in the crook of her elbow as she walked faster now, trying to catch the lights before they went out. She'd forgotten her gloves and stuffed her hands inside her coat pockets to keep them warm. Her fingers felt the strip of matches she'd stolen from him the other night in Soho, tracing the outline of the embossed gold writing on the front of the matchbook. Her breath quickened. It occurred to Tommie that she could just telephone Mr Jackson about the meat in the morning.

Rolling the strip of matches between her fingers, Tommie hesitated for just one moment and then quickened her pace. If she put her best foot forward then she could be in Soho in no time.

Half an hour later she turned into Carlisle Street and checked her reflection in a shop window. It was still early and Tommie felt sure that he'd be at home now. By coming at this time, she hoped that they could make a proper night of it – maybe even go out dancing later. She imagined leaning seductively in his doorway, saying the right words to entice him. He would smile and then invite her in, pouring her a drink before suggesting they go to all his favourite places. Walking into bars and clubs on his arm . . . Dancing in front of everyone . . . She felt a ripple of anticipation fizzing through her and began to walk quickly past the familiar shops and coffee bars until finally she reached the corner of his street.

Up ahead she could see the outline of his building. Tommie began to imagine his face when he opened the front door to find her standing there. She rehearsed clever things to say . . . the way to say them, with a half-smile. Teasing him gently until he invited her upstairs, because he could never turn her away.

Tommie was on the other side of the small garden in the square when the door opened. Out of the corner of her eye, she saw a glimmer of something recognizable . . . Afterwards, she thought it was probably the girl she saw first. Not his usual type – no, this one looked like a church mouse. Shiny, neat chestnut-brown hair clipped back behind one ear, slender figure, almost athletic in build, a sensible navy coat all buttoned up to keep out the damp, freezing air and a cream leather handbag slung casually over one shoulder. Her arm was tucked through his, holding on to him as they rushed across the road through the evening mist and cold. They passed by her, walking quickly. He hadn't noticed her but the girl glanced in her direction.

Tommie felt slightly dazed by the sight of them, as if someone had struck her hard and now whatever had been real felt strangely blurred around the edges of her reality. Who *was* this girl that she'd never seen before? The Cheryls and other old friends of his were ten a penny and Tommie knew exactly who she was dealing with . . . but this girl was different. Tommie imagined her smelling of lemon soap and a faint floral perfume.

She was gaining on them again now and could hear the girl laughing. Tiny peals of amusement that landed like daggers, and he was laughing too, but not in a way that Tommie had ever heard before.

Maybe she's his sister, Tommie thought and the idea pleased her. Yes, that must be it. A family reunion. He was probably taking his sister to an early supper before putting her on the train home.

Her imagination flared in coloured strands of hope and despair. They were coming up to the wooden doors of an Italian trattoria and Tommie waited to see if they would go inside. They slowed down a little . . . and so she slowed down too, pretending to look in shop windows at green satin dresses and silver shoes. She didn't want to get caught in the light of the restaurant, so she hung back in the misty gloom, shivering as she watched them go inside. The burly waiter kissed the woman on both cheeks as if he knew her, before settling them at a table in the window. *The waiter knows her . . . then she must be his sister.* She exhaled and thought about walking away . . . but there was something about the way that girl was looking at him.

Tommie couldn't tear her eyes away as the table filled with a carafe of red wine and a basket of bread, followed by plates of steaming spaghetti. She pressed herself into the shadows, out of his eyeline, and pretended to be looking at the menu in the window. Reading descriptions of pasta and their sauces.

Whoever she was, he couldn't take his eyes off her: this fresh-faced girl with the shiny chestnut-brown hair. He was clutching her hand across the table and at one point warming it with his breath when she must have complained about the cold air. The girl giggled shyly and wrinkled her nose as she laughed. The way he looked at her . . . she *wasn't* his sister. Tommie knew that much.

He smiled at her, hanging on her every word and then feeding her with his fork. Twisting strands of spaghetti and cupping the palm of his hand underneath the fork so it didn't fall on to the tablecloth. Pouring her a small glass of red wine until she placed her hand firmly over the top of it to refuse him. The power of that refusal. To look him straight in the eye and ask for what you wanted, or tell him what you didn't want. Tommie couldn't imagine what that must be like.

She slunk back into the misty shadows so that she could no longer see his face but only the girl's. This shiny box-fresh girl smiling up at him.

A new thing, then . . . Tommie felt sick. She was shivering with cold and the shock of seeing them. She couldn't walk away and leave them to it. She had to know how their night would end.

Edie had woken up that morning craving her old life – before Frank. The girls at the biscuit factory and the fun they used to have. On her line of fancy biscuits, the women had stood in a row facing each other across the conveyor belt, with icing bags at the ready to draw wiggly pink lines across the top of the iced biscuits. On other days she was on packing, which was another long line of women all standing next to each other, scooping up a dozen biscuits – no more and no less – to go into tins with 'Marshall's' painted across the top in bright pink letters. At first, the work was overwhelming as everybody was so quick, and Edie found that her hands and brain were not quite in co-ordination, leading to some awful mistakes. But eventually, she caught up.

Edie prided herself on being one of the quickest girls on fancies. Her hands worked without her mind needing to be there and that left plenty of time for chatting or daydreaming. At the end of a long shift, her feet ached right up to the back of her calves, but after a quick sit down and a bite to eat, Edie would soon be ready to go dancing. Of course, then she met Frank . . .

The ugly wallpaper in her attic room offered no comfort, and Edie switched to the other end of the bed where she could see the sky. White-grey clouds, and a heavy fog starting to swirl outside her window. Edie closed her eyes and imagined what the inside of the biscuit factory was like in this kind of weather. The strip lights would be switched on early in the day and everyone would have a strange yellow glow cast over them. The enormous windows had thick bottled-glass panes that you couldn't see through and that let in only greyness even on the sunniest day. The paint was a horrible pale green, peeling along the metal frames.

Bad weather made all the girls quiet for some reason. The weird yellow glow stopped all the chatter and they worked steadily, heads down, icing bag in hand.

Edie hadn't seen any of the women she'd worked with for such a long time, apart from Violet Crim. She missed the others. The younger girls' stories about their dates or their nights out, and the older ones, who all had husbands they liked to moan about, or medical conditions, which they talked about as if they were badges of honour.

She'd heard the front door slam several times that morning and assumed Tommie had gone to work. Phyllis seemed to be out, too. Edie sighed and stretched her arms up towards the ceiling. The fog was getting worse now. So thick you could lift up handfuls of it. Edie rolled over on to her side facing the door to her room. She had a tiny glimmer of an idea. A crazy idea, but she felt desperate enough to go through with it.

Edie got dressed, fastened her coat and knotted her headscarf under her chin. She would have to take two buses, but then if she got off at the end of the road, by the gas works, she could walk from there if the foggy weather held. It was set in for the day, Edie was sure about that.

The first bus was crowded but Edie didn't make eye contact with anyone around her. The second bus was late and crawled along so slowly she worried about someone seeing her from the street. She kept her head down, trying not to lean against the window, and sat waiting until someone rang the bell for her stop. She stayed in her seat until the last possible minute and then, just as the bus slowed to a halt, she scrambled past people and leapt off.

She could see the great, black iron gates of Marshall's in the distance. At lunchtime the girls would come pouring out of there, smoking their cigarettes and heading to the café on the corner for egg, chips and a slice of fried bread. Sometimes the supervisors would take themselves off to the pub for a shandy and a sandwich, and come back giggly, willing to overlook one too many girls popping off to grab another cigarette break in the afternoon. If they were in a really good mood then you could get a little sing-song going on the factory floor. Edie loved those times. All the girls singing away until Mr Thwaite appeared at the top of the metal staircase where the offices were, shouting at them to 'get back to bloody work and stop that wailing'.

Edie hid across the road from the black iron gates surrounded by the fog and sheltered by the remnants of a bombed-out house. She could see the girls coming out in twos or threes, arm in arm, running to grab a good table in the café or the pub. A wave of longing passed through Edie. She wanted to run over to them, throw open her arms, but it was too late for that. She had messed everything up good and proper. There could be no more singing on the factory floor, or egg and chips in the café. No more nights out dancing or hen do's at the pub.

'Sadie, wait for me!' The voice was as familiar to Edie as her own. Pat had stood next to her on that 'fancy biscuit' line, drawing her wiggly lines or packing up her tins of biscuits. Her stocky little legs were running to catch up with Sadie, who was tall and took great galloping strides across the road without worrying about the others.

Sadie brought the football pools coupons around for her Uncle Bert, who used to be the agent, until he hurt his back and couldn't walk around the streets any more. Sadie's stern rat-tat-tat on the door was unlike anyone else's, and Uncle Bert would shout from the back room, 'Get that, love, will you? It's the pools woman.' He would sit at the kitchen table chewing the end of his pen and deliberating carefully whether one football team might draw with another one on the weekend. He'd once won five pounds and took Edie to the pub to celebrate.

Edie coughed and tried to do so quietly. The fog was getting to her throat and the damp cold was making her shiver. It would be warm in the café, she thought, with a mug of tea and a chip butty. The butter oozing out of the ends and sliding down her fingers. The rest of the girls were right in front of her now – so close she could reach out and pluck at a sleeve. Edie drew back, afraid of being seen. These were new girls that she didn't know. Four long years had passed since she'd given up her job at the biscuit factory. Lots of faces she didn't recognize. In fact, it was only Sadie and Pat that she'd worked with out of this lot.

The others were probably all married now with kids, or had moved on to other jobs. The button factory down the road paid good money for half an hour less each day, or some girls tried out for dress shops so they could get the discounts, but those jobs were hard to get if you didn't speak nicely or look the right way. It was all gone now . . . the life that Edie was lonely for. She felt foolish searching for her past in the fog.

Edie turned away and began to walk back towards the bus stop. It wasn't her life any more. She'd given it all up so easily, and for what? She felt tears slipping down her cheeks and wiped them away with the back of her hand. She missed the old Edie – that was it. Not her friends or the factory but the girl she used to be when she was dancing on top of that table and laughing all the time. What happened to *that* girl? But she knew the answer. Frank happened . . . and now here she was hiding away from everyone.

A bright red double-decker crawled around the corner, belching black smoke out of its exhaust, and Edie ran to jump on board, settling herself on the top deck. An old man squeezed in next to her, sitting too close, with his elbows rubbing against her arm. A newspaper lay on his lap, folded over like a dinner napkin. As he settled himself in, he unfolded it, opening out the front page, and Edie felt the air forced out of her lungs as she caught the thick black words inked on to the front page.

'MAN FOUND DEAD'.

Two Years Earlier

Edie was trying to cut sandwiches the way Frank liked them. They would have a houseful after the funeral and she really didn't want anything to set him off today. Since Mrs Budd had passed away, Frank had spent more time out of the house than in it.

On the odd occasions she'd waited up for him, it had been difficult to say anything without a row breaking out. He'd accused her of spending too much on housekeeping now his mother was dead. Her pension had stopped and so they were forever short of cash. He watched Edie walking around the kitchen as if she were a stranger to him. Once he'd started an argument over a bit of ham being cut too thick or too thin – Edie couldn't remember which crime she'd been guilty of that day. The argument had become vicious, wounding words flying across the kitchen table like little knives. Edie tried to be quiet and not answer back. She knew he was grieving for his mother, but even worse than that: he was on a losing streak.

The day after his mother had died, Frank had gone out to his usual bookmaker's and placed all the money he had left in the world on a nag called Heaven Sent at twelve to one, taking the name as a sign that his mother was looking down on him and about to bless him with a level of abundance he hadn't enjoyed while she was alive.

The horse pulled up lame on the home stretch, and Frank's dreams of a windfall disappeared.

At first he'd thought it was a fluke, but in the weeks that followed he had gone on to lose every single bet he'd placed, every game of cards he'd played. His luck would not change, no matter what he did. Frank was furious. He had *always* been lucky. His life had been saved during the war by a man getting up to stretch his legs while they were hiding in a dugout somewhere in Normandy. Frank had only been eighteen years old, but even so he'd realized that the man who died right in front of him had saved his own young life. He was immortal, and charmed. It gave him a swagger when he walked; an attitude that nothing could touch him. All that was gone now. The swagger had disappeared, and he had the stumbling walk of a man who drank his troubles away, only to find more troubles had arrived when he wasn't looking.

Edie didn't know the exact details of Frank's doings outside the house, but she knew enough to see that life was not going the way he'd planned it. His temper was short. The funeral had had to be delayed several times – the first delay due to the Christmas holidays and then again because the January freeze had made the ground too hard for the gravediggers to work. And all the while, Frank Budd couldn't catch a break. He was starting to get a stink about him. Other players didn't want him in their card games and the bookmaker looked the other way when he came through the door. His credit was no good and he owed money to some men that he'd rather not owe money to.

When he was at home, Frank and Edie spent their time in silence with only the sound of the radio for company. Then he would suddenly get to his feet, grab his jacket off the hook behind the front door and disappear to the pub. When he came home, he stank of booze. Edie had got into the habit of leaving him a cold plate of food on the kitchen table and going to bed without waiting up for him.

She would hear the front door go, though, and hold her breath as he came up the stairs, before he slid into bed beside her, his hands cold as ice. Those nights, he buried himself in Edie's flesh as if he was trying to change his luck somehow, to make something different.

Afterwards, Edie would lie on her side, her back turned to him. She had nothing to say and no comfort to offer. This was a man that Edie didn't recognize. She tried to remember the old Frank – the charming smile and how she'd wanted him. The touch of his fingers sliding across her skin and his mouth hot against her neck. His fingers drawing circles on her knee on that first date. Ever-widening circles of pleasure.

*

The funeral service was mercifully short. The vicar's words about Mrs Budd were nice, considering he barely knew her. Frank had chosen not to speak, which was just as well as he'd been drinking since after breakfast. Edie could smell it on him. At least nobody would mind that today.

The skies were blue, a frosty winter's day with the brown sludge of a recent snowstorm on the frozen grass verges of the churchyard. The earth had thawed enough to allow the gravediggers to hollow out a coffin-shaped mound. Frank went to the graveside with the men while Edie piled the sandwiches on plates and set about slicing up a fruit cake one of the neighbours had made for the occasion. It wasn't a very good one, as the currants had sunk to the bottom, but she sliced it and arranged the better pieces on the top, hiding the others from sight. The girls from the biscuit factory had dropped off a box of broken biscuits, but Edie was worried about putting them out in case it set Frank off again. She didn't want him to think his mother wasn't worth the trouble of proper biscuits. But they had no money left and biscuits all tasted the same, broken or not.

A few of the wives and girlfriends were scattered around Edie's living room sipping on the last of Uncle Bert's cream sherry. He'd turned up with two bottles on the morning of the funeral, and Edie was grateful. If it had been left to Frank, she would have been serving cups of tea and toast, with nothing but beef dripping to go with it.

The key on the piece of blue wool rattled up the door, signalling the return of the men from the graveyard. They trooped in one by one with their black ties and dark suits led by a red-eyed Frank. They must have had a little nip of something at the graveside because Frank seemed drunker than he had been at the church.

Edie busied herself passing around plates. She'd bought ham and cheese on tick, as she couldn't very well serve fish paste at his mother's funeral. Not when the old woman had disliked it so much. As it was a funeral, Mr Travers the grocer had been too embarrassed to turn her down, but Edie knew he had wanted to and there wouldn't be a next time.

Frank wouldn't eat the sandwiches. He wanted something stronger than cream sherry, but there wasn't anything. Edie carried on cutting extra slices of bread; the mourners were stuffing their faces full of food that she couldn't afford to give them. Frank came up behind her, stepping so lightly Edie hadn't been aware of him, until his arms wrapped around her waist and he buried his face in the back of her neck. The knife trembled under her hand. She turned to look at him; his eyes seemed so lost and sad that she felt herself soften towards him.

'You all right, Frank?' she whispered.

'You're all I've got now, Edie. You're all I've got left in the world,' Frank said.

13

London, October 1958

Phyllis was quite partial to a rum and peppermint. It was the drink that her father had loved and for her it brought back happy memories. The tang of the peppermint and woody smell of the rum felt like home to her. Most people considered it the wrong kind of drink for a lady but that didn't bother Phyllis. She liked what she liked.

She still wasn't quite sure what she thought of the 'new' Phyllis with her yellow helmet hair and her best dress. She'd even put on a pair of nylons, hiding her blue-veined legs inside American Tan stockings. It was certainly a different-looking woman who slipped into the usual shabby worn winter coat and decided to forgo her trusty headscarf lest it ruin the yellow helmet.

Shortly after eight o'clock, she pushed open the lounge door to the Admiral public house with some trepidation. There would be people inside that she knew. Neighbours . . . almost certainly couples who would know all about Terry Collier and his exploits. Phyllis braced herself – shoulders back, head held high. She would venture into the lounge bar and purchase a rum and pep. It was a perfectly simple proposition. Her sister Dora worked behind the bar and so there would at least be one friendly face and someone to talk to if necessary – Phyllis would never have dared go in on her own otherwise. She was a respectable woman, after all.

The lounge bar was half-empty. Dora was reluctantly polishing glasses with a tea-towel and chatting to a lone man who was standing at the bar supping a pint of beer. There were couples at two of the tables, but nobody that Phyllis knew to say hello to. It was a foggy old night and she was glad to get inside and see Dora's friendly face. Her sister's eyebrows raised as she took in the new Phyllis, but she nodded approvingly and smiled.

'Well, look at you – all dolled up. Usual?'

'Yes. Just a small one though. I'm not stopping.' Phyllis felt the man at the bar eyeing her up and down, trying to work out who she was and what she wanted there. She felt her fingers go up to the back of her new hairdo, teasing the strands into place, feeling suddenly self-conscious. Dora filled a small glass with a shot of rum and a tiny splash of peppermint cordial before setting it down on the bar. Phyllis placed half a crown on the wooden bar and took a tiny sip, swilling the minty rum around her mouth before she swallowed. The man was still staring at her and it was beginning to be irritating.

She would have liked to settle herself on a bar stool and have a good chat to Dora in between customers but the man was spoiling that idea, so she sidled away to a round wooden table, cupping her drink between the palms of her hands.

Sure enough, within a few minutes the man appeared next to her table, taking hold of the other chair and pulling it out to sit down. Phyllis sighed. She wasn't in the mood to talk to strangers. She'd just wanted a night out – and maybe a fish supper to take home with her. The new yellow hair felt all wrong now, as if it was sending out messages and Phyllis wasn't in control of what they said. The man was in conversation with her dyed blonde hair, and barely looking at her – at her 'respectable' face and manner that should tell him she was not the kind of woman to be trifled with.

'Don't mind, do you?' he said but Phyllis very much did mind. She pursed her lips and took another small sip of her drink. She couldn't stop him sitting there anyway. Dora gestured to her as if she'd struck gold, the man being some sort of prize that Phyllis was lucky to win. A full house at the bingo.

He was an ordinary-looking sort of a chap. Going thin on top but his hair was combed back so it wasn't noticeable at first. *You'd soon notice it though*, Phyllis thought. His face was ruddy, as if he worked outdoors, and his fingers yellow with nicotine-stained tips. He gulped at his beer, great swilling mouthfuls, and licked his lips as he waited for Phyllis to say something.

'It's a free country . . .' she said and then thought that was the wrong thing to say as it sounded as if she'd wanted him to sit down but was playing a little game with him. Flirting, even. Phyllis Collier had never flirted in her life and she wasn't about to start now.

'That it is . . . made sure of it . . . did my bit,' he said, holding up his half-empty glass of beer as if he'd won it.

'Yes, everyone did their bit.' Phyllis was tired of hearing men talk about the war. She'd had a war too. Bombs dropping and queuing for rations. He should try making meals out of dried egg and tinned spam. She didn't go on and on about it though. Half of them had never even seen action, they were so far behind the lines. They'd heard a bit of gunfire or a bomb in the distance. She'd had bombs falling just a street away. The whole street nearly went up one night and every fire engine in the city had come out to douse the flames. He'd come home safely, hadn't he, so what did he have to complain about? A spark of anger flickered and then died inside Phyllis. The rum was nearly gone now, but the man was still staring across the table at her.

'Get you another of those, shall I?' He was already on his feet, hand wrapped around her glass before she could say a word.

*

Across town, Tommie's feet felt as if they were frozen to the floor. She'd followed him and the girl with the shiny chestnut-brown hair back to his flat. Now, she was hiding in the little gardens opposite his building like a fugitive, tucked away in the darkness, watching the lights go on in his rooms.

First the living room where no doubt he was pouring the girl a nightcap – or maybe she wouldn't want one, given the way her hand had lain across her wine glass to signal enough. Maybe he'd boil a kettle and make them tea? No, that felt too domestic, too cosy for a seduction. Was that what this was? Tommie was determined to find out. She thought long and hard about ringing his doorbell, making him explain to her what he was doing up there. Him telling her to clear off or to come back later when his 'friend' was in a cab on her way home.

Shaking with cold now, Tommie clutched at the neck of her coat to try and get a tiny bit more warmth out of it but there was no comfort to be had. She could feel the foggy damp on her chest and felt sure she'd be coughing her guts up come morning. She had to know, though, just how much of a fool she was. The bedroom light flickered on and then off again. Tommie couldn't work out if they'd adjourned to the bed or if he'd just gone into the room to fetch something he needed. She was getting a crick in her neck from staring up at the windows and it was surely getting late if the girl needed to get home. A shadow passed across the thin curtains – the girl was walking around.

Then the lights in the living room went out and Tommie could see a familiar light in the bedroom coming from the bedside lamp with its small red shade.

She felt her chest constrict and her throat tighten.

She'd always been stubborn, ever since she was a kid. Too stubborn for her own good. Now, as she stared up at the bedroom window, an unwanted memory drifted into her mind.

Five years old, standing on the platform at Paddington Station. Her chubby little arms wrapped tightly around her mother's knees and her little gas mask bumping against her chest each time she tried to get closer. She was screaming at her mother, begging her not to put her on the train and send her away with the other children. Her mother tight-lipped, chain-smoking and staring hopelessly at the steam trickling out of the train engine.

'Tommie . . . stop it.'

They wanted to send her away to Wales, somewhere with cows and countryside, but Tommie clung on fiercely, refusing to be put on the train. Her mother was weary . . . too weary to fight her off and so in the end they went home again, hand in hand. Her mother cried all night long.

Later, when the bombs came, they ran into the shelter, jumping down into the blackness while her mother fumbled with matches to light the old oil lamp. Tommie hated the shelter. It was damp and full of spiders. She had nightmares about being buried alive in there. Her mother said she'd get used to it, but Tommie never had. She'd cried and begged every time the air-raid siren went off. That mournful howl, making her dread the darkness.

She shook her head trying to rid her mind of the past. She was so cold now that she couldn't feel her fingers and her teeth were chattering. How long would the girl stay? That would tell Tommie what she needed to know. He was particular about who stayed and for how long. It had taken him a long time – months and months – to let her stay for an hour or so afterwards. He didn't like anyone staying the night, he said. Liked to sleep alone, and he'd rather pay the cab fare than face chatter over breakfast. Tommie would have been silent given the chance but she was *never* allowed to stay.

She sat down on a damp bench in the gardens and lit a cigarette, gently inhaling and exhaling her feelings with the cigarette smoke. It was dark now, inside and outside. She imagined him kissing the girl, touching her and then eventually rolling away and wanting her to leave. The thought pleased Tommie that he would demand his usual sacrifice for the pleasure of being with him – don't chatter and take the cab fare. Even better if you left quietly and found your own cab home.

Four cigarettes later, the crushed lipstick-stained butts lay at her feet and still the flat was in darkness. It had been over an hour now. Tommie heard a clock chime somewhere and thought it was probably midnight. She stood up and decided to walk around the gardens to keep warm. Slapping her arms against her chest to get the blood flowing but never taking her eyes off the windows of the flat. On and on she walked but the flat remained in darkness.

Tommie couldn't get her breath. The shivering wouldn't stop and even walking, her arms clasped to her chest, made little difference. She wanted to cry, or maybe to scream. Scream so loudly that he would hear her and come outside to talk to her. Even as she thought it, Tommie knew that he wouldn't do anything of the sort. She was all alone and he'd found somebody else. A girl he wanted to stay the night after all. There would be no midnight cab ride home for her. Tommie couldn't imagine what it would be like to wake up next to him and have something as ordinary as breakfast, as if she belonged inside instead of out in the street looking up at the black windows.

In the distance, she could hear a couple walking by, arguing over something he'd done. The girl's voice was sharp and demanding. Tommie couldn't make out the words but she could hear the anger and the boy being defensive and sullen. Then they were gone and the street was empty.

Tommie had seen enough. She turned away and

walked back through the streets of Soho, grimy with dirt and strewn with cigarette ends. The sounds of music were still blasting from the jazz clubs and late-night drinking dens but the smaller places were starting to pull down their metal grids and shut up shop for the night. Wasn't much doing tonight. Girls plastered in their club make-up but now dressed in their street clothes – ordinary skirts and blouses like an army of shorthand typists going off to work – passed her by, only the slight orange pan-stick of the stage make-up giving them away. The false eyelashes and the too-red lipstick that never faded away.

Even Monty Daniels had called it a night and Tommie walked on by ignoring the occasional leer from a drunk in a shadowy doorway.

She wondered about the girl, and of course about him. When she might see him again and lie there wrapped up tight in his arms, as if she was safe and everything was fine in the world.

The lights were still on in a bar at the end of the street, but the customers were long gone. Just the man clearing up and watching her walk by.

'Fancy a drink, darling?'

Tommie hesitated just long enough for the man to speak again.

Two Years Earlier

Frank was eyeing Edie in a half-drunken way as he slumped across the kitchen table wearing his old white vest and a pair of dirty striped pyjama bottoms. It had been months since his mother had died and things, if anything, had got worse. He took an enormous greedy bite out of his bacon sandwich and then another until it was all gone. Every last bit. He licked the grease off his fingers and wiped the back of his hand across his mouth before gulping down his tea.

Edie couldn't take her eyes off him as he walked over to the dresser and got a small painted wooden box out of the drawer. He usually spent his Saturday mornings making tin models of things and he was quite particular about them. When he made little tin soldiers, he took great pains to get the details of their uniforms right. Once he'd even taken himself off to the public library to find out about the colour of a sash and got into quite a bad mood when he realized that he didn't have the correct yellow model paint for it. Edie was trying to pick the right moment to say what she had to say.

The tin soldiers were lined up on the kitchen table. Edie carefully moved the teapot and the sugar bowl out of the way. And all the time she watched him and waited . . .

She busied herself washing up the dishes, scrubbing the iron pan until all traces of the bacon fat were gone and then wiping down the surfaces until they sparkled. Edie hadn't eaten since yesterday, but she'd given Frank all the bacon for breakfast in the hope it would put him in a better mood. Still she waited. She said nothing. She needed to change the sheets and wash out her smalls but Edie didn't want to leave the kitchen. She had to do it now before she lost her nerve again.

She fussed over things that didn't need fussing over and cleaned the same surfaces several times. She rinsed and wrung out dishcloths until a fine layer of sweat started to form on her forehead. Finally, she leaned back against the cooker and exhaled.

Frank looked up and saw her staring at him. 'What are you looking at, Edie? You're putting me off and this is delicate work. It's bloody hot in here. Open a window, would ya?'

She pulled up the latch and pushed open the window a crack so a breeze wouldn't disturb his tin soldiers. He was focused intently on the tiny details of their cap badges, his tongue lolling out of the side of his mouth. He grimaced and for a moment Edie held her breath, but Frank just swore and got up to fetch a damp cloth. He'd smudged his paint and had to start over.

Edie untied her pinny and slipped her arms out of it before hanging it up on the back of the kitchen door. Frank walked over to the sink, rinsing the edge of his cloth under the tap before heading back to the kitchen table and his soldiers.

Edie wished she could just go out for the day, maybe go to the pictures and see a nice film. She could stop somewhere and have a cup of tea and an iced bun. She was partial to an iced bun . . .

They were scrimping on everything but there was never enough money to last the week. Any spare cash took Frank straight down the pub. Edie was so glad to get rid of him that she didn't think to complain that she was never included.

Frank had taken to doing more occasional 'jobs' with friends of his, but whether those jobs were entirely legal or not, Edie couldn't guess. She took a deep gulp of air. It was now or never . . .

'I was thinking about helping Mrs Travers out at the grocery shop . . . you know her husband has been in hospital with his hernia? Just a couple of mornings. It's not like I'd be going back to the biscuit factory, or doing anything full-time.' The words came out garbled as she rushed to make sure that Frank understood this was a different situation.

In reality it was only different because they were more desperate these days than they had been when they'd first got married. Frank was still on a losing streak with the gambling and Edie had grown embarrassed to keep asking for tick that they couldn't pay off at the end of the month. Everyone knew that Frank wasn't in what you might call 'gainful employment' and she had started using shops that were further away when she did have her housekeeping money as those shopkeepers were at least polite. Always calling her 'madam' or 'miss' with a cheery smile.

Mrs Travers was the only one who was nice to her, even though she knew they owed money. It was possible that she'd suggested a couple of mornings because she'd recognized Edie's desperation – noticed that Edie couldn't look her in the eye when she asked for tick, or promised that next Friday she would of course pay something off her bill.

Frank stared at the kitchen table for a few moments and frowned. He put down the tin soldier and the thin paintbrush and took a deep breath.

'NO! She can find somebody else to help her out. I'm the man of this house and I pay the bills. My wife does *not* go out to work!'

'But, Frank . . .' Edie stumbled over her words and was silenced by Frank getting to his feet, unsure of what he intended to do. But it seemed that the matter was closed.

'Right then. I need to have a wash and a shave. Put the kettle on for some hot water, would ya? I've got a card game later on. Going to be lucky today, I can feel it.'

Edie held the old kettle under the tap until it was full and then put it on the gas stove. Frank stretched out his arms in a wide yawn and then held them open to Edie.

'Come here, you . . . There's no need for you to worry about working while I'm here. My luck's about to change, Edie. I know some people – important people – and they can help . . . Anyway, it's time you had a baby. That's what you need. It's nearly two years now since we got married. We need to get on with it.'

Edie shuffled forward, trying not to look unwilling but at the same time not really wanting to step into Frank's sweat and beery fumes. He wrapped both his arms around her, pulling her close to him. She breathed in the sour smell of him and waited until he released her. If she tried to wriggle free there would just be another row. Edie was so tired of fighting for the smallest piece of her life, but what choice did she have? Uncle Bert couldn't take her in, and probably wouldn't. She could imagine him sucking on his old pipe before turning to her and saying, 'You're a married woman, Edie. You belong with your husband.' Nobody could hear her screaming inside. *If he slurps his tea one more time or comes home drunk and rolls on top of me* . . . She wanted . . . Edie didn't even know what she wanted. All her mind ever said was *NOT THIS*. But it didn't offer alternatives.

'You haven't lit the gas, Edie. I'll be waiting on that kettle all day to get hot.'

'Oh, sorry, I was miles away . . . I'll do it now. You go on up to the bathroom and I'll bring the kettle when it boils.' Edie was glad of the opportunity to move away and busy herself with lighting the gas. Frank, satisfied that everything was in order, left her to it and she heard him whistling all the way up the stairs.

She stared out of the kitchen window at the back yard, and wondered what it might be like to go dancing again, like she used to do. The kettle began to boil and without thinking she reached out a hand to grab it. A red welt formed across the centre of her palm.

14

London, October 1958

The floor of Edie's room was covered with both the daily and evening editions of every available newspaper. Her knees felt sore from the time she'd spent kneeling over them, poring over the words on the pages. 'MAN FOUND DEAD' – and it wasn't him. A stranger, beaten and left on an old bombsite in Lewisham. Eventually she reached the back cover of the very last newspaper and leaned back against her bed.

Turning to face the mattress, Edie shoved her hands underneath it to feel for the brown envelope. She felt a pulse of determination as she slipped off the thick elastic band to release the cash. Licking her fingertips, she counted out the notes and then, scarcely able to believe how much was there, she counted them out again for good measure. Spreading them over the bed, the sight of them filling her with a strange pleasure. It was £250 all told. Edie had never seen so much money in her entire life, and now she knew just how much was there, she had the worry of exactly where she should put it, as shoving it back under the mattress didn't seem the best idea. She rolled up the notes with the five-pound notes on the inside and the fifties on the outside, tucking them back inside the envelope and snapping the thick elastic band around them twice for good measure.

Edie sat back on the floor, nibbling at her fingernails until an idea occurred to her, and then she pulled the wooden chair over to the closet and stood on it. The top shelf held her little cardboard suitcase and Edie reached past it until she couldn't reach any further, placing the envelope right at the back of the closet, hidden by the suitcase.

For a moment she felt peaceful, as if she'd somehow solved all her problems. Nothing had happened after she'd seen Violet. There wasn't anything to concern her in the newspapers as the 'man found dead' wasn't anyone she knew. No one had come to Dove Street looking for her; she hadn't been followed. Somehow, she had got away with it all, and was free to choose somewhere to go and then buy a ticket. She could find a little hotel to stay in while she looked around a bit. Finding your feet in a strange place would take a bit of time but an envelope full to the brim with money would let her do exactly that. *Just pick a place now, Edie, my girl*, she said to herself. She'd go to the railway station and buy a ticket first thing in the morning and after that . . . well, the future was yet to be written. For the first time in a long while, Edie felt a glimmer of hope.

*

It was the early hours of the morning when suddenly a car door slammed outside in the street and Edie heard loud voices: a man talking and a woman giggling. The sound of it startled her at first and she scrambled to look out of the window. A flush of dread flowed through her as she imagined it was Violet leading someone right to her door, but it couldn't possibly be her.

Down in the street a black car was parked haphazardly under the street lamp, and Edie could just make out the back of a man trying to pull Tommie up from the pavement where she must have fallen.

Tommie was leaning against the car with her head thrown back, laughing at something she clearly found very amusing. Every time the man tried to lift Tommie up from her resting place, she sank back down again and sat there like a peculiar rag doll with her legs splayed out in front of her and her head lolling backwards against the car door. The man was getting exasperated now.

'Come on, doll . . . you *gotta* stand up now. You've had a bit too much to drink.'

'Shhhhhhhhh.' Tommie placed her finger over her lips and the man dropped his voice to a whisper.

'Let's get you inside, shall we? Your nice skirt is getting ruined on that pavement. You'll catch your death sitting there. Need to get you out of those damp clothes.' The man smirked, apparently at the thought of Tommie undressing, and continued trying to pull her up by her arms but she just allowed her body to flop back down again.

'Come on, love. Brought a little chaser with me . . . if you fancy it?' The man drew a small bottle of gin out of his jacket pocket and Tommie smiled up at him.

'Got a smoke?'

'Yeah, but you have to get up first.'

'I like it here. The world looks nice. You should come down.'

The man reached into his jacket pocket and pulled out a pack of cigarettes, taking one out with his teeth and lighting it. Passing it down to Tommie, he watched her as she took a long drag and then let out a long, complicated sigh that even Edie could hear from her window.

'Getting up now?' He took the cigarette out of Tommie's hand, storing it between his lips.

'If I have to . . .' she said.

'You *have* to . . . Come on, let's go inside and carry on our little party.' The man bent down catching Tommie under her arms and dragging her to her feet. Propping her against the car, he shoved the cigarette back in her mouth so she could take another drag and stood there admiring her.

'You're quite the party girl, Tommie.' He put one arm around her waist and started to walk towards the front door with her.

Tommie giggled. 'I am THE party . . . Do you know that song "Stupid Cupid"?'

'Sure, I know it.'

'That's me.'

'What? You're Stupid Cupid?' He laughed.

'No, I'm the *victim* of Stupid Cupid. I am. That song is my life. You're laughing but it's not funny.' Tommie wagged her finger in his face and then clung on to his arm to stop herself falling back down to the ground again.

They were almost at the front door now and Tommie wanted him to hold her tight, but he was busy trying to get her to stand up while he searched her small brown handbag for her keys.

'Hold me tight . . .' Tommie whispered as her eyelids fluttered shut.

'Wait a minute, doll . . . There we go . . . let's get inside.'

Tommie tripped over the front doorstep and sprawled face down across the ugly olive-green carpet runner, which started her giggling again, but it didn't last long. The giggles turned into tears quite suddenly and the man clearly didn't know what to do with her now.

'Oh, doll . . . no . . . no . . . no . . . no crying. C'mon, up you get. Where's your room? Upstairs?'

Tommie nodded but the tears wouldn't stop falling and her mascara started to trickle down her cheeks in wet black streaks. The man tucked one arm around her waist and tried to get her to walk but with no chance of success. Then he seemed to have a brainwave and picked her up in his arms. She leaned into his chest, her head bouncing back and forth against him as he struggled to climb the steps. About halfway up to Tommie's room the timer light switched off and they were both plunged into darkness. Tommie didn't know whether to continue crying or start giggling again, so she wrapped her arms around the man's neck and breathed in the smell of him. Beery fumes and some cologne she didn't recognize. She liked it.

'You smell nice . . .' she muttered, her eyelids closing again.

'So do you, doll. Where's the light switch?'

'Somewhere . . . *over the rainbow* . . .' Tommie started to sing and then giggled again. It was all so funny.

'Put the light on. I can't see where I'm going.' They weren't making much progress up the stairs. Tommie was sure he was probably in two minds whether to call it a night and just leave her there, but her room wasn't far away. He'd invested a good few drinks in her; surely he'd want to keep her company. He heaved her up another step.

Suddenly the light snapped on, casting a dim yellow glare and taking them by surprise. Tommie looked up, feeling a surge of embarrassment wash over her when she saw Edie at the top of the stairs staring down at them. She looked back at the man from Soho, who blinked up into the light. Then, quite suddenly, Tommie saw his face change, a look of pure astonishment washing over his features as he stared at the girl upstairs.

'Pete . . . I . . .' Edie couldn't say another word. She stood there open-mouthed, gaping in horror at the sight of him.

What on earth was Frank's best man doing here? She wished that she'd left Tommie alone. *Why did she have to come down to check on her?* But it was too late now and the two of them took turns to stare at each other. Edie's heart thudded against her ribs. A raw fear clenched at her insides making her feel sick.

Shaking his head from side to side, Pete blinked quite slowly, 'I *know* you . . . you're Frank's missus, ain't ya? What are *you* doing here?' He frowned at her, a puzzled look on his face as if he was trying to make sense of how his evening had turned out.

'I'm visiting a friend . . .' The lie slipped out easily but she couldn't tell if he believed her. He nodded and was about to say something when Tommie lifted her head from his shoulder. Her skirt was covered in dirt and stains from the road and her face streaked with tiny clouds of mascara tears. She registered Edie's presence and her face broke into a wide grin.

'Edie . . . we're having a party . . . shhhhhhh.' Tommie sniffed loudly and then vomited all over herself.

'Oh *Christ* . . .' Pete quickly dropped Tommie on to the stairs, shaking his arms free of her, a look of pure disgust on his face. 'That's *enough* now. I'm off.' And giving Edie another curious stare, he stomped back down the stairs, slamming the front door behind him.

'Oh . . .' Tommie gave an exasperated cry and then folded, child-like, bent over her arms, in a heap on the stairway. A trail of yellow vomit leaked from the corner of her mouth and down the front of her blouse.

A wave of panic flooded through Edie. She needed to get out of number 73 before Pete had a chance to tell people that he'd seen her. As she turned to run back up the stairs to her room, Tommie raised her head and began to sob.

'I'm *sorry* . . .' she cried. 'I saw him with a new girl . . . and the next thing . . . look at me. *Look at the state of me* . . .' Her chest heaved as she gulped for air.

Edie was torn. She couldn't just abandon the girl in this state. Maybe she could get her sorted and then escape . . . after all, it was late. She was probably safe until Pete had the chance to tell someone and that wouldn't be until tomorrow . . . *she hoped*. Maybe he'd believed her lie about visiting a friend – after all, if there was nothing in the newspapers then he had no reason to think anyone was looking for her. As long as she left at first light, then she'd probably be all right.

Edie sighed and looked down at Tommie lying slumped on the stairs covered in vomit. She couldn't leave her there. 'It's all right. Let's sort you out.'

Edie clasped Tommie's hand in hers and pulled her up off the floor. Tommie followed her meekly into the bathroom and stood obediently as Edie ran a basin full of hot water, the little Ascot heater blasting away, chewing through the pennies in the meter outside the door. Edie wrung out a hot damp flannel and used it to wipe away the sooty streaks on Tommie's face. 'You need to get out of those things.'

Tommie smiled weakly. She stood, arms hanging by her sides, as Edie unfastened her clothes and they dropped to the floor.

'You'll be fine. Give me your door key and I'll fetch you a clean nightie. I'll be back in a tick.'

Tommie handed over a small brass key, and Edie slipped quietly out of the bathroom, leaving the other girl staring blankly at the walls, her vomit-stained clothes pooled at her feet. Once inside Tommie's room, Edie quickly searched the closet shelf for a nightdress, finding one in blue cotton with small yellow pansies embroidered on to it. Then suddenly a wild panic washed over her as the horror of her close encounter hit her and she collapsed into a wooden chair, rocking back and fore. She was running out of time.

Phyllis Collier had fallen asleep on her sister's settee. It had been good to catch up with her after closing, but she'd woken up cold and desperate for her own bed. Stepping into the hallway of 73 Dove Street, she could hear the sounds of the milkman on his rounds – and, more importantly, she could smell something strange.

A nasty combination of bleach and a whiff of vomit in the air. She sniffed, wrinkled up her nose and looked around to see if she could spot anything that offended her sensibilities, but everything looked just as it had when she'd left home the previous evening.

She sighed a bone-weary exhalation and took off her coat, hanging it on the hook by the entrance to her back kitchen, and proceeded to put on the lights so she could see where she was going. Phyllis caught a glimpse of herself in the little kitchen mirror and sighed again. That awful yellow hair! Her night out had very much not gone as planned. The dreary man had sat at her table boring her with his war talk and every time she'd tried to signal to Dora that she needed rescuing, Dora had shaken her head and waved her onwards. Onwards to what exactly, Phyllis couldn't tell. Her fresh start had hit the buffers. The hair was all wrong – giving out calling cards to the kinds of men she didn't want calling. She'd have to go back to see Val and ask her to change it, although whether you could dye it back to mousy brown with grey was another matter.

The strange smell bothered her. *What had those tenants been doing?* Up to no good, she imagined. Fiddling about with bleach at this time of night . . . as if she didn't have enough to contend with.

She'd enjoyed the rum and pep though. It was very nice to dress up a bit and go out to the lounge bar. It had been a long time since that had happened. Maybe she could try again but without the yellow hair. Blondes didn't have more fun, as far as she could see. They just got more annoying people trying to talk to them all night long.

Phyllis was about to go to bed when she heard the sound of footsteps coming up the garden path and then a delicate tap-tap-tap as somebody tried to shove something through the letter box. Whatever it was seemed too big to fit, but still, whoever was on the other side of the door carried on trying and the letter box clattered away.

Maybe it was the man from the pub . . . he might somehow know where she lived. Phyllis gripped the wooden handle of her mop in one hand and slowly made her way to the front door. She bitterly regretted not making her husband fit a security chain so she could just open it a few inches to check who was there, but it was too late now.

Phyllis tightened her grip on the wooden handle ready to thrust it into the face of any late-night visitor who might be up to no good. She carefully turned the door latch and pulled it open a few inches. Tutting loudly, Phyllis scowled at the man on the other side of the door. There, bold as brass on her front doorstep, was a drunken Terry Collier – carrying a box of Milk Tray chocolates as if they were the crown jewels.

Two Years Earlier

'Hello, love, haven't seen you for a week or two? Everything all right?' Mrs Travers was a kind woman and she always spared your feelings if she could. Everyone knew by now that Frank had lost big at cards again and was now indebted to the Costello Brothers, small-time gangsters who had their sticky fingers in too many pies around their way. The gossip had spread through every pub and back around the shops where the wives filled their baskets with groceries. *Did you hear about Frank Budd?* Their mouths twisting around the delicious gossip. Feasting on her life and smacking their lips in satisfaction afterwards.

Edie had woken up that morning determined to change her fortune and Mrs Travers was her first call. She was tired of being talked about and even more tired of being poor. Scrimping and scraping for every meal. She was sick of begging Frank for every last penny only for him to tell her she couldn't have it, and then take the money down the boozer. Today she was going to disobey him and Edie didn't care what he thought about it. She wanted to look people in the eye again, to not owe them money. Edie wanted an occasional night out or a new dress. She'd waited for Frank to make something of himself but all he ever wanted to do was hang out at the pub or the betting shop. It was no kind of a life and she was tired . . . bone-weary tired of struggling.

'I was wondering . . . if you still needed someone to do those mornings you talked about. I'm a good worker.' Edie was keen to emphasize that she was not like Frank although she didn't speak his name.

'What does your husband say about you working here?'

Edie held Mrs Travers's gaze and she heard herself say that Frank was perfectly fine about it. A bare-faced lie and there it was. She couldn't take it back now. It was done.

'When can you start?' Mrs Travers smiled now and Edie smiled back.

'Tomorrow . . . if you like.'

'Tomorrow it is then. Nine o'clock sharp and don't be late.'

'I won't be!' Edie could have skipped out of the door she was so happy. It didn't seem all that much but the idea of having her own money in her pocket made her smile all the way home. She'd have to make up an excuse to go out every morning but she usually did her shopping then, so as long as she arrived home with something for dinner he'd never guess. Then, after a while, when it had become a regular thing, she could tell him, maybe after buying them something nice.

She walked slowly back towards their street, trying to ignore the neighbours who liked to gossip. A gang of children were knocking on doors and running away. They almost knocked Edie off her feet as she turned the corner and she could see in the distance that Frank was talking to the bloke across the road. He caught sight of her coming down the street and waved, his face breaking out into a wide grin as it used to do when they were first courting. Edie raised her hand and gave a limp wave in return, her good mood fading. She would have to tell him . . . but not yet. *Couldn't she just have one thing of her own for a little while?*

Frank was leaning against the front door, watching her walk towards him. He took the shopping bag from her hand as she got closer.

'Can't have you carrying heavy loads now, girl . . . you never know, you might be pregnant already. That would be something, wouldn't it?' And he walked into the house taking the shopping bag all the way through to their little kitchen.

'Yeah, that would be something . . .' she said in a dull tone, watching the sharp bones of his back as he walked away from her.

Edie hung up her coat on the metal hook and looked away as she passed the mirror. She couldn't stand to see her lying eyes reflected back at her.

15

London, October 1958

Edie balanced on her tiptoes in order to get a good view of the street below. Her little cardboard suitcase was neatly packed and tied up with the piece of string once again. She'd hadn't slept a wink as Tommie had insisted on talking for most of the night, but now Edie needed to leave while everyone was still in bed.

As she checked the street to make sure that nobody was watching the house, Edie felt a familiar pulsing ache behind her eyes. She rubbed at her temples and sent up a silent prayer that it wasn't a migraine. Once one began, there was no way out. So far, the street below was quiet and ordinary. Out of the corner of her eye she could see the milkman further down the road about to begin his round.

Edie gulped down a breath and blinked her eyes. The street lamp seemed too bright and the edges of her vision grew speckled with colour. She blinked again and moved away from the window.

Maybe she could have a cup of tea and a ginger biscuit. That might help. The lack of sleep had probably set her off. Yes, a quick cup of tea should do it but there was something funny about the water this morning. Everything tasted off – metallic and sour in her mouth. The stress of hiding out was starting to take its toll.

She reached for her tin of ginger biscuits but the tin was empty. They were the only thing that settled her stomach these days, but she didn't want to go outside for something so trivial. Edie tried to remember back to a time when she wasn't anxious and didn't wake up feeling sick with worry but it was so long ago. She tried to pluck a happy memory from the far reaches of her mind.

The roar of a motorbike engine screamed down the street, leaving a trail of black smoke in the air. Edie thought about Frank and their trips to Margate, before everything had gone so wrong. Maybe it had always been wrong but there were happy times too. The day he'd won a teddy bear for her at the fun fair. Throwing little wooden hoops until one landed over the small brown bear. He'd presented it to her as if it were diamonds and they'd eaten candyfloss on the seafront, until a great big bird came along and tried to steal it. They'd laughed about that all the way back to the hotel. The big white seagull with pink candyfloss stuck to its beak.

Edie couldn't imagine Frank not being alive in this world, but he was as dead as could be. She would never see him again in this life. The thought made her feel afraid and the worry made her feel queasy again.

The past couple of nights she hadn't been able to close her eyes without seeing his face in her dreams. Waking up haunted by his presence.

Her head pounded and her breathing became shallow. Black spots gathered before her eyes as flashing lights began their strange dance. A peculiar dizzy feeling flooded through her. She would have to lie down until it passed. She felt wrung out with the lack of sleep and the constant worry and sank down on to the bed. Exhausted, she took several deep breaths. Running a hand across her forehead, feeling it, as if it would predict her future. Clammy . . . not clammy . . . Did she have a fever? No . . . Oh, the last thing Edie needed was to get sick in this strange house with nobody to look after her. Sometimes her headaches lasted for hours but once a particularly bad episode had made her take to her bed for a whole day. They would come for her now. She had to get away.

Edie raised her head from the pillow but quickly sank back down again . . . it was hopeless.

Tommie was shucking oysters, dozens of them. Her hands were red and freezing cold from prising open the little shells and laying them on the slab of ice that had arrived that morning. The ice had been delivered by the most bad-tempered man and he'd left it at the back door so that Tommie had had to lift it up and find a suitable spot in the kitchen, so it didn't melt everywhere. She'd woken up with a splitting headache, having barely slept a wink, but she'd shovelled down two aspirin and drunk enough tea to float a battleship. All she had to do was get through this dinner party, fall into her bed and forget all about the night before.

The Beef Wellington was already in the oven but as Tommie couldn't see what was going on inside, she kept opening the door to make sure it wasn't burning. Consequently, the pastry still looked as pale and uncooked as when it went in there. She sighed but didn't reach for the cooking brandy. Tommie had sworn off the booze and her Soho nights for the foreseeable future. The vague memories of being washed with a flannel by Edie made her cheeks flush crimson – not to mention the thought of that barman . . . whoever he was. Tommie never wanted to see *him* again, that was for sure.

If only she hadn't seen the new girl and followed them home. What was *he* doing now? Were *they* together? The questions burned and part of Tommie didn't want to know the answers. Still, the familiar hunger deep inside began to scratch at her. She could feel her longing welling up, just to be held again for those few moments. Aching to be close to him.

Tommie shook off all thoughts of Soho, determined to get through this terrible dinner party and go straight home. She should go and say thank you to Edie, really – she was a good sort, picking her off the floor and cleaning her up like that. And if she hadn't appeared on the stairs at that very moment . . .

who knew what might have happened, as that barman didn't seem to be taking no for an answer. A fleeting image of Phyllis returning home to find Tommie naked in bed with a drunken stranger made her cover her face with both hands.

A slight whiff of burning brought Tommie right back to reality and she flung open the oven door, waving away clouds of steam and retrieving the Beef Wellington just in time. It needed to rest, and in the meantime she would take the oysters upstairs and lay them out for the guests. Speaking of which, it occurred to Tommie that she hadn't heard the doorbell ring. Mrs Vee had hired an agency girl to open the door and pour drinks, while Tommie cooked and served. The girl would clear and help her wash up afterwards.

If the agency girl had left the front door open for visitors to wander in by themselves, then Tommie was sure that Mrs Vee would not approve. She liked each guest to ring the bell and be greeted as if they were the only visitors that mattered. The girl was supposed to take their coats and offer them cocktails as quickly as possible, so that Mrs Vee could move to the part of the evening she liked the best, which was making small talk with people who adored her.

Tommie rested a cold plate of oysters on her arm and picked up two more in her hands. It was a delicate balancing trick but she was well practised at it. She'd forgotten to take her apron off but rather than put the oysters back down on their ice slab, Tommie decided she would be so quick that Mrs Vee wouldn't notice and she could send the agency girl to call the guests through to eat.

The table looked beautiful, if Tommie said so herself. A crisp, white linen cloth covering the rectangular oak table. The dining chairs like regimented soldiers in their red livery. On the table itself the best silver and china, with crystal glasses sparkling under the lights. Flowers were arranged along the full length of the table: deep reds and purples to match the crimson dining chairs. Delicate tapers giving off small pale yellow flames. Tommie felt satisfied with her day's work. She only hoped the Beef Wellington would not spoil everything by being bloody and uncooked when she cut it.

Tommie laid the oysters down carefully next to the flowers and away from the candles. She would tell the girl to get the guests in now so the oysters wouldn't spoil. Then she would go down and cut the Beef Wellington and pray.

The agency girl was a sallow-cheeked youngster wearing a shabby hand-me-down black dress that was too big for her and a white lacy hat which sat crooked on her head. She leaned against the wall in Mrs Vee's hallway next to a silver tray of glasses that were filled to the brim with now quite flat champagne. Her face was a picture of wretched boredom.

'What *are* you doing?' Tommie said sharply, for the

girl was just staring into space and all of Mrs Vee's best champagne was going to waste.

'Waiting . . . as I was told to do,' the girl replied in a sullen tone that suggested she didn't have much time for Tommie.

'Where are the guests?'

'Well, how would I know? Nobody has turned up yet.' The girl inspected her fingernails, removing a dark rim of dirt from one and casually flicking it on to Mrs Vee's parquet floor.

'What do you mean, nobody has turned up yet? It's gone eight o'clock. The invitations said seven thirty prompt. Mrs Vee don't like people coming late. It spoils things.' Tommie stared at the girl, puzzled now, as if she had hidden the missing guests away somewhere.

'Well, nobody has arrived, so I guess they'll be late, won't they?'

'Where is she?' Tommie gestured upstairs and the girl shook her head.

'She's in the drawing room with her glass of champagne . . . waiting . . . like the rest of us.'

Tommie frowned. She was about to say something but then the telephone rang and Tommie picked it up, repeating Mrs Vee's number exactly as she had been instructed to do, and asking how she might help the caller.

'Oh, hello . . . Just wanted to let Gladys know that we can't make it this evening. I'm afraid Howard is not feeling well at all. So sorry for the late notice but it's been quite the day, I can tell you . . . do give her our love, won't you?'

Before Tommie could say a word, the caller hung up without giving their full names but she presumed that Mrs Vee would know who Howard was. So at least two of them were not coming now.

The doorbell finally rang, sparking hopes of a stream of apologetic visitors, but when the girl opened the door with a fixed smile plastered to her sallow face it was the boy from the florist shop standing on the doorstep, carrying an enormous basket of white calla lilies. A stiff white card was tucked amongst their stems, which Tommie retrieved and put on the small silver platter that Mrs Vee liked to use for calling cards and letters.

'Stay here!' she hissed to the girl and wondered whether she should retrieve the oysters before dealing with Mrs Vee, but decided to take the flowers and the card into the drawing room. The hall clock chimed for a quarter after eight. It seemed unlikely that anyone would arrive this late. The telephone rang again, and this time Tommie scooped up the basket of lilies with one hand, gesturing to the girl that she should answer it.

Tommie tapped lightly on the drawing-room door and entered, carrying the lilies, wearing her most accommodating smile, the one that she reserved for times when things were really going wrong. Inside,

Mrs Vee was all dressed in purple silk, with a strange feathered turban wrapped around her head.

'Did I hear the door, Tommie?' Mrs Vee looked up hopefully, but the hope faded as she glanced upon the basket of lilies.

'Flowers . . . There's a card. I'm afraid some of your guests telephoned to say they've been taken ill . . . Howard is sick, I believe.' Tommie spoke as authoritatively as she felt able to do, considering she had no idea who had called, as she'd forgotten to ask their names at the beginning of the call, even though Mrs Vee had instructed her to do so on multiple occasions.

'Oh . . .' Mrs Vee seemed crestfallen. 'What time is it now?'

'It's a quarter past eight.' Tommie stood awkwardly with the basket of lilies hanging from her arm, not quite sure where to put them now that she'd brought them into the room.

'Leave the flowers in the hallway for now. I wonder if there's been some kind of traffic accident? Do you think so, Tommie?'

'I really couldn't say.'

'Seems quite odd that *everyone* is so delayed . . .' Mrs Vee swallowed and looked down at her hands, which were fidgeting in her lap. Clasping and unclasping. Tommie felt a rush of pity for the old woman. It was just bloody rude that nobody had turned up.

Mrs Vee was wearing her best jewellery too, the stuff

she only got out of the vault on special occasions. Tommie chewed on her bottom lip and wondered what to do next. The oysters would be ruined unless she returned them to the ice very shortly and then there was the Wellington . . .

'Can I get you anything?' Tommie ventured.

'No, it can't be helped . . . You can let the agency girl go. Nobody can expect a full dinner service if they arrive at this time. It would be considered the height of bad manners in my day . . .' Her voice tailed away.

'How about I make a nice bit of supper and bring a tray up for you?'

'Just a small plate then . . . shame to let it all go to waste. And a bottle of champagne.'

'Be right with you!' Tommie sounded unnecessarily jolly now as if this awful dinner party was all going to plan.

'And, Tommie . . . if anyone calls, you can tell them that Mrs Vee is no longer receiving guests this evening.'

16

London, October 1958

At Dove Street, Phyllis couldn't settle no matter what she did. She'd spent all day thinking about Terry and wondering what to do. In the end she'd taken to her bed rather earlier than usual, only to find she couldn't sleep no matter what she tried. After hours of tossing and turning, Phyllis had picked up her box of Milk Tray and begun to read a novel.

Her library book had turned out to be the kind of romance novel that bored her. The man was very much the strong, silent type but she preferred men who spoke about interesting things. The heroine fluttered her eyelashes and swooned at regular intervals, which Phyllis couldn't see the point of at all.

'Silly girl,' she muttered under her breath and then considered getting up to fetch a little bicarbonate of soda in water for her acid stomach. It was surely the after-effect of all those chocolates, she thought as she lay back on her pillows. The house would be cold now the fire was out and the thought of getting all chilly again when she had the pleasure of a hot water bottle on her feet filled her with dread. It was hard enough to get warm at night and the chasm on the other side of the double bed seemed wide and too empty.

'Hmm,' Phyllis muttered to herself, rubbing at her chest now and trying to ease her heartburn. Those chocolates were very nice on the way down but not so nice now. The cheek of it – bringing her chocolates to try and get her to take him back.

And what if she did take Terry back – what then?

New rules . . . Oh . . . Phyllis sighed and let loose with a deep belch which eased the sharp pains in her stomach and chest. At least she could belch in comfort. There was something to be said for living alone. She was too old to make new rules and what was the point? Terry Collier had always pleased himself since the day he'd left his mother's house. Brought up as 'my little prince' for whom no woman made of flesh and blood would ever be good enough. Terry had believed it and kept on looking long after he'd settled on Phyllis. She'd worried that he had what they called a 'roving eye', as if it was a sport. A *roving eye* indeed. 'No harm in looking,' he would say. There had been good times though . . . before the war came and changed everything.

Phyllis rubbed at her belly as the acid burned. She would not eat a lime cordial barrel again, that's for sure. They disagreed with her.

She'd never looked at another man and she should have. Phyllis thought of all the years she'd wasted, cooking and cleaning for a man who would put on the clean shirt that she'd carefully starched and ironed to go down the pub without her. Buying other women drinks, most likely, and behaving like a daft old fool.

She picked up her library book and then put it back down again. The words on the page melting into a blur of black ink; her eyes filled with tears as she considered her lot. *What had she ever done to deserve this?*

The house seemed unusually quiet. The only sound was the faint rattling of the windowpanes as a cold October wind blew against them. She was quite alone. Phyllis suddenly remembered a Barbara Stanwyck film where she couldn't get out of her bed, and the husband had arranged for someone to murder her. The thought made Phyllis pull the bedspread up around her neck. Silly to think thoughts like that. Besides, Terry Collier would be hard pressed to arrange for clean shirts on laundry day never mind a murder.

The thought of Terry irritated her. She wriggled about trying to get comfortable, but to no avail. Phyllis couldn't sleep and neither could she read.

She thought about the first time she'd laid eyes on Terry Collier. She'd just turned eighteen years old and was working in the local grocer's shop. She was good at it too. Could cut a quarter pound of cheese just by eye and was rarely wrong. He'd come in one day for some tinned peaches for his mother, and then again the next day for a few slices of ham . . . By the third day Phyllis realized that this young man was in fact coming in to see her and she'd said to him, 'You'd better ask me out before you spend all your money in this shop.' And he'd laughed – a nice, boyish laugh.

That night Terry took her out dancing and they'd stayed on that dance floor until it was time for the band to pack up their instruments and go home. They didn't want to let go of each other. A year later they were married . . .

Phyllis pulled a face at the thought of the years that separated her from that day. She'd worn a drop-waisted blue chiffon dress with flowers in her hair. She was lucky, everyone said, because there weren't many young men left with all their limbs intact or unscarred lungs. So many of them had breathed in mustard gas or were broken by the horrors they'd witnessed. Never the same again. Terry had been much too young to fight in the first war though. He was strong as a bull and full of fun.

Phyllis tried to imagine herself as a very old lady lying in her bed all alone, unable to move around properly. Nobody to talk to about all the days of her life. Nobody to remember when she was young and full of fire. Only Terry would remember and she didn't want to talk about it with him.

It would be nice to have someone to talk to but she didn't even have a cat. *Maybe she should get a cat for company? Old women did that, didn't they?* Phyllis had never liked cats though – sly little creatures, always getting in the bins and making a mess. The bedside lamp flickered and then the bulb made a strange popping noise. The light disappeared, leaving Phyllis in the half-gloom thinking about a young girl in a blue chiffon dress and all the years she'd forgotten about.

The empty pillows seemed to mock her and Phyllis picked them up and threw them on to the floor, only just missing the bedside lamp with her poor aim. She shifted over in the bed, lying out in the centre and feeling the chill of the cold sheet underneath her bare legs. She hated this time of night. She'd turned in early hoping to fall asleep long before now but with no luck. These were the lonely hours and everything seemed as bleak and miserable as could be. Phyllis lay back in the darkness, tossing and turning for several minutes . . . but it was no good. The acid pains swam over her and she belched again. She shuffled her ice-cold feet into her slippers. She would have to get something to soothe her poor belly or there would be no sleep for her at all. She blamed Terry Collier for everything – her acid stomach and her worries. She could live alone . . . plenty of people did.

But somewhere deep inside she compiled a long list of new rules for Terry Collier to obey just in case . . .

As she stepped out into the hallway Phyllis heard a loud thud, but by the time she'd got to the bottom of the stairs to check, there was nobody there.

Upstairs, the attic room was in darkness. Edie had dreamed of being trapped inside a small cage that she couldn't escape from and woke up with a start to find that it was already late in the evening and she'd slept all day long. She'd eventually fallen asleep after hours of lying there with no respite from her headache and was relieved to find that it had passed.

Gingerly Edie sat up and, when that went well, she got to her feet, smoothing down her rumpled clothing and taking a deep breath. She poured some cold water from the kettle into a cup. Drinking thirstily, she gulped it down and wiped her hand across her mouth. Running her hands through her hair, she sighed . . . she would go now. At least if she got sick again, she would be on a train . . .

Oh, but then the thought of being ill outside was as bad as lying here in her single bed and being discovered by Pete. Yet he could come back at any moment. No . . . it was no good . . . she would have to take her chances and leave. Edie reached for her coat and scarf. Once her coat was buttoned, she grabbed her handbag, checking the envelope was safely inside. Then she picked up the cardboard suitcase, clutching it to her chest as she crept out on to the landing.

Treading silently, she edged down one step at a time in the dark, stopping at the turn of the stairs on the first floor to listen for any signs of life. Edie's heart began to race as the steps creaked and groaned when she trod on them. Desperately trying not to make a noise, she stepped as lightly as she could on to the bottom stairway . . . just a few more treads to go. Edie could see the street light reflected through a piece of glass over the front door and in her haste to get to it, she stumbled on the step. Her cardboard suitcase crashed on to the stairs as it fell from her arms.

Suddenly, the downstairs was flooded with light.

Two Years Earlier

Frank was late. Edie started to fret that there had been an accident but someone would have told her by now. She'd put the casserole back in the oven and turned the gas down low, so as not to ruin it. The kitchen table was laid ready for his dinner. His knife and fork next to his favourite plate. Salt and pepper next to the sugar bowl. A teacup ready to be filled when he asked for it. No detail forgotten.

The familiar bounce of the key rattling against the front door alerted Edie to his presence. She got up from her place at the kitchen table and moved towards the stove to put the potatoes on to boil. There was no greeting from the front door. Just the stomp of heavy work boots on the linoleum as he arrived in the kitchen doorway.

Frank stood there, leaning against the doorframe, watching her moving back and forth between the stove and the cupboard. Edie added a generous pinch of salt to the potatoes and covered them with the metal saucepan lid. She didn't bother to look at him.

'You're late. I made a casserole. Hope it's not all dried up.'

'I stopped off at the pub on my way home.'

Edie kept her back turned to him. 'Dinner won't be long.' Her voice faltered and she went back to lifting the lid on the saucepan and putting it back down again.

'Well, it's a funny thing because I got talking to a few of the lads in the pub . . . and guess what they told me?'

Frank hadn't moved from the doorway. His broad shoulders filled the frame, and Edie suddenly became aware that he was drunk. Cold, angry drunk. Fear slid over her like treacle until she couldn't stop her hands shaking. The lid of the saucepan rattled in her hand as she tried to cover the whirling water in the pan.

'What was that then?' Edie asked, trying to sound casual but inside her heart was racing. She'd asked the question but she didn't want to know the answer.

'They told me . . . that *my missus* was working for old Travers in the grocer's shop up in the High Street.' Frank spoke slowly and deliberately. Emphasizing her crime of disobedience.

'I . . . I don't know what you mean . . .' Edie felt her throat tighten and trap all the lies deep inside. She couldn't speak. She could only wait.

Frank took two steps from the kitchen door, looming over her. 'Gerry's missus saw you working in the shop. Said you served her. He put his fucking hand on my shoulder . . . and *do* you know what he said?'

The spray of Frank's spittle was landing on Edie's cheek as he spoke, but she couldn't move away. Her feet felt frozen to the spot. She shook her head.

'He said, "Never mind, Frank, it's not your fault if you can't keep your wife in Dolly Mixtures." And then he *laughed* . . . right in my face. Laughing at me . . . because of *you*.'

Edie's mind churned with things to say but when she spoke, the words belonged to somebody else. 'Funny thing to say . . .' She wanted to keep her voice light and failed. The words came out garbled and hesitant. She tried to smile at him but her lips wouldn't move. Her face felt as if it was made of plaster and if she moved, then everything would crack into a million pieces. A cold feeling of dread crept over her. Frank had often raged at her but this was somehow different – harder, with a meanness she didn't recognize.

'*You . . . lied . . . to . . . me.* You won't be going back there, you hear me?' Frank breathed out the words but the fury behind them turned his face to a mask of rage. Edie clenched her teeth and tried to put some distance between her and Frank, but to no avail. As she took one step backwards – he took one step forwards. On and on they danced until Edie backed up against the wall. All she could think about was offering him some explanation to make him stop, but there was nothing that she could say.

The saucepan started to spit and hiss on the stove

as the water boiled over the sides. She wanted to turn the gas down but Frank was standing between her and the stove.

'Frank . . . I can explain . . .' The words hung in the air between them as he stared her down. He backed away as if readying himself and then just as Edie was about to offer some plea in her defence, his right arm swung down and the back of his hand swiped across her cheek.

Edie watched his arm rise and the hand glide towards her, and in an instant, she crumpled to the floor. The blow shooting through her cheekbone into her jaw. Her ears ringing with the pain and shock of it. All these years she had wondered if Frank was capable of this. He'd sulked at her, raged at her and once twisted her wrist until it was bruised purple but he'd never raised his hand to hit her – until that moment.

There would be no turning back now. Edie knew she would never again be a woman who couldn't be hit. Frank's arm came towards her, his fist curling around the top of her apron as he yanked her on to her feet.

'YOU LYING BITCH! You've made me a right laughing stock.' The second blow was a fist to the side of her head, causing the room to spin and Edie swallowed down her urge to be sick. Her eyes tried to focus on him – to say something . . . anything to make him stop but Frank didn't stop. He wouldn't stop.

The Frank that knew how to stop was gone forever.

All that was left was this man pounding his fists on Edie's broken body until his rage was exhausted.

At dawn Edie came to, lying on the kitchen floor. She could taste her own blood, dried inside her open mouth and over her lips. Her face felt swollen and when she breathed in, a sharp pain seared through her chest. There was no sign of Frank and the kitchen was dark. Edie sat up, propping herself against the cupboard, and tried to inspect the damage. She couldn't breathe properly. Her head hurt but her legs could move. Her right arm hung limply by her side but the left arm was able to reach out.

Edie spat a lump of dried blood out of her mouth and watched it land on her kitchen floor. She was one of those women now. Getting gossiped about and pitied. People would look on her bruises and then look away again. They would roll their eyes and purse their lips. Blaming her . . . looking for fault. What did she expect?

There was no way out. Her life stretched before her, one day after another. Good days when she would manage to please Frank no matter what he wanted or needed, and the bad days, which would be infrequent at first . . . and then gradually, Edie knew, there would come a time when she would no longer be able to tell the good days from the bad days.

She lifted her left hand and gently touched her lips. Feeling the swelling under her fingertips and wincing when they touched a cut. Closing her eyes and remembering the girl who danced on tables and the man who came calling with a bunch of pink carnations wrapped in brown paper.

A light flicked on at the top of the landing and Edie heard Frank's footsteps thumping down the stairs. Coming closer and closer. Lights glowing fiercely in the dark – until the kitchen was bright and Edie turned her bruised and bloodied face to the door.

Frank didn't look away. He didn't shuffle his feet and mumble as if he was sorry. He glared at her as if he thought she had got exactly what she'd asked for and he had paid up in full.

17

London, October 1958

Tommie sent the agency girl packing and finished the cleaning up all by herself. She gave the rim of the sink a last wipe down with the dishcloth before rinsing it out and hanging it over the tap until morning. She untied the strings of her apron and hung it on the peg behind the kitchen door. There was something about the sadness of the whole evening that was still bothering her. Mrs Vee had barely touched her supper, picking at forkfuls and sipping at a glass of champagne. Eventually she'd gone up to her bedroom without saying a word.

Tommie picked up her coat and handbag but as her hand gripped the back-door handle, she found herself hesitating.

Oh, you are a soft touch, Tommie . . . She sighed as she draped her coat over a kitchen chair and placed her handbag on the table. *Five minutes . . . that's all. I'll just see if she wants anything, before I go.*

Tommie made a bargain with herself and then ran up the stairs to Mrs Vee's bedroom. A gentle pool of lamplight under the bedroom door suggested she was still awake and so she tapped softly.

'Do you need anything before I go, Mrs Vee?' she whispered but the old woman didn't respond. Tommie turned the door handle, opening the bedroom door, intending only to turn the lamps out if Mrs Vee had fallen asleep. The old woman was propped up on her peach satin pillows dressed in an ivory silk nightgown. She'd taken the time to roll up two fat curls either side of her face and tie them up with a pink bandana to hold them in place. Her cloudy blue eyes gazed at Tommie but she didn't say a word.

Stepping closer, Tommie noticed the box of violet creams had been upended all over the peach satin bedspread and moved quickly to the bedside. 'I'll tidy those away for you, shall I?'

The cloudy blue eyes didn't blink or move. Tommie put her hand on to the bedspread to straighten it but a cold shiver crawled up her spine. 'Mrs Vee?' she whispered but the vacant blue eyes just stared back at her. Suddenly her chest tightened, her breath wouldn't come and she found herself gasping for air.

Tommie backed away from the bed in a wild terror. Stumbling over the edge and falling into a heap on the Turkey rug as she tried to get away. She couldn't get her breath and neither could she get to her feet. Mrs Vee's bedroom seemed to fade away into another smaller, darker room and Tommie began to gasp and sob. A sense of shock flooding over her, her chest like a steel cage, trapping her lungs so they wouldn't work properly and then Tommie started to wail . . .

That night, she'd refused to go into the bomb shelter. Screamed at her mother not to make her do it. She hated the dark and spiders. Her little face red and furious with tears. Her mother finally gave in, weary from war and arguing. So they cuddled up in the cupboard under the stairs. Her mother holding on to her so tightly; Tommie falling asleep knowing that nothing bad could ever happen to her, until the bombs woke her, roaring louder than ever as they fell. Shattering explosions all around them. The house shook and Tommie heard the sounds of glass breaking. There were splintered shards of wood covering her head and at first she didn't understand what was happening. Something was wrong. The walls were on the floor and everything seemed topsy-turvy. Clouds of thick dust made her cough and splutter. Tommie wriggled free of the shards of wood and reached for her mother's arm, which had been tightly wrapped around her. Her mother's hand was still warm and Tommie kept picking it up and then watching it fall back to the floor again. There was blood in a dark crimson pool, but she couldn't work out where it was coming from.

Tommie crawled closer to her mother, trying to open her eyes with her tiny fingers. Her mother didn't move. Her mouth fell open so that she gaped at

Tommie. Her tongue lolled strangely in her mouth. Then a strange bitter smell of burning and the sound of bells clanging somewhere. Tommie couldn't hear properly – there was only ringing. So many bells . . .

She crawled over to the cupboard door and tried to push it open but it was wedged tight. The bells got louder and louder. Tommie crawled back over to where her mother lay, trying to make her wake up. Shaking her mother's hands and giving her cheeks tiny slaps until a thin trail of black blood began to ooze out of the corner of her lips.

A cold terror rising inside her, she backed away from her mother's body, pounding the cupboard door with her little fists. She couldn't catch her breath for the choking dust and the fear. Tommie felt as if her lungs were being crushed tightly and her breath wouldn't fill them up. Suddenly, there was a loud cracking sound and a man's hand appeared, clamping hold of Tommie and pulling her through the shattered wood.

She clung to him, her little body shaking with shock and fear. The man held on to her . . . tightly . . . oh so tightly until Tommie fell asleep in his arms.

Tommie stood in her usual spot on the pavement, staring up at the house with the pink curtains as if they held all the answers. It felt as if it was just yesterday rather than eighteen years ago.

The treadle of the sewing machine rattling back

and forth, her mother's back bent over it. Snapping cotton with her teeth and shifting the pink material from side to side. Neat hem stitches and then a song under her breath. The radio playing Vera Lynn and an old pink dress chopped up to make curtains for Tommie's bedroom window. It was another life.

She'd walked for hours and hours. One foot in front of the other, feeling nothing at all. Neither cold nor rain. The ambulance had come and taken Mrs Vee to the mortuary. The two men carrying her body out of the peach satin sheets and on to a stretcher where they covered her with a rough grey blanket.

Tommie stayed behind to clean up as if she were in a trance. Some awful dream that had once again left her trapped in a room with a dead woman. Except that she was no longer a child and was perfectly able to open the door and leave that room. She hadn't done so though – not for hours. Mrs Vee sat there staring through her lifeless eyes while Tommie choked for breath and sobbed until she had no tears left to cry. Then she'd calmly picked up the telephone and called for help as if this was something she did every day.

One foot – then another foot. Pavements and wide streets. Great sand-coloured buildings and then familiar narrow streets. Neon signs that flashed on and off as if she were being hypnotized. Then a front door that she couldn't stop knocking on.

He'd come down in his wine-coloured bathrobe. His hair was messy as if she'd got him out of bed.

Tommie had no idea what time it was except the neon sign on the corner had stopped blinking.

'Tommie – what the fuck are you doing?' He ran one hand through his hair, sweeping it back from his face. His eyes screwed up in a frown as he looked at Tommie with her blotchy red face shivering in front of him. She stared back at him as if she had no idea who he was or why she'd come. She just wanted someone to hold her.

'Are you all right? What's the matter?' His voice sounded soft to her ears and she gazed up at him searching for the answers. Her lips moved but no words came out.

'Tommie . . .' He stepped aside and gestured to her to come in but she didn't move.

'Come in if you want to or I'll get you a cab home.' Still she could do nothing but stare at him.

'*Well . . . ?*' he said, impatiently this time. He was shivering standing on the doorstep in nothing but his dressing gown. His feet were bare, his toes stretching up away from the cold floor. Tommie shook her head and walked away.

18

London, October 1958

After the light flooded the hallway, Edie had heard Phyllis Collier muttering to herself. Grabbing her suitcase, she had scurried back up the stairs in a panic. She couldn't take the chance on Phyllis seeing her sneaking out in the middle of the night. She'd have to wait and make sure everyone was fast asleep before she tried to leave.

As she reached the turn in the stairs, Edie hesitated, nervously smoothing over the outside of the suitcase with her fingertips and playing with the knotted string that held it all together. Edie's stomach churned and she had to sit down quickly on the stairs to put her head in her hands. Another moment and her mouth filled with the same sour metallic taste as earlier. Swiping a hand across her mouth, she ran to the lavatory, abandoning her cardboard suitcase in the passageway. Sinking to her knees, Edie vomited until the retching stopped. She lay slumped across the red linoleum of the lavatory floor, feeling as sick as could be.

She began blowing out tiny breaths to calm herself down. Her forehead was clammy and she felt light-headed and queasy. It was an altogether strange sensation and she bowed her head between her knees to see if that might help. The more she tried to avoid thinking about feeling ill, the worse she felt. Her mouth filled with saliva as her insides churned. Suddenly her stomach gave a mighty retch and she leaned over the toilet bowl and vomited over and over again until there was nothing left except the empty heaving of her belly.

Wiping her mouth with the back of her hand, Edie flopped against the lavatory wall, breathing heavily and clutching her knees to her chest. She wasn't one for vomiting even when she had a bad headache. She must have eaten something that disagreed with her. She worried that it might be food poisoning and she would be stuck here for days until she felt better. Edie couldn't bear the idea of staying for another night.

The thought of Pete telling everyone that he knew where she was and Edie being too sick to do anything about it made her eyes glassy with tears. She was filled with fear. She'd had her dream again earlier, waking up in a cold sweat, feeling as if she were choking, dangling from a thick yellow rope. Edie tried to get up off the floor, her agitation demanding that she moved. She couldn't get sick now . . . she had to get out of this house . . . out of London . . . before it was too late. Her stomach clenched, and she flopped back down to her knees and vomited another stream of yellow liquid.

When she was done, Edie spat into the toilet bowl, trying to empty her mouth of the awful metallic taste that wouldn't go away. She sucked in a deep breath and blew out smaller ones until the strange queasy feeling was gone. Gradually she was able to pull herself up, going into the bathroom to wash her hands and face in the sink. Her red-rimmed eyes and deathly pale skin reflected back at her in the mirror. Edie smoothed down her hair and splashed cold water over her cheeks until she felt better.

It was only last night she'd been stripping Tommie of her vomit-ridden clothes and now here she was doing the same thing. If she wasn't sure that Tommie's vomiting had been caused by drinking too much, she'd think it was one of those awful sickness bugs going around. She'd only eaten vegetable soup . . . no . . . there was a piece of ham left over from a sandwich yesterday. It must have gone off. Hopefully whatever she'd eaten was gone now.

A devastating thought suddenly bloomed at the back of Edie's mind. She sat down on the edge of the bath, her mouth gaping at the dawning realization. *How long had it been? It wasn't possible* . . . She began to count . . . desperate days gone by . . . but how many of them? Inside her a tidal swollen feeling, a growing tenderness that she hadn't noticed until that very moment.

Edie just had enough time to let the thought take hold before her stomach gave its little warning and she scrambled back to the lavatory for another bout of vomiting. She *couldn't* be . . . not now. Oh, not now . . . She murmured the words like a prayer, trying to banish the thought of it.

Yet as Edie clutched the toilet bowl with both hands, she knew quite certainly that she was pregnant. That changed everything. You couldn't just hop on a train to who knew where and start over with a baby. *How would she work? What could she do?* The old horror stories of unmarried mothers who ended up with the nuns came flooding back to her. Babies ripped away from their arms and handed over to anyone who wanted them. She remembered her friend Margaret knitting her little yellow booties and struggling to make the best of things.

It couldn't be . . . but when she thought back it was weeks since she'd last had her monthlies . . . at least two months. She hadn't noticed . . . Why hadn't she noticed? And still her silent prayer continued: *Oh, not now . . . not now . . . not now.*

Edie churned over the possibilities. She had nowhere else to go but she couldn't stay here either. Desperate thoughts scattered across her mind and the more thoughts that arrived, the more unsure she became about what to do next. Paralysed by her own fear and indecision, in a tangle of her own making. She felt like a spider trapped in the middle of its own web. She couldn't leave while she was being sick, but the longer she stayed the more chance there was of getting caught.

It was several minutes before Edie felt well enough to retrieve her suitcase and make her way back up the stairs to her attic room. She gnawed at her fingernails and put her suitcase down on the bed. If only the night would end. Maybe daylight would bring fresh answers – maybe she was mistaken. A horrible mistake. Yes, she'd just frightened herself. She'd eaten some bad ham and with all the stress . . . The thoughts scattered and bled into each other but Edie *knew* . . . The question was what could she do about it? She had to get out of this house before it was too late . . . but a baby changed everything. *Oh, not now . . . not now . . .*

A splatter of fat raindrops on the windowpane startled her and then a sudden burst of heavy rain made her stand on her tiptoes to look at the street below. It was pouring down. Rain hammering on to rooftops, trickling down gutters and pooling over drains. Edie groaned. She hoped it might ease off before she had to leave. Whatever happened she couldn't spend one more night under this roof. Pete could turn up again at any moment and this time he might not be alone.

She was about to turn away from the window when something caught her eye. A shadowy figure made eerie by the greenish glow of the street lamp.

There in the middle of the road, standing in the pouring rain . . . was Tommie.

*

Tommie had been standing outside number 73 Dove Street unable to bring herself to go inside. Her front-door key was wrapped tightly in the palm of her right hand. Both hands were curled into little fists, but Tommie carried on standing in the road, blankly gazing at the house. Her bedroom window was in darkness but there was a light on in Edie's attic room. Now Tommie's feet had stopped moving, she could no longer get them to go one in front of the other, so she stared up at the windows hoping to find out what she should do next.

The raindrops started to fall. Sploshing on to the road and then forming tiny puddles. The water gleaming black and oily under the street light. Then a heavy cloudburst and Tommie felt water cascading down through her hair and running off her face. Her clothes were sodden and Tommie suddenly realized that she'd left her coat behind at Mrs Vee's house. Her blouse was soaked through . . . and still she couldn't move out of the road.

The street was empty – all the houses in darkness and even the neighbour's cat had crawled under the nearest hedge, taking shelter from the rain. Only the light from Edie's room shone brightly into the night sky and Tommie couldn't take her eyes off it.

Shaking the rain from her head, she stuck out both hands to catch the drops. She was shivering quite badly now and the sight of the little brass keys in the palm of one hand reminded her of something, but Tommie couldn't remember what.

There was nobody to care what she did now. Everyone died and left her alone in the end. Tommie let the rain carry on running over the palms of her hands. Her mind unable to grasp what she should do now, other than stand quite still and wait.

The front door of number 73 suddenly flew open and Edie came running towards her, holding a coat over her head. Tommie watched her and wondered why she was there. She put her hands down and stared at Edie. Her lips were moving and there were words floating around in the air.

An arm went around her shoulder and then her feet remembered what they could do. The two women shuffled slowly back towards the house, closing the front door behind them with a silent click.

Two Weeks Earlier

That morning, Frank rolled out of bed as usual. Took his morning swill at the sink while barking orders at Edie. She carved two thick slices of white bread off the heel of the loaf and spread them thick with butter. Frank took himself off down the garden with the racing pages and his cigarettes as Edie kept one eye on the lavatory door. It was the only time she could relax when he was at home, and let the burning anger flush through her. The skin on her face felt taut and swollen from yet another late-night slap. Since he'd started on her two years ago, he'd barely stopped, and she'd learned to cover it up with pan-stick make-up as best she could, but the purple edges were there for everyone to gossip about no matter what she did. There was something about Edie that made Frank want to hurt her. She hadn't noticed it on all those long nights they courted but these days she witnessed it only too regularly.

The worst part for Edie were the times she saw the old Frank surface; worse than the pain of all the beatings were times when the man she'd loved would emerge with those charming pale blue eyes, but they were never directed at her. Sometimes it was a neighbour or a barmaid from one of his local pubs. He loved to charm barmaids and if he bumped into them in the street, he would raise his cap from his head and say, 'Well, you're a lovely sight this morning, Rene or Bet or Pats.' And they giggled and sometimes congratulated her on how charming her husband was, while Edie with skin the colour of purple grapes under her frock would have to nod and laugh along with them.

Those nights Edie lay on her back looking up into the darkness as he pushed himself inside her, a fresh bruise throbbing on her cheek and her body racked with pain. Some nights Edie wished she was poison. She lay there praying with every thrust that Frank was dying and she was the one poisoning him. Some mornings the disappointment of waking up and finding she had not actually poisoned Frank made her want to scream. At other times she dreamed of ripping open her frock and walking down the street, showing everyone the yellowing bruises, but she knew she never would. Edie felt nothing but shame that she was beaten and part of her wondered if she deserved it. She'd begun to urge him on, provoking him at times because her life now was just pain sooner or later, and she would rather know it was coming than be taken by surprise. There was nowhere to go and no one to tell. There was just a dream of the poison inside her and it didn't seem to be working . . .

*

Edie curled her hand into a small fist and thought about breaking the glass of the kitchen window; she wanted to shriek until somebody came to rescue her. The chances of anyone bothering to knock on the front door if they heard her screaming were slim. People kept themselves to themselves. Men shouting and women screeching attracted little attention in her part of the world. The regular Friday night 'few clips' to show a woman the error of her ways were laughed off in the local boozer. She wanted to run away and start again somewhere else but there wasn't anywhere to go.

Instead, she kept busy . . . wiping and scrubbing, folding and tidying . . . She bustled about the kitchen, shaking out cloths and moving the sugar bowl to the other side of the ketchup bottle on the table. None of it mattered but Edie's hands needed something to do. Every time she stopped moving, her fingers flew to her mouth where she gnawed at them. Tearing the skin violently, making herself bleed.

Suddenly, out of the corner of her eye, she saw something. A bulging brown envelope had fallen on to the floor under the kitchen table. It must have dropped out of Frank's pocket when he'd got up to go to the lavatory. Edie knelt down and picked it up, inspecting it, feeling the weight of it in the palms of her hands. It was crammed full of cash. More money than she'd ever seen before. The envelope was so full with notes that it had to be held together with a thick rubber band to stop them spilling out. Edie scrambled to her feet, keeping one eye on the lavatory door at the bottom of the garden. It was still tightly closed.

She placed the envelope carefully on the kitchen table next to Frank's breakfast plate with the stains from the yellow egg yolk and the piece of fried bread with his perfect teeth marks. Edie stood there for a moment, her fingertips stroking the sharp edges of the envelope while she stared out of the window, waiting for the lavatory door to open and her torment to begin again.

For one precious minute she was alone in the kitchen with the greasy smell of breakfast hanging in the air, and under her fingertips this bulging envelope stuffed with money. She found that her fingers wouldn't let go of it.

The radio played soft music and for a moment Edie imagined being somewhere else. Dancing like she used to do. Wearing pretty dresses again. Being a real person and not just somebody that gave things on demand to a man who was always angry at her for something.

There was nobody left in the world that was on her side. Her family were all gone now. Uncle Bert had been the last man standing but he'd died of a stroke in his armchair last year. They'd buried him on a beautiful summer's day. And who would mourn her if she died? For Edie was sure that one of these days Frank would go too far.

She wiped away a teardrop. More likely they'd find her with her head in the gas oven. Isn't that what women did when their lives grew too much for them and the misery too great? Edie stared at the kitchen floor and tried to imagine lying there on her knees, her body half in and half out of the oven. What would Frank say? Who would he turn to when he wanted to hurt somebody and there was no Edie to beat with his angry fists?

Her fingers curled around the brown envelope. Holding it . . . claiming it as her own. The lavatory door opened and Frank began to stride back up the garden path, his racing pages tucked under his arm and a cigarette dangling out of his mouth. She watched him walking towards her but Frank couldn't see her standing there yet. Another few steps and he would look at her through the kitchen window. The same glare he always gave her these days, as if she was doing something wrong. But for now, he couldn't see her. Her heart skipped a beat and then gave a mighty thud as her fingers gripped the brown envelope. Edie wondered if she had gone mad. *What was she thinking of?* She couldn't say. But still her fingers wouldn't let go of the envelope. One more step . . .

'Did you want another cup of tea? That one will have gone cold now . . .' Her voice light as a feather . . .

'Go on then.' He barely cast a glance at her as he smoothed out the pages of his newspaper.

Edie's hands shook as she poured the tea but Frank was looking down at his racing pages and didn't notice. The soft music playing on the radio was a tune he liked and he hummed along with it, his pencil outlining the names of sure winners and their odds. Edie put the teapot back on to the table and smoothed down the creases in her apron. Her fingers skirted over the bulge in one of her pockets.

I'll just say I found it, which is true, Edie thought, safe in the knowledge that no harm had been done yet. She'd found an envelope in her kitchen. Under her table. On the floor she cleaned every single day. On the parts of the lino where she'd scrubbed her own dried blood from the swirled patterns of the orange floor. She'd found something and was just about to tell Frank the news. *LOOK!* she would cry. *It's only in my apron pocket because you looked parched and I wanted you to have a nice hot cup of tea first. No harm done at all.*

Frank would look at her with that frown he got when she annoyed him, but not the face that comes before the beating. No . . . not that face, for that face is blank. It belongs to nobody and thinks nothing, except about the rage and how to get rid of it.

Her heart thudded against her chest so loudly that she was sure Frank would hear it. Edie was afraid because she didn't know why she had Frank's envelope full of money in her pocket. She couldn't think what she intended to do with it. He finished his hot cup of tea and she cleared away his plate and cup.

Silently Edie carried on wiping and tidying but she said nothing. The money was right there inside her pocket, almost next to her bruised skin . . . so close. She felt the weight of it, solid and reassuring. The very heft of it felt like freedom to her.

Frank got up from his chair, filling the space between Edie and the table. 'What are you doing with yourself today?' he asked without looking at her.

'The usual . . . thought I might get some sausages for your dinner. I could do some mash and a bit of gravy.'

'Sounds all right to me. I don't know what time I'll be back . . . leave my dinner in the oven if I'm late.'

Edie nodded meekly. 'I will . . .'

She watched him walk away without checking his pockets or giving the envelope a second thought. That would come later, Edie thought. But it occurred to her that, by then, she might be gone.

19

London, October 1958

Edie quickly shifted her little cardboard suitcase off the bed and placed it on the floor. She steered the rain-soaked girl towards the edge of the mattress so she could sit down. Tommie's hair lay in damp tendrils around her face and drops of rain fell from her clothes as she moved. Dripping rainwater all the way up the stairs and into Edie's attic room.

Pulling the eiderdown off the bed, Edie wrapped it around Tommie's shoulders and helped the girl to sit down. She began to shake with cold even though the gas fire was turned up as high as it would go. She watched the blue-yellow flames crawling up the white blocks.

'I'll make you a hot drink . . . warm you up a bit. You're soaked through.'

Edie shook the tin kettle to check for water and, finding with some relief that there was some left in there, proceeded to make hot tea. While she waited for the kettle to boil, Edie studied Tommie out of the corner of her eye. All her usual smart answers and sharp wit had disappeared. The girl stared blankly at the wall, not even sweeping back her wet hair as it trickled over her cheeks. Every trace of the make-up that Tommie usually wore was gone and her face looked wan and strained.

Edie fussed about watching the tea brew while silence enveloped them.

'Tea won't be long . . . and then we need to get you out of those wet things,' she said, sounding more in control of events concerning her late-night visitor than she felt. She slopped a teaspoon of powdered milk into the cup and stirred it briskly before handing it over. 'Here . . . drink this.'

Tiny lumps bobbed about on the surface of the tea before gradually melting away but Tommie didn't seem to notice as she gathered the cup between her palms and warmed herself. 'Thanks . . .' she whispered. Her eyes flitted from one end of the room to the other, taking in the strange combination of belongings that weren't hers. Eventually they paused on the small suitcase resting on the floor. 'Are you going somewhere?' she muttered.

'Never mind that . . . Drink your tea. You *do* need to take those wet clothes off though, before you catch your death. You should get some rest and not be worrying about me.' Edie pushed the suitcase out of Tommie's view with her foot and bustled around wiping up the sprinkles of powdered milk off the counter top next to her gas ring.

Tommie leaned back against the pillows and blew

on her steaming hot tea to cool it down while silent tears began to slip down her cheeks. 'I'm *sorry* . . . I just . . . My old lady died tonight.' She blew out a long, jagged breath. 'Mrs Vee . . . I don't know why I got so upset . . . It just reminded me . . .'

Edie nodded but Tommie seemed to want to talk now, albeit in a rambling and incoherent way.

'It was a shock, you see. We were having a dinner party but . . . anyway, that doesn't matter. Nobody came . . . and then she died . . .'

'You'd worked for her a long time, hadn't you?' Deep inside, even as she made polite conversation, Edie felt the itch of anxiety as if she was about to be found out. All she could think about was the fact she was *pregnant*. She was sure now. So sure she would swear to it on the bible. As Tommie spoke, Edie's mind wandered, unable to believe the situation she'd found herself in. How could this be? One minute she was dancing on top of a table, having such fun . . . Was it really five years ago? And now . . . What would she do? How could she take care of a baby? There was nobody to help her . . .

Tommie cut across her thoughts with her words but Edie found it hard to concentrate on them. 'Yes, a long time now. I'm sorry . . . You've been very good looking after me . . . last night and now this . . . I'm not usually like this. Honestly, I don't need *anyone* to take care of me . . .' Tommie's voice faded away and she wiped the back of her hand across her face, reminding Edie of a small child pretending to be a grown-up as she sipped at her tea.

'Shall I top that up for you?' Edie just wanted an excuse to move around, to busy herself with things to do. All the time terrible dark thoughts took hold inside her. She was trapped. Her silent prayer offered up, *Oh, not now . . . please not now. What am I going to do?*

'No, that's fine. I'll be OK now.' Tommie sounded as if she was about to leave but she didn't move. Edie didn't want to rush her out but at the same time she didn't know how to help the girl and neither was she sure that it wouldn't mean more trouble for her. After all, if Tommie knew Frank's best man there was no telling who else she knew.

Desperate thoughts flitted through her mind. She wanted to speak them out loud but she didn't dare. Words formed into conversation but Edie wasn't listening or even aware of what she was talking about. Filling silences . . . trying not to break down and sob on Tommie's shoulder. To beg the girl to help her . . .

Edie wanted a friend to confide in but not at any price. She waited until Tommie had drunk the rest of her tea and seemed more like her usual self before broaching the subject of the previous night. It seemed as if it might be a good idea to find out exactly who Tommie knew before she thought about asking her for help.

'Did you *know* that boy you brought back here last

night?' She hesitated, not wanting to go too far. Leaving herself space to back out and return to casual chatter if necessary. Edie was planning all the time, even as she spoke: she would leave at first light or sooner. When this girl stopped talking and went back down to her own room, Edie would run . . . and run. They would never catch her. Somewhere deep inside a small voice rang out, *How are you going to run, and run with a baby?* Edie swiped the thought away and tried to focus on what Tommie was saying.

'Who? Oh no . . . I was stupid and upset. He kept pouring me drinks and I kept on drinking them. You saw the rest . . .'

'So he doesn't know who you are?'

'No. Never clapped eyes on him before and probably won't ever see him again if I can help it. Wasn't my finest hour.' Tommie managed a rueful grin.

'Right . . . but he *knows* you live here?' Edie was wondering how much further she should go with this conversation.

'He's not likely to come back. There're a thousand girls like me looking for someone to pour them too many drinks.'

Tommie snuggled deeper into Edie's quilt, her hands pulling the heat from the teacup as she held it between her palms. Her shivering had subsided and she pushed her wet hair back off her face.

'You seem to know a lot of people in town.' Edie felt bolder now.

'Yeah, to say hello to, but none of them are friends exactly.'

'Well, if you're feeling better . . .' Edie gestured to the cup that Tommie was holding tightly. She hoped the girl would take the hint and leave but instead she smiled and handed it over. 'OK then . . . twisted my arm.'

Edie sighed. She hadn't been offering more tea. She'd expected the other girl to say, *Thank you. I must be going now.* But she didn't and now Edie was stuck. She picked up the kettle and then frowned. 'Oh, I'll have to go down and fill it up. Won't be a minute and I'll try not to wake Phyllis.'

Edie ran down the stairs to fill the kettle, and back up again, without putting a single light on, tripping over a piece of loose carpet and stumbling in the dark but managing to catch hold of the banister just in time to stop her tumbling over.

Back in the safety of her little room she lit the flame on the gas ring and waited. Tommie's eyes were closed tight and for one minute Edie thought that the girl had fallen asleep on her bed. She looked so peaceful lying there. Breathing softly, her chest rising and falling. That same itchy feeling of anxiety pulled at her. She tugged at a loose strand of hair and twisted it around her fingers. Maybe she should just go now while Tommie was asleep. She was safe enough and warm. The kettle started to hiss steam and Edie switched off the gas and poured the boiling water over the same stewed black tea leaves before slotting the lid of the teapot into place.

When Edie turned around, she found Tommie wide awake, sitting at the other end of the bed where she was running her fingers across the stringy knots of the cardboard suitcase and looking puzzled.

'Edie, can I ask you something?'

Edie could feel trouble approaching and her throat grew tight. Her voice seemed small as she whispered: 'What is it?'

'What are you running away from?'

Two Weeks Earlier

'*Where is it?*' Frank's face was red and furious. He had barely reached the end of the street before realizing he no longer had the envelope in his pocket and returning home in a temper.

'I don't know what you're talking about!' Edie answered him, holding his angry stare with a determined gaze, her little chin jutting forward indignantly.

'The envelope – I had an envelope full of cash and now it's gone.' Frank was standing so close now that Edie could feel his spittle hitting her cheeks and smell the sourness of his breath.

'Well, I haven't seen any envelope. I don't know what you do with your money. That's your business.' The sharp creases of the little brown envelope poked into Edie's breasts, tucked away as it was inside her brassiere, but the outline was thankfully not visible under her apron. She felt the sharp edges and imagined that freedom was within her sights . . . if Frank didn't kill her first.

Edie wiped down the cooker, scooping up tiny grease pocks and crumbs with a damp cloth. She busied herself cleaning and tidying, shaking out tea-towels and trying to look as if she was not, in any way, worried about Frank's accusations. Inside her heart thudded against the bars of her ribs. A drumbeat of alarm, but on the outside, she was just Edie wanting to get the breakfast cleared away, so she could get to the shops to pick up something for dinner as usual.

Frank stepped forward, looming over her now. 'I *have* to find that envelope . . . it's not all my money. It's from a job.'

'What *kind* of a job?' Edie was suddenly suspicious. Frank wasn't the type of man to be afraid of anyone without good reason. This wasn't gambling winnings. The fear in his eyes told her that. It was probably something to do with the Costellos.

'Never you mind what kind of a job. It's not all my money and I need it by this afternoon.' Frank's voice rose an octave, becoming more agitated by the second.

Edie turned away, stacking egg-stained plates and teacups in the sink to be washed. 'I haven't seen any envelope. I told you,' she said, while turning her face to the kitchen wall. The angry stare pierced her. Frank could surely see she was lying if he looked closely enough. The sharp edges of the envelope and the weight of the roll of notes sat between her breasts. It was all Edie could do to stop herself putting a hand to her chest to check that it was safe and secure under her blouse. She couldn't bring herself to undo what she had done. She couldn't find the words to say, *Don't you worry, Frank. Here it is, safe and sound.* Something inside her felt sharp and cold as steel.

What would happen to him if she didn't say those words? Edie discovered that she didn't altogether care. Maybe some of those men she'd seen going in and out of the pub at night with their broken noses and silvery knife scars on their cheeks would give *him* a beating for a change. Edie would be glad if they did. Let him feel the pain of stiff purple bruises and soft skin split by raging fists. She allowed the faintest smirk to play on her lips for just a few seconds. Visible only to her in the reflection outlined in the kitchen window.

Frank ran his hands through his hair and paced around the kitchen, his eyes scouring the floor and surfaces – looking for the small brown envelope.

'Maybe you dropped it in the pub?' Edie said as she clattered about wiping down forks and slamming them into the cutlery drawer.

'No . . . I had it right here – I'm sure of it.'

Edie sounded helpful but her heart was ice-cold and pulsing slowly. She breathed on to a knife and then polished it with her cloth until it shone. Outside, it was another grey morning. A sly marmalade cat helped itself to something from the bins next door.

'They'll *kill* me . . . I've got to find it,' he muttered to himself.

'You should retrace your steps – that should do it. Unless someone has picked it up.'

Frank stopped pacing around the kitchen and marched towards the front door, pausing only to grab his jacket from the metal hook. The door slammed hard behind him; the key rattled on its wool chain. Edie sank down into the nearest chair and exhaled.

20

London, October 1958

Edie sat down tentatively on the edge of the bed, feeling the weight of Tommie's clear-eyed gaze. Her damp hair was scrunched back off her face now, revealing an earnest expression combined with a dangerous curiosity.

'You can trust me, Edie. I'm not daft. I've been around long enough to know when something isn't right. I could see it the first day you moved in here. Standing there plastered in make-up with a purple bruise hiding underneath. Why are you asking me about that guy I picked up? Are you in some kind of trouble?'

Edie swallowed a gulp of air and raked her teeth over her bottom lip. She couldn't meet Tommie's eyes and the story that was buried deep inside her was reluctant to be exposed to the air. She frowned and tried to think of something to say. It was clear that Tommie wasn't going to let it go until she'd got something out of her. Her reluctance only seemed to make the other woman more curious, if anything. Edie had to tell her something . . .

She drew a sharp breath and then said, 'It's my husband, Frank . . . When he died . . . well, he liked to bet, you see? Horses . . . dogs or card games. He wasn't very good with money and he owes people . . . you know, the kind of people you don't want to owe money to?' Edie wasn't even sure which bits were true and what were lies any more. Her words were just stories falling from her lips. She'd embroidered them into her truth . . . a life that she'd lived. It *was* the truth though, wasn't it? She married Frank and then all the bad things happened . . . one after the other . . .

Tommie nodded thoughtfully. 'So, you think that fella who came back here might tell these people where you are?'

'Yes. He knew my husband. It's nothing to do with me but . . . Oh, it's so hard to explain. I just need to leave as soon as I can. I was going to go tonight but then I saw you standing there in the pouring rain and I couldn't just walk away and leave you all upset like that.'

Tommie chewed on her bottom lip while she appeared to consider the options. 'Where are you going?'

'I don't know.' Edie shrugged her shoulders as her nervous fingers picked at the seams of the sheet on her bed. She was telling stories . . . but not the one about the baby . . . That story was too real. She wanted Tommie to understand, but how could she understand when Edie couldn't possibly tell her about all the terrible things she'd done? It was all her fault now. There was no point blaming Frank, for he was dead . . .

'Do you know anyone outside London?' Tommie kept on questioning, searching for answers.

'No . . .' Her voice cracked and for a moment she felt stupid, exposed as a child with her thinking that she could just get on a train and step down in a strange city with no friends to help her.

'Do you have a plan? I mean, what are you going to do?' Tommie was all matter of fact and businesslike, as if this was an everyday occurrence.

'Not really . . . I hadn't got that far yet.'

'You need to think it all through. Make some arrangements first or you could end up jumping out of the fat and into the fire.'

Edie's face folded into misery. 'I *know* . . . I just can't stay here in case they find me.' The words were on the tip of her tongue. Tell *her* . . . tell her the truth right now. Maybe she could help . . . but the words wouldn't leave her tongue. Her voice warbled with the threat of tears and Tommie reached across and squeezed her arm.

She was quiet for a moment and then her face brightened and she turned to Edie. 'I've got it! I've got somewhere you can stay for a week or two. After that you'll need to leave . . . but for two weeks, you'll be safe. My old lady, Mrs Vee – I've got the keys to her house. There's nobody else to clean up so I'm supposed to keep an eye on the place for a week or so. I had to call her solicitor because there's not much family, you see. She didn't really have anyone left, except some distant cousins. The solicitor told me they'd pay me for two weeks . . . so you could stay there.'

'But suppose someone comes . . . ?'

'He's never met me. We only spoke on the telephone tonight. If someone comes, just tell them you're Tommie Lane. How will they know?'

Edie's eyes widened and she thought about it for a few seconds. Couldn't be worse than her current situation, that was for sure. She nodded. 'Are you sure I won't get into trouble?'

'I don't see how you could . . . you're not breaking in and it won't be for long.'

The thought of even a few days of safety would give her the breathing space that Edie craved to make her arrangements – and maybe Tommie could help her? She knew so many people. If anyone would know how to find a safe place to go, it might be Tommie. It was worth a chance. 'OK . . . I'll do it.'

'Let's wait until morning. Must be not far off dawn now.' Tommie yawned and stretched her arms open wide.

'But suppose Phyllis sees me with my suitcase?'

'I'll keep her talking while you sneak out the front. I'll meet you in the café around the corner and take you to the house.'

'All right . . .' For the first time in so long Edie felt a warm flicker of hope deep inside. She had a friend and somewhere she could go for a little while to get her thoughts straight and to plan what she was going to do next. 'You've been so kind to me,' she whispered softly.

'You've been nice to me, Edie, and I appreciate it. Especially tonight. I don't know what came over me. It was the shock, I think . . . finding her dead like that. I don't do well around dead people . . .'

Tommie shook her head and her face set into a glassy smile. Edie knew not to ask any more.

'I'll go down to my room now,' Tommie said. 'Let's try and get some kip, eh?'

Edie twisted the sheet under her fingers. 'Are you sure we couldn't just go now?'

'I need to sleep for a bit. Tell you what . . . come and call me at first light. Will that do you?'

Edie nodded. 'Yeah, that would do.'

'And bring a cup of tea down with you. I'm not a morning person by rights.' Tommie got to her feet and smiled at Edie. 'Don't worry. Get some sleep yourself. You look done in.'

Edie watched as Tommie laid the eiderdown back on top of the bed and slipped quietly out of the door. Carefully locking it behind her, Edie sank down on to her bed. Lying back, exhausted, she closed her eyes for a second and then darkness draped over her.

21

London, October 1958

Tommie was as good as her word. As soon as they heard Phyllis moving about downstairs, she ran down and cornered her in the back kitchen. Edie slipped silently down the stairs, stopping only to listen out for their voices, before descending to the hallway and eventually the front door.

'I still don't know this area all that well, you see. Where would you recommend?' Tommie's voice rang out deliberately loud and clear. Phyllis Collier's replies were softer and more muffled, but some kind of conversation was going on, keeping both women inside the back kitchen and away from Edie.

Edie hesitated with one foot on the very bottom step. She twisted around to check that the kitchen door was closed. It was slightly ajar but Tommie's back was blocking any view that Phyllis might have, and so Edie clutched her little cardboard suitcase and scampered towards the front door. It was still all locked up as nobody had come or gone this morning. She bit down on her lip and tried to twist the door latch as quietly as she could. Once that was done, with a final glance over her shoulder, Edie stepped outside into the chilly morning air.

As she pulled the front door closed there was a noise, louder than she'd hoped for, and Edie began to run down the garden path and out on to the pavement. Once there she turned left and trotted all the way down the street until she was out of sight of number 73 and could see the café sign ahead of her.

Inside, Edie ordered a cup of tea so the woman behind the counter wouldn't bother her, and took a table as far away from the window as she could manage. The tea tasted slightly stewed, as if it had been in the pot too long waiting on a customer. She wrinkled up her nose and pushed it away from her. She couldn't see people coming and going from where she was sitting until they got right past the window, so it took her by surprise when Tommie suddenly appeared in the doorway of the café, gesturing to her to come outside.

The two women walked briskly across the road to the bus stop, hopping on the first bus that came along and paying for their tickets. They sat side by side, Edie with the cardboard suitcase crushed on to her lap as there was no room to stow her case in the luggage rack, which was full with a baby's pushchair that wouldn't fold down. Tommie didn't say much but jingled a set of keys nervously in her hands as the bus rumbled through the streets, its journey only interrupted by the sound of the bell ringing, announcing the inevitable tide of passengers coming and going.

In the seat just in front of them, an exhausted mother struggled to keep hold of her child. The boy was squirming away from her grasp, stretching his grubby little hands over the back of the seat towards Edie. His cheeks were blistered red with a furious rash while his eyes screwed up in distress, and he was resisting all attempts to sit him back on his mother's lap.

Edie couldn't take her eyes off the child and his exhausted mother. The never-ending battle of wills. The boy began to cry and hit out at his mother. His tiny fists pounding at her, wriggling and full of rage now. Something was hurting him – a tooth, or a stomach ache. He gave exasperated cries and then waited in silence for a response. The woman patted at his head and murmured, 'Hush now . . .' but the child wouldn't hush. His tiny fists coming closer to Edie as she sat, unable to take her eyes off her future. Her silent prayer being offered up: *Please not now . . . not now . . .*

'. . . Of course, you must be very careful not to damage anything – although I don't suppose anyone would know. It's not as if Mrs Vee will care . . .' Tommie's voice cut through the baby's cries and then trailed off.

'I'll be careful. Thank you for doing this. I don't know what I'd do otherwise. I'll leave just as soon as I can.' Edie sounded as if she meant it but even as she spoke a wave of nausea swept over her and she swallowed hard. Her skin felt clammy and she could feel small beads of sweat on her brow. She couldn't be sick here, yet the smell of fumes from the bus exhaust was making her feel worse. The child's cries turned from pitiful mewling to anger, sharp and piercing. The noise and the fumes combining in an unbearable marriage causing Edie a hot, feverish distress. *Not now . . . not now . . .*

'Is it far from here?' she whispered.

'No, it's the next stop . . .'

Edie gulped and wiped the back of her hand across her forehead. The baby shrieked, drumming his fists on the top of the seat. Her stomach gave a mighty retch and she uttered a small cry.

'Are you OK?' Tommie turned to inspect Edie for the first time since they'd met at the café. 'You look white as a sheet. You're not coming down with something, are you?'

'Do you think we might get off and walk from here? I think I'm going to be sick.'

Tommie got to her feet and rang the bell, dragging Edie and the cardboard suitcase behind her. She eyed the clippie, whispering conspiratorially, 'She's going to throw up. Best let us off here.' The clippie nodded, ringing the bell in a sequenced code of four abrupt rings that she used to tell the driver to stop quickly, and sure enough the bus started to slow just long enough for Tommie and Edie to leap off and land safely on the pavement. The clippie dinged the bell twice more and the bus rolled away, gathering speed.

Tommie took the cardboard suitcase out of Edie's

arms and started to walk after the bus. Edie took a deep breath, swallowed hard and followed along. The wave of nausea eased off and she exhaled a gentle stream of air in relief. Her thoughts were still desperate and muddled. *What am I going to do?* There was a time she would have been happy about having a baby. Years ago, when she still believed in a future for her and Frank. She knew better now. *Oh, not now . . . not now . . . please not now . . .*

The two women walked in silence until they reached the sandy-coloured pillars of a large town house. There were stone steps running down to a basement kitchen and black metal railings all along the front of the house. A navy-blue front door with a gleaming brass knocker stood in the centre of the house, with two severely pruned potted bushes either side of the porch.

'Down this way. We'll go in through the kitchen as usual. Don't want to get the neighbours talking.'

Tommie ran down the stone steps and slotted a small black key in the lock. The thick wooden door sprang open, revealing a large, rather gloomy kitchen, but Edie was just relieved to get inside and away from the chances of anyone seeing her.

Dumping the cardboard suitcase on the table, Tommie started fussing around the kitchen. 'Come on then . . . I'll make us something to eat later. Do you want to see the house?'

Edie wasn't sure that she did, in all honesty. Part of

her would have been just as happy to curl up and sleep on the kitchen floor, as the thought of invading the rooms of a woman who wasn't yet in the ground made her feel uncomfortable. Yesterday Mrs Vee had been planning her outfit for a grand party and now . . . Tommie breezed on ahead flicking on lights where necessary and opening doors, proclaiming this room 'the drawing room' or 'the dining room' and then up several flights of stairs to the bedrooms. Hesitating at the door of one of the bedrooms, opening it a crack so that Edie caught a glimpse of a peach-coloured satin bedspread neatly folded back exposing a bare mattress.

'I stripped the bed . . . after . . . One of the guest rooms is made up though. You can sleep in there.'

Edie felt enormous relief that she wouldn't have to spend the night in the same bed that Mrs Vee had so recently died in.

The guest room was at the other end of the landing with pretty pink chintz wallpaper and thick cream curtains. The bedclothes felt soft and fresh under Edie's fingertips. Nothing smelled of damp in this house. There was a faint aroma of lavender whenever you touched the bedclothes. Next to the bed were polished bedside tables and, on top of them, lamps with fringed mustard shades. Taking up most of one corner of the room was a heavy oak wardrobe and in the opposite corner a matching dressing table that held a set of silver hairbrushes and a hand mirror.

Edie had never seen such a beautiful room. Everything was fresh and expensive, soft as could be, or built to last through generations. Tommie insisted on carrying her suitcase up the stairs for her, even though Edie pleaded to be allowed to do so. She set it down carefully on top of the thick quilted eiderdown. Small blue flowers mixed with strands of green leaves on a cream background. The cardboard suitcase looked shabby, broken down and completely out of place in this room filled with finery.

'Are you *sure* this is a good idea? I don't want to get you into trouble.' Edie hoped that Tommie wouldn't change her mind but at the same time the idea of sleeping under this fine roof all alone seemed terrifying to her.

'Nobody will know. Look, I had to drag the solicitor out of bed to tell him Mrs Vee had died. He barely said three sentences on the telephone. Couldn't wait to get rid of me, so I doubt he's going to bother himself. Come on, you make yourself comfortable. The guest bathroom is across the landing. You can use that. I'll make us something to eat. The larder is full of food and it will only go to waste.'

As Tommie turned to walk back to the doorway, Edie reached out and grabbed her arm.

'What is it?' Tommie said, spinning around to face her.

'You're a good friend. Thank you.' Edie managed a wan smile.

'It's nothing. You still feeling a bit queasy?' Tommie looked at her anxiously.

Edie nodded. 'A bit . . .'

'Why don't you have a nice bath to relax? It's probably all the stress making you feel sick. I'll get us something to eat and that will make everything seem brighter.'

Edie nodded, swallowing down another wave of nausea and wondering just how long she could go without having to tell Tommie the truth.

Phyllis Collier had wasted quite enough time that morning chatting to people. First of all, her tenant Tommie, asking all sorts of questions about the area and what shops to use, or where to get her shoes cobbled properly. On and on she'd gone until Phyllis was on the point of being rude and asking the girl to let her get on, but then suddenly Tommie had stopped talking in mid-sentence and dismissed her with a curt, 'Must be going. Thanks so much.' Leaving nothing but air where she'd been standing just a few seconds ago.

Then the milkman had knocked for his money. He'd run out of Gold Top that morning and hoped she'd been able to make do? Well, it seemed to Phyllis that making do was all she did these days but what choice did she have? It was Terry who liked Gold Top anyway so it wasn't a hardship to go without it. She should cancel it but somehow Phyllis had not been able to bring herself to cancel the things that reminded her of him.

After the milkman came, the young coalman arrived, abandoning his coal sack on the front porch . . . and in the rain . . . rather than taking it around the back to the coalhouse, as she had asked him to a million times. Phyllis was about to give him a piece of her mind but he disappeared down the garden path leaving her to cope as best she could. As she put a hand either side of the neck of the coal sack and tried to drag it through the hallway to the coalhouse, Phyllis felt a sharp pinging sensation in her lower back. It was enough to make her let go of the coal sack straight away and mutter to herself, 'Oh . . . Ow . . . Oh dear . . .'

Phyllis was stuck, unable to straighten up and unable to proceed. The coal sack and its contents lay at her feet, heavy and defiant. She leaned back against the wall of the hallway and tried to use that to inch her back upwards into a tall column. It was no good. It hurt no matter what she did. Phyllis could neither stand tall, nor could she move very well while she was bent over. And whatever route she took, there was no possible way to lift the coal sack or drag it even an inch inside the front door. 'Oh . . . blast it . . .' she cried but there was nobody to hear her.

She was firmly stuck and quite unsure what to do next. She called out meekly, giving kitten-like yelps, hoping for one of her tenants to turn up, but with no luck. She tried to straighten up one more time but a sharp arrow of pain made her cry out. From her bent-over position, she suddenly heard the welcome metal rasp of the front gate opening and a pair of familiar old work boots plodding up the path.

'What on earth have you done to yourself, Phyllis?'

Phyllis groaned. Of all the people she wished not to see her in this position, Terry Collier was top of her list. Out of the corner of her eye, if she squinted a little, she could just make out a bunch of flowers in his hands. Terry had come a-courting again. First a box of Milk Tray that had given her indigestion and now a bunch of pink chrysanthemums.

'If you must know, I've pulled something trying to lift this coal sack. I've told them a thousand times to take it around the back but they just ignore me and now look . . .' Phyllis wanted more than anything to stand up straight and look Terry Collier in the eye. Instead, she was standing there in her ancient day dress, bent over like an old witch in a fairy tale.

'Let's get you inside, shall we?' Terry set the chrysanthemums down carefully next to the stubborn coal sack and placed a firm hand gently on Phyllis's arm. She sighed long and hard before leaning on him and allowing Terry to guide her into the bedroom.

Phyllis edged her way gingerly on to the bed, eventually leaning back against a sea of plumped-up pillows that were carefully placed at crucial angles by Terry. She was all right as long as she didn't laugh or move.

'Right then. I'll make us a nice cup of tea and maybe a biscuit or two, eh?'

'This doesn't change anything between us, you know, Terry. It's a bad back. I've not gone soft in the head and there's nothing wrong with my memory neither.'

'I know that. I'm not pretending things didn't go on that shouldn't have . . . But if I walk out that door now, *who* is going to look after you? You're still my wife, Phyl.'

'You should have thought about that . . .' She didn't mean the words to sound as bitter as they did but when they hit the air between them it was too late.

'I'll make us that tea.' Terry, suitably chastised, turned away, his shoulders sagging under the weight of Phyllis's vinegary words. She lay there regretting them . . . not regretting them. Wanting to hit her target over and over again . . . wanting to lean into his warmth and feel cared for. Wanting . . .

Phyllis laid her head back on her pillows and stared up at the ceiling, tracing the lumps and bumps of uneven plaster, until Terry appeared in the doorway carrying a tea tray and a repentant smile.

'I'll put a little bit of sugar in for you. Make you sweet . . .' It was an old joke they'd shared and Phyllis felt hot tears start to sting her cheeks. Terry stirred the teaspoon of sugar into the cup and handed it to her. A Lincoln biscuit idled in the saucer.

'Come on, Phyl . . . it's not like you to get all

teary-eyed.' Terry stood there, gazing down at her, and for a moment Phyllis felt the anger – her beautiful, righteous anger – crumble into hurt. The tears glided silently down her cheeks and even as she attempted an almighty sniff to capture them all again, they continued falling like little raindrops on to her pillow.

'Hey, what's wrong, Phyl?'

Phyllis shook her head. 'Everything is wrong, Terry . . . just about everything is wrong as could be.' The tears turned to reluctant sobs. 'You know, I nearly did such a silly thing because of you . . .' Her voice was cracked and broken as the tale of the gas oven and her knitted yellow cardigan rushed out of her before she could stop it. 'That's what you drove me to . . .'

Terry sat down awkwardly on the edge of the bed, his face showing a quiet agony. He reached out a hand and patted her gently on her arm. Nodding as if he was listening, even though Phyllis was silent . . . and then he spoke. 'I'm so sorry, Phyl . . .'

She could feel the warmth of him right next to her knees. His hand on her arm. Phyllis tried to take a sip from her cup of tea, but her throat felt closed and tight. All she could do was lie there quietly sobbing, while Terry stared down at the scuff marks on his work boots.

Two Weeks Earlier

Edie had spent most of the day sitting on the low black wall outside the Red Lion public house and, as if that wasn't humiliating enough, she had the neighbour's dog Tipper tied to a bit of string and lying at her feet. From time to time the dog whined and his large pink tongue flopped out of his mouth, desperate for water. A few yards away the same neighbour's children were kicking a dead creature whose bloodied carcass lay stinking in the street and she had to tell them to stop, mostly because it was making her feel sick. The kids stopped briefly at the sound of her voice but then started again through sheer boredom.

Edie wished that she hadn't offered to keep an eye on them while Tony the Fish (as they called him) was inside the public house enjoying a pint of beer, but the fact was that she had to sit on that wall anyway, waiting for Frank, and had therefore become the general minder of children and pet animals while their owners took refuge inside.

Frank had returned from his first expedition to the Red Lion complaining that Rene the barmaid didn't come on duty for another hour and nobody else had seen his missing brown envelope. He was in a foul temper, insisting that Edie come with him on his second trip so that she could search outside while he questioned Rene inside.

Edie of course had sat down on the wall without searching for anything. There being no point, as the missing brown envelope was still very much attached to the inside of her brassiere and held firmly in place by a small but sturdy safety pin. She waited . . . and waited for Frank to return. All the time Edie thought about how to get away and where she might go if she could find the courage.

Part of Edie had begun to believe that he would find it and they were all just passing the time outside the Red Lion with an overheated dog and some rowdy children that didn't belong to her. Yet the little brown envelope remained fastened carefully to the inside of her brassiere. She could feel the weight of it close to her heart. She liked the feeling it gave her but beyond that, Edie really had no idea what might happen next.

Across the street she could see Violet Crim getting off the bus by the chemist's shop and heading back towards where she was sitting. Edie grimaced, for she had been sitting in the exact same spot when Violet Crim had got on that bus to go wherever she was going, around two hours earlier. At least the pub should be throwing out soon and they could go home.

As Violet Crim came closer to where she was

sitting, the woman raised her hand in a friendly wave although Edie wasn't stupid, she knew Violet pitied her. Didn't they all pity her? There was a time when she'd been the envy of them all. She was the best dancer by far; at nights Edie would shimmer and shine as she twirled and bounced, arms flailing and legs stomping to the latest craze. She would end the evenings shining with sweat and aware of men's eyes all over her. That was before her life with Frank, she thought bitterly.

Just as Edie thought about him, Frank appeared in the doorway of the Red Lion. He walked in a straight line towards her with a smile for the neighbourhood children but he couldn't fool Edie. He was half plastered already and his eyes were glittering hard and cold.

Edie stood up and greeted him with a tight smile. 'Did you find it?' she asked softly.

'No.' Frank spat out the word, striding across the road and leaving her scurrying behind him, the poor dog abandoned to the care of the neighbour's kids. She sighed to herself and put a hand to the inside of her blouse to check for the package. All she had to do was call out, *Frank . . . look what I've found. You must have dropped it right here. Lucky you that I found it first.* And he would take her in his arms and hold her tight like he used to . . .

Edie's thoughts were interrupted by Frank snarling over his shoulder for her to hurry up. She increased her pace, keen not to annoy him any further. She'd wait until he was asleep and then Edie was going to leave him for good. She had no idea where she might go or how she might do it. But she wasn't going to be punched and kicked or spat on or shaken or slapped any more.

She hadn't counted the money inside the envelope but Edie knew it was the kind of amount that might put you on a train or a boat. You could wake up in a different city or start a new life. Edie's dreams of a new life were complicated for when she really thought about it, she couldn't have told you what her first steps might be on the road to this future. She only knew that she wanted one.

22

London, October 1958

Edie undid the small pearl buttons of her blouse and dropped it on to the shiny black-tiled floor. Next, she unhooked her brassiere and let it fall. Her wool skirt she hung on a silver hook on the back of the bathroom door, and the stockings she balled up and placed near the large basin ready for her to rinse out. Lastly, she wriggled her knickers down her legs and stepped out of them, running her hands across her belly.

Growing inside her was a baby that at one point in her life she might have welcomed. A child to make them happy and bind them together. It was too late for that. Edie knew better. She couldn't think about it now.

The bathroom was so clean, everything in its place with crystal bottles filled with coloured oils – all to make bathing more pleasurable. Edie emptied almost a quarter of a bottle of amber liquid into the water, and the air was filled with a delicious aroma. Steam from the large enamel bath rose into the scented air. She could smell orange blossom and spices. An expensive cocktail to bathe in.

Sitting down on the edge of a hard chair, the back of which was covered in elaborate gilded curls and flowers, Edie pondered her situation while the taps ran.

Soon, the bath was almost overflowing with its pale amber water and Edie sank down into it, trying to let the steam melt her worries away. There must be a way out and she would think of it. She lay there until her skin began to prune and the water grew tepid, but still Edie couldn't find a solution to her problems. She had to get away – but if she managed that how would she cope? The rest of her life stretched before her – struggling to raise a child alone. A child she didn't even want to have – that much was true. Edie didn't want this baby. She knew it deep in her heart.

The thought of a child with those same glittering angry blue eyes staring at her. A son who would grow broad and tall like his father. Edie couldn't do it. She could barely take care of herself. It occurred to her that in many ways she'd been a child when she married Frank. Certainly, she hadn't understood the bargain she was making, signing up to obey someone who wanted to hurt her as much as he wanted to breathe clean air.

She got to her feet, spilling drops of water over the side of the bath, and reached for a plush pale peach towel to wrap herself in. There was no way out of this life for her. She'd chosen a man who smiled and kissed her as if she was the only thing that mattered on this earth. Now she had no choice about her future. Where did women in her position end up? Nowhere good.

Edie's mind churned and churned but there was no answer to her problems. The money she had would run out. And then what?

Maybe Tommie could help her . . . but she couldn't tell her the whole truth. She might call the police. Maybe she could tell her some more soft white lies about Frank and having to get away. She could just disappear and make a new life . . . but then she came back to the baby . . . Edie felt trapped in a maze of her own making. There was no way out.

A light tapping on the bathroom door and the sound of Tommie calling out that lunch was ready startled her. 'I'll be right down!' Edie answered, her voice forced and cheerful.

She stepped out of the bath and leaned over to pull out the plug. The water gurgled away and Edie dried herself. Glancing at the mirror, she saw her anxious face, pink with heat, staring back.

Tommie untied her apron, throwing it on to the back of a chair, and cleared some of the debris from her lunch preparations out of the way. She couldn't bring herself to go upstairs to lay the table in the dining room; the kitchen table would do fine for the two of them.

She'd taken a leftover fish pie that she'd made the day before for Mrs Vee's lunch and reheated it with some green beans. They could have some cold apple tart for pudding. The kitchen was warm from the oven heat and strangely cosy in the gloomy autumn daylight. Tommie had a thought and scampered off to the dining room, where Mrs Vee kept her favourite bottles of wine in a special Chinese lacquered cabinet by the window. Tommie helped herself to one of the bottles that had been laid carefully on its side before hurrying back down to the kitchen to wait for Edie.

Moments later, the other girl appeared. Her hair was slightly damp at the ends and her skin flushed from the heat of the water and dressing too quickly.

'Here, drink some of this . . .' Tommie poured a large measure of red wine into one of Mrs Vee's crystal goblets and handed it to Edie. She watched as the girl took a tiny sip. One sip led to another and then one more – the wine flowed through her, and a long sigh escaped her lips as Edie pulled out a chair to sit down.

'Fish pie all right for you?' Tommie heaped a spoonful of buttery mash with lumps of white fish hidden in the creamy sauce on to a china plate and offered the dish of wilting green beans across the table. Edie sat opposite and picked up a mouthful with her fork.

'Mmn – it tastes good. I didn't realize how hungry I was.'

Tommie watched as she gobbled it down, only

pausing to drink more of the red wine. Once the pie was dispensed with, Edie refused the apple tart and Tommie lit up a cigarette.

'Can I have one of those?' Edie asked timidly.

'Sure . . .' Tommie pushed the packet of Woodbines across the table and sparked a match to light it.

Edie took a deep lungful and blew out the smoke. 'Thanks for doing this. It's all a bit of a mess . . .'

Tommie drained her wine glass and leaned her elbows on the table. 'It's all right. I want to help you . . . but at some point, you *are* going to have to trust me, Edie.'

'I *do* trust you . . .' Her voice quivering, giving away the lie.

'It's OK that you don't but the way I look at things, you need help to get out of London, and quickly. I need to understand what the truth is, so I can help you. I don't think you've told me everything that's going on with you. It's fine – I mean, we hardly know each other and now look at us . . . me hiding you out in Mrs Vee's house. Sat here drinking her best wine . . .' Tommie's voice faded away as she imagined the old woman as she used to be – upstairs with her violet creams and never-ending demands.

'It's complicated. I just need to get out of London. Get away somewhere nobody knows me. There are things . . . I don't know how to say . . .'

Tommie refilled their wine glasses but Edie pushed hers away, her face suggesting that she was already regretting the strange combination of red wine, fish pie and Woodbines after a day of worry.

'Frank . . . my husband . . . he used to beat me . . .' The words tumbled out of her mouth, as though once out they could not be put back in again. Tommie leaned back in her chair and stared at her across the table. She exhaled softly but her eyes never left Edie's face. The girl stared back at her, unflinching and questioning.

'What happened to him?' Tommie didn't lower her gaze but her tone softened slightly.

Edie took a deep gulp of air. 'Heart attack . . . Just dropped dead one day.'

'But he used to hurt you?' Tommie nodded as if that somehow explained Edie.

'It wasn't always like that . . . not in the beginning. In the beginning he was lovely. So handsome . . . All the girls used to say he was like a film star. Blue eyes and dark hair: he could have been a movie star . . . but of course he wasn't. He was just ordinary, like me. I thought you found a handsome prince and lived happily ever after like in the fairy stories . . . but it wasn't like that. He changed . . . got harder . . . colder. Frank had always been a gambler and he started losing big time. He did owe money – that much is true. You owe that money and you have to do things to pay it off, I guess.'

Tommie shifted her gaze a little, waiting patiently for Edie's explanation. Weighing and examining each word for particles of truth.

'One day . . . he came home with an envelope filled

with cash. I don't know where he got it from. It was a lot of money. More money than we'd ever seen. Two hundred and fifty pounds. Can you imagine?'

Tommie nodded, remembering the fifty-pound note she'd seen on Edie's floor that first night.

'I just wanted him to stop hurting me. He wouldn't stop, you see . . . he kept on hitting me all the time. If the weather was bad – or he couldn't light the fire – or the horses lost – or he was in a bad mood . . . It didn't matter what I did because we always ended up the same way. I never thought I'd be one of *those* women . . .'

'*One of those women?*' Tommie frowned, puzzled now.

'You know – a "battered wife". You've heard them talk. You must have . . . Laughing in the pub about giving the missus a "Friday night special" – a good slap to keep her in line . . . That was *my* life except it was every single day. Sometimes really bad – a proper beating with his belt – and other times just a swipe across the cheek. I'd forgotten what it was like to go through a day without him hurting me . . . So, I'm not sorry that he's dead . . . but I took that money anyway.'

Tommie crushed out her cigarette and looked away. The girl was painting a picture of her past but there was something bothering Tommie. Something not quite right.

Edie seemed to be waiting for her to say something. 'Don't you believe me?'

'Yes . . . if that's your story . . .' Tommie said softly but part of her was unsure.

'I'm telling you the truth, Tommie.' Edie stared across the table, her voice deadly serious.

Tommie searched the other girl's face and, finding what she took for truth, nodded. Reaching across the table, she took hold of Edie's hand. Squeezing it gently, she said, 'Tell me all of it.'

'I took his money and I hid it. He was out of his mind with worry but I didn't care. I thought he deserved what was coming to him. But then . . . he just dropped down dead right in front of me . . .' Edie's voice faded away into silence.

'And you've still got the money?'

Edie nodded. 'It wasn't his money though. The Costellos will come looking for me. They might work out that I was the one who took their money. And it's the *truth*. I've got to get out of here before they find me.' Her eyes desperately pleaded with Tommie to understand.

'Is that everything?'

'Yes, that's what happened. I swear . . . Cross my heart.' Edie swiped her fingers across her chest as Tommie studied her. Was she telling the truth? Tommie frowned and sucked her teeth, trying to decide.

'OK. I'll help you. The Costellos don't know that you've done anything. They can't prove a thing. Probably best to move on though – as soon as you can.

You need to decide where to go . . . and then I'll go to the railway station to buy you a ticket. When it gets dark you can make your way to the train and off you go. Nobody will ever find you.'

'You make it sound so easy . . .' Edie's voice cracked and tears filled her eyes.

'It's not that complicated – if we act fast. You could choose a place and make a hotel booking for a couple of nights. Use the telephone here to do it. Just so you've somewhere to stay . . . then you can plan from there. Get a job and a place to live. They'll never find you. There's . . .'

Edie's face crumpled and she began to sob uncontrollably – first quietly and then as if her heart was breaking into a million pieces.

Tommie stared across the table helplessly. 'What's wrong? You'll find somewhere to go . . . Oh, don't cry . . .'

Edie shook her head. 'I'm having a baby, Tommie . . .' The words sliced through the air, stunning both women into silence as Edie sat there with tears dripping off her cheeks.

'You're sure?'

Edie gulped back the tears. 'Yes, I've missed my monthlies. I've been queasy and sick every day since I moved into Dove Street. I feel different . . . This skirt is getting tight on me now. It used to hang off me. There's no mistake.'

Tommie exhaled a soft whistle of breath she hadn't even realized she'd been holding. 'Well, that changes things around . . .'

Edie's face screwed up into misery and she started to cry again. Desperate, soft, pitiful cries. 'I don't know what I'm going to do . . . I *can't* go back . . . I just can't do it. I've got to get out of here.'

'How will you manage with a baby?'

'I don't know . . . but I have to get away. You don't know what it's like to be trapped like that. No money and a husband that won't stop hurting you . . . This is my one chance to start again. If you won't help me then I've got nobody who will.' She buried her face in her hands as her chest heaved and her entire body was racked with sobs.

'You could go to one of those homes for mothers and babies?' Tommie offered hesitantly.

Edie sat up, shaking her head fiercely. 'NO . . . I don't want to go through all that and then have some nuns take it away. You don't know what happens to those kids. What kind of a life do they have? I *want* to be free but I don't want any child of mine to end up like I did.'

'Well, it's either that or you keep the baby and try to find a place to live or work where they don't mind.'

'Nobody decent is going to take in a pregnant woman without a husband. We both know the only kind of work I'm likely to find.' Edie sounded angry now at the bleakness of her choices and her frustration with them. 'I've messed everything up, haven't I?'

Tommie churned over solutions, trying to find an answer for Edie but there wasn't one. The possibilities stacked up as one dead end after another. 'You'll work something out once you get out of London,' she said hopefully.

The girl stared at her eagerly as if Tommie might provide the answer to all her problems.

For a second Edie seemed as if she had almost believed Tommie's sweet lies . . . that she could just run away and start over as if nothing had happened. Suddenly her face folded in despair and Edie's soft cries turned into desperate, racking sobs that split the air.

'I don't *know* what to do – I don't want it. I don't want to have Frank's baby . . . I don't want to have anybody's baby. I want to be free . . . I want my own life again. Is that wrong? I've got a chance now that he's dead . . . I could be happy someday. I might even meet somebody who cares for me . . .'

There was nothing that Tommie could say that would make Edie feel better. 'I don't know what to tell you. I'm so sorry . . .' The other woman was clearly in despair but there was something bothering Tommie: she could feel Edie was holding back – yet her cries were real enough.

'There must be *something* I can do . . . anything . . .'

The unasked question hung between them for a few moments until Tommie got to her feet. She started to clear away the dishes and then stopped what she was doing, turning to face Edie. Whispering softly under her breath, 'I know a woman who can help you . . . if that's what you want.'

Edie blinked and looked up at Tommie. Their eyes checking that they both understood the situation. 'Is it safe – only I've heard some awful stories . . .'

'I don't know – yes, probably. I'm not trying to force you into anything you don't want to do. Just saying that I know a woman . . .'

Edie considered the situation for a moment and then swallowed before saying, 'This woman. What's she like?'

'I've heard girls say she's all right . . . It's not nice but it's over quickly. It's your choice. If you like I can go there tomorrow and see about fixing you an appointment this week and then once it's over and you feel better, we can go back to our plan for getting you on a train somewhere . . . Is that what you want?'

Edie wiped her face with the palms of her hands and sniffed loudly. She stared down at her hands for a moment and then she took a deep breath, looked straight up at Tommie and nodded her head.

Two Weeks Earlier

Frank appeared in the doorway, scowling furiously, as Edie searched the pantry for the last of a minced beef pie that she'd made but there wasn't any left. There were two small lamb chops and they would have to do. One was supposed to be for her own meal but she would give it up to please him . . . again.

'I'm doing you a couple of chops and fried potatoes. That's all there is. I can't go shopping with fresh air in my pockets . . .' Edie heard herself talking but couldn't for the life of her understand why she was saying these things. It would only make him angry. He'd been ever quicker to fly off the handle since he'd failed to find his envelope of cash. She was bending over the pantry shelf, reaching for the plate with the chops, when she felt his hand on her hair. Pulling at it . . . at her.

'You're hurting me! LET ME GO!' she cried.

'You can't talk to me that way, Edie. D'you hear me?'

'Let go . . . I'm s-sorry . . . OK, I'm sorry . . .' She put her hands up to cover her face and he released her. Edie watched him turn away, putting her fingers to her head, feeling tentatively for any damage. A small tuft of hair came away in her hands and she could feel that the small brown envelope had shifted slightly. She smoothed down her hair before securing it. She would *never* give the money back . . . He deserved all he got.

As Edie reached for the chops, gently unwrapping the greaseproof paper, she could see him out of the corner of her eye, sitting at the kitchen table waiting for her to feed him. A wild fury rose up from somewhere deep inside as her eyes grazed across a small tin on the pantry floor that Edie had forgotten about. For a moment she considered the contents. Her mind seemed to have made a decision without the rest of her paying much attention to it. Her future opening up in front of her.

She sniffed, then turned away, picking up the lamb chops and walking quickly back to the kitchen. Throwing the chops into a pan of sizzling lard, watching them browning while she added some leftover boiled potatoes to go with them.

Frank sat at his usual place, angry and brooding over his misfortune while Edie piled fried potatoes and chops on to a dinner plate. The back of her head aching where he'd pulled at her hair. Her fury turning white-hot as she carried the plate over to the table, feeding him . . . waiting on him . . .

'There you go. Eat it while it's hot.' Her voice quivered as she spoke and she coughed to disguise it, before turning away. He grunted at her, his face screwed up into worry about the money and what he might do. Moving away from him, Edie leaned against the gas cooker, watching him shovelling fried potatoes into his mouth. Her white-hot fury solidifying, her blood turning to ice-water as she watched him chewing . . . the brown envelope pressing against her heart.

23

London, October 1958

Tommie opened the door to a shop in the West End, and a sharp 'ting' of a bell echoed slightly throughout the room. It was a poky little costume shop smelling of the oil heater that was wedged in a doorway leading to the back office. Behind a thick, dark red velvet curtain lay a small winding staircase leading up to a set of rooms that Tommie had never visited, yet had heard all about from various girlfriends over the years.

As soon as the door opened and Tommie stepped inside, she realized there was an official-looking man standing at the counter, talking to the owner, Mrs Broad. The man was tall and thin with a sour expression on his face. In his hands, he held a black leather notebook with the pages flipped over, and he was writing quite carefully with a half-chewed stump of a pencil. Tommie hesitated in the doorway, unsure of whether to go on in, or to step back out into the safety of the street.

The shop was stuffed with racks of costumes in all colours, bright glittering chiffons and leotards for showgirls and theatrical companies. Gold and peach satin, black silk tops with silver spangles, pink ballerina outfits. Exotic bejewelled headdresses and ribboned skirts.

Behind the counter where Mrs Broad was speaking in hushed tones to the man were large wheels of ribbon of varying widths in a rainbow of colours. As soon as Tommie closed the shop door behind her, she could see the neat dark hair of Mrs Broad's daughter, Marjorie, tidying away boxes of pink ballet shoes in the far corner.

'Margie, serve the lady while I deal with this *police* detective . . .' Mrs Broad said softly while her face remained impassive. Tommie, although startled, tried to keep calm – after all it was a costume shop and she could be there for anything.

Margie got to her feet and gestured to Tommie to come in. 'How can I help you?' the girl said as they huddled in the corner. When Tommie glanced nervously at the police detective, Margie didn't miss a beat, 'So have you come back for those ribbons?' she asked breezily.

Tommie hesitated and the girl nodded once – quite firmly.

'Yes, that's right. Decided to take them after all.' Tommie tried to follow the girl's lead.

'Remind me again, was it one to two yards you wanted, or more than two?' The girl held Tommie's blank stare, willing her to understand the clumsy code.

Tommie pretended to inspect a small pink ballet

shoe on the shelf and said casually, 'I'm really not sure but let's say more than two to be on the safe side. It's for my friend. She's made a right mess of her dress and now she needs ribbons . . . or the dress will be ruined.'

'Not to worry, we can soon sort that out. Nice bit of ribbon is a quick fix.' Margie shot an anxious look at the back of the police detective just as he flipped the pages of his notebook over, putting it and the pencil back inside his coat pocket.

'Well, like I say, we don't have any leads as yet but you could try offering a small reward. It's unlikely we will retrieve your takings – how much was it again?'

'Two hundred and fifty pounds all together.' Mrs Broad frowned at him and started to walk towards the shop door.

'It's a lot of money to keep on the premises. You should take it to the bank in future.' The police detective followed her to the door. 'You must sell a lot of costumes for that money.' He laughed, suddenly pleased with himself.

'It was for my stock. We buy in once a year.' Mrs Broad glared. 'Don't suppose you will ever catch them?'

'Never say never, Mrs Broad, but with no fingerprints . . . unless we get a tip-off it is quite unlikely. I'll keep you informed but it's over two weeks now and so far we have nothing to go on.'

Mrs Broad ushered the policeman out of the door and stood there with her arms folded as if to bar him entry to her shop again. Tommie pricked up her ears at the amount of money. It was surely a coincidence that Edie had taken the same sum from her husband, or so she said. Her stories still bothered Tommie. There was something that didn't quite add up. But she pushed the puzzle to the back of her mind for the moment. There were more important things to think about.

'Your friend will be paying in cash. Two guineas . . . for the *ribbons*,' Margie interrupted and Tommie nodded.

'She can collect her ribbon on Wednesday, but she has to get here before twelve as it's our half-day. Make sure she's not late. We wouldn't want her to miss out. She has to follow the instructions . . . Got it?'

Tommie listened carefully as Margie explained what Edie would need to do and committed it to memory.

The policeman wandered off up the street and Mrs Broad shut the shop door, flipping the sign to 'Closed' and letting out an exasperated sigh.

'Can't trust anybody these days,' she said. 'Lock up, Margie, when you've finished serving.'

'Yes, be right there. This lady has ordered some ribbons for her friend. I've told her to come and pick them up on Wednesday.'

Mrs Broad eyed Tommie knowingly. 'Tell your friend not to be late. I won't open the door to anyone banging on it. We close at twelve o'clock sharp.'

'I'll tell her,' Tommie said. With that she walked

back to the front door with Margie trailing in her wake. The bell made the same sharp 'ting' as she opened the door and as soon as Tommie took a step outside, the door was quickly shut behind her, the blind hastily lowered and she could hear the sound of a key being turned in the lock.

Shoving her hands in her coat pockets to stop them getting cold, Tommie crossed the street. A neon sign suddenly flashed on, advertising 'EXOTIC DANCERS'. The neon light glowed bright orange in the twilight. Tommie hesitated, wondering where to go next. She watched the orange neon sign flash on and off as the little costume shop was plunged into darkness, except above the windows where the word 'SPANGLELAND' glittered silver under the lights.

24

London, October 1958

'Here you are, Phyllis.' Terry Collier was fussing around her like a wasp buzzing around a jam jar. Cup of tea and then a glass of water . . . a library book . . . her reading glasses . . . a cloth to wipe her reading glasses. Phyllis was tucked up on the rather lopsided sofa in the parlour. Terry had lit the fire and was doing his best to appear the attentive husband.

He had not moved back in – Phyllis was very clear on that point. He was merely going to stay for a few days to help her out until her back got better. She was able to take painful steps in an emergency, but mostly Phyllis needed to lie down on the sofa and allow Terry to wait on her hand and foot. Issuing a list of demands to keep him busy. A general busyness replacing the need to talk about what had happened.

'Thank you.' Phyllis took the cloth and rubbed at the smudges on her glasses made by her fingers, which clouded the words on the page. There was a lot she needed to say to Terry but there was no way to begin – and what would her tenants think if she just let him come back after all his carryings on?

Terry, for his part, moved around the room, seemingly afraid of the silence that might smother them if he stopped for a moment. When he came to the mantelpiece he leaned down, taking hold of the iron poker and stoking the coals until the yellow flames began to climb.

'Got a good fire going in this grate, I'll say that.' He carried on playing with the coals until his eyes came to rest on the wooden picture frames lying face down on top of the mantelpiece. He put the poker back in its resting place and sighed. Phyllis watched him, her reading glasses in her hand and a library book spread open on her lap. A tartan blanket was draped across her legs to keep her feet warm. She could hear him breathing and then his fingers reached towards the wooden picture frames, picking one up.

Phyllis took a sharp gasp of breath as if she felt a sudden pain. Terry turned the frame over and stared at it for the longest time. She looked away, unable to bear it. She couldn't look at that photograph – not now.

A small boy of about five or six years old smiled fiercely out of the frame, his tiny smile pocked with little gaps and his eyes shining with merriment. Terry sniffed loudly and carefully placed the photograph back on the mantelpiece, only this time it was standing proudly, so the little boy's face smiled out at anyone coming into the room. Phyllis pulled at her fingers and then her hands clutched at each other for support. Her eyes grew glassy and her lips moved without parting.

The second photograph Terry picked up was the same boy but now he was a young man. The same bright smile, standing tall in a khaki uniform that was badly fitted. Phyllis remembered the day he'd had it taken. She'd insisted one sunny morning before he'd left. It was the very last time she'd seen him. There had been brief letters as if they'd sent him away to a boarding school.

Dear Mum and Dad,

I'm well. Training was hard but now we should finally see some action. Food is terrible. Miss your cooking, but will hopefully see you before too long.

Your loving son,
David

David was shot down as they ran on to the beaches at Normandy. Killed outright, they told her. Wouldn't have suffered or known a thing about it. It was a clean shot. They had a church service for him on a warm summer's day with the sky as blue as could be. Phyllis could still feel the sun beating down on the back of her neck as she stood there with her flowers, but there was no grave to place them on. In the end she'd left them on a stranger's grave and hoped that some other mother was doing the same for her boy.

Phyllis couldn't even see him as that young man in his khaki uniform and brass buttons. She dreamed of him as the gap-toothed child with his eyes shining and all Phyllis wanted to do was crawl under the cold earth to be with him. To hold him one more time.

A stifling silence fell over the room as both Terry and Phyllis refused to part with the words inside their heads. The flames crackled in the fireplace and a lump of burning coal fell on to the hearth. Terry swiped the poker at it, trying to push it away from the edge so it couldn't burn anything.

Phyllis frowned. There were some things that went beyond words. It was fourteen years now. She'd just turned thirty-nine then and felt full of life. David had just had his nineteenth birthday. Overnight Phyllis and Terry had become unable to speak about him. Their days filled with talk of 'What's for dinner?' and 'Where's my clean shirt?'

A smothering silence hung between them and then Terry whispered, 'I miss him dreadfully, Phyl . . .' His voice cracking a little. 'He'd be in his thirties now – maybe we'd have grandkids . . .'

'STOP IT!' Phyllis shouted and tried to move, but a shooting pain in the base of her spine made her wince and sink back down into the cushions.

'We never talk about him. We *should* talk about him. He deserves to be remembered.'

Phyllis struggled to sit up, furious with Terry for talking about her son that way. 'Do you think I don't remember him? Is that what you think? Do you think a minute of a day goes by when I don't wonder what he would be doing with his life now? I carried him inside me . . .' Phyllis lay back on the cushions exhausted from her outburst. She didn't want to cry but the tears came anyway.

Terry was silent for a moment, his face collapsing into misery. Kneeling on the floor beside her, he took hold of her hand. 'I didn't mean to upset you, Phyl. It's just there between us all the time. We used to be different . . . don't you remember that?'

Phyllis did remember. The days of laughing as they'd painted this room side by side. She'd ended up with tiny speckles of paint on her face and Terry had wiped them off one by one, as tenderly as if she were a child. They would run down the street arm in arm to catch last orders at the pub, or squeeze into the back row of the cinema delighting in the nearness of the other, Phyllis leaning her head on Terry's shoulder. She couldn't imagine ever feeling that way about the man kneeling in front of her, yet they had been so happy for such a long time. Always laughing together.

Then one day she'd been fixing her blackout blinds. They were so bored with war and it was nearly over . . . everyone said that. The invasion had begun and that would mean the end. Quick march all the way to Berlin and then peace. She was standing on a chair at the window when she saw the postman coming through the front gate. It was a beautiful summer's day and

Phyllis had waved. The postman pretended he hadn't seen her. He looked away and just like that she knew. Phyllis looked again and realized he was carrying a yellow telegram and her heart broke.

After David was killed, she couldn't go out. Phyllis had tried but one day she was in the post office queue and a well-meaning old lady had greeted her, 'Phyllis! I haven't seen you for a while. How's that handsome boy of yours?' She had run away, shoving past people and fighting to get back outside into the fresh air. She couldn't explain. Phyllis couldn't bring herself to say the words. *He's dead. My son is dead. They didn't even send his body home in a box covered in a flag. They let strangers bury him in the cold damp earth and then expected me to carry on living. I can't do it.* That was the truth.

For three months Phyllis had taken to her bed and stared at the walls. She'd refused all but mouthfuls of food and wouldn't be comforted no matter what Terry tried. He'd read her stories and fixed up her radio so she could listen to her favourite programmes but it was no good.

Terry went off to work every day and came home at night to cook and clean. When he was in the house, he rarely left her alone. She hardly raised her head from the pillow to notice him at all.

Then one day Phyllis had finally looked up and noticed that he had a button missing on his shirt. The shirt hadn't been ironed properly. It was a small thing but it suddenly bothered Phyllis that her husband was going out and about in that state. She looked around and saw there was a filmy layer of dust over the bedside tables and the whole house held an air of misery and despair.

The next morning, she got out of her bed. She put on her old day dress with her apron and she dusted and polished. She swept and mopped. She ironed shirts and cooked food.

Phyllis rattled around the house wiping and cleaning until she could no longer think. Terry at first was relieved to see her washed and dressed, taking care of things with her old energy, but his relief was short-lived. His lovely, laughing Phyllis was gone forever.

Terry laced his fingers through hers. Toying with them and struggling to find the right words. If he said the wrong thing she would clam up and they would never speak of this again. Gnawing at his bottom lip, he thought carefully and then said, 'We let it go on too long, Phyl . . . this state of things. We were a team you and me . . . and then it was like I was living alone.'

It was the wrong thing to say and Phyllis's mouth tightened in anger. She snatched her fingers away from his. 'There was always a clean shirt and a cooked meal on the table. I kept this house going . . . You never *wanted* for anything, Terry.' She sat up, indignant now, her back pain subdued by her anger.

'I wanted for *YOU*, Phyl . . .' His voice was thick with emotion. Terry's eyes turned watery and he looked away, appearing embarrassed by it. The stifling silence returned as he sat back on his heels and stared at the dying piece of coal on the hearth.

Phyllis didn't know what to say. All this time she had blamed him for everything. It was easier to be angry with Terry for all those years than feel the weight of her own grief. It was Terry who had encouraged David to join up. He could have got him a job on the railways where he would be safe, but part of Terry felt he'd missed out on two wars now. As if it was some kind of a Boy's Own adventure – a game they could all recover from. David would come home a hero and Terry could bask in pride at his son's exploits in a war he didn't attend in person. No matter what Phyllis had done, the man on his knees by the side of her had turned away too. He'd hurt her with his carrying on.

'But *that girl* . . .' The tears streamed down her cheeks, dripping off her face as she tried to wipe them away with the backs of her hands. Her cheeks flushed pink. Phyllis couldn't stand the thought of it. The pain and unbearable grief of losing her child, the aching torment as she watched Terry slipping away from her and then the final betrayal . . . finding him undressed with a naked girl in her own home. 'You *humiliated* me in my own home. Made me feel like I was nothing to you.'

'I *know* I did. I don't even know why . . . She didn't mean anything to me. She was just friendly at first . . . but I was so lonely. It's been fourteen years since

David died and in all that time you've never said more to me than "Pass the salt" or "Do you want more tea?" You left me, Phyl, and I couldn't get you back no matter what I did.'

'You didn't try. What did you ever say except "Where's this?" or "Where's that?" You treated me like I was your housekeeper.'

'You *behaved* like you were my housekeeper. When did you last behave like you were my wife? He was *my* son too, Phyl . . . I loved him and I miss him . . . I grieved for him every bit as much as you did, but I had to get up every morning and go to work. I couldn't just lie down in bed next to you or what would have become of us?' His voice rose – a burst of anger and his face wet with tears. The sight of it made Phyllis's chest ache but her pride wouldn't let her give in. The sight of him standing there with that naked girl giggling on the mattress would never leave her.

Phyllis sat, blinking away more tears, her lips clamped together. She felt a flame of anger but deep down inside she knew that Terry wasn't entirely wrong. Maybe she had cut him off. In the beginning she couldn't bear to see his grief because it mirrored her own, so she'd turned her face to the wall. Later she'd found that she couldn't turn back to him because there was too much she didn't want to talk about.

She'd placed the photographs face down on the mantelpiece and neither of them had picked them up when the other person was in the room . . . until this day. Phyllis used to dust them quickly, without looking at David's sweet face, and Terry . . . when did he look at them? She wondered whether there had been moments of grief that she'd missed and then, because she hadn't witnessed them, had mistaken that for a lack of feeling on Terry's part. Watching his face now, with tears falling, Phyllis could see that he missed David as much as she did. He missed his son . . . and the way they used to be a family. She dabbed at her eyes with the corner of the tartan blanket and then sniffed loudly several times.

Phyllis turned to face Terry and stretched out a hand to wipe a stray tear from his eyes. 'And what now?' she said quietly under her breath. Her words hanging there between them. Terry caught hold of her hand and kissed it softly.

'We can begin again, Phyllis . . . if that's what you want.' He clasped her hand between the palms of his hands as if he was at prayer. This time Phyllis didn't pull away.

'Is that what *you* want? Are you sure?'

Terry nodded. 'I'm sure.'

'You don't want to be out there with those other women? Younger, prettier women than me . . .'

'There's no one for me but you, Phyllis Collier. Never has been and never will be.'

'I don't know if I can ever forgive you. It won't be easy to forget . . . *things*.'

Terry pressed his hands tightly around hers. 'We

can try. I know it will take time to mend, but I think we can if we both want to. That girl . . . It will *never* happen again, Phyllis. I swear to you. It was a stupid foolish thing and I wish I hadn't done it. If I could take it back you know I would . . . I love *you*, Phyllis Collier . . . and I always will. Let me make it up to you? Let's try again, Phyl . . . What do you say?'

Phyllis nodded . . . the tiniest movement of her head signalling a new beginning.

25

London, October 1958

Edie was standing across the street from the costume shop, watching people coming and going. She kept checking her watch to make sure that she was neither too early nor too late. Tommie had made sure she understood exactly what to say and what to do. Her heart pitter-pattered with nerves and her stomach clenched. She felt as if she might be sick, standing there right in the middle of the street.

The silvery 'SPANGLELAND' sign was dull in the morning light, faded and peeling. The dusty windows were crammed full of little gold costumes, leotard bodies with spangles and pearls sewn on to the bodices. Some costumes had fringes attached to them while others had glittering satin skirts with slits up each side.

It was very nearly twelve and Edie began to cross the street. As she approached the front door, she was relieved to see that the shop was empty. The bell gave a sharp warning as Edie opened it, and in she went.

Mrs Broad was sitting behind the counter, crocheting a large pink circle of blanket. Round and around she went, her little crochet hook looping and pulling until another pink rose joined the rest of the blanket. At the sound of the bell, the woman looked up and, seeing Edie standing inside the doorway, eyed her curiously and waited for her to speak.

'I've come to pick up some ribbons for my dress.' Edie had rehearsed the words all morning, afraid that she would get them wrong in some way.

'What colour ribbons were you after, dear?' Mrs Broad said.

Edie took a deep breath and repeated exactly what she'd been told to say. 'Something blue . . .'

Mrs Broad nodded. Rolling up her pink blanket and slipping the crochet hook into her pocket, she walked over to Edie and put a gentle hand on her shoulder, a light comforting squeeze before she turned the latch on the door and flipped the sign to 'Closed'. Pulling down the blinds on the door, Mrs Broad said softly, 'Up you go – just through there.' She gestured to a winding staircase that was half hidden by the thick red velvet curtain. 'Have you got the money, dear? Only I don't like to bother you for it afterwards.'

Edie counted out two guineas and offered it to Mrs Broad.

The woman nodded her approval, pushing the money deep into her pocket. 'Good girl. Soon be over. Up you go now . . .'

The stairs were wooden and uncarpeted. Edie's feet made the wood groan and creak as she climbed. At the top of the staircase was a narrow passageway leading to a kitchen. It had dark green linoleum and a bare lightbulb hanging down in the centre of the room. There was a cream stove and a stained Belfast sink, some old wooden cupboards with loose-fitting doors and, in the centre of the room, a large wooden kitchen table with no chairs. Under the table was a rusty metal bucket.

In one corner of the room was an enormous stack of old newspapers piled high on the floor. There was a window overlooking the back of other buildings. Every small window glared at another small window in the distance.

Mrs Broad bustled into the room behind Edie. Pulling a pair of thin blue gingham curtains together to cover the window, she put the overhead light on. Edie noticed the kitchen table had been placed quite deliberately underneath the only bulb, which hung down and let out a bright whitish glow that made her blink furiously. The woman filled a saucepan with water and lit the stove. It was all so casual that for a moment Edie imagined she was about to be offered a cup of tea.

Mrs Broad set about laying out pads of old newspapers on the kitchen table, while Edie tried to breathe and not think about what was to come. There were headlines on the pages about politicians and one about an actress. The woman was beautiful and posing for the camera. Edie nibbled at her fingernails and wondered how much it would hurt. It couldn't be worse than all the nights that Frank had slapped and punched her. It couldn't hurt worse than not being loved and cared for. She gritted her teeth. She would be free of every part of him – she could start a brand-new life and get it right next time.

'You can hang your coat on the door, dear – I usually tell people to take their stockings off because of the splashes, but you can just roll up your dress to your waist.'

Edie looked at Mrs Broad, a question hanging in the air unasked. The woman smiled a sharp, tight smile intended to be of comfort. 'It's the blood, dear . . . you don't want it on your stockings.'

Unbuttoning her coat, Edie found her clumsy fingers struggling to work properly. The buttons felt too big and awkward, and her hands were trembling a little. Eventually she slipped her arms out of her coat and hung it neatly on the back of the door. Placing her shoes just underneath it, side by side, she carefully unclipped her stockings from her suspender belt and rolled them down her legs. The stockings curled into tiny balls which she put neatly inside her shoes for safekeeping. Then she pulled down her knickers and, not knowing what to do with them, shoved them hastily into her coat pocket.

Mrs Broad put on a large navy-blue apron that covered her from her neck to her knees and, just as the saucepan started to boil, Edie was horrified to see the woman slip a hand into her pocket and pull out the crochet hook, which she then dropped into the boiling water. Edie must have made a noise, a faint gasp of surprise, because Mrs Broad moved towards the wooden cupboard at the far end of the kitchen and retrieved a bottle of gin with a thick glass tumbler. Filling the glass to a quarter full, she handed it to Edie, saying, 'Drink this! It's your first time, is it? You'll feel better for a nip of gin then. It will be over quick as you like.'

Edie hesitated, looking at the colourless liquid for a moment, and then she opened her mouth and drank it straight down. The alcohol at least made the shaking stop, which Edie was grateful for. For a moment she thought about grabbing her neatly balled-up stockings and shoes and running back down the stairs, but then what would she do?

There was nobody to look after her. If she was rich, she could pay to go to a fancy doctor but she would never be rich, and this was all that was left for her. If she kept the baby, what kind of a life would they have? No job, no home of her own, no family – this was the only way out. Edie tried to think about a life afterwards. One where she was older and wiser. Maybe a future where there might be hope . . . or even love.

Mrs Broad emptied out the boiling saucepan and ran the crochet hook under the cold tap to enable her to hold it. Edie noticed that the woman hadn't washed her own hands at all and she could see her lacquered pink fingernails. The polish had been picked away at the base of the nail exposing the pale half-moons.

'Come along then – up you get.' Mrs Broad gestured to Edie to climb up on to the wooden table. She patted the thick wad of newspapers, 'Place your bottom on there and roll your dress right up like I told you.'

Edie obeyed, pulling up the skirt of her dress until it was all bunched under her waist. She could feel the soft pad of newspaper under her skin; the chill of the unheated room turning her flesh to goosebumps and she shivered a little.

The woman was at the other end of the table now and Edie could see the crochet hook in her hand. She swallowed hard and tried to erase the stories she'd heard of girls bleeding to death, or dying of putrid infections. The girls at the biscuit factory were always warning each other in hushed whispers of the price to be paid for slipping up. There was no way out except this.

Edie took a deep breath and stared for too long at the bright white bulb above her. Her eyes were dazzled for a moment by the light and she blinked hard. She felt Mrs Broad's hands positioning her so that her knees were raised and her legs splayed apart.

'That's it, dear . . . now this might hurt a bit but I'll be quick as I can. It's very important that you don't move at all. Very important . . . Do you understand me?' the woman murmured, and Edie could see her bending over the table between her legs, her head almost level with Edie's private parts; then came the push of Mrs Broad's pink lacquered nails and the warm steel of the crochet hook on her flesh. Inside her. Pushing deeper and deeper inside her.

Edie bit down on her bottom lip as she felt a dull ache, and then a sharp, pinching pain. She wanted to cry out and her mouth opened, but Mrs Broad glanced up and said, 'Don't make a noise, dear. Nearly there.' Then another fierce burst of pain as the crochet hook was pushed all the way up inside her. A silent scream gathered at the back of her throat. She could feel it stabbing at her, scraping her insides and then a fierce cramping agony seared through her. She gasped and breathed hard through clenched teeth. A strange, garbled moan escaped from the back of her throat.

'That's it . . . all done, dear. Lie quietly for a minute.'

Edie felt the pain subside into a dull ache and then she heard the clatter as Mrs Broad dropped the crochet hook into the kitchen sink. Underneath her, Edie could feel a pool of dampness trickling out of her and she tried to sit up to see what was happening, but the woman placed a hand on her shoulder and pushed her back down.

'Not yet. We need to give it a few minutes and then we can clean you up.'

Edie felt tears of relief starting to roll down her cheeks. It was all over. She laid her head back down against the hard wooden table and felt the trickle increase, then another large spasm of pain deep inside her, and finally something was released in a flood over the wads of newspapers.

'Don't look, dear . . . I'll clear everything away.'

The blue gingham curtains were stained at the edges with something brown and Edie stared at them while Mrs Broad collected the bloody newspapers, piling them into an old coal sack that she tied at the top. 'I'll get Margie to get rid of this and then we can get you sorted out to go back home.'

Edie could feel that she was bleeding but the cramps had eased and she felt able to sit up. Mrs Broad handed her a thick sanitary pad and a small safety pin as Edie started to move. 'Use this for your journey home. You will need to go to bed. Best to manage without aspirin if you can. Put a hot water bottle on your tummy if you're in pain. It should feel much better in a day or two.'

As Edie swung her legs over the side of the table and got to her feet, she found that her limbs were jelly-like and seemed unused to bearing her weight. She clutched the sanitary pad between her legs, trying to stem the flow of blood, and inched her way to the door, so she could retrieve her knickers from her coat pocket. Mrs Broad washed out the crochet hook under the tap and placed the coal sack outside in the passageway for Margie to collect and dispose of. Edie could smell the thick sour metal of dried blood. The crochet hook was gently slipped back inside Mrs Broad's dress pocket and it was all over.

Edie fumbled with her stockings, ripping a ladder in the left leg. She put her coat on but couldn't manage the buttons, instead holding it around her. Her legs still felt heavy and boneless. She took a clumsy step towards the door and Mrs Broad said, 'I'll go first and let you out. If you get a fever and you have to call a doctor, don't mention my name, dear, will you? We really don't want a fuss.'

Edie reached down to get her shoes and noticed for the first time that the dark green linoleum was covered with stray spangles off the costumes. Silver, gold and blue, glistening under the bright white light.

26

London, October 1958

'Here, I brought you a hot water bottle. That might help with the pain.' Tommie slid the pink rubber bottle under the sheets and Edie took it and placed it on top of her abdomen. She grimaced a little as she did so, clenching her teeth. A sheen of feverish sweat lay glistening on her forehead.

'Does it hurt a lot?' Tommie asked softly as she sat down on the edge of Mrs Vee's guest bed. Edie nodded weakly. She didn't have the energy to talk until the wave of deep cramps had gone. The pain had been ebbing and flowing since Edie arrived back at the house, her face deathly white and dark clots of crimson blood between her legs. Tommie cleaned her up and put her to bed but that was the extent of her nursing skills, and she worried about what she might have to do if Edie got worse during the night. The girls she'd worked with had spoken about saltwater baths to clear up infections, or drinking brandy for the pain, but there were other stories – darker, sadder stories that Tommie didn't want to think about.

There'd been a girl once in cooking school. She was

a silly thing, always laughing at something stupid, plus she was a terrible cook. One of those daft posh girls who failed at everything, so turned up for cooking lessons paid for by their disappointed mothers.

One day Tommie had found her crying all alone. She had an appointment but she was scared to go. She wanted Tommie to go with her but Tommie had said no. She was going to the pictures on a date, and anyway she didn't even particularly like this girl. They weren't friends. Florence, her name was – named after an aunt who was an opera singer. She had told that story to everyone. Tommie made her terrible excuses and left Florence wiping away her tears. It wasn't Tommie's problem.

The next day, when she'd arrived at her cookery class, the other girls were gathered around in a sombre circle. Florence had bled to death in her bed, next to the childhood dolls arranged neatly on the shelf by her window. Tommie kept telling herself that it wouldn't have made any difference if she'd gone to keep her company, but deep down, she wondered.

It wouldn't be that way with Edie. Mrs Broad was well known for her skills. Nobody had died there, although they sometimes had a rough few days afterwards. Tommie put her feet up on the bed and lay back against the pillows next to Edie.

'I should really get going. I need to sleep.' Tommie yawned as if to prove her point.

Edie looked panicked and sat up in bed. 'Oh, you

can't leave me tonight. Please . . . I don't want to be on my own . . .'

'OK . . . no need to worry. I can stay if it bothers you that much. You're over the worst now. The fever has almost gone and it's just a bit of pain. You'll be right as rain tomorrow, I reckon.' Tommie was trying to sound more cheerful than she felt, but her confidence seemed to encourage Edie and her face became hopeful.

'Do you think so? There's still a lot of blood and the cramping is really bad.'

'I'm sure you will.'

The women lay back on the bed side by side, their shoulders almost touching. They didn't speak and the room was silent apart from the sound of their gentle breathing. Edie sighed long and deep.

'Tommie – do you believe in heaven and hell?' she whispered so softly that Tommie could barely hear her.

'Not really. Why are you thinking about that?' she replied.

'If I died right now . . . would I go to hell for what I've done?' Edie peered at Tommie, seemingly willing her to say something that might offer comfort.

'Don't talk about things like that! You'll be fine in the morning. I know lots of girls who've done the same thing and none of them have died . . .' Tommie hesitated as she remembered poor silly Florence.

Edie lay back down on her pillow and took small comforting breaths. Tommie could hear the sound of her breathing in the darkness, and for a moment she felt a great fondness for this nervous girl who had wandered into her life one day.

'Are you sleepy?' Tommie asked.

'No. I know it sounds silly but I don't want to go to sleep in case I die.' Edie's voice broke slightly as she appeared to contemplate the idea of never waking up again.

'You *won't* die . . .' But even as Tommie spoke, she felt Edie's hand clutching at hers.

'Hold my hand for a bit, would you? I feel safer with you here . . .'

Tommie took hold of Edie's cold hand and tightened her grip on it. 'It's going to be fine – you'll see . . .'

'I don't want to die yet. I haven't done anything with my life. Haven't been anywhere or seen anything really. All I've done is been a silly girl . . . fell in love and got a good hiding for it . . . and now this. There must be more to life than what I've had so far. It's not been much but even so . . . I really don't want to die like this—' Edie's voice cracked and Tommie gripped on to her hand as if that could stop her dying.

'Hush now, stop talking nonsense. You need to get some sleep.'

'I'm scared to close my eyes. I don't like the dark.'

'All right then, we'll just talk – take our minds off things. I'll go first if you like. What's your favourite colour?'

'Blue. Yours?'

'Yellow, I should think.'

'Favourite food then?'

'Pie and mash!' Tommie licked her lips in anticipation of an imaginary dinner.

Edie laughed. 'But you're a cook. You can't just say pie and mash.'

'Why not? It's lovely. What about you?'

'Oh, I dunno . . . um . . . fish and chips probably.'

Tommie paused for a second to think of another question and Edie shifted slightly in the bed, adjusting the hot water bottle.

'How's the pain now?'

'Not so bad . . . Keep talking: it helps to take my mind off things.'

'What are your favourite things to do?'

'Dancing . . . I used to love dancing. Every Friday night I'd get all dressed up and go to the Rivoli. My friends always wanted to meet boys, but me . . . I wanted to dance. As soon as I heard the drumbeat start to play, my feet would start tapping, and off I'd go.' Edie giggled to herself. 'That's how I met Frank . . . I was dancing on top of a table with a sailor.'

'You don't strike me as the type of girl to be doing that.'

'Can't judge a book by its cover, Tommie. I'd go dancing every night if I had my time again.' Edie sighed and her face grew sad. 'I doubt I'll ever go dancing again now.'

'Of course you will. You've had a rough old time, that's all. But you're free now. Frank's dead and soon you'll be out of London, and nobody will ever find you. You could go anywhere you liked in the world. Think of that . . .'

'I don't know where I'd go. I've only ever been as far as Margate and it was Frank who took me there.'

'Well, let's think . . . Where have you always wanted to go?'

'Maybe America? It looks nice in the films. And they all speak English, so that would help me, wouldn't it?'

'There we go then . . . this time next year you could be dancing in Hollywood.'

Edie smiled a tired smile. 'Where would you go?'

'Oh, me . . . I'd go to Paris to a nice cookery school. One of those fancy ones. Learn to do everything properly and then I'd go and work for the Queen – or a rich movie star. See, maybe I'd end up in Hollywood too!'

'Do you think we're allowed a second chance, Tommie?' Edie whispered.

'I don't really look at life that way. You get what you get.'

'I like to believe that we all get another chance. I'm always hoping for that.'

'That's nice . . . that you still have hope for things. I'm not sure I do any more . . .' Tommie sounded sad and weary.

A stillness fell over the two women and they lapsed into silence again until Edie spoke.

'I'm so sorry, Tommie. You've been a good friend to me. If I don't wake up, I want you to know that I really am sorry.'

'Sorry for *what*? Edie . . . what have you done?'

Two Weeks Earlier

'Make a pot of tea, will you?' Frank said. No please or thank you. Just issuing commands for Edie to follow. She lit the gas and put the kettle on to boil. When it began to bubble and steam, she tipped a little water into the old brown teapot, swilling it around to warm the pot before emptying it out. Then she took her green tin of loose black tea down from the shelf. Running her fingers over the Chinese dragon on the top of the tin, Edie carefully spooned the tea into the pot. Then she stopped . . .

Edie held the teaspoon in the air for a moment. She was about to stir the pot and let it brew but she didn't. The air around her seemed to change. It became lighter and clean. She felt perfectly calm as if nothing could hurt her. Her heart pulsed gently and her hands were steady as she opened the tin of rat poison.

She hadn't even known it was next to her. She didn't remember picking it up from the pantry floor and carrying it back into the kitchen with the chops. Later she wouldn't remember this part, where she spooned the brown powder into the teapot and stirred it vigorously. Edie slotted the tiny lid of the teapot into place and closed her eyes.

She imagined her freedom coming around the corner. How long would the poison take to work? Edie was quite some way into her fantasy of Frank choking on poison, just long enough for her to tell him exactly what she thought of him, and how he would never lay a hand on her – or any woman – ever again. She'd started to silently mouth the words and was about to act out the scene to great applause from her imaginary audience when he looked up at her. Somewhere she could hear her name being called.

'Edie. EDIE . . . I'm waiting for my tea here . . .' Frank sounded irritated. If she pushed him now, he would slap her. Maybe even take off his belt. It was his new trick. Belt buckles ripping into her flesh until she bled. He would hurt her until he stopped hurting. Maybe this time he wouldn't stop at all.

Edie clenched her jaw and picked up the teapot. She walked slowly across the kitchen floor and put the pot down on the table. Frank had gone back to his racing pages and didn't bother to look up. Looking for a winner . . . something to solve his problems, Edie thought. He didn't speak.

She told herself she wouldn't do it . . . she would stop in a minute. She would make an excuse and throw the pot of tea away.

Edie poured a splash of milk into his favourite teacup and then poured the tea. The pot wasn't full. She'd only made enough for Frank. One cup and probably a bit of top-up was his usual habit. She stared at the tea . . . you couldn't tell. It was the same sea of dull milky-brown as ever. Frank reached his hand across and grabbed the cup, wrapping his palm around it.

Edie took a breath; her mouth opened to shout a warning . . . but the warning never came. He swallowed it down in two large gulps, before demanding his usual top-up. She stood stone-like, pouring more tea into the cup. Watching him drink it down while she waited to be free . . .

Frank began to grimace as if, somewhere deep inside, something was bothering him. He let out a guttural cry and stretched a hand towards her. Then he hit the floor with such force that Edie almost jumped out of her skin at the shock of him lying there flat on his back with his eyelids fluttering open, his mouth kind of lopsided and strange. His chest in arching spasms. There was white drool at the side of his mouth and his whole body was convulsing. Edie watched . . . fascinated by the violence of it, how helpless he was. She couldn't take her eyes off him.

Then she walked slowly to the spot where he lay staring up at her. His pale blue eyes were puzzled now . . . frightened . . .

'You are *never* going to hurt me again, Frank Budd. You're *never* going to hurt anyone ever again.'

For a moment Edie felt the taste of freedom as if

her jailer had gone away and left the cell door open. A sense of euphoria came over her and she wanted to cry and dance. She was free.

A loud thumping on the front door brought her crashing back to reality. She snapped out of her euphoric haze and felt her heart drumming inside her chest. For a moment she thought it must be the police come to arrest her.

Frank lay there perfectly still now. She'd *killed* him.

They would take her away and eventually they would hang her by the neck. She put her hands to her throat and tried to imagine the air being choked out of her. Her icy calm replaced by sheer terror at the consequences of what she'd done. Another loud thumping alerting her to the fact that whoever was knocking was not going away.

Edie moved as if in a dream towards the front door. She pulled the kitchen door tightly shut behind her and wiped her hands on her apron. She could hear gruff male voices calling Frank's name as they pounded their fists on her door and Edie suddenly realized who they were.

In all her revenge fantasies, she had not for one moment given thought to what might happen if the men he owed money to actually turned up. The envelope crumpled inside her brassiere but Edie took a deep breath and opened the front door a crack. The two men wore dark suits, like undertakers, and thin ties, their hair slick with too much Brylcreem. When they saw her peeping through the door at them, the shorter man grinned as if she were prey and he the hunter.

Edie took a long nervous breath before saying, 'Yes? Can I help you?'

'We're looking for your husband. He's late for a very important meeting. Is he home?'

The taller man kept one hand in his suit jacket pocket and Edie could see the outline of a thick brass knuckleduster. A long dark car was parked in the street behind him with the motor running. Another man sat waiting in the driver's seat.

Her heart thudded against her ribs. She thought of Frank lying on the kitchen floor, possibly dead by now. His lifeless eyes staring up at the ceiling. A brief vision of him flashed through her mind as he was on that first night, grinning at her as she danced on the table. His hand in hers . . .

Edie wasn't a girl any more. She was so very tired. He'd made her sick with worry, beaten her until she could barely breathe, and what would become of her? In a split second she considered her options, weighing them carefully. She could just hand over the money, and these men with their knuckledusters would go away satisfied . . . but something inside Edie couldn't part with the little brown envelope and all the things she might do with it.

The shorter man leaned forward, inserting his shiny winklepicker shoe into the doorway. 'Where is he?' he said.

Edie hesitated for a split second and then she pulled the front door wide open and said in a strong clear voice, 'He's not here . . .' The taller man stared her down but Edie didn't look away. 'Come in and check if you don't believe me. He's *never* here. Probably in the pub or the bookies – as usual.'

Her impression of an exasperated wife seemed to satisfy them and the shorter man backed away. 'Well, when he comes home tell him we're looking for him.'

'Who shall I say called?' Edie pursed her lips and gave the men an impudent stare.

The two men smirked at her but didn't answer. They climbed back into the long dark car, slamming the doors hard. The taller man glared at Edie out of the back window as the car crawled away down the street.

Slamming her own door shut, she stared wildly around the hallway, catching sight of herself in the mirror.

Taking the stairs two at a time, she pushed their bedroom chair up to the wardrobe so she could stand on it to reach the cardboard suitcase, which had lived on top of it since their wedding. Edie didn't stop to think. She threw her night things and as many clothes as she could manage into the suitcase and picked it up by its handle. The handle came away in her hand and the damn lock wouldn't shut properly.

Edie had a ball of twine in her sewing box that she'd found somewhere and stored away in case it came in handy. She pulled her sewing basket out from under the bed. A large bag of different coloured cottons and bits of wool spilled out on to the floor. Next to them was her big green tin that she kept full of assorted buttons and a pair of scissors sharp enough to cut fabric if needed.

Fastening the string around the case and tying a neat little knot to hold everything in place, she unpinned Frank's envelope from deep inside her brassiere and shoved it into her handbag.

Edie had no idea where she was going or how she would manage but, as she scrambled down the stairs in her coat, clutching the cardboard suitcase to her chest, she didn't care.

27

London, October 1958

Edie felt a gnawing pain in her belly as she lay in Mrs Vee's fancy guest bed staring up at the ceiling, Tommie beside her, watching and waiting for her to speak.

She'd murdered Frank. She, Edie Budd – Edie Fletcher as was in her single days – she'd murdered somebody. Not just anybody, but Frank. Then there was the little matter of the Costellos. It was, after all, their money she was carrying around with her as if she owned it.

She'd heard stories about them for years – badly beaten bodies turned up in canals or on wasteland. Old bombsites where bloodied remains lay waiting for someone to claim them. Sometimes the bodies were not found at all, but everyone *knew* what had happened. They had displeased someone important, owed money, or picked a fight with the wrong person.

They'd come after her when they heard about Frank . . . but there was still nothing in the newspapers. She'd *killed* him and nobody seemed to care. The police would care though – they would catch her and hang her for it. She shook her head . . . It wasn't possible. She would get out of London and then they wouldn't find her. She could change her name and just melt away as though she'd never existed.

She'd *killed* him, as if she'd never cared for him at all . . . but of course she *had* cared – long ago. Back when he used to crush her to him and smother her with kisses, bringing her little gifts, or she would finish up a long shift at Marshall's and find Frank sitting astride his motorbike, holding his spare crash helmet that he'd bought just for her.

They were happy together . . . weren't they? Happy – not happy. Edie couldn't remember when the unhappiness had started. Maybe it had always been there, seeping in like damp until one day everything was ruined and beyond repair.

Tommie was still waiting. Edie felt a cold fear press itself around her heart. She'd done so many terrible things, and now she was surely going to pay the price for them. The burden of keeping so many secrets was crushing her and finally she looked across at Tommie and spoke.

'I haven't been honest with you . . . You've been so good to me and I've kept things from you.'

'What kind of things?' Tommie shifted her weight so she was facing Edie. Her face was suspicious and wary.

'I've lied to you . . .' Edie lay staring up into the darkness, pain shooting through her. 'If I die tonight, I want you to know the truth about what happened.'

Tommie sat bolt upright, waiting. 'What is it? You can tell me . . .'

'Frank didn't just drop dead one day . . . It wasn't a heart attack.' Edie turned to face Tommie but her face was shrouded in darkness.

'Are you saying what I think you're saying?' Tommie let go of Edie's hand, turning away and reaching for her packet of Woodbines on the bedside table. The match flared, showing her serious face, and Edie regretted her words, wishing she could take them back now . . . but it was too late.

'It wasn't an accident . . . I put something in his tea . . . he fell to the floor and that was it.'

'What did you put in his tea?' Tommie sucked on her cigarette and exhaled a loud gasp of smoke. Edie watched the glowing tip of the cigarette and raked her teeth over her bottom lip, reluctant to say the words.

'Rat poison.'

'You *poisoned* him?'

Edie nodded, although Tommie couldn't see her face clearly in the faint glow of her burning cigarette.

'Oh my God . . . you *killed* him . . . !' Tommie blew a stream of smoke up towards the ceiling. She swung her legs off the bed and planted her feet firmly on to the carpet. 'You *murdered* your husband and you didn't think to tell me? I could be an accomplice!'

'I'll say you didn't know a thing – and it's true. If they catch me, I'll tell them that I lied to you. It wasn't a lie about the beatings . . . he *hurt* me for years. I just couldn't take it any more.' Edie started to sob – pathetic, pleading sobs.

'Why are you telling me now?' Tommie demanded, her friendly overtures all halted now and replaced by her usual weary distrust of people. She'd felt there was something off about this girl – something she was keeping back – and now she knew what it was.

'Because if I die tonight, I don't want to go to hell . . . I don't *want* to die here, Tommie . . .' Edie's chest heaved, her misery plain. 'Not like this.'

Tommie gave a weak sigh. 'Oh, Edie, you're not going to die tonight. I keep telling you.' The girl was so pathetic and helpless that Tommie couldn't just abandon her. She didn't want to get in trouble with the police though. Her mind began to race through possibilities.

'I am sorry, though, for lying to you . . .' Edie's hand reached across searching for hers.

Tommie sighed and leaned back against the pillows, allowing the girl to clutch at her hand for comfort.

She lay there, chain-smoking and listening to Edie crying softly in the darkness. She smoked her cigarettes right down to the tip, eventually throwing them into her water glass and listening to the hiss as they died. She had to get this woman on a train somewhere and then wash her hands of the whole thing. She could deny all knowledge – after all, nobody knew she was at Mrs Vee's house hiding out. Tommie could say the girl had moved in to number 73 Dove Street, and then just as quickly moved out again. As far as everyone was concerned, that was the truth.

The thought occurred to her that it might not be that easy. After all, this was murder, not someone stealing a few quid that didn't belong to them. She needed to talk to someone – ask their advice – but who? There was only one person she could think of to confide in . . . but whether he would help was another matter.

A weak band of sunshine formed an arc across the bed where the curtains let in a crack of light. Tommie threw her arms across her face to shield it as she blinked herself awake. They must have been sleeping for hours. It was so peaceful in Mrs Vee's house compared to anywhere else she'd lived. People didn't make much noise around rich people.

Tommie coughed a little and then leaned back on her elbows to sit up. Edie's hair was strewn across her face. Her lips were parted but her skin seemed strangely pale and waxy. For a moment she felt a rising terror. She leaned over the sleeping girl, shaking her awake and calling her name.

'Edie! Wake up!' Tommie shook her until eventually Edie sniffed and gulped a reply.

'What? Why are you shouting?' Edie swiped her hair back off her face and turned to face Tommie.

'Oh God . . . I thought you were dead for a minute.'

'Well, shouting at me wouldn't have helped.' Edie sat up in bed and threw the now cold rubber water bottle on to the floor.

'Sorry . . . you gave me a fright. How are you feeling?'

'I don't know yet. All right, I think. There's no pain at the moment.'

Tommie got up from the bed and straightened out the creases in the dress she'd slept in all night. 'Look at the state of me. I'll make you a bit of breakfast first and then get myself sorted out. You need to eat something. Got to keep your strength up.'

'Thanks. I could murder a cup of tea but I'm not really hungry.' The unfortunate choice of words hung in the air between them until Edie grimaced and said, 'Sorry . . .'

Tommie gave a swift nod. She had to get Edie out of here as soon as possible but first she needed some advice and there was still only one place she could think of where that might be available. She wondered if he was home alone.

'I was thinking . . . if you decide where you're going, I could pop into the railway station and buy your train ticket for you. You don't have to leave right away. Stay another night until the bleeding stops and you feel more yourself.'

'Thank you . . . you've been so kind to me . . .' Edie said softly but her expression revealed her despair.

'Do you have any idea where you'd like to go?'

Edie shook her head. 'I don't know . . .' She shrugged her shoulders helplessly.

'Can't you just pick a place and then I'll get the ticket?' Tommie encouraged but the girl just shook her head and looked as if she might cry.

'I don't *know* where to go. I've never been anywhere . . . Can't you choose for me? It doesn't matter much to me where I end up,' Edie pleaded.

'But that's not right. It's *you* that has to live there.' Tommie frowned at her, beginning to feel a flood of frustration that she'd somehow got caught up in this.

'I just want to get out of London. I know you probably wish that you hadn't got involved but *please* can you just do one more thing for me? Just *choose* a place and I'll be out of your hair.'

Tommie sighed. 'OK, I'll get off after breakfast. I might be gone a while today. There's a couple of things I need to do first. Are you going to be all right on your own?'

'I'll be OK. You don't need to worry about me. You won't forget though – about the railway ticket?' Edie managed a weak smile but her face was shrouded with pain.

'I won't forget,' Tommie said.

28

London, October 1958

Tommie started walking her familiar route, a half-smoked Woodbine dangling from her lip as she rang the doorbell. There were no signs of life and so she pushed it again, leaving her finger on it for too long. Eventually the front door opened and there he was.

'Oh, it's you . . . What are you doing here, Tommie? Not like you to be visiting in daylight.' He frowned at her but his voice was soft – undecided maybe. She searched his eyes for something and didn't find what she was looking for.

'I need to talk to you. Can I come up?' Tommie was trying to be calm. She didn't want him to send her away before she'd said her piece.

'I don't know what's got into you lately. What the fuck was the other night all about? Come on then.' He opened the front door and then turned his back on her and walked away, expecting her to follow along behind. Tommie threw her cigarette on to the pavement, crushing it out under the tip of her shoe. She stepped inside the hallway and closed the front door, watching him climb the stairs.

By the time she reached the door of his flat, he was already pouring them two brandies but he didn't make a move towards the bedroom. He watched as she took off her coat and folded it neatly over the back of his sofa.

'You're alone then?' The words came out with a bitter edge.

'Apparently . . . I am allowed visitors, you know.'

'Of course you are. I didn't mean it like that.' Tommie took the brandy glass, her hand grazing against his for a second. She was losing her train of thought now he was standing in front of her. She'd been very clear what needed saying when she'd set out that day.

All night long she'd thought about Edie's situation and realized that she needed some guidance. There had been no doubt in Tommie's mind how this conversation would proceed but now, as she sipped on her brandy and felt the warmth of his hand, she suddenly wasn't sure what she was doing here, with this man who didn't care.

He sat down in the armchair, cradling his drink and apparently slightly enjoying her discomfort.

'Come on, Tommie, spit it out . . .' He took a drink of brandy. Suddenly, his face darkened. 'You're not pregnant, are you?'

Tommie sat down on the sofa, her eyes taking in his reactions. The panic. What would he do? Give her money and send her to Spangleland to buy some ribbons? No, he'd know someone in Harley Street. Probably kept a number in his little black book just in case. Men like him always knew someone who would clean up their messes.

'No, don't worry, it's not that.'

'Then what is it?'

Tommie thought about the first time she'd set eyes on him in the café where Cassie worked. He was sitting, drinking coffee and reading a book. He looked so odd compared to all the other blokes filling the jukebox or trying to grab at passing girls, but he'd just sat there reading, then quietly closed his book and got to his feet. Tommie had walked right up to him – brave from the brandy she'd drunk earlier that evening and said, 'Hello, is your book interesting?'

He'd laughed softly as he'd looked her up and down. 'Not all that interesting. Fancy a nightcap at my place?' and she'd gone with him – just like that.

The old familiar ache started to build inside her – but she tried to damp it down, stay focused on what she'd come to say.

'I need some advice on something . . . a friend of mine is in trouble. Well, she's not really a friend . . .' As Tommie spoke, she began to realize how pointless it was to tell him about Edie. He couldn't help her.

He frowned. 'What kind of trouble?'

She bit down on her lip. 'It doesn't matter . . . I shouldn't have come here.'

'What is going on with you these days? You used to be a fun girl. Now you're driving me nuts. You leave in the middle of the night without a word. You turn up on my doorstep at all hours. It's too much fucking drama, Tommie.'

She glared at him . . . hating him . . . wanting him.

'You know you've never taken *me* out on a date?'

'A *date*?' He almost laughed but caught himself at the sight of Tommie's earnest face staring at him. 'I don't know what's got into you . . .'

'Yes, a date. It would have been a nice gesture.'

'I don't know what you want from me. I've never lied to you about what this is. You came back here that first night, and I took you at your word. A bit of fun . . . that's all.'

'After all this time, didn't you ever think that I could be more than a bit of fun?' Tommie stared down at her shoes rather than meet his gaze.

'No . . . no, love, I've never thought of you like that.' He finished his brandy in two gulps but stayed there cradling the empty glass. 'I'm sorry if that hurts your feelings.'

Tommie shook her head. 'Why? What's *wrong* with me?'

'There's nothing wrong with you . . . You're just not that type of girl, that's all.'

'What type of girl? I'm the same as anyone . . .' She could feel tears starting to seep slowly from under her eyelids.

'You're not though. You're . . . I dunno . . . kind of broken. It's like there's just something inside you that I can't do anything for.'

'*BROKEN* – is that what you think I am? Are you *seeing* that girl?' Tommie raised her voice, trying to let her anger stop the tears.

'What girl?' he said sullenly.

'That girl you took for spaghetti the other day – I saw you with her.'

'Have you been *following* me?'

'Don't change the subject. Are you seeing her?'

'Yes, if you must know. She's a nice girl and I'm seeing her.'

Tommie stood up, grabbing her coat from the sofa and fighting back the tears. 'So, she's not broken then?'

He shook his head, regretting his cruelty for a moment. 'I didn't mean it like that. It came out wrong. I just meant that you're hurt – I can see it. Everyone can see it, except you. I can't help you . . . I *am* fond of you – you know that?'

'Fond of me . . . but you're never going to love me, are you?' Tommie's voice cracked as she watched him trying to think of something to say that wouldn't sound callous.

'No . . . I'm *never* going to love you, Tommie. I'm sorry if you thought that's where we were heading. It wasn't my intention to lead you on. I thought we were both clear about what this was. Just a bit of fun.'

'But we've been seeing each other for nearly two years . . . that's got to mean something?'

'It's not like that for me. Two years ago, I thought

you were a fun girl and I liked seeing you. I still think that. I haven't changed.'

'But you must *feel* something to stay with me all this time?' Her voice rose, angry now. 'I thought the longer it went on, the more you *cared* about me? Why would you let it drag on for two years if you didn't have proper feelings for me?'

'It's not like that for guys, Tommie . . . maybe for girls . . . but longer don't mean deeper. I'm sorry, love.'

He got to his feet and walked towards her. Tommie's shoulders sagged with disappointment and she stared down at the carpet again, trying not to show how much he'd wounded her.

'I'd better get going.' She slipped her arms into her coat and wrapped it around her.

He was close now – so close she could smell his cologne. He smiled in that way he had. Boyish, not wishing to be found guilty of anything. Trying to make it better because he'd gone too far. He reached out a hand and picked up a loose strand of Tommie's hair with his fingers, twirling it gently.

'You can stay for a bit if you like. No need to rush off. I am fond of you – you know that. I'm just being realistic. I don't have to go anywhere for an hour or so. Come on . . . let me get you another drink?'

He was trying to sweet-talk her now. A wave of anger swept through her and she shook her head. 'No, I'm going. I won't be coming back.'

'You're always welcome here if I'm on my

own – you know that? It may not be everything you want, but it's a good thing we've got going . . .' His fingers were still playing with her hair. Saying sorry the only way he knew how.

The anger flooded over her and poured out of her mouth. 'I'm *not* broken. I might be hurt. I've lost things in my life that you can't understand because you haven't lost anything yet. But you will . . . because we *all* do. And I deserve someone who wants to buy *me* spaghetti.' She gave him a defiant look.

'Wait a minute . . .' he said but Tommie was already walking away.

It was clear to Tommie that getting Edie on a train and out of Mrs Vee's as quickly as possible was the only way out of this pickle. Staying another night had been a bad idea. She chewed on her lip fretting over the situation.

She'd just deny all knowledge of Edie's plans . . . that was it. She'd simply buy the ticket and say the girl asked her to get it. She'd no idea Edie was a murderer, otherwise of course she never would have bought it for her.

Satisfied with her imaginary alibi, Tommie strode purposefully into the ticket hall. The railway station was crowded, filled with travellers. Big and small suitcases, wicker baskets packed with sandwiches and thermos flasks. The noise of people like an out-of-tune orchestra.

The ticket office had a small queue and one bored man sat behind a glass counter. Every single person who approached the window had too many questions to ask about routes or times. Tommie grew impatient, shuffling along behind a woman with two small boys. One of the boys was making engine noises as he pretended to fly a wooden aeroplane in circles. On and on he purred, while the line for the ticket counter moved ever slowly forward. She sighed . . . she just wanted to get the ticket and wash her hands of the whole situation. Tommie shuffled exactly two paces forward in the queue and weighed up what she knew about Edie.

If what Edie had said was true, then her husband deserved his fate. Who could blame a woman if she was pushed that far? If he beat her like that – well, then it was self-defence, wasn't it? Tommie justified it to herself.

On the walls of the ticket office were posters of everywhere you could visit by train. Families with buckets and spades at the beach, green rolling hills of the countryside. Tommie eyed the destinations, trying to find one to suit Edie.

None of them seemed suitable. *Where was the best place to hide out if you were wanted for murder?* She really didn't seem like someone capable of killing her husband but he must have driven her to it. Tommie put Edie on trial in her mind . . . and found her not guilty. As both judge and jury, she was satisfied. She would help the girl get away and start a new life.

Tommie sighed. The little boy in front waved his wooden aeroplane at her. 'Brrrrummm,' he screeched. She waved him away but he didn't move.

'Brrrrrummmm,' he shouted again, only this time the tip of a wooden wing hit her elbow, causing Tommie to glare at the child.

She had quite enough on her plate without this. Poor Mrs Vee was gone, and she'd have to find another job now. Everything felt as if it was ending. All the things she'd come to rely on were over. She tried to imagine a life without Mrs Vee to fuss over – a life without her Soho nights. Nothing would go back to how it used to be. But where did that leave her?

The woman with the two small boys finally bought her tickets, then fussed about putting her change back inside her handbag.

'Excuse me, but I am in a bit of a hurry,' Tommie said sharply. The woman finally snapped her handbag shut, scooped up the hands of her children and marched them out of the ticket office, leaving Tommie next in line.

The bored man behind the counter didn't bother to look up at her. 'Where to?'

Suddenly, all the pieces fell into place. She imagined Edie sitting at a table in the little teashop on her postcard. Tommie took a deep breath and then stated her destination.

The man ran his finger over a timetable and then squinted up at her. 'Single or return?'

'Single, please.'

'That's all?'

The man started to write out the ticket. 'So, one single . . .'

Tommie didn't know what the future held, but something inside her felt it must be different. She thought about her mother, and imagined the little pink curtains blowing in the breeze without her to see them. Slowly another idea formed at the back of her mind . . . There was nothing to keep her in London any more. She needed a fresh start.

'Actually, it's *two* tickets . . . two singles . . .' and she smiled for the first time that day.

Once Tommie had got back to number 73 Dove Street, she sank down on to her single bed and wondered if she'd done the right thing. Edie might not want her tagging along, and she still didn't know if the girl was even telling her the whole truth. Of course, Edie could always go her own way once they arrived . . . or Tommie could. There was no need for them to be stuck together, but it might be nice to have at least one friend in a strange place. Starting over alone felt like an impossible task, but with two of them, maybe . . .

Pulling down her large brown leather suitcase, Tommie began to pack her clothes inside it. Folding her sweaters and pretty dresses carefully, pushing her shoes down the sides to save on space. Tommie felt lighter already. A decision had been made and even a bad decision was better than none at all.

She had a quick soak in the tub and fixed her hair, before hastily writing out a note to Phyllis to give her notice. Tommie wasn't one for goodbyes. She would leave it on the table in the hallway and try to sneak out without being seen. They could stay at Mrs Vee's for one more night until Edie felt better and then off on the evening train to a new life.

She felt a small bubble of excitement rising inside her at the possibility of starting again. Nobody to know you or judge you for any past mistakes or silliness. She could be a whole new Tommie . . .

Once she was ready to leave, other darker thoughts began to intrude . . . Edie was on the run for murder. Tommie didn't want to get caught up in that, although in some ways she already was. She decided to take one step at a time. First get out of this place and then see what happened. The vague plan felt as good as anything at that particular moment. The matter was settled . . . for now.

Putting on her coat, she took a deep breath and looked around her room for the final time. The postcard of the teashop was still pinned to the wall. Tommie pulled it from its pin, shoving it into her coat pocket. Straightening her shoulders, she reached down to close her suitcase. It was the end of life at 73 Dove Street – time for a new beginning.

Suddenly she heard a loud pounding on the front door. Fists hammering, determined to get a response. Pulling back her bedroom curtains with one finger, she peeked out to see who it was.

Down in the street a familiar black car was parked right outside the house. Her heart sank. Tommie thought about ignoring it but then there was the worry that Phyllis might open the door and let him in.

She raced down the stairs and cautiously opened the front door a crack to see a man standing there, who might have looked more familiar to her had she not been so drunk the last time they met.

'Ahh, you're here then?' Pete said.

'Now's not a good time. Tell you what, why don't you come back tomorrow?' she said and moved quickly to shut the front door. Suddenly the door crashed open, smashing against the wall of the hallway and forcing Tommie to take a step backwards. A man she didn't recognize stepped right in front of Pete and glared at her.

'What *are* you doing?' Tommie spluttered as he came closer.

'Is this the right house then?' the man barked.

'Yeah, this is the girl I told you about . . . Edie was here. I saw her with my own eyes.' Pete stepped away from the front door, edging back towards the car as if his work were done.

'What do you want? There's nobody here . . .' Tommie yelled indignantly as the man tried to shove past her and into the hallway. 'Who *are* you?'

'I'm looking for Edie Budd. She was right here, so Pete reckoned. *Where* is she?'

'She's not here. There's nobody of that name here—'

The man pushed past her, striding towards the staircase shouting, '*Where's my wife?*

29

London, October 1958

Frank shouted at the top of his voice: 'EDIE . . . get down here now!'

'But you can't be . . . I thought you were—' Tommie's mouth clamped shut but too late.

'Did she *tell* you what she did to me? I could get the police on her. She should go to jail . . . Where is she?' Frank marched up the hallway, still yelling. 'EDIE, COME DOWN NOW!'

Tommie ran after him, trying to stop him going up the stairs. 'There's no one upstairs. She doesn't live here.'

'She's got something that belongs to me and I want it back.' Frank shrugged her off and continued his bellowing. 'EDIE, come down here now! I *know* what you did—'

'There's nobody here of that name. You've got the wrong house—'

'You don't want to lie to me. I could go to the police and tell them everything. How she tried to kill me – and stole money from me. Now I want my money back, so someone had better tell me where she is.'

'I don't know where she is. She wasn't here long . . . She left.'

Frank stopped and gazed at her. His pale blue eyes searching her face for lies. He smiled at her – a soft, charming smile. 'Look, this is nothing to do with you. Are you protecting her? She's crazy. I bet she's told you a pack of lies about me. She could have *killed* me . . . It was only by luck that she didn't manage it.' His voice was soft now – beguiling. His smile poured over her.

Tommie stared back at him. At that moment, he didn't seem like the kind of man who would hurt someone. She didn't know who to believe. 'She's not here . . . honestly.'

Frank sighed. 'I *loved* that girl – more than my life. I'm not perfect – far from it – but she never wanted for anything. No reason for what she did to me. Now *please* tell me where she is . . .' His pale blue eyes fastened on Tommie, pleading.

'She says you *beat* her.' The words just slipped out of her mouth.

'That's a lie! I *never* touched her. She's mad – a crazy woman, making up stories to cover up what she did to me. She should be in prison. Now *where is she*?'

Frank pushed past Tommie and put one foot on the bottom stair. 'EDIE . . . EDIE . . . GET DOWN HERE . . .'

The parlour door flew open and a perplexed Terry Collier suddenly appeared in the hallway. 'What's going on here?' He glared at Tommie. 'No gentlemen callers. The rules are quite clear.'

Tommie briefly registered the shock of finding Terry Collier back in the house as he stormed past her, but she had no time to say anything as the next minute he'd grabbed hold of Frank's arm. Terry yanked him backwards off the bottom step but Frank was in no mood to be stopped, and before Tommie knew what was happening a scuffle had broken out between the two men.

She opened her mouth to shout for Phyllis, but out of the corner of her eye she could already see Pete running back up the path towards her. 'I'll call the police if you don't get out of here and take him with you,' she screamed.

The message must have got through, because Pete began to pull Frank away from Terry Collier until eventually he was back outside the house.

Tommie slammed the front door shut and leaned back against it breathing heavily. 'Oh my goodness . . .' she panted.

Terry Collier dusted himself off and glared at her. 'I don't want to see him here again. Got it?'

'Yes . . . OK.' Tommie couldn't explain and anyway she really didn't care what he thought. The only thing going through her mind was that Frank Budd was very much alive and she needed to talk to Edie right now.

Running back up the stairs, Tommie left Terry Collier huffing and puffing by the parlour door. She could hear Phyllis shouting, 'What's going on out there? Terry?' but Tommie didn't hang around to hear the answer.

She stood to one side of the curtains, trying to look out into the street without being seen. Pete and Frank were standing by the car and, judging by the gestures, an argument was going on. Pete looked like he wanted to get out of there, as he kept opening the car door and then closing it again while Frank waved his arms around angrily.

Tommie tried to work out what she should do. She couldn't go out of the front door but, somehow, she had to speak to Edie.

If Frank wasn't dead then at least Edie wouldn't be wanted by the police . . . although there was the small matter of the £250. *Suppose she had lied though about the beating . . . Suppose Frank was telling the truth? Suppose she had played her for a fool?* Tommie didn't know what to think, or who to believe. She needed to have it out with Edie right now and get this cleared up.

Tommie crept down the stairs, watching and listening for anyone who might stop her. The parlour door was tightly closed and she could hear the quiet hum of voices coming from behind it. Inching her way towards the kitchen, she checked over her shoulder to make sure that neither of the Colliers were about to descend on her, before unlocking the back door and stepping out into the yard.

The door leading to the back alleyway was swollen

with rain and Tommie had to pull and pull at it to get it to open. Eventually the door gave way and she ran as hard as she could until she reached the safety of the street.

Tommie had pennies for the phone box clutched in the palm of her hand. A young girl was inside the box, giggling and chatting.

'That's what you say . . . Cheeky, you are . . .' The girl giggled again as she saw Tommie standing there waiting. She turned her back and carried on the same low, flirtatious laughter as if everything was too funny. Tommie rapped on the glass and when the girl turned to glare at her, she put on a pleading face.

'Please . . . it's an emergency,' she cried. The girl tutted and rolled her eyes but after another few seconds of giggling, the black receiver was put down and the door swung open. Tommie caught hold of the door before it swung shut. Her hands shook as she dialled Mrs Vee's telephone number, praying that Edie would answer. The phone began to ring, sounding shrill and urgent in her ear. First once, and then again, and again.

30

London, October 1958

The old gramophone had been Mrs Vee's pride and joy at one point in her life but now made a strange crackling noise as the music blared. A sort of tinny squawk accompanied each of the old records Edie had uncovered and was currently amusing herself by playing.

She felt slightly dizzy when she stood up for too long but the bleeding had eased and Edie felt as if she was over the worst of it. The music was quite old-fashioned but there was a good drumbeat, her fingers tapped along and her body began to sway as she lay on Mrs Vee's sofa flicking through a pile of old 78s in paper sleeves.

She imagined a time when she might be able to go dancing again – or play music to her heart's content with nobody to tell her off. It was a ridiculous dream – her most likely outcome was prison . . . or, even worse, a hangman's noose. Edie stroked her delicate neck with her fingertips and felt a wild fear flare inside her.

She was still weak from the loss of so much blood, but at the same time she could feel a new strength building inside her. By not dwelling on Frank and what fate might indeed await her, Edie allowed herself exactly seven minutes of happiness humming away to old songs.

Then the dark thoughts began to crowd out the happy ones. A life where she would be forever punished for what she'd done. In her mind she could hear the loud bass tones of her childhood preachers shouting about hell and damnation. *But what is hell other than what I've been living in for all these years? What more can they do to me?*

Still, the darkness was everywhere; worries about the future and the past greeted each other like old friends. Edie gnawed anxiously at the skin around her fingernails and wished that Tommie would hurry up. She felt safer having a friend who knew all her secrets now. As if the secret contained half the power for having been shared. All she needed was her train ticket and she could start again . . .

The record finished and Edie got up to change it. Feeling stronger until a wave of dizziness made her sit back down and put her head on her lap until it passed. A sudden noise from the hallway made her sit up straight, braced for a stranger to enter the room and demand to know what she was doing there, but it was only Tommie.

The girl was out of breath and her face was flushed pink. 'Oh God, you're OK . . . I ran all the way. When you didn't answer I thought something had happened to you . . .' she gasped and then bent over, leaning heavily on the door handle until she managed to get her breath back.

'I'm fine. Just a bit dizzy.' Edie looked at her puzzled.

'I've been *calling* you. Didn't you hear the telephone?' Tommie wheezed out between breaths.

'No, I was playing records . . . Has something happened?' Edie was suddenly alert to the fact that something had gone wrong.

Tommie straightened up and gave Edie a hard stare. 'Yes, something's happened. Frank's *alive* . . . He came to number seventy-three looking for you with that bloke I picked up from the bar.'

Edie's face didn't change but she nodded slightly to herself. She didn't say a word. Tommie felt a rush of anger at having raced over to warn her. The girl just sat there, swallowing hard.

On the journey over, she had come to think that Edie was a practised liar. After all, she'd told her tale after tale, but only when Tommie had forced her. Trying to arouse her pity by telling her a sob story about beatings . . . but maybe the truth was that she was just a common thief? Edie seemed such an innocent, and she had felt sorry for her – it was the first proper friend she'd made in the longest time. But the distrust that Tommie wrapped around her like a shield was starting to win through, and she glowered at Edie.

'You need to come clean with me. It's been a pack of lies from start to finish. I'm nobody's mug – *got that*?'

Edie's lips parted but still she didn't speak. Shaking her head from side to side, staring up at Tommie. 'He's *alive*?' she repeated and then fell silent again.

'Yes, he's *alive* . . . if any of what you said was even true. He says you tried to kill him to steal his money. He was shouting the odds – barged right into the house yelling your name. Old man Collier almost got into a fight with him.'

Edie's face crumpled in with agony. 'I have to get out of here. *Please* help me. I need to go tonight. He'll *kill* me if he catches me. I swear he will.'

'I don't know. I bought your train ticket. There's a place I know . . . but now . . . well, to be honest, I don't trust you, Edie. You've lied to me from the beginning. You've told me so many different things . . . the sob story about him beating you . . . He *told* me he never touched you. I don't know what to *believe* any more.' Tommie stood there with her arms folded, guarding herself against feeling pity for the other woman.

Edie exhaled a long miserable sigh and calmly got to her feet, looking straight at Tommie as her fingers fumbled with the buttons of her blouse. Steadily she undid them, slipping the blouse off her shoulders and arms, letting it float down to the floor. Unzipping her skirt, letting that fall over her hips until it, too, pooled at her feet.

Then Edie turned . . . slowly and carefully . . . letting the other woman see her uncovered body for the first time.

Tommie grimaced as she took in the faded yellow and purplish masses that covered Edie's skin. Faded as they were, she could see every mark was the result of a fist. The edges overlapped from creamy-yellow to the palest bluey-purple. Edie slowly turned around, revealing yet more scars and bruising.

Across her back were welts from a belt buckle, dozens of angry, pink ridges flayed across her skin. Tommie gasped, putting her hand to her mouth, shaking her head in disbelief.

'Now do you believe me?' Edie's eyes shone wet with tears as she gave Tommie a defiant look. Then she took a deep breath, gathering up her clothes, fixing zips and buttons until she was covered up. Only then did she sit back down on the sofa, waiting for Tommie to say something. Her fate was resting in the other girl's hands.

'Oh, Edie . . .' Tommie couldn't say anything else as her throat wouldn't expel the words. A wave of desperate pity for the poor, beaten woman in front of her swept over her at the awful sight of her skin . . . the map of Frank's brutality etched across her.

Edie nodded. 'I told you the truth. I didn't do it all in the right order . . . but it was all true. I stole his money because I wanted to leave him, and then I poisoned him . . . but it looks like I even got that wrong. I wish he was dead. He took *everything* from me. The girl I used to be – he killed her. I wish I had killed him.'

'Yes, but the police won't be after you now, so you can make a fresh start. You can leave right now!'

Edie shrugged. 'Where am I going to go? He'll find me and they'll make me go back to him, because he's my husband. I can't do anything without him. I've got nobody . . . no family, no friends, no job, and that money I took will run out one of these days and then what will happen to me?' Edie's despair wrapped itself around each word and Tommie's heart softened towards her.

'Look!' She reached into her coat pocket and pulled out the postcard, handing it to Edie. 'I went to this place once with my mum when I was a kid and it was so beautiful. We had a cream tea in that teashop and it's always been my favourite place. The memory of that day . . . I've kept this postcard for years, always thinking that one day I'd go back there and sit in that same teashop.'

Edie ran her fingers over the creases in the postcard and nodded. 'It does look lovely.'

'It's a long way from here. The thing is . . . I bought *two* train tickets there . . .'

'Two?' Edie's eyes widened as she stared back at Tommie.

'I hope you don't mind but . . . I bought one for me.'

'You're coming with me . . . ?' Tears began to glide down Edie's cheeks. 'Really?'

Tommie nodded. 'There's nothing here for me any more, and I could do with a fresh start. We'd be safe there . . . at least for a bit. We could start over and have a new life . . . maybe even a better life, like you're always saying. You don't have to hang around with me – I'm not saying that—'

'No, I'm *glad* . . . honest I am. What made you decide to come?' Edie smiled up at Tommie.

'I don't know. Maybe you're right that everyone gets a second chance. Nobody would know anything about us. We could be whoever we wanted to be – at least for a little while. I'd like a second chance . . .' Tommie's eyes welled up at the thought of it.

'That's settled then.' Edie beamed. 'A fresh start.'

'Right, well, we had better make a plan.'

'What are we going to do? He didn't follow you here, did he?'

'No, I went out through the alleyway. I'll need to go back though and get my things. Here's what we'll do . . . We'll have to leave tonight. I'll see you at the railway station.' Tommie undid the clasp on her handbag. 'Here's your train ticket . . . I'll meet you on the platform at seven o'clock sharp. There's a train leaving at quarter past. Got that?'

'Seven. Yes, I've got it.'

'If I'm held up for any reason, you get on that train. Do you hear me, Edie? You *have* to get on that train.'

'I will . . . but you'll be there, won't you?'

Tommie nodded. 'I'll be there.' She moved towards the door, giving a brief smile to Edie.

'Wait . . . what about your postcard?' Edie held out the wrinkled picture of the teashop but Tommie shook her head.

'You hang on to it for me.'

'Are you sure about this?'

'I'm sure. Now I'll get back and sort things out. Seven o'clock – on the platform.'

Edie repeated the instructions, committing them to memory, and then Tommie was gone. The kitchen door slammed shut behind her.

The record player made a crackling noise as the needle went back and forth over the same groove, unable to move forward. She stood up and switched it off, returning the record to its paper sleeve. On the sofa lay the white paper train ticket, next to Tommie's postcard – a brand-new future, waiting for her to pick it up.

She looked over at Mrs Vee's fancy gold clock ticking the time away. There were hours to wait and she hoped the dizziness would pass long enough to let her get to the railway station and on to that train.

As long as she stayed in London, Frank would find her. But if she could disappear somewhere . . . Edie felt a faint whisper of hope, and she clung to it.

31

London, October 1958

At six thirty exactly, Tommie clicked the locks shut on her brown leather suitcase. Taking a deep breath, she turned the lights out in her room. She stood by the window, peering through the crack in the curtains at the street below for a few seconds. It was dark outside and a fine mist swirled around the light of the street lamp. Tommie could see no signs of life, other than a neighbourhood cat with its tail crooked into a question mark.

She picked up the suitcase by the handle and pulled it off the bed. The weight of it reminded her that carrying it for long distances rubbed the skin off the palms of her hands, but there was no choice. She would get the tube and then she wouldn't need to carry it so far. Taking a last look at the empty room, she carried the suitcase outside and then crept to the top of the stairs without it, to check the coast was clear.

There was, thankfully, no sign of Phyllis, although Tommie could hear the soft strains of music playing in the back kitchen. The door was closed and she scurried back up the stairs to collect her suitcase. Trying not to bump it along the edges of the treads and make a noise, she edged her way down each step as carefully and quietly as she could, until she was standing in the hallway.

She could hear a man's voice and then a woman laughing; Mario Lanza was singing a love song on the radio. Tommie opened her handbag and took out the note she'd written to Phyllis, placing it carefully on the hall table. Phyllis wouldn't be happy to lose both her tenants but maybe she and Terry could use some time together. Tommie thought back to the night she'd come home to find the house smelling of gas, and felt glad not to be leaving Phyllis all alone.

She took a last look around. 'You're getting soft in your old age . . .' she murmured, before opening the front door and stepping out into the misty night.

A quick glance at her watch told her she had less than thirty minutes to get to the station, which would be plenty of time if she didn't dawdle. She grabbed her suitcase with her right hand, hooking her little brown handbag over the crook of her elbow, before proceeding down the garden path and out of the front gate.

Tommie looked left and then right but there was no sign of anyone hanging around and she breathed out softly, muttering, '*Right then . . .*' to chivvy herself along. Her shoes clipped along the grey pavement, making a strange hollow sound that seemed to echo around her. The mist was thicker than she'd imagined and Tommie quickened her pace, suddenly wanting the safety of lights and crowds of people in the underground.

Her breath came in heavy bursts, the hairs on her

neck prickling as she approached the railway bridge. There was a pool of misty darkness in the centre of the bridge where you couldn't quite see the lights on the other side, and Tommie suddenly felt a blaze of fear.

There was a sound . . . barely detectable, but she knew at once what it was. A pair of men's work boots behind her. She swung around, her eyes searching the blackness, but there was nobody there. The only sound was her breathing, jagged and strained.

Tommie turned back in the direction of the underground station and started to run as best she could with a heavy suitcase: great limping strides until she reached the steps leading down into the light and the people. Queuing up at the window to get her ticket, she placed her suitcase on the ground beside her. It would only be a handful of stops, and she would be there.

She felt her shoulders relax and then it was her turn to be served. Out of the corner of her eye she caught a glimpse of the shadow of a man who darted away quickly out of her line of vision. Tommie stretched out the tension in her neck, wishing she was on a train.

Taking a deep breath, she asked the ticket clerk for 'a single to Paddington, please'. Clutching her ticket, she carried her suitcase along the tiled corridor and ran down the steps as she heard the familiar rumble of an underground train approaching.

The doors opened and she staggered into the carriage, finding a seat with enough room to stow her suitcase by her feet, glancing around carefully so it didn't seem as if she was staring at people. She could feel somebody looking at her from the window of the next compartment but when Tommie checked there was nobody there.

A woman rushed on just as the doors were closing, getting her heel caught in the wooden slats of the floor and then stumbling over Tommie's suitcase. She started to protest, all the while rubbing at her shin and Tommie smiled a weak apology, wishing that the woman would move away and stop making such a fuss.

The train rumbled into the dark tunnel. The metal sounds of wheels on the rails reverberated through the carriage. The train picked up speed, rattling from side to side, then slowing as it arrived at a station where other ordinary-looking passengers got on and off. Tommie's palms were clammy with sweat, even as the rest of her shivered a little with nerves, but inside she was calm with a steely determination. Two more stops . . . one more stop . . .

The train crawled to the platform and the doors opened. People rushed off and crushed on to the escalator. Tommie was caught for a moment in the throb of the crowd pulling her this way and that. Squeezing her forward, then moving slowly – oh so slowly – upwards towards the light. Eventually she could see the station concourse straight ahead of her and all the passengers milling around. She walked briskly to the nearest platform and stood where she could be seen very clearly. Glancing up at the station clock and watching as the hands showed it was very nearly seven o'clock, Tommie placed her brown leather suitcase at her feet, straightened her shoulders and waited . . .

Edie walked up and down the platform, clutching her cardboard suitcase to her chest, but there was no sign of Tommie. The station clock said two minutes after seven and the train had already arrived at the platform; its doors were all flung open and people were ready to board. The porters scurried back and forth, carrying trunks and expensive cream leather suitcases to the baggage car.

A small burst of steam escaped from the funnel of the engine, the noise hissing around the platform, making passengers nervous at being left behind. Edie stood on her tiptoes, trying to see over the heads of the crowd as there were so many people coming and going, kissing and hugging their goodbyes.

'Where *are* you?' Edie muttered to herself and then decided to do one more circuit of the platform in case she'd somehow missed Tommie on her previous laps. A worrying thought nagged at the back of her mind that maybe she'd got the wrong train . . . and so she stopped, pulling out her ticket to check. Then Edie spotted the guard in his uniform and, to make absolutely sure, headed towards him. Shoving her train ticket under his nose, she asked, 'Is this the right platform for the night train?'

'Yes, miss, and it's going in a few minutes so best get on board.' His little silver whistle was held in his left hand, and he looked past Edie to where some passengers were dawdling with their bicycles. He tutted and left her standing there while he went to usher them towards the guard's van.

She wandered up and down for a few seconds, but then began to worry that the train would leave without her. Placing her little cardboard suitcase on the ground, Edie looked again, both ways, but there was no sign of Tommie on the platform anywhere. Her right hand urgently pulled at the fingers of her left hand. The guard, having dispensed with the bicycles and the passengers who owned them, headed back towards her.

'Get on board, miss, or we'll be leaving you behind,' he said gruffly and the little silver whistle hesitated by his bottom lip. Edie took a deep breath and climbed up into the train corridor, placing her suitcase in the overhead rack of a second-class compartment. Then she went back out into the corridor and pulled down the window as far as it would go, hoping to find her friend. The guard slammed the train doors, checking it was all clear. Leaning out as far as she could, Edie searched the crowds for Tommie . . . but there was no sign of her.

The guard finally placed his silver whistle between his lips and blew a sharp warning blast. A whirl of steam rolled around them and the train lurched forward. Edie fell backwards against the compartment door, almost colliding with a family who had rushed down the corridor at the last minute, delighted at having found almost an entire compartment to themselves.

The mother snapped the windows shut and settled herself in the seat opposite Edie. The platform emptied as the train rolled away into the distance.

She sighed. So Tommie hadn't come after all, and she was quite alone again. The train gathered speed and London rushed past the windows. All the houses with their tiny people and small glowing lights disappeared into the darkness as Edie leaned back in her seat and closed her eyes.

At exactly a quarter past seven, a train rolled on to the platform at Paddington Station where Tommie was still standing in clear view. The doors opened and a mass of people emptied out and then quickly dispersed. The steam hissed as the doors were slammed shut and the empty carriages prepared for another journey.

Tommie could see Frank Budd very clearly now at the top of the platform, no doubt waiting for Edie to show up. She smiled to herself and waited another minute to make sure that it was too late; then she picked up her suitcase and slowly walked over to where he was lurking.

'She's gone,' Tommie said, unable to keep the triumph out of her voice.

Frank looked puzzled, as if trying to work out what she was talking about.

'Where is she?' he said.

'You'll never find her.' Tommie smirked as she watched his face darken; the charming smile was gone, and the fury that he carried with him as a permanent passenger began to rise. Frank took a step towards Tommie, looming over her, but she wasn't as small as Edie, and somehow it didn't have quite the same effect.

She didn't flinch, and she didn't move away. Standing there clear-eyed, staring right back at him. The smirk playing on her lips. 'You think I didn't know you were following me? You're not very good at it, Frank – I saw you the minute I left the house. Did you really think I was going to lead you to Edie so you could carry on torturing her?'

'I'm her husband! Where's she gone? I've got *rights* . . . She stole money from me. I bet she didn't tell you that, did she? She's told you a pack of lies about me. She's my wife and you need to tell me where she's gone.' Frank's voice rose but still Tommie stood there unblinking.

'Oh, she *told* me all about you. I think you gave up those rights when you took your fists and pounded on that poor girl until she was black and blue. Men like you make me *sick* . . .'

Frank's fist lifted until it was right under Tommie's chin. At first, she thought he was going to grab her coat but his fist just curled and hovered in mid-air, as if he wasn't quite sure what to do next. She wondered what would happen if he hit her and how much pain his fist could bring with it. The memories of Edie's yellowing bruises flashed in front of her eyes, but Tommie didn't have it in her to back down.

Frank snarled at her, 'You'd better tell me where she is, or else . . .'

'Or else what? What are you going do, Frank? I'm not scared of you. If you lay one finger on me, I'll scream the place down.' Her voice shook slightly as she spoke and she was certain that Frank could smell her fear.

He was so close now that Tommie could feel the warmth of his breath on her face, but she couldn't step away.

He tried a different tack. Softer now . . . wheedling. The smile was charming but his blue eyes were cold. 'Look, I'm not interested in *you*. This is none of *your* business. She's my wife – she belongs with me. Now tell me—'

'I don't *know* where she's gone. All I know is, she's not coming back. It's a big old world out there and you are *never* going to find her.' Tommie tilted her chin towards him defiantly.

'You *need* to tell me where she's gone . . .' His voice was cold and threatening now. The rage seemed to well up inside him and spilled over in a flash of fury. 'Where is she? TELL ME!' he screamed at the top of his voice, grabbing at the collar of Tommie's blue coat.

People turned to stare but, thinking that Tommie was his wife, they looked away again and let the man conduct his business as he saw fit. Frank, realizing that he was being watched, slowly released his grip on Tommie's coat.

She stretched out her hand, catching hold of his fist, holding it away from her in mid-air. She was feeling more rage than fear at that moment, and that anger was icy cold. 'You don't scare me. You're just another bully, Frank.'

Tommie could feel a tide of fury washing over her. She wanted to hurt this man. For a moment she wished that she had the strength to hit him. He could kill her with one punch but she had nothing left to lose.

She couldn't stop herself from talking and she couldn't walk away. 'What's the matter, Frank? Does it only work if a woman is begging you to stop hurting her?'

His fist tightened and his other hand grabbed hold of her wrist. Twisting it. The brute force of him hurting her. Out of the corner of her eye Tommie spied a police officer wandering up and down the station concourse chatting away to passengers.

She grimaced in pain. 'Oh, *look*, there's a police officer . . . shall I call him over?'

Frank released her wrist and took a step backwards. Fists still curled ready to hurt her. His face dark and furious. Tommie rubbed at her wrist and then picked up her suitcase.

'Now get out of my way . . . and if you ever try and make trouble for Edie, I'll go straight to the police and tell them everything I know about a certain robbery in the West End . . .'

Frank's face was like thunder but his fists slowly

uncurled. Tommie breathed a sigh of relief. She'd been right about the costume shop. As he backed away from her, Frank glared at Tommie for a few seconds, but then his face caved into misery.

Angry and defeated now. Trying to explain things that he had no words for. The same old tired excuses. For some reason Frank needed to tell Tommie how it used to be. His pale blue eyes pleading with her to understand him.

'You don't understand. Edie was *my life*. We were so happy . . . She disobeyed me, that's all . . . If she hadn't disobeyed me, none of this would have happened . . . I *never* meant to hurt her . . .'

Tommie clutched her suitcase tightly in her right hand, giving a long, exasperated sigh as she took a step towards him. 'Of course you *meant* to hurt her, Frank. That was the whole fucking point. The only way men like you can feel good is if women like Edie are in pain. Now, get out of my way . . .'

Frank's face registered the shock of her words but Tommie knew within a few seconds he would want to lash out at her. She shoved past him and didn't look back, running as fast as she could down the steps, back into the underground station, leaving Frank Budd staring after her. She would wait down here, then come back up when he'd gone, make her way to Euston and follow after Edie.

Threading through the crowds with her suitcase, Tommie eventually managed to get on to the platform where she stood trembling for a few moments, watching the trains rush in and out of the tunnel.

After a few moments she felt calm enough to set her suitcase down by her feet. Gathering her wits, she opened her little embroidered cigarette case, taking out a Woodbine, tapping it gently on the case before putting it in her mouth. The crowds began to crush around the edge of the platform, and she thought about the teashop. The flowers trailing up the walls that her mother had liked so much. Tommie took a step backwards, fumbling around in her coat pocket, searching for a light.

Her fingers discovered the book of matches, a stolen souvenir. Her lucky charm. The old familiar ache rose inside her. Striking the match, she caught the end of her cigarette and watched as it glowed into life. Extinguishing the match with a swift breath, Tommie threw it away and stood at the edge of the platform, thinking.

There was another train in the morning. She could always catch that one . . .

Flicking the book of matches between her fingers, she spun them around, and all the time she could feel the aching deep inside her. The scratchy hunger . . . There would be other trains. There would be other days.

Tommie hesitated. Then sucked in a deep lungful of tobacco, blowing a tiny smoke ring that curled up into the air and disappeared.

Epilogue

Edie was sitting in the teashop for the third day in a row. The rosy-cheeked girl behind the counter had begun to treat her as if she was a regular, pouring her a cup of tea and offering her the pick of a plate of pink iced buns, carrying it over to her usual table, where Edie could see the entrance to the railway station. There were only two trains that came in or out each day and, although Edie didn't know why she was doing it, she'd made a deal with herself that she'd give it a week.

She sipped at the tea, picking a sliver of pink icing off the side of the bun with her finger. Checking the clock on the wall of the teashop, Edie imagined that the morning train had probably arrived in a cloud of steam as usual, and the passengers would have started to drift out on to the platform. Licking the pink icing off her finger anxiously, Edie watched the entrance to the railway station, desperate not to miss an arrival.

Out they came – men, both tall and short; children running out to greet waiting relatives; women, fair and dark – and then the station was empty once more.

She sighed and picked at the pink icing again, its sweetness comforting her. The rosy-cheeked girl came out from behind the counter, wiping down the small tables with her cloth and straightening the chairs. It would be another few hours until the afternoon train arrived.

'Your friend not made it, then?' the girl said cheerfully.

'No.' Edie gave her a shy smile.

'Not to worry. She'll probably be on the afternoon train, I expect.'

'Yes,' replied Edie. 'I expect she will . . .'

Acknowledgements

Huge thanks as ever to my team at Penguin Michael Joseph for showing so much love and care for my work. Everyone works so very hard yet retains so much passion for each book that is released, and I am thrilled to be published by them. To everyone who has helped to produce this book in hardback, digital and audio and sold it to booksellers, I am so grateful for all your efforts. THANK YOU!

Once again, I am blown away by the gorgeous jacket design from Lauren Wakefield and Matty Newton. You make my book look so beautiful on bookshelves that it's a dream come true.

None of this would be as much fun to do without my brilliant editor Clio Cornish, a woman who asks such ridiculously difficult questions that it makes my brain ache but inevitably makes my work better. Huge thanks to Maddy, Liv, Sophie, Steph and Jessie for being the best team a woman could want on her side, to Nick and Richenda for their careful work, and to my agent Nelle for continuing to champion my best interests. Special thanks to Georgina Moore, Hannah Bright and the team at Midas PR for their brilliant work.

Big shoutout to all the book bloggers and booksellers whose passion for reading and readers makes this all worthwhile. Love to the brilliant Frances Quinn, Jodie Chapman and Laura Shepherd-Robinson for offering to read early copies. Authors who support and champion other authors are the best of the best.

Last but not least, thanks and all my love to my husband Sean who keeps this show on the road.

During the dark, bleak days of a winter lockdown and the months that followed it, I wrote *73 Dove Street*. It was a hard book to write and the first time I've written to a deadline, knowing that somebody was waiting to publish it.

I've dedicated this book to my grandmother Lilian. Although this is not her story, there is so much of her in everything I write. She smoked woodbines, sheltered from bombs under the stairs, cleaned up after eccentric rich people and lived a tough life. Her favourite phrase was 'Wish in one hand and spit in the other. See what you get first.' Yet she wasn't a cynical woman and she remained so proud of me and my efforts to live a different life from hers.

I was born into a working-class family populated by strong women with few rights or choices. Many of them had been 'forced' to marry due to a youthful fling that resulted in pregnancy. They lived hard lives, finding joy where they could, but too often suffering from the whims and behaviour of the men they felt shackled to. Those tough resilient women hid from bombs falling, from people they couldn't pay, they cleaned up after the rich and tried to find a spark of joy in music, dancing or nights out to the cinema.

In writing the women of *73 Dove Street*, I wanted to show the wounds and injustices of their lives but mostly the courage that it takes to fight back and choose more than you've been given. In a world where we see increasing evidence of women's rights being rolled back, I believe this book is a timely reminder of what happens when we take away those choices.

I hope you love Edie, Tommie and Phyllis as much as I've loved writing them.

Julie x

Turn over for
an extract from
Julie's new novel
Circus of Mirrors

WHICH BOOK WILL YOU READ NEXT?

Berlin, August 1961

Annette was sitting in the dark, smoking a cigarette. She could barely make out the hands of the clock on top of the sideboard, but she could hear it ticking. Outside was a violet sky and the promise of a new day. She hadn't slept at all. She wasn't sure that Leni had either. The apartment was still draped in a bitter silence – but the dull yellowish glow of a bedside lamp shone from under the bedroom door, and Annette thought that she could hear her sister moving around: the gentle tread of her footsteps and the creak of the floor.

Crushing out her cigarette in the glass ashtray, she walked over to the window. Outside, the streets were empty, and she felt completely alone. Running her fingertips across the side of her face, Annette winced. It felt sore and tender – a bruising reminder of just how much her sister hated her.

She had nobody now. She'd lost everyone she'd ever cared for. Annette felt sorry for herself, even as she realized that it was probably her own fault. Hot tears spilled down her face as she contemplated her future. Where could she go? There was nobody waiting for her. Wiping away her tears, she cast another glance towards the tiny pool of light.

There was something she should have done years ago. It was probably too late to make any difference now. But Annette needed to at least try and explain things.

She took a tentative step towards the bedroom door before hesitating just outside with her hand raised. Finally, inhaling a deep breath, Annette gently tapped on the door with her knuckles.

There was no answer, yet she was sure that her sister was awake. She waited for a few more seconds, her hand hovering in the air, unsure of what to do. Then, Annette knocked again – and, this time, she didn't wait for an invitation.

PART ONE

Berlin, August 1926

I

Dieter's finely manicured fingernails made gentle tapping sounds on the side of his tin cheek as he surveyed the state of his desk. Leaning back in his wooden chair, he lit a Turkish cigarette and exhaled. The cloud of smoke curled menacingly in the direction of Herr Keks – a small white cat that was fast asleep on top of a large pile of bills. The bills lay stabbed through the heart with an enormous steel hat pin to stop them escaping into the random piles of paper that were scattered in all directions.

He rubbed anxiously at the edges of his face – the place where the tin met the skin. He had left the rest of his cheek on a battlefield in Belgium. One moment he was a man in his prime, with not unattractive features – and the next minute a violent explosion had blown him off his feet, the skin on his cheek melting away as if it had never existed, leaving him with nothing but a bloody pulp. Now, at nearly thirty-five years old, Dieter was so very tired of his face. The raw skin was kept hidden away under a tin mask, which was painted with a single brown eye, to replace the one he'd lost – his left. Most of his mouth remained intact, but the left edges of his lips had gone, too, replaced by a rather strange painted smile.

This gave Dieter a peculiar way of speaking, and meant that people never quite knew whether he was really smiling at them as his metallic brown eye stared blankly and his painted lips were permanently turned upwards – as if he were privy to an amusing joke that he refused to share.

Now, his good eye blinked furiously at both the sleeping cat and the pile of unpaid bills. The cigarette he was smoking made his throat itch, and he coughed, first delicately and then as if his life depended on removing the smoke from his lungs. Eventually, Dieter leaned forward in the wooden chair, which creaked ominously under his weight, before spitting a small yellow ball of mucus into his empty coffee cup.

Herr Keks woke grumpily, jumped down from the desk, raised his tail in a haughty fashion and disappeared through the open door. The door to Dieter's office was always left ajar, but it was meant only for the cat to come and go – not, under any circumstances, for people to use. Especially women.

The girls of the Babylon Circus, with their tears and tantrums, their fights and jealousies . . . Dieter let out a long, miserable sigh at the thought of them. Dancing girls, singing girls . . . *Why was his life so very difficult?* It was, he thought, because he was always surrounded by women. Dieter preferred the company of men. They were less likely to complain or cry. He still shuddered at the memory of the time one of the dancers had sobbed all over his shoulder. He had patted her on the back of her head – with rather less affection than he reserved for Herr Keks when handing him a small piece of fish.

Outside his office, Dieter heard a shriek of loud screeching laughter that he recognized as Berolina. The Babylon Circus employed a range of 'artistes', mostly sweet singers and girls who might dance with the 'guests' until later on in the evening, when the lights were lowered and the dancers took over the stage. The final part of the night required girls like Berolina. Loud, skilled at strangely exotic tricks, and mostly naked.

A riptide of amusement echoed once again right outside his office door and on through the dark brown passageway leading down to the dressing room. For reasons that escaped Dieter, given they had a perfectly good room with a door that closed, the corridor was always filled with girls fixing their feathery headdresses or hoisting their silk stockings, smelling of face powder and perfume. Several of the dancers liked to stand around smoking there, although Dieter was sure he had told them a million times to go somewhere else and stop cluttering up the passage with their smells and laughter and complaints.

They were always complaining. It was too hot or too cold. The customers were too mean or too rough with them. There was never one day where these girls were happy for the entire shift. He coughed again, a light rattling machine gun that ended with nothing except his fist pounding his chest. He wasn't a well man. They could at least afford him a little peace in his life.

Dieter adjusted his tin mask again. The edges felt tight today. They irritated him, making his skin red and inflamed. His cough irritated him. Berolina's laughter irritated him. It was too early in the evening to feel this irritated. There was a whole night ahead.

He glanced at the bills on the desk. Now the cat had vacated his position, Dieter could clearly see the amounts demanded. He would need to put the prices up again. Lately, once the customers had paid their three marks to enter the club, they were content to ogle the dancers yet refused to buy more than one bottle of champagne for their table, which caused him great distress. The mark-up on the champagne was enough to pay if not all the bills on his desk, then at least a good number of them, if only bottles were bought. He would have to speak to the girls about enticing these guests to drink more . . .

Berolina shrieked with laughter again. Dieter chewed angrily at the inside of his mouth and crushed his cigarette out in his mucus-filled coffee cup. 'What could be so funny that people need to keep on laughing?' he muttered out of the part of his mouth that still worked. He should fire them all. Annoying creatures. But then what? No girls meant no customers. *But why couldn't they just be quiet?*

Suddenly, a loud, heartrending scream replaced the laughter and was swiftly followed by an anguished cry. It wasn't Berolina this time, but Adele, who was howling, 'NO!' over and over.

Dieter got to his feet. His knee hurt from an old shrapnel wound when he tried to sit or stand. The aching made him rub at his right leg as he set off in the direction of the wailing. He would tell them to shut up or be sacked on the spot. He was the manager after all. They should listen to him and show more respect.

By the time he reached his office door a cacophony of wailing and crying was pouring out of the dressing room, the howls of anguish increasing with every step he took. Dieter muttered swear words under his breath, cursing his lot in life – the girls and their noise, his aching knees, the sore point at which the tin mask rubbed against his left cheek. Oh, his life was all pain today . . . He just wanted five minutes of peace and quiet.

Dieter shuffled along the empty passageway, shaking his head and preparing himself for battle. He was only one man and they were many, but there had to be silence today or his head would burst with pain.

The door to the dressing room was wide open. Every surface appeared to be covered with sobbing half-naked women.

'WHAT IS GOING ON?' Dieter roared at them out of his lop-sided mouth. A now weeping Berolina turned to face him. Her large breasts were covered by only the smallest of silver stars, while a ballet skirt of the thinnest pale green gauze parted dangerously to show the milky white of her legs. She fixed him with a serious glare, her eyes quite pink now from sobbing. 'Rudolf Valentino *died* . . .'

Dieter slowly shook his head. Valentino. The loss of a movie star famous for parading around in silly costumes meant nothing to him.

'Well, this caterwauling won't bring him back,' he snapped before slamming the dressing-room door shut on the women who tormented him so. Muttering to himself, Dieter strode purposefully back towards the safety of his office – only to find his path blocked by yet another agitated young woman, who appeared to be waiting to speak to him.

'I . . . I'm looking for work. I can wait on tables . . . or whatever you need.' She looked up at him with wide pleading eyes. The girl looked no more than eighteen or nineteen years old – no doubt she would be just as annoying as the other women at the Circus. He grimaced slightly as he considered the matter.

As it happened, his cigarette girl had quit suddenly that week and he did need to replace her. Dieter looked this young woman up and down disapprovingly.

'I'm very reliable,' the girl added hastily. Taking in her nervous demeanour and shabby cotton dress, he let out a deep sigh.

All he wanted was five minutes to himself. Yet, as he raised his one good eye to the heavens, Dieter understood there would be no peace for him today.